MARIANA'S KNIGHT

LEGENDS OF THE DESERT, BOOK 1

MARIANA'S KNIGHT

THE REVENGE OF HENRY FOUNTAIN

W. MICHAEL FARMER

FIVE STAR

A part of Gale, Cengage Learning

GALE
CENGAGE Learning

Farmington Hills, Mich • San Francisco • New York • Waterville, Maine
Meriden, Conn • Mason, Ohio • Chicago

LIBRARY OF CONGRESS CATALOGING-IN-PUBLICATION DATA

Names: Farmer, W. Michael, 1944– author.
Title: Mariana's knight : the revenge of Henry Fountain / W. Michael Farmer.
Description: First edition. | Waterville, Maine : Five Star Publishing, [2017] | Series: Legends of the desert ; 1
Identifiers: LCCN 2016058124 (print) | LCCN 2017005913 (ebook) | ISBN 9781432833923 (hardcover) | ISBN 1432833928 (hardcover) | ISBN 9781432836900 (ebook) | ISBN 1432836900 (ebook) | ISBN 9781432833886 (ebook) | ISBN 143283388X (ebook)
Subjects: LCSH: Fathers and sons—Fiction. | Missing persons—Fiction. | Revenge—Fiction. | BISAC: FICTION / Historical. | FICTION / Westerns. | GSAFD: Historical fiction. | Western stories.
Classification: LCC PS3606.A725 M37 2017 (print) | LCC PS3606.A725 (ebook) | DDC 813/.6—dc23
LC record available at https://lccn.loc.gov/2016058124

First Edition. First Printing: May 2017
Find us on Facebook– https://www.facebook.com/FiveStarCengage
Visit our website– http://www.gale.cengage.com/fivestar/
Contact Five Star™ Publishing at FiveStar@cengage.com

Printed in the United States of America
1 2 3 4 5 6 7 21 20 19 18 17

To Corky,
My Wife and Best Friend

ACKNOWLEDGMENTS

Melissa Starr's editing was a guiding light for this book. Her insightful comments kept the focus of the story where it needed to be and I owe her much for a job well done. Bruce Kennedy provided many helpful comments and enlightening information from his historical research on the time and place of this story. Jann Arrington Walcott's encouragement and insightful comments were an inspiration for the original Hombrecito manuscripts. When I return to New Mexico to do further research on its land and history, Pat and Mike Alexander open their home to me. They are a constant source of encouragement. I thank these friends and colleagues without whom this book would not have been possible.

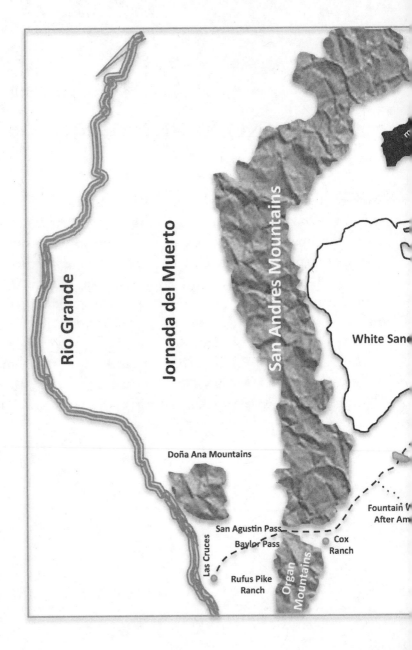

Rio Grande

Jornada del Muerto

San Andres Mountains

White San

Doña Ana Mountains

Fountain V
After Am

San Agustin Pass

Baylor Pass

Cox
Ranch

Las Cruces

Organ
Mountains

Rufus Pike
Ranch

A Knigh

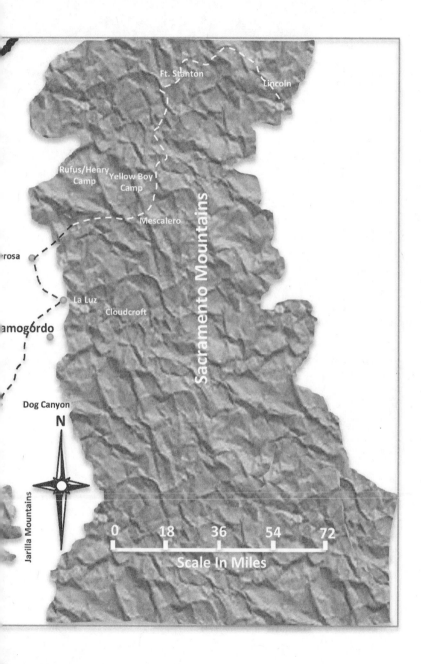

Ft. Stanton

Lincoln

Rufus/Henry
Camp

Yellow Boy
Camp

Mescalero

Sacramento Mountains

rosa

La Luz

Cloudcroft

amogordo

Dog Canyon

N

Jarilla Mountains

0   18   36   54   72

Scale In Miles

untry

PREFATORY NOTE

"The pursuit of truth, not facts, is the business of fiction."
—Oakley Hall, author of *Warlock*

Mariana's Knight is a novel. The characters of Yellow Boy, Rufus Pike, Henry Fountain (after age eight), Jack Stone, Red Tally, Charlie Bentene, and Sarah Darcy are fictional. The Fountain family members, Oliver Lee, Pat Garrett, and most of the characters and events leading up to the disappearance of Albert and Henry Fountain in the desert near White Sands, New Mexico Territory, are true historical figures.

What actually happened to Albert and Henry Fountain and who was responsible for their apparent murders have been fiercely debated for nearly a hundred and twenty years. Those who knew the truth went to their graves without telling the story, or if they did, historians have not heard or believed it. Logic dictates that eight-year-old Henry Fountain died with his father, but life, filled with unexpected events and inconsistencies, is not logical. What if Henry survived? This story assumes Henry's survival and is constructed from actual and fictional events to create a myth for what devotees of western legends might wish had been.

The story of Henry Fountain's survival was first published in 2005 as *Hombrecito's War,* which was a Western Writers of America Spur Award Finalist for Best First Novel and a 2007 New Mexico Book Award Finalist for Best Historical Fiction.

Mariana's Knight retells Henry's story from a different perspective to make it more accessible to a wider audience. It is the first in a series of historical novels that are developed around true events in the southwest that became legends as the generation that settled in the New Mexico and Arizona territories, beginning about 1880, began their lives in a hard, brutal land, survived against all odds, and lived until the mid-twentieth century.

W. Michael Farmer
Smithfield, Virginia
15 August 2015

PROLOGUE

History records that my father, Albert Fountain, and I vanished one cold, dreary afternoon in the Tularosa Basin near White Sands, New Mexico Territory, the first of February in 1896. I am told experienced lawmen, Mescalero Apache trackers and ranch hands who rode the Tularosa Basin range every day searched for weeks for some sign of us. They found nothing.

My father, an attorney, politician, and newspaper publisher had many enemies. Near the top of the list was a widely respected rancher, Oliver Lee in the Tularosa Basin country, who battled with him often over range justice and politics. Lee lived by an unwritten Texas range code that oft times clashed with New Mexico Territory law my father vigorously enforced. Lee was a Democrat, my father a Republican, and dirty tricks were common on both sides in rough-and-tumble New Mexico politics.

On the day we disappeared, we were returning from Lincoln, New Mexico Territory. My father had just obtained thirty-two grand jury indictments of small ranchers, itinerant cowboys, and known bandits for cattle rustling. Included among them were indictments for Oliver Lee and a few of his friends, making them logical suspects for our supposed murders. Within a month after we disappeared, Pat Garrett, raising race horses in Texas, and famous for killing Billy the Kid in 1881, was brought out of retirement to solve the case by territorial governor William (Poker Bill) T. Thornton.

In 1899, a trial was held in the picturesque little mining town of Hillsboro, New Mexico Territory, at the base of the Black Range over seventy miles north of Las Cruces, where our family and their supporters lived. Lee and his friend James Gililland, charged with my murder, were supported by a large group of family and friends who came to Hillsboro from all over the territory. Another of my father's enemies, Albert Fall, and three high-powered attorneys defended Lee and Gililland. After eighteen days, including several nights of testimony from a long line of witnesses, the case was given to the jury. The jury deliberated eight minutes and found Lee and Gililland not guilty. Thereafter, the countryside was divided into two factions that have never stopped arguing and literally fighting over the guilt or innocence of Oliver Lee in our supposed murders.

By 1950, only two men knew the true story of the murders and the hard, bloody retribution that followed. One was my Mescalero Apache mentor and adopted father, Yellow Boy, and the other was myself, Dr. Henry Grace, also once known as Henry Fountain. In 1950, I persuaded Yellow Boy to tell me his life story and to let me write it down as he told it. Over many afternoons and weekends I wrote his oral history. At each session I read back to him what I had captured in the previous session and rewrote it until he said I had it right. His story has filled several journals.

When I finished Yellow Boy's story and read it back to him as a complete piece following the "tracks of the *Indah* (white man) on paper," he nodded, smiled, and looked at me with his shining, black obsidian eyes, and said, "Now, *Hombrecito,* you must make the tracks that tell your story. Others will want to know. It must not be lost. It will be told around the council fires for many harvests. All men, *Indah* or *Indeh* (Apaches) place a high value on courage."

So it is that I have filled more journals with my own story, and here my story begins.

Dr. Henry Grace
Las Cruces, New Mexico
June 1951

Chapter 1
Knighted

When I walked up to the parlor, my mama was dabbing her eyes, and I knew she had been crying again. My father stood puffing a cigar and looking out the window, his back to the door, as though trying to ignore her. We'd already had supper, and they had a warm fire crackling in the fireplace. The cedar-like smell of burning piñon wood mixed with the sharp, tingling smoke from the big Cuban cigar as the wind whipped and whistled around the corners of the house, made me glad I was inside. It was a harsh January night in 1896, the last evening my father was alive to enjoy time with us in that house, and the last time I would spend in that parlor again for many years.

I stood by the doorway until my mother saw me, smiled, and motioned for me to sit beside her. That night, she wore a cactus flower perfume that smelled wonderful and left the nicest trace of her in any room through which she passed. Her shiny, black hair was twisted into a bun at the nape of her neck, and her teeth were white pearls against her coffee-colored skin as she smiled at me and said, "*Enrique,* your father and I have been talking." I immediately understood from the tone of her voice that this was to be a serious conversation.

"Your father has to go to Lincoln," she said, and her hand shook a little as she raised her handkerchief to dab her eyes again. "He has to make a presentation to a grand jury to get indictments of men he believes have been stealing cattle from some ranchers he represents. He's found evidence that can put the thieves in prison for many years, and some of them are well-known, prominent men. When word gets out about your father's plans, there's likely to be a lot of trouble. His life will be in danger."

I nodded, narrowing my eyes to a serious squint, as if I were a grown man, and asked, "Is he afraid of those men?"

She took my hand and said, "No, Henry. I wish he were, but he's not." I felt a surge of pride in my father because that's what I'd wanted to hear.

Mama squeezed my hand gently and said, "I've begged him to stay here, but he insists he must go if he's to do his duty for his clients and keep his honor. He's stubborn and full of pride. He'll go, regardless of what I say."

Mama sniffed, then held up an index finger, and said, "But I know how to protect him. *Enrique,* I want you to go with him. Your sister Maggie and I don't believe anyone would attack a man traveling with a little boy." I always liked it when she called me *Enrique,* which was my name in her native tongue. She usually reserved it for tender moments, when her love for me seemed to be at its strongest.

She paused for a moment, as if gauging my reaction. I felt a sense of pride, understanding she was asking me to do something brave. I knew I was just a spindly, half-Mexican kid, and some even said I looked sickly, but I was just tall and thin for my age, the last of twelve siblings. My brothers often played rough, adolescent games with me. Trying to survive around them made me a lot tougher than I looked.

Mama placed her hand on my shoulder and continued in a soft voice, "Your father has insisted that he go alone, but Maggie and I have been equally insistent that you go with him because, with you along, no harm will come to him. Tonight, he agreed that you could go with him, if you want to go. What do you say?" She smiled and squeezed my shoulder. Her deep, brown eyes were pools of kindness and understanding. I loved her so much that if she had asked me to jump into the parlor fire, I wouldn't have hesitated.

I swelled up bigger than the bullfrogs I'd caught playing down by the Rio Grande. When they puffed up for a croak, they could be heard in El Paso. I sat up as straight as I could and said, "Yes'm. I'd sure like to go."

Smiling, she reached into a knitting basket at her feet and handed me an ivory horse head watch fob. "This was your grandfather's," she said. "Your grandmother gave it to him because he was her *caballero*—her knight and her protector. Now, my son, you can be the knight for me, Mariana Pérez de Ovante Fountain, protecting your father. I'm very proud of you. Keep it with you, and remember you're my *caballero.*"

I took it and turned it in my hands, examining it from every angle, before saying, "I will, Mama. Don't you worry."

My father turned, casting a baleful eye on me, half-serious, half-humorous. His mouth was a tight, straight line. I could tell he wasn't happy about my decision, but in my excitement, I plunged forward and shared my first great idea for the trip. I said, "Daddy, since I'm gonna be ridin' shotgun with you—"

Before I could finish, he held up his palm and said, "Whoa, stop right there, little man. You're just along for the ride. You'll get to visit the town of Lincoln for a while. It's bad enough folks are liable to think I'm hiding behind a little boy, but it's downright idiotic for a boy to think he can protect me with a damn gun. Do you understand?" He ground out the words between clenched teeth, obviously straining to maintain his self-control, and I could sense his fury below the surface. I realized he was frustrated by the iron will of my mother, and this made him speak more directly than usual. I also knew it was very rare for her not to go along with what he wanted. He just didn't have much practice in dealing with her when she insisted on getting her way.

"Yes, sir," I mumbled, looking at the floor, and then I thought of something that would justify our taking and my shooting his rifle. "I was just gonna ask if we could do some target shooting on the way. Maybe we'll see a bear or mountain lion when we cross the mountains, and we can get us a hide for Mama's floor."

I knew how to handle the '73 Winchester carbine standing in his gun rack. He and my brothers had taught me to shoot cans and bottles when they went out for target practice in the desert or in the big arroyo east of town. He had even let me shoot his Schofield pistol a few times, but I liked the rifle best because I couldn't hit much with his pistol. It was too heavy and hard to cock. I couldn't shoot it accurately, even holding it with two hands.

"Well," Daddy said, as a grin started to grow under his mustache. "Yeah, we could do that, Henry, but you'll be responsible for that rifle if we shoot it, so I'll expect you to clean it. We'll keep it in a scabbard under the buggy seat." He walked over, tousled my hair with his big hand, and said, "I've got some business to take care of first thing in the morning, so we'll leave at noon and camp in San Agustin Pass before rolling on to Tularosa the next day. I'll carry your clothes in my valise, and we'll use the buggy with Sergeant and Buck rather than ride saddle horses because I've got to carry a trunk full of grand jury papers, too."

Sergeant and Buck were a big black and a big white, high-stepping horses Daddy had bought from a farm in Tennessee. They could really cover ground and had more endurance than any horses I'd seen before or since that trip. With our light wagon, I knew they could go like the wind for miles.

CHAPTER 2
STRANDED ON SAN AGUSTIN PASS

My father was never late. He said if you were late to a meeting it was an insult, so we were ready to go right at noon the next day. The sky was bright blue with lots of puffy, white clouds sailing across it, but the wind was cold and gusty. I shivered as I climbed up on a buggy wheel to hug Mama and kiss her good-bye.

"Don't worry, Mama," I said. "I'll take real good care of Daddy. Nobody's gonna get us." She managed to smile and nodded. Then Daddy held her close and whispered something in her ear. She smiled again, but her eyes were near tears as she and Marta, our cook, handed us a basket and stuffed a big, heavy blanket with a dog-head pattern over our laps. On Mama's orders, Marta had fixed us a big basket supper and a bag lunch for the following day.

I was wrapped in a red wool Mackinaw that had belonged to one of my brothers when he was ten or twelve, and it was about three sizes too big for me. Daddy wore his army overcoat with the collar pulled up high around his neck and his campaign hat pulled down tight on his head. We also carried a buffalo robe, just in case the blanket wasn't warm enough. He looked over at me and asked, "Warm enough, son?" I grinned and nodded.

Just before we left, he said, "Mother, my ears are about to freeze off. Do you have anything I can wear to keep them warm?"

She thought for a second and then held up her wait-a-minute

finger. Without a word, she ran into the house. Returning in a couple of minutes, she brought him a *rebozo,* her favorite head shawl, to tie around his head. "Now don't you lose that, Albert," she said, her teeth chattering through an I'll-be-brave smile, her lower lip trembling.

Daddy smiled and hugged her good-bye once more. "Don't worry, Mother, I won't lose it. We ought to be back around the first week in February. If you need anything, call on the boys to get it for you or to help you. If there's an emergency, send me a telegram. We'll be staying at Mrs. Darcy's boardinghouse in Lincoln." She nodded, crossing her arms and shivering in the wind.

I leaned out of the buggy and gave her a final good-bye kiss and a couple of comforting pats on the back. She smiled, hugged me, and said, "*Adios, Enrique.* Mama loves you, and we'll miss you. Have a good time. Make Daddy come back home as soon as he can, and you two stay warm, or you'll catch pneumonia."

"Yes'm. We'll be back soon." Daddy clucked to Buck and Sergeant, made a little slap with the reins, and we were off into the wind and down the street at a fast trot. Most of the ride between Las Cruces and the mountains was so gentle I couldn't feel we were climbing, even in a horse and buggy, until we got to the climb past Organ village, but then the horses started pulling hard, and the going was slow up that grade. The wind made us huddle up close and hunker down under the blanket. Daddy kept the horses stepping along, and he cracked little jokes about how cold it was, such as, "Son it's colder than a well digger's rear on Halloween night in the Yukon." His jokes made me laugh aloud in the pure joy of getting to take a trip with him, and he laughed with me.

We stopped in San Agustin Pass at about five o'clock. The shadows were long from the setting sun. It was much colder and windier up there than it had been in the valley. We camped behind some boulders that were close to a little spring to get out of the wind. It was like having a nest on top of the world. The view of the valley and the road back toward Las Cruces stretched forever in the last light from the sun falling behind the Florida Mountains on the edge of the world far to the west. We could see a few lights down in Organ, and, later, when it was pitch black, we could see a dim glow out of the valley and points of light from the streetlights in Las Cruces and Mesilla.

Daddy fed and watered the horses and put me to work gathering up brush we could burn for a fire. He was particular about his animals. They were skittish that evening, hard to handle in getting them out of harness and rubbing them down, and I think now they probably smelled a big cat or a bear.

Daddy led them to water at a little pool fed by a slow spring leaking out of the boulders below us. Then he tied them to picket stakes out of the wind and fed them. Finally, we got to eat that nice basket supper Marta had fixed for us. I was starving and the taste of steak, fresh-baked bread, and hot coffee filled my mouth with pleasure after bouncing around in the wind on a cold buggy seat half the day.

While we ate, I got Daddy to tell me a story or two about his Indian fights. When we finished, it was fully dark, and the stars were out. We built up the fire and rolled up together in the buffalo robe right next to it. Daddy kept the Winchester within easy reach, and checked the load in his Schofield pistol before putting it under the blanket he used for a pillow.

"Best get some sleep, now, little man," he said, and I snuggled in close to him. It was the first time I had spent an evening with Daddy sleeping on the trail. Of course, I had slept out with my brothers Tom, Jack, and Albert on some of their jaunts over to ranches or hunting. I knew what to expect, but, even so, I had a hard time getting to sleep and wiggled around some. Then the warmth of his body and the hot glow from the fire had me sleeping as well as I did in my own bed at home.

The next morning, Daddy was up before dawn. He broke up some kindling and soon built up the fire from the coals that survived the night. He let me stay wrapped in the buffalo robe watching him in the weak light of the coming dawn. After he had a nice fire going, he told me to roll out and get ready to go. Then he filled the grain buckets for the horses and walked around the boulders to where they had been staked. Much quicker than I expected, he came stomping back, cursing under his breath. He looked mad enough to bite the head off a grizzly bear.

"What's wrong?" I asked.

"The horses are gone. Somehow they pulled out their picket stakes and took off." I went to look for myself, came back, and found Daddy muttering to himself as he took a slow walk around the camp trying to figure out where they had gone. I followed him, and we could see their tracks led back down toward Las Cruces. Although we couldn't find any other tracks, Daddy said he was certain some varmint had scared them off. After that, he didn't say much as he dug in the supplies and fixed us a little breakfast.

I was just about in tears. The only options I thought we had were to walk back home or hope somebody would come along and help us. I knew I wasn't strong enough to walk all the way back to Las Cruces in the cold, and I was too heavy for Daddy to carry. Daddy and I looked down the road from both sides of the pass, but we didn't see a soul or any animals moving for miles. I sniffled over the hot bread and coffee, trying not to cry, and said, "Daddy, what are we gonna do?"

He flashed one of the most confident grins I've ever seen and said, "There's not much we can do, Henry. I can tell the horses are headed back to town. I figure they'll wander into the stable for feed sometime this afternoon at the latest. Somebody at home will find them and figure out something has happened for them to get away from us like that. They'll probably bring them back here within a day or two, but if they don't, we'll just catch the mail wagon back in four or five days."

Hearing that changed my attitude. I realized I had at least a day or two to play up high in the mountains. *What a stroke of luck,* I thought. *Daddy might let me shoot the rifle, too.*

I scouted around and found a long, straight yucca stalk for my rifle, and then I spent most of the day either playing hunter or hiding behind rocks around camp pretending to be an Indian fighter. I'll bet I killed a thousand redskins, and they got me a few times with their arrows.

Daddy got out his legal papers from the old, red trunk, and, sitting on a rock next to the fire, spent most of the day reviewing evidence and making final preparations for his presentation to the grand jury.

We bundled up again after supper and slept sound and warm until about midnight when the scream of a mountain lion woke us up and made every hair on my head stand straight out. Daddy opened one eye, gave a big yawn, and said, "Go back to sleep, Henry. Don't be afraid. It's just an animal. Men are ten times worse than some hungry cat. Why, if that cat comes around, we'll give him a new eye in his backside with the Winchester. Just like you said, we'll skin him up and have us a new rug for your mama." I faked a yawn and forced myself to be still. I finally got off to sleep again, but it took a while.

At mid-afternoon the next day, Daddy walked out to the road and looked down the pass toward Organ and Las Cruces. He was gone so long I walked out to the road looking for him. He was there, sitting on a boulder in the sunshine. He pointed to tiny figures on horses plodding up the road each leading a horse and said, "That's Albert and his father-in-law, Antonio García. They'll be here in about an hour, and they have Sergeant and Buck with them. Let's go get the Dutch oven and cook us a good supper."

Sure enough, Albert and *Señor* García showed up in about an hour. Boy, was I glad to see them, and so was Daddy. Albert rode up to the fire with a big grin on his face and gave a smart military salute, which Daddy returned. He said, "Pa, you and Henry had us all worried to death when Sergeant and Buck showed up at the barn. Mama and Maggie thought somebody had attacked you. But I told them the horses probably just ran away and you needed them back, and, as you see, here they are. Mama had me bring you some more food, too. Antonio wanted to come with me, said he hadn't been up in the pass in a long time, and I was sure happy to have his company."

Daddy shook hands with *Señor* García saying, "Antonio, I much appreciate you coming way out here with Albert. I know he was glad for the company."

The old man grinned under his big *sombrero* and said, "*De nada,* it is nothing, Alberto. It is a good thing to find you so easy."

Daddy, showing nothing but teeth under his mustache, said, "Albert, I sure raised you right. You figured it out exactly like I thought you would. Gentlemen, climb down and tie those horses to the buggy wheel. I'll feed them. Henry, you get the plates, and we'll eat in a little bit. I can feel my backbone rubbing my navel."

While we ate, Daddy leaned back against a boulder and talked a while with *Señor* García about a land dispute arising from local politics. There was a long pause in the conversation while the coffeepot was passed around for refills, then Daddy said, "Albert, it's clear to me that it was foolish to bring Henry along on this trip. I want you to take him back home with you, and I'll go on alone."

Señor García frowned and Albert just stared at Daddy, his mouth half full of beans and biscuits. He stopped chewing, swallowed, then looked at the ground and shook his head. At first, I could hardly believe he did this because it was forbidden for us to argue with our parents. My older siblings could get away with arguing a little with Mama, but when Daddy told us to do something, it had better be "Yes, sir!" or we could expect a quick trip to the woodshed. However, Albert was a grown man, and I could tell he'd try to rebut Daddy's order.

"Pa, why would you want to do that? Henry seems to be doing just fine, and I thought you agreed with Mama and Maggie that you'd be safer if he came along."

Daddy pulled two cigars out of his coat pocket, gave one to *Señor* García, lighted them, and then fixing Albert with a hard stare that would have scared me, said, "Albert, you're not to argue with me again. Do you understand? This had best be the last time it happens. I'll let you off this time because you were so prescient in bringing the horses back to us as quick as you did. However, this is a trail, not some eastern highway. If something happens to the horses or buggy out in the desert, or if we get attacked, Henry's just not strong or mature enough yet to survive. I don't want him hurt."

I blurted out, "Daddy, please don't send me back. I can survive in the desert. Albert and Jack's told me all about what to do. Please, Daddy."

Albert said, "Henry's right, Pa. He does fine when we play hideout in the desert. He nearly always finds me after I've ridden off and hidden from him." What he said was true. Playing hideout was the same as playing hide-and-seek, except the play-

27

ers ranged over much larger areas using horses, and I was good at it.

Albert continued, "He's a good shot with the Winchester, too, even if he is just a little kid. Mama and Maggie want him with you, Pa, and I think you owe it to the women to keep Henry with you so their minds will be at ease."

Señor García, blowing a puff of his cigar into the still air, said nothing but nodded he agreed with Albert.

Daddy stared at Albert for a moment, then just threw his arms up and said, "Oh, all right. Henry can stay. But this sure as hell is against my better judgment." Then he turned to me and said, "You and Albert clean up the dishes here, and I'll look after the horses. They're not getting out of here tonight."

We had a good time sitting around the fire that evening with *Señor* García telling us about hunting cats and bears in the mountains and Daddy telling us stories about his days down in Texas and joking with us. It got late, and Albert and *Señor* García laid out their bedrolls across from us as Daddy and I crawled under the buffalo robe again beside the fire. We all slept peacefully, but it was cold up there, even out of the wind.

Daddy was up before dawn, building up the fire, making coffee, packing up the buggy, and harnessing the horses. Unlike the morning before, he said, "Get out of that robe, Henry. We've got to get ready to roll down this mountain. There's a long day's ride in front of us. Pick up your stuff now, and get it ready for packing."

After some hot coffee and hard bread left over from supper, Albert hugged me and said, "So long, Henry. I know you're going to have fun. Bring Daddy back safe."

I stood as tall and straight as I could and said, "Don't worry, Albert. I'll bring Daddy back safe and sound."

Albert and *Señor* García shook hands with Daddy. Albert

said, "Be careful, Pa. There are some bad *hombres* down in that basin." *Señor* García frowned and nodded in agreement. Albert continued, "We'll tell Mama that you and Henry are getting along just fine."

Daddy nodded at *Señor* García and hugged Albert, slapping him on the back a couple of times. Then Albert and *Señor* García saddled their horses and started back down the pass toward Las Cruces. Daddy and I packed up the buggy and started rolling down the other side of the pass as the sun began to rise, casting orange and red light that bathed the desert in soft purple shadows.

CHAPTER 3
El Tigré

I was glad to get down the Tularosa side of the pass and watch Daddy drive the horses. It was so cold that, as the morning came on, I began to wish Albert and I hadn't talked Daddy out of sending me home. My lips and cheeks were chapped. My eyes watered from the cold, and my feet were so numb I kept a steady rhythm tapping them on the wagon floor just to be sure they were still attached. Even so, I didn't dare complain after begging Daddy to keep me with him. The sun finally warmed things up a little.

After we rode for a while, Daddy decided I needed to learn to drive the wagon. He showed me how to hold the reins and coached me on the kind of commanding voice to use when telling the team gee, haw, or whoa. He put the reins in my hands, then wrapped his arms around me and covered my hands with his. He guided me along that way for a little while as he continued to let Buck and Sergeant step along in a fast walk that ate up the miles. When we got to a long, straight stretch of ruts down in the flats, he released my hands and sat back with his arms crossed.

As I drove, he kept telling me, "Sit up straight, Henry. Just relax, son, and let the horses do the work." Often, he'd ask, "Are you tired yet, Henry? Want me to take the reins?"

I'd shake my head and say, "No, sir, I've got 'em." Somehow, I managed to drive the wagon for nearly an hour before my shoulders started to cramp so badly I became afraid I'd drop the reins. At that point, I handed Daddy the reins but asked, "Can I drive some more later on?"

He roared a big, strong laugh, but I barely heard him because the wind started gusting and stole it away. He said, "Henry, you're going to be a first-class wagoner. I'll let you practice some more after lunch."

We rode along, making jokes again about how cold the wind was. Figuring he was in a good mood and wouldn't turn me down, I begged him to tell me his *El Tigré* story. *El Tigré* was a bad outlaw who had sworn to kill Daddy after Daddy's posse broke up the Kinney gang and killed one of his *amigos* in Rincon. I knew he'd already told my brothers that story, but I hadn't heard much of it.

At first, Daddy told me I was too young to hear about all that fighting, but I kept begging him to tell it. Finally, I said, "Please, Daddy. I promise I'll never tell Mama you told me." Apparently, that was the dealmaker.

"Well, Henry," he said, smiling, "when the posse and I ambushed the Kinney Gang in Rincon, there was a big shoot-out. Lots of bullets were fired on both sides. However, the boys and I caught 'em with their britches down. We managed to kill most of the gang, and only one of our men was even wounded. Element of surprise, I guess. They just didn't believe we could travel that far that fast and get ahead of them. Just like old Nathan Bedford Forrest used to say in the Civil War, 'Git thar fustest with the mostest,' and we did, too. Why, they were planning to ambush us in Rincon themselves. Hard work to surprise your enemy always pays, Henry. Don't forget that."

He looked over at me as if checking to see if I'd taken his words to heart. I nodded and said, "Tell me more about what happened after you got to Rincon."

Daddy took in a big breath, let it out, and said, "I was lucky. I shot and killed Kinney's right-hand man, Doroteo Saenz, just as he was about to shoot Israel Santos. But then one of the meaner bastards, *El Tigré,* got away."

I almost never heard Daddy use profanity, so I understood right then that he had absolutely no use for *El Tigré.* Daddy continued, "I figured he must have slipped off and hidden in the Bosque along the Rio Grande until he got close to El Paso and then rode across the river into Mexico. I decided I'd be patient and wait for him to come back, I knew he would, and then I'd nail his tail, and that would be the last of the Kinney gang."

"How long did you have to wait?" I asked.

"A couple of months. I was working in my office with the windows open to the street, enjoying the nice air around harvest time and the sounds of nighttime coming. Then José Padilla came in. I think you've met him before. Do you remember him?"

Again, I nodded as a vague image of a middle-aged Mexican man came to my mind. Daddy said, "José rode with me in the early days and was one of the best trackers I knew. When he came into my office, I looked up, realized he was in bad shape, and jumped up to help him. His nose looked like it was broken. His face was covered with bruises; his right eye was swollen shut, and his left arm was wrapped in splints."

"Who beat him up?" I asked, eager to hear the rest of the story.

Daddy smiled and said, "Patience, boy, I'm getting to that. I said, 'Good God, man. What's happened to you?' He croaked, '*El Tigré* . . . He's staying with a whore in Concordia down by El Paso. I saw him in an El Paso cantina last night. I was minding my own business just having a little tequila, when he recognized me about the same time I saw him. He walked over, and just stared at me. I stared back. I was ready to trade shots with him or use my hands to defend myself, when he drew his *pistola*. Ayeeeee, Alberto, he was a lot faster than me. My *pistola* never got out of the holster.' "

I said, "Daddy, was José that slow or *El Tigré* that fast?"

Daddy looked over his shoulder at me and grinned. "That's a good question, Henry. I'd say José was about as fast I am." I could only shake my head and say, "Then *El Tigré* was mighty fast."

Daddy nodded and continued. "José said, '*El Tigré* just stood staring at me and pointing that cocked *pistola* at my guts. He started to grin as I stood there with the sweat running down my face waiting to die. He let the hammer down, and, before I could move, like a striking snake he swung the *pistola* hard sideways and broke my arm. Then on the upswing he smashed it across my face while the good-for-nothing Mexican crowd just stood there and watched him. Everyone, they are afraid to cross him. It was quiet as a grave in that place. I remember the silence. It roared in my ears as I heard him grunt to use his strength to swing that *pistola* through the air. I tried to cover up against other swings but he beat me good.' "

The wind rolling across the desert made me shiver from the excitement of the story and the cold, but Daddy wasn't shivering. He was hot just thinking about what *El Tigré* did to José.

"José said, 'Finally, he got tired. He say loud enough for everybody to hear, "You sorry old dog, you tell that bastard Fountain I'm looking for him. When I find him, I'll rip his guts out and string them across El Paso like the tiger I am. Your whipping is just the beginning, you old son of a bitch. When I'm through, even my woman can whip you if I tell her. You tell Fountain. You tell him. I'm here waiting to kill him good."

" 'He spat a stream of nasty tobacco juice on me, took bottle of whiskey and poured it on my face and shirt, it burr like the fires of hell, *Señor* Fountain. Then he stuck ou' elbow for his woman to grab, and he and the whore walk into the night like nothing happened. He was laughing loud too. The bartender sent old Cardenas to get Dr. Bright, and he put splints on my broke arm. He said there wasn't anything else broke and that there wasn't a lot he could do for the bruises and swelling. He gave me a bottle of laudanum for when the pain gets bad. It works pretty good too. I used a little of the laudanum to kill the pain, and the swelling in my face is down some, I think. It don't hurt too bad now.' "

Daddy's face got blood red as he told the story. I could see it even under the chafing from the wind. I'd never seen him so angry, and he was just remembering how José looked and what *El Tigré* had said.

Then Daddy said, "I drove him to his place just downriver from Mesilla. When his wife Maria saw him, she started to cry. After I promised her he'd be all right in a few weeks, she got control of herself and helped me get him into the house. I gave Maria some money and told her to get whatever medicine she needed for José and to come see me if she needed more."

As Daddy spoke, I could see everything in my mind, even the parts he didn't tell. I pictured José's wife with coal-black hair, a chunky, middle-aged woman, gingerly wiping José's bruised face with a wet cloth, and I knew Daddy was thinking about what to do next. "Did you ride for El Paso that same night?" I asked.

"No, son. That would've been too far to ride on horseback. I headed straight back to Las Cruces and found Israel Santos putting up stock at Lohman's Hardware. Do you remember him? He's a second or third cousin of your mother's. He's kinda short, but very strong. I've seen him roll around hundred-pound kegs tilted over on their edges, one in each hand at Lohman's. He's fearless, and a dead shot with a pistol in either hand."

I nodded, though I wasn't perfectly sure I remembered him. Daddy continued, "I motioned him outside into the shadows, told him *El Tigré* was back, had beaten José to a pulp, and that I was catching the five-o'clock train to El Paso to catch him. I asked if Santos wanted to come with me. He did, and we were in El Paso by six thirty the next morning. Then we rode as fast as we could over to Concordia. Neither one of us spoke a word the entire ride."

I could picture them riding out on their dangerous mission on horseback, but I didn't understand their silence. "Why didn't you talk during the ride?" I asked.

Daddy sighed and said, "Son, it's a matter of focus. Once you set your mind to do something like that, you just have to keep your mind in the right place. You don't talk until you need to talk."

While I tried to absorb that, he continued, "Just outside Concordia, we met a toothless old woman trudging toward the El Paso market with vegetables in a basket on her head. When we asked her about *El Tigré,* she pointed out the adobe house where he and the whore were staying."

Daddy had used the word *whore* once before in this story, and I hadn't understood it, so this time I stopped him and asked, "What's a whore?"

Again, he sighed and then paused to think for a moment. "You know the type women who wear clothes your mama doesn't approve of?"

I asked, "You mean the ones she says look like they don't care if their bosoms spill out of their clothes?"

"The very ones, Henry."

I frowned and asked, "Why doesn't Mama like them? What do they do?"

A line of red began creeping up Daddy's collar, and he said, "They sing songs to drunks in the saloons."

"So *El Tigré* liked singing?" I asked.

"That he did," Daddy said. "Anyway, we walked the horses

35

down the backstreet where the whore's house sat and checked it for windows and doors. The windows were too small for *El Tigré* to crawl through, so I put Israel at the front door and told him when he heard me bust through the back door to come in the front ready to shoot and not to hesitate to shoot the whore if she got in the way."

I frowned, not believing I'd heard Daddy right. "You mean you told him to shoot a woman?"

Daddy squinted and said, "Henry, those women often carry pistols or knives, and they can kill you just as dead as any man can. Don't ever forget that, son."

I nodded as I squinted out toward the mountains trying to look serious and he continued his story. "I took my pistol out at the back door and made sure it was loaded." Then Daddy paused again, leaned down so he was eyeball-to-eyeball with me, and said, "Always be sure your gun is loaded. An empty gun will get you killed in a hurry."

Again I nodded and he continued, "Taking a deep breath, I was just reaching for the door handle when it turned, and the door swung open. There stood *El Tigré* in his long johns, boots, and gun belt, yawning and heading for the privy out back. As soon as he saw me, he tried to slam the door shut, but it hung on a rug and wouldn't close. He saw my old Walker Colt was cocked and ready and knew I wouldn't hesitate to kill him if he tried for his pistol, so he put his hands up. If we hadn't caught him like that, there'd have been a hell of a fight.

"I called out, 'Israel. Come round back and see the skunk I've caught!' Then I yelled into the doorway, 'Lady, you stay inside, and stay quiet, or my man will make you wish you had!' Israel came running around the corner of the house with his shotgun in one hand, both hammers cocked, and a revolver in the other. I said, 'Israel, disarm *El Pussy Gato* and put the shackles on him.' Israel holstered his revolver, walked over to him, and said in a low voice, 'José Padilla *es mi amigo,* you son of a bitch.' Then he smashed *El Tigré*'s face with the butt of his shotgun and broke his nose. And that's how we caught *El Tigré.*"

I liked it when Daddy said words in front of me Mama would object to because I knew he was talking to me as if I were a man. Daddy grinned at me as if he'd finished the story, but I frowned, sensing there had to be more to it. "How did you get him back to Las Cruces?" I asked. "Did they hang him for riding with the Kinney gang?"

Daddy tightened Mama's *rebozo* over his ears and said, "Israel saddled *El Tigré*'s horse while I kept an eye on him and the whore. He found a brace of the new Smith and Wesson pistols in *El Tigré*'s saddlebags, but most of the money he'd stolen was gone. I figured the whore probably had most of it, but I decided not to pursue it, since I really was out of my jurisdiction. We threw *El Tigré* over the saddle and tied him on. As we headed out for the train depot, the whore stood in her doorway and yelled, '*El Tigré* will keel you, Fountain. He'll keel you.' I just grinned and called back to her, '*El Tigré* isn't going to do anything except go to hell.' After breakfast, I sent a telegram to the sheriff in Las Cruces asking him to meet us at the station to pick up *El Tigré* and put him in jail.

"The ride home was quiet; however, as we got close to the depot, *El Tigré* seemed to revive and started growling about how he'd get free and shoot us in our heads and cut our *cojones* off. I got tired of hearing it, got up to stretch my legs, and walked back to where a Texas Ranger was sitting. The Ranger told me I ought to fix my pistol like his, which had a lanyard around the handle with the other end tied to his belt. He said it had saved his bacon several times when he had scuffled with prisoners and had his weapons knocked out of his hand. I thought that was pretty smart thinking, so he gave me a string of rawhide and showed me how to rig my pistol up that way."

I knew Daddy was telling me this for a reason, and I could guess what it was. "Did *El Tigré* try to knock your gun out of your hand?" I asked.

Daddy nodded, smiling, and said, "There was a big crowd waiting with the sheriff on the station platform when we got to Las Cruces. I reckon people just wanted a look at a famous outlaw. Israel and I got off the train with *El Tigré* between us. I had hold of the shackles chain between his wrists. As soon as we stepped off the train, the sheriff ran up to us with a big grin on his face, held out his hand, and said, 'Well done, Fountain. Well done.'

"Like an idiot, I relaxed my grip on the chain as I shook his hand. *El Tigré* instantly pulled free and tried to jerk my pistol out of its holster, but my new lanyard jerked it out of his hands. Then, quick as anything, *El Tigré* jumped off the platform and ran for the desert.

"Israel had unloaded his shotgun for the ride back and was cursing and yelling that he couldn't fire. The sheriff and his deputy froze and just stared at *El Tigré*'s fast disappearing backside. I used the lanyard to jerk my big Walker Colt revolver back as I yelled at him to stop. I dropped to one knee to steady myself, knowing I'd have only one shot, and a long one at that, to stop him. Just as he was about to disappear into the mesquite, I fired, and the forty-four-caliber ball from that six-pound revolver struck him square in the back. It hit him so hard he did a somersault forward and landed faceup. I felt bad I had to shoot the man, but I wasn't about to let him get away after the beating he gave José and the threats he'd made about killing me."

I looked at Daddy and felt mighty proud to be his son. For a long time, I sat looking over the yuccas, mesquites, creosotes, and brown, black, and white patches of sand between the far blue San Andres Mountains and us. I thought about all he had told me. The lessons I had learned from his story have stood me in good stead for a lifetime.

CHAPTER 4
ROY TIBBETS, COWBOY

On the way to Tularosa, Daddy stopped about a mile from the first road leading through White Sands and checked the loads on his long-barreled Colt revolver and the Winchester. In those days, outlaws who had been run out of Texas liked to make hideouts around there, so he kept the rifle on his knees during the ride through the Sands. Daddy was supposed to meet a man in Tularosa, but he wasn't sure he'd be there because we would be two days late.

We stopped for dinner that night at Pat Coghlan's store and cantina in Tularosa. Charlie Esparza ran it then. It was a clean, well-lighted place with a small bar at one end, and it had Mexican waiters who didn't keep us waiting for our supper. We sat at a table close to a fireplace so big I could have walked into it if there had been no fire. I was a little short for the chair, but sitting on one leg made up the difference. That night, the house special was *caldillo*. Charlie Esparza's wife used the best beef, potatoes, onions, and fiery chilies and cooked it just right. My mouth still waters when I think about her stew. I remember Daddy leaning toward my ear and saying, "Careful, Henry, this *cadillo* will be hot coming and going." I grinned a moment later, when I figured out what he meant.

While we were eating, a cowboy walked through the door, looked around, and then came over to our table. He was wearing a soft, buckskin coat with lots of fringe; a rough, wool vest buttoned top-to-bottom; and shotgun chaps that showed thousands of scratches. He had a big, blue bandanna tied around his neck, and on his left hip, he carried a big, long-barreled Colt revolver in a fine, double-loop holster. It was the first time I had seen a cowboy up close, so I couldn't help staring at him and taking in every detail. I was a townie, and Daddy didn't let me play where cowboys liked to congregate in Mesilla or Las Cruces. When he saw me staring at him, he grinned and winked. I winked back and immediately liked him.

Daddy stood up, shook hands with him, and introduced him to me as Mr. Roy Tibbets. When Roy shook my hand, I noticed his hand was rough and powerful with short, stubby fingers. My daddy's hands were powerful, too, but his hands had long fingers with well-manicured nails, and they were smooth like my mother's.

Roy's hair stuck out from under his hat like old, weathered straw falling out of a barn, and he hadn't shaved the scraggly beard around his big, swooping mustache in quite a while. He smelled of sweat and tobacco, and I could tell that his squinting eyes took in every detail about us.

After we'd made our introductions, Daddy said, "Pull up a chair, Roy, and tell us what you have for me."

Roy pulled up a chair and sat up straight, looked Daddy in the eye, and said, "I been working for a rancher named Fremont. He told me to ride over to Tularosa and give you some pieces of cowhide."

Even I knew who Mr. Fremont was. He owned one of the biggest ranches on the east side of the Black Range, and Daddy did a lot of legal work for him. Daddy nodded and said, "I've been expecting you. Won't you have dinner?"

I don't think Roy had eaten for a while because he went through two bowls of *caldillo* as fast as he could pitch it down with a big spoon. He was done with two bowls before I'd even finished one. He wiped his bowl clean with a flour tortilla, ate it in three bites, and, sighing with contentment, wiped the outside of his mouth and mustache with the back of his hand. He leaned back, patted his lean belly, and belched so loud everyone in the cantina must have heard him. Then he reached in his vest and pulled out a sack of tobacco and some cigarette papers. While rolling himself a smoke with one hand, he pulled the sack's drawstring closed with his teeth.

Daddy had finished his meal, too, and pulled a cigar out of his coat, which he'd thrown over the chair to his right. He'd also hung his pistol belt there, out of sight but within easy reach. He struck a sulfur match and used it to light up for both of them.

Roy said, "Sorry about eatin' like a wolf, Mr. Fountain, but I've been sittin' on ol' Claude since 'fore daylight, and the wind off them mountains is downright cold. I'd expected to meet up with you in Lincoln tomorrow, but when I saw you in here, I figured I was just lucky and decided I'd gotten my days confused, which ain't that hard for me to do."

Daddy nodded his head appreciatively and said, "I'm glad you showed up when you did, Roy. We got delayed a couple of days in San Agustin Pass ourselves. Horses ran off and left us stranded. Fortunately, they went back home, and my son Albert and his father-in-law brought them back to us. So being a little late actually saved a little time in the long run." He looked over at me and winked like we were fellow conspirators.

Roy nodded and grinned. "Yes, sir, horses, they's just like women, can't live with 'em, can't live without 'em." We all had a good chuckle, although I had no idea what he was talking about.

Then Roy glanced over at me and said, "You got a good-lookin' son there, Mr. Fountain. You ever done any ranchin', boy?"

I answered, "No, sir," but I got kind of puffed up, thinking I must look older than my age if he was asking me that kind of question. Daddy just grinned, stuck his lower lip out, and slowly shook his head.

Roy took a draw on his cigarette and asked Daddy, "You wanna wait till later to discuss business?"

Daddy shook his head and said, "No, sir. Henry knows to keep his mouth shut, and he does. He's my assistant. Tell us about what you have."

Roy and Daddy talked in low voices for nearly an hour. I had to sit up on the edge of my chair and lean forward over the table on my elbows to hear what they were talking about, and even doing that, I didn't catch it all.

I heard enough to piece together that when Roy had butchered a couple of Fremont's cows for a *fiesta* back before Christmas, he'd noticed something odd about the brands on the hides. Mr. Fremont's brand was the Bar F. He had just bought some stock from Charlie Bentene, who was trying to start a little ranch called the Circle Eight over in Black Canyon. Bentene's brand was a fancy, straight-sided eight with a circle around it.

One of the steers Roy had slaughtered had just been bought from Bentene, and one was from Fremont's original herd. When Roy compared the flesh sides of the Circle Eight hide next to the one from the Bar F, it was easy to see the Bar F brand had been changed to make a Circle Eight. However, Roy said a man wouldn't have been able to tell it if he was sitting on a horse ten feet away from the branded cow. Bentene had used a running iron on stock from Fremont's ranch and then sold the stock back to Fremont. I had to work to keep from grinning. I thought it was a pretty clever trick. Roy said Fremont and some of the other big ranchers were hopping mad about tricks like that, and they wanted blood.

CHAPTER 5
WOLF EYES

As we sat there in Pat Coghlan's place, Daddy took out a little notebook and wrote down everything from Roy Tibbet's story he thought he might use in Lincoln at the grand jury presentations. Daddy had just reached over and dropped his notebook back into his coat pocket when the cantina door swung open and was slammed shut by the wind. Two well-dressed men walked in. They might have been cowboys, but their clothes weren't covered with dust like nearly everyone else's. They were younger than Roy, wore stockman dress coats, and carried big, heavy revolvers. One was tall and skinny with a big, hooked nose and crooked teeth that stuck out under his walrus mustache. The other was short but walked with a cocky strut. His face was clean-shaven. He grinned and nodded hello to everyone. His hat, a big-brim, white Stetson, was pushed back on his head, letting his straw-colored hair hang down toward blue eyes that were hard and piercing. When he looked at me, I felt like a wolf was sizing me up for a meal, but I felt safe with Roy and Daddy there.

Both of the men were red-faced, like they had been out in the wind most of the day. They pulled chairs out and sat at a table close to the bar across the room. In loud voices intended to bring a waiter on the run, they said they were ready to put some firewater and *caldillo* in their bellies. I watched as a waiter came around, and they ordered their supper. They sipped short glasses of whiskey the waiter brought them, laughed and joked with a few men sitting nearby, and looked around the room, apparently sizing everyone up. When Wolf Eyes saw Roy talking to Daddy, his eyes narrowed to a squint as he nodded toward us to catch Hook Nose's attention.

Grinning, they stood up and started twisting between tables as they moved toward us, Wolf Eyes in front with Hook Nose behind him, grinning like a school bully ready to pick on some little kid. I saw them coming, and when Roy saw me staring at them across the cantina, he glanced in their direction. His jaw muscles rippled as he grew silent. His hand moved off his knee and slid down to ease the tie off the hammer of his revolver. I saw Daddy move his right hand under the back of his coat, and I knew he had it on the handle of his revolver when I heard its hammer click back.

Daddy whispered, just loud enough for me to hear, "Henry, if any trouble starts, move away from Roy and me as fast you can." I nodded that I understood.

Wolf Eyes came up to the table, a toothpick hanging out of the side of his mouth, and stuck his hand out toward Daddy. He said with a grin, "Howdy, Mr. Fountain. I'm Jack Stone, and this here is Charlie Bentene."

Daddy's gun hand didn't move as he hooked his left thumb into his vest pocket, and, for a few long seconds, didn't speak. I'd never seen him refuse to shake hands with anybody. Stone's eyes narrowed as he lost his smile. Daddy leaned forward in his chair a little with his right hand still inside his coat as he continued to stare at Stone.

I could tell by how quiet he was that Daddy was angry. I started looking around the cantina to find a shelter if trouble started. Finally, Daddy nodded at them and said, "Gentlemen? Mr. Tibbets here and I were discussing some personal business. If you want to wait, I'll be glad to talk to you after we're done."

Stone looked taken aback, and he said, "Well, Mr. Fountain,

I just hope you ain't believing anything this old son of a bitch has told you." He spat the words out as if he'd bitten into bitter weed as he stared straight at Roy. Roy, silent and poker-faced, not blinking an eye, stared right back at Stone and Bentene. His hand rested unmoving and relaxed on his revolver.

I'll never forget the look on Daddy's face. His eyes narrowed to slits, and his voice became a hard, flat, threatening monotone that made the hair on the back of my neck stand straight up. He said, "Watch your foul mouth, Stone. I don't want this young boy hearing rough language like that. I don't want to hear any more threats, implied or otherwise, toward us now or later. Understand me?" He was furious, and Stone's eyes showed surprise.

Daddy's eyes never left Stone's. The way Daddy said the words, precisely and slowly with deadly calm, was enough to make any man back away from starting a fight. Right then, I knew I wanted to be just like my daddy—fearless and a man to be feared.

Stone suddenly seemed to relax. He grinned and gave a little nod, but Bentene's eyes were wide and his mouth open. Stone looked like a wolf showing his fangs trying to keep a grizzly bear off him. He shook his head, held up both hands with his palms out, and waved Daddy off. He said, "Sorry, Mr. Fountain. I didn't mean no harm, just teasing old Roy here. He's the da . . . I mean he's the durndest, wild storyteller a feller can listen to here in Tularosa. I just wouldn't want you to take anything he told you too seriously."

Daddy said, "I'll take it any way I think best, Stone. I'll use it too, understand me?"

With a twisted little grin, Stone shrugged and nodded. He said, "That's fine. See ya later, Tibbets." He turned from our table and led Bentene back to theirs where their *caldillo* was already sitting with steam rising off the top.

Daddy never moved until they sat down. I'd never seen Daddy stare somebody down like that. In fact, I'd never seen two grown men seem so ready to fight, and my heart pounded for a while as I thought about it. Daddy finally relaxed, and I heard the hammer ease down on the Colt. Roy took his hand off his revolver, but he left the hammer tie loose.

Daddy pitched some coins on the table for dinner and said, "Roy, let's go over to our room at *Señora* Esparza's boarding-house, and you can show us those hides." Roy just nodded and followed us out the door.

Neither he nor Daddy ever looked back toward Stone, but I did. Stone was watching every move we made as he slowly spooned up his *caldillo*.

Roy disappeared into the cold darkness while we walked over to our room. He showed up with a roll of hides under his arm just as we were entering the boardinghouse. We walked single file down the narrow hallway to our room, with Roy's spurs making a pleasant jingle as he moved behind Daddy and me. When we got in the room, Roy unrolled the two hides and spread them out on the floor.

Even I could tell the Bar F brand had been changed to a Circle Eight. Daddy looked at them and grinned. He said, "Now we have enough evidence to arrest those thieves. Two of them are sitting in the cantina right now. Roy, you've earned your pay for this one, my friend. I'm sure Mr. Fremont will be grateful." Roy just squatted by the hides, nodding and grinning all the while, as if he had struck the mother lode.

Daddy said, "Roy, I'll keep these hides and show them with the one Les Dow is bringing. If you find out about any more anywhere in the next week or two, let me know. I'll be in Lincoln for the next two or three weeks. For your safety, I think you need to get on to Lincoln soon. Why don't you ride along with us? Two guns are better than one anytime. We're leaving about an hour before sunup. I'll call you before the grand jury in the next two or three days, and then you can get on back to Fremont's."

Roy took out his tobacco sack from a vest pocket and started rolling another cigarette. He said, "I was just thinkin' the same thing, Mr. Fountain. I'll ride on over to Lincoln with y'all and tell my story, the sooner the better. I'll be glad to hang around Lincoln and ride back to Cruces with you, if you want. Y'all are gonna have to be real careful goin' back, 'cause the cat's gonna be out of the bag."

"No, that's all right. You can get on back to the ranch after you testify, because I have a first-class bodyguard right here," Daddy said, squeezing my shoulder.

"Then I'll go on back to the ranch as soon as you're done with me. If I find any more of these hides, I'll let you know. Wisht I had a bodyguard like you do. I'd feel a sight more safe." Roy looked in my direction and winked, and I wished mightily I were a cowboy so I could ride with Roy. I was ready to go anywhere with that man.

As Roy was clinking out the door, Daddy said, "We'll be fine on the ride up to Lincoln with our friends, Colt and Winchester. I expect to have my work finished soon. Good night, Roy. See you in the morning. You're a great help."

Roy nodded and touched his hat with a two-fingered salute before he disappeared in the dark. We got settled to bed, but I didn't sleep well that night because I kept seeing Jack Stone's eyes boring into mine and feeling that he was about to do something bad to us. Daddy appeared to sleep easy, but I wasn't sure he was really asleep. I usually heard him snoring at home when he was sleeping in bed with Mama. He was mighty quiet in bed with me that night.

Way before sunup, Charlie Esparza served us up a big breakfast of *huevos rancheros*. Then he harnessed Sergeant and

Buck and brought the wagon around for us. When we finished breakfast, Roy was waiting outside sitting on Claude and had his Winchester across his saddle pommel.

Daddy loaded up our Winchester, lunches, trunk of papers, the valise, and Roy's hides. We said *adios* to the Esparzas and headed down the dark road to Lincoln in the dark, freezing air, Roy's horse trotting along beside us. It was still over an hour before sunup. I sat next to Daddy, wishing it would get light soon so Stone couldn't jump out of the bushes and start shooting without us seeing him first.

CHAPTER 6
JACK STONE

The tall, tree-covered mountains, ominous and scary, rose around us. I knew some gang of outlaws and murderers was going to charge us out of nowhere shooting and yelling as they filled us full of holes. It didn't relieve my fear any when Daddy kept that loaded Winchester across his knees. I figured Roy could get to his pistol quick enough if he needed it.

While we were passing a wide meadow where the chances of attack, or so I estimated, were low, I asked, "Daddy, who's Jack Stone?"

Daddy shook his head and said, "He's a mean, no-good, greedy son of a bitch." Again I delighted in having him talk to me just as if I were a grown man. "He owns a small spread in a canyon over on the San Andres side of the basin. He has a few cattle, and I'll bet nearly all of them are stolen. He's a greasy thief, a murderer, and a con man who talks a great line about how all the small ranchers in the Tularosa Basin have to stick together if they want to survive. He keeps talking about open-range law."

I frowned and asked, "What's open-range law?"

"Well, Stone claims the unwritten open-range law says that if you find an unbranded calf on your property, then it's yours, regardless of the mother's brand. Naturally, he says, if you keep the calf and its mother is there, then you ought to keep its mother, too. He likes to say, 'That's the way it is in Texas, ain't it?' And folks think, *Well, if that's the way Texans do it, then we should, too."*

I frowned because his idea conflicted with what Mama had taught me from the Good Book about doing unto others as you'd have them do unto you. It seemed to me if someone's cow had a calf on your property, you should give them both back to the owner. Stone's idea of open-range law just didn't seem right to me. "Why would people think that way, Daddy?" I asked.

Daddy handed me the reins and let me drive while he lit a cigar, but instead of taking the reins back, he looked to our friend and asked, "How can I explain that, Roy?"

Roy laughed and said, "I reckon you know better than me."

Daddy sighed and said, "The drought that started in eighteen ninety is still hurting all the ranchers, big and small. It's dried up most of the water supply and, with too many cattle already on the open range, it's wiped out the gra'ma grass. Ranchers who are about to go under will listen to anybody who says it's right to fight any fight to keep cattle that aren't their own or even to kill in order to keep what little they have. Stone got several of the small ranchers to form an association. They all agreed to put money in a pot to help Stone fight against what they felt were illegal and unwarranted attacks against them by the big ranchers and their attorneys."

I frowned and asked, "You mean they gave him money to hire a lawyer?"

Daddy shrugged and said, "I doubt he's hired a lawyer. I think they use the money to pay thugs to—" Instead of finishing the thought, Daddy said, "Regardless of that, I know Stone just wants to steal cattle to build his ranch into a major operation. He's been accused several times of killing or running off range detectives that were nosing around small ranchers' herds. Whenever the sheriff tried to develop evidence to bring Stone to trial, the association ranchers all kept quiet and made sure their ranch hands kept their mouths shut. For all I know, association members might have helped him with the killings. If I don't put a quick stop to the rustling, there'll be a major shooting war between the big and small operations, just like fifteen years ago in the days of Billy the Kid, and if the shooting starts, a lot of blood is going to be spilled."

"Ain't that the truth," muttered Roy.

By this time, the sun had come up, and I felt safer, being able to scan the woods around me. It made me proud to be out with Daddy helping to set wrongs right.

Sometime late in the afternoon, when the lunch Mrs. Esparza had fixed for us was long gone, I was ready to start chewing on cactus, I was so hungry. Daddy was hunched down in his army coat with its big collar turned up as high as it would go, and I was shivering from the cold, but Roy just loped along beside us and casually rolled his cigarettes whenever we stopped to rest Buck and Sergeant.

At one of our stops, I kept rubbing my hands and slapping myself to keep warm. Roy grinned and asked, "You cold, Henry?" All I could do was nod. He said, "Aw, it ain't so bad. Why you'd get used to it quick if you was a-cowboyin' out here for a month or two." For the first time, I thought, *Maybe I don't want to be a cowboy after all.*

CHAPTER 7
MRS. DARCY'S BOARDINGHOUSE

When we got to Lincoln a little before dark, Daddy rented a room at Mrs. Darcy's boardinghouse on Main Street, almost right across from the two-story courthouse where the grand jury met. Roy helped us unload our gear and carry it to our room. Then we drove over to the livery stable, and Roy stabled his mustang and said he was headed for a saloon. Daddy said, "Be careful not to drink too much, Roy. I need you to testify in a day or two, so you have to be clear-eyed and sober."

Roy raised one hand as if he were being sworn in at a jury trial and said, "Mr. Fountain, I ain't no drunk. Just want to warm my innards with a meal and a little shot of good whiskey. You can count on me when you need me."

Then Roy turned to me and said, "Get on down to the boardinghouse and get big on Miz Darcy's good cookin', Henry. I'll see ya 'fore I leave." He slapped me on the back and took off down the street toward the saloon.

Mrs. Darcy was a widow lady, generously broad across her backside and big in the bosom. Her gray-streaked, blonde hair rode in a big twist on top of her head, and she was as gracious and kind a person as I've ever met. She took a shine to me right off.

When Daddy and I got back from the livery, she said, "Now you gentlemen just go right on to your room and get comfortable. I'll be serving dinner promptly at six o'clock, so come hungry. There'll be plenty for everybody, especially Mr. Henry."

After hanging our clothes up nice and neat, we washed up, combed down our hair, and slapped the dust out of our riding clothes. We walked downstairs to stand by the fire in the dining room as the other boarders were coming in.

Mrs. Darcy had a full house, and every place at the dinner table was taken. There was a rancher from over near Roswell who never took his hat off, inside or out; a Methodist preacher who rode a circuit between Roswell and Las Cruces; an army lieutenant with wavy, black hair and a droopy little mustache from Fort Stanton; and an old-timer with bright, dancing eyes behind silver-rimmed glasses. The old-timer sat next to me and extended his hand for a shake and said, "Howdy, young feller. I'm Rufus Pike. I own a small ranch up in the Organs behind Tortugas Mountain."

I liked him right away. I shook his hand and gave it a couple of pumps saying, "Pleased to meet you, Mr. Pike. I'm Henry Fountain."

"Just call me Rufus, son." Rufus talked to me all through a dinner of pot roast with potatoes, carrots, and onions. He and Mrs. Darcy were the only ones in the room who actually paid any attention to me.

I learned that he and Mrs. Darcy's husband had ridden in the same company of dragoons in the days before the Civil War, when the militias were fighting Apaches all over the southwest.

About halfway through our meal, I told him I was helping my daddy bring thieving cattle rustlers to justice. Then I asked, "What brings you here, Rufus?"

"Why this lady right here," he said, hooking a thumb toward Mrs. Darcy. "Two or three times a year, I ride my big, gray mule, Sally, over to Lincoln and make repairs on Miz Darcy's house in exchange for her good cooking and some extraord'narily fine hospitality." He had an extra twinkle in his eye when he said this, and Mrs. Darcy blushed like a schoolgirl.

★ ★ ★ ★ ★

Most of the folks staying with Mrs. Darcy were gone in a day or two. The preacher was there until Sunday, when he held a church service somewhere in town, and then he moved on. The rancher was gone the next day, and so was the lieutenant. I was glad Rufus stayed around for a few days because he was fun to talk to. Since I didn't know anyone my own age in town, I offered to help Rufus with his work while Daddy was at the courthouse. Rufus grinned and said, "I reckon I can use all the help I can get, especially from a strong, young buck like yoreself."

It wasn't long before we were great friends. I followed him around like a pup, listening to his stories and helping him repair fencing and other stuff around Mrs. Darcy's place. His stories were the first I'd ever heard about the Apache wars from somebody who'd actually fought the Indians. My daddy wouldn't talk about his soldiering days. Rufus had an unlimited supply of stories, and he was a great storyteller. We'd work a while, and then he'd get a cup of coffee and relax before refreshing the wad of tobacco he kept in his cheek. While he was resting and drinking coffee, he'd tell me about his past adventures.

CHAPTER 8
RUFUS'S STORY

The first Sunday after we arrived, Rufus had seen Daddy with his Winchester and commented on what a fine weapon it was. Daddy told him we'd be going out shooting later that morning and invited him to come along and try it out. Rufus thought that was fine idea and said so several times. Soon we hitched up Buck and Sergeant and drove a couple of miles outside of Lincoln for target practice in a little canyon that fronted the river. Rufus watched closely as Daddy cranked a couple of cartridge loads through the Winchester, never missing anything at which he pointed. Then Daddy let me shoot a load while he and Rufus encouraged and coached me. After I managed to hit four targets out of twelve shots, I was beginning to feel a bit cocky as Rufus nodded and winked at me. Daddy just stood behind me with his arms crossed, looking serious.

When it was Rufus's turn to shoot, he hit every target at every distance available. He was a better shot than Daddy, and Daddy said so. Rufus had one round left in his load after turning a rock the size of his fist twenty or thirty yards downriver to dust, and in one smooth motion, never pausing to aim, he whipped the Winchester up and killed a grackle sitting on a bush cussing at us at least fifty yards away. After the shot, there wasn't anything left except just a few black feathers floating to the ground. It was a remarkable shot, and Daddy asked, "Where'd you learn to shoot like that, Rufus?"

Rufus just grinned and said, "Why, in the old days, a feller learned to do that or die in Indian country."

After shooting, we rode down the river looking for some good, deep fishing pools, but most of the water was gone. It was just too dry.

When we got back to Mrs. Darcy's in the middle of the afternoon, her house was filled with the aroma of baked apple pies. She invited us to come sit around her kitchen table next to her cooking stove, warm up, and keep her company while she cooked the evening meal. We didn't hesitate to accept the invitation.

As we sat at the table, Daddy and Rufus told stories and drank coffee while we ate pieces of pie so fresh it scalded our mouths if we didn't blow on it first. We put butter and some hard sauce on it, and it was sweet and fruity all the way down. I had milk with mine, and I've never had better apple pie anywhere. Mrs. Darcy rattled around her kitchen getting *chiles rellenos* ready for dinner while we ate.

Rufus said with a chuckle, "You know, havin' sugar in coffee's a rare treat fer me. Why if'n I tried keeping sugar out'n a fancy sugar bowl on the middle of the table at my place, the ants and waspers would come fight me fer it. They'd probably win, too. I wouldn't fight no wasper fer no sugar. No, siree."

Mrs. Darcy came and sat down with us for a while and told Daddy and Rufus they were welcome to smoke or chew. Rufus excused himself to get his spittoon. He was back in two ticks of the clock and already had a chew started. He plopped back down in his seat and said, "This here is mighty kind of you, Miz Darcy, feeding us some of yore deelicious pie, then lettin' us indulge in our nasty habits."

She tilted her head down and looked up at him with a smile. "Your company is worth it all, gentlemen, especially young Henry's. Now he's a real gentleman." I sat up a little straighter, a man among men. Daddy wet his cigar, grinning, and, with a wink at me, lit up.

Mrs. Darcy teased Rufus about carrying a spittoon during his scouting days, and that set him to telling us a story about a close scrape he had with an Apache named *Caballo Negro* (Black Horse).

Rufus said, "Back in 'fifty-five, I was a-scoutin' fer Cap'n Ewell and his Sixtieth Dragoons. We was a-chasin' and a-fightin' Apaches down in Texas on the El Paso to San Antonio road. In those days, the Mescaleros was a-wipin' out any freight outfits that wasn't protected by soldiers.

"Cap'n Ewell was determined to have some satisfaction fer all the murderin' and robbin' they'd done. We chased those damned Apaches all over hell and half of Texas. We had a few running battles with them, but they never stood and fought till they was cornered. Then they was the devil to pay. We musta lost ten or fifteen men in those fights."

"What if they captured you?" I asked, hoping to draw out some gruesome details, the sort I'd heard my older brothers tell. I wondered if their tales were true.

Rufus frowned and said, "Lord help ye, if they ever caught ye alive. They knowed how to torture a feller so's he stayed alive fer days, and they did it so's they'd git more power from his sufferin'. Ewell told us that in any Indian fight to always save one bullet fer our own use. We did, too. I knowed a few fellers that had to pull the trigger on their own heads, stuck the business end of those old Walker Colts right up against an eyeball and pulled the trigger, they did."

I was thrilled to hear this story, told in graphic detail my mother wouldn't approve of. Then I wondered if Daddy had forgotten I was there and decided with joy that he hadn't, that he counted me man enough to hear this talk.

Rufus continued, "Well, sir, it got on into late fall, and we'd just about rode our horses to death a-chasin' those red heathens.

I found us a nice spot on the Rio Grande up in the Bosque about twenty miles north of El Paso. Ewell, he decided to hole up there to escape bein' attacked by *banditos* and Indians and to rest the animals and men fer a while. I tell ye, I was mighty glad not to be in the saddle fer twelve hours a day in wind and dust that cut just as bad as any Mescalero blade.

"After we'd been camped fer four or five days, I reckin those Apache devils got lonesome fer us 'cause we woke up one morning with half the stock gone and the sentry with a second mouth cut across his windpipe. Nobody had heard a sound. That's how tired we all was and how quiet them Apaches was in takin' 'em. I 'spect the sentry just dozed off, and that there was the end of him. He was my friend, but he made a big mistake and paid fer it, so I didn't have a whole lot of sympathy fer him. Ye just didn't make those kinds of mistakes and expect to live in those days. Ye know what I mean don't ye, Mr. Fountain?"

Daddy took a pull on his cigar and, after blowing a long stream of smoke toward the ceiling, he said, "Yes, sir, Rufus. I'm afraid I know very well from long, hard experience."

Rufus winked at us and said, "Yes sir, Mr. Fountain. Yore reputation as an Indian fighter runs a far piece in front of ye. Anyways, Ol' Ewell just stood on the edge of the river and stared off in the distance toward the Organs and Franklins fer a long time. The rest of us jest sat around the fire tryin' to get warm and cursed those red heathen fer their damned, slick trick. Finally, Ewell yelled, 'Rufus Pike!' I come a-runnin' with a salute and said, 'Yes, sir.' 'Rufus,' he said, 'Go find where those Mescalero are. Then come back and get me if they ain't killed all the stock they stole by runnin' 'em to death.' So I saddled up with the best horse that was left 'cause they'd taken mine, and I started after 'em."

By this point, I tingled with excitement. "He sent you out by yourself?" I asked. "How did you know where to look?"

Rufus grinned and said, "Yep, I tracked 'em by myself, and them devils was smart. They rode about twenty mile up river then started across the desert toward Baylor Pass as a group. Then a rider with three or four horses would peel off the main group and head out alone."

Rufus gestured first to the right, then to the left, with his hands. "Some went over the Organs by Baylor Pass; some, over San Agustin Pass; a few went through Bear Canyon; and some, through Soledad Canyon. Before long, the only tracks left was from four animals and three riders who finally split up.

"I knowed what was a-gonna happen when that first group split out. When I seen them last tracks I stopped and sat a spell, tryin' to figger out where they'd rendezvous. I guessed it had to be near a spring over in the Jarilla Mountains since it was on their way to some camp up in the Sacramentos. Only a few old *gringo* desert rats like me knowed 'bout that spring, but all the Mescalero knowed where it was.

"I figgered I'd ride over there and set myself up a little ambush fer the early birds. Maybe get 'em all if they came in slow. At least I could keep 'em from water so's the horses would move real slow. I knowed I'd get there first, 'cause they's riding 'round the desert in all different directions tryin' to confuse anybody that followed 'em. I wasn't sure enough about their meeting spot to go back and get Cap'n Ewell, though. Ewell's animals needed rest bad, so I went Apache huntin' on my own. That there was a big mistake."

Daddy was puffing his cigar and nodding as he listened. When Rufus paused, I asked, "Why was it a big mistake, Rufus?"

"Well, son, I got over to the Jarillas about dark and found me a good place to make camp up a little draw behind a mesquite thicket where I could watch the spring and not be seen. I was plum wore out and didn't want to risk no fire, so I hid my horse and just rolled up in my blankets and went to sleep. 'Bout daylight, I felt this here sharp prick on my neck and thought some sticker had blowed on to me during the night. I opened one eye and looked into the narrow, slanty eyes of an Apache face that had the ugliest scar I'd ever seen on a man." Rufus took a finger and drew its pattern down his face while I sat watching his every move. Mrs. Darcy fanned herself.

Rufus said, "That there scar run from his scalp line across his forehead, down by his left eye, across his cheek, and just kinda fell off the edge of his jaw. He had this big Bowie knife ready to cut my throat, and he was grinnin' like a cat with a cornered mouse. I found out a few years later his name was Fast Hand, and he had fought and killed two men in his own clan who'd objected to him takin' a couple of Mexican women fer wives. That's how he'd got that there scar, but nobody objected to the Mexican women bein' around after the fight. No, sir. They shore didn't.

"I knowed I was a-gonna die. In fact, I couldn't quite figger out why I was still a-livin'. He had me dead to rights. I did a deadly stupid thing by going to sleep when Apaches was around, and I knowed I deserved to die. They's nothin' I could do about it 'cept die quick or, if I couldn't pull that off, not scream too loud while he tortured me. He was a-grittin' his teeth as he held that blade against my windpipe, and he motioned to a young man that was with him to come over beside him."

Rufus paused, looked at me, and said, "That young man was older'n ye are, must have still been in his teens, probably on his first raid. He didn't have no shirt, and he had streaks of black running the full length of his arms and on one side of his face like the man's scar. That damn Indian who had me at knife-point was a-wantin' him to cut me. Fast Hand motioned fer him to pull out the skinning knife he was packin'. The cutting wasn't a-gonna be just around my face and neck, either, if ye know what I mean."

I saw Mrs. Darcy blush, and I knew why. My brothers had told me that Indians would cut a man's *cojones* off. Rufus said, "Lordy, lordy, I knowed I was a-gonna suffer, and I decided when the cuttin' was about to start I'd try to kill myself by pushing my throat against that big blade against my windpipe. Then the young man turned to Fast Hand and said something in Apache I couldn't understand. Fast Hand nodded and, without a word, pulled the blanket off me. He took my big hawg leg Walker Colt and my skinning knife, checked me fer other weapons, and motioned fer me to take off my boots, shirt, and pants. Now it was cold, let me tell ye, and I wondered if they'd decided to let me die naked, a-freezin' to death.

"Then Fast Hand asked, *'Habla Espanol?'*" Rufus paused and explained to Mrs. Darcy, "He wanted to know if I spoke Spanish, and I told him I did a little. Then Ol' Fast Hand told me that the boy had said there was no power in killin' me this way. He wanted strong enemies to defeat. He said I looked as weak as a woman and told me, 'Go, get strong, and come again if ye can survive in the cold. We'll kill ye when it's worth our trouble.'

"I said, *'Gracias, hombre.* I'll come again in the spring to get yore hair.' Fast Hand nodded and said, *'Bueno.* Come. It's good to kill ye then. Tell Ewell we look fer him, too. Now go.' I got up real slow and started a-shiverin'. I was curious about the young man who didn't seem to be cold at all. I asked him in Spanish what his name was, and he said, *'Me llamo Caballo Negro,'* meaning, my name is Black Horse."

Rufus paused for a moment to spit and cut another chew, and I waited, spellbound for him to finish his story.

After he got his chew started, he said, "Well, sir, I'm here to tell ye he might be called Black Horse, but he shore as blue blazes stood in my book as White Horse fer not killin' me. I was mighty grateful he'd decided not to practice cuttin' on me.

Why, he'd made a friend fer life after the fool stunt I'd pulled. Didn't matter none, though, 'cause I knew we'd probably try to kill each other the next time we met.

"They took everything I had 'cept my long johns. I knew there was a little ranch about twenty miles away over toward El Paso, and I figgered if I trotted the whole way I could keep warm enough not to freeze and could probably make it in four or five hours if I didn't run into no more Indians.

"Well, sir, I got to that ranch before midday. I reckin it must have taken me 'bout five hours, and onct I got there, I could barely walk. I'd run through so many sticker plants there wasn't a place on my body that wasn't bleedin' a little and hurtin' like hell, but, by God, I was alive. The Morales family pulled the stickers out, washed me up, fed me, and put me to bed. Sometime into the next day, I got strong enough to head back to Ewell. Mr. Morales let me take a horse, some clothes, and a pair of boots, and I promised to come back and pay him later. Then I lit out to Ewell's camp."

I giggled and said, "It's a good thing you didn't have to ride back to Ewell's camp in your long johns, Rufus."

He smiled, spat into his spittoon, and said, "Yeah, and it's a darn good thing I had that horse. My feet wasn't in no condition fer me to hafta hoof it back." He cut another chew of tobacco and said, "I found Ewell and the troops late the next day. Ewell was glad to see me. He didn't look too disappointed when I told him I hadn't been able to find the stock. Said he'd decided he was gonna ease on up to Mesilla now that I was back and rest the company till after the spring winds. I was glad to hear that. So I collected my pay, rode back and paid Mr. Morales, and joined them at Mesilla. But by this time, I'd decided I was done scoutin' fer the army. I quit after I got to Mesilla, telling Ewell it was just too hard and risky. Ewell said he hated to lose me but understood why I wanted to leave."

Rufus sat silent for a moment, apparently finished with his story.

"Did you go back and look for *Caballo Negro* that spring? Did you take his scalp?" I asked.

"Naw, Henry, I figgered that would be a little hard and risky, too. Instead, I found me a spot in a canyon up in the Organs behind Tortugas Mountain. It had good water, and there was enough grass so I could do a little ranchin', just enough to get by. I didn't want a big spread. I stocked it with some wild cattle rounded up outta Mexico, and, in a couple of years, I had a poke big enough to live on and had built myself a comfortable, little shack outta timber I hauled up from Las Cruces. One of these days, I'm a-gonna make a house outta rocks and a little lumber jest like old Frenchy Rochas made over to Dog Canyon."

Forgetting the manners Mama had taught me, I asked, "Can I come and see you at your ranch sometime?" Then I saw Daddy's disapproving eyes on me.

Daddy reminded me, "Son, never invite yourself. Let someone else do the inviting."

Rufus just laughed and said, "Henry, why don't ye come out to see me at my ranch sometime? Ye can bring yore daddy if'n ye like. Ye can even bring yore mama, but I doubt she'd think much of it."

"Could we do that, Daddy?" I asked.

Daddy chewed his cigar for a moment and said, "I reckon so, once we get our business squared way."

CHAPTER 9
YELLOW BOY

That evening, Mrs. Darcy had a special meal of steaks, fried potatoes, *chiles rellenos,* and southern-style cornbread with butter. I'd never eaten southern-style cornbread, but I liked it, especially with butter melted into a piece. While we were eating, I asked Rufus, "Did you ever hear any more about Fast Hand or *Caballo Negro*? I mean, do you think they're on the reservation now, or did they ride with Geronimo and get shipped off to Florida?"

Daddy took a swallow of coffee and looked over at Rufus. Apparently, he was wondering the same thing. Rufus said, "Naw, they didn't ride with Geronimo. Ol' Fast Hand wasn't so fast after all. A Mexican army patrol run into him by accident when he was leadin' a raiding party tryin' to steal women from Aqua Blanco, a little village he'd terrorized for years. The Mexicans shot him and his raiders so fulla holes all they had left to bury was air."

I giggled, trying to imagine how an Indian might look and be nothing but air. Rufus said, *"Caballo Negro* is dead now, too, but he had a son called *Muchacho Amarillo."* He glanced over at Mrs. Darcy, who was listening, and said, "That means 'Yellow Boy' in English. Yellow Boy must be close to thirty-five or forty now, and he stops by my place fer water ever month or so. He eases down into Mexico to visit his second wife for a moon. She's a-hidin' in a camp of Apaches in the Sierra Madre. That bunch includes about all what's left from those that run off with

Geronimo in one of his breaks from San Carlos, a few from other bands, some *banditos,* and even an Americano or two who's after cattle owned by rich Mexicans. Them from Geronimo's band is still there 'cause they played it safe and didn't come back across the border with him on his raids.

"Yellow Boy has this old, lever-action Henry rifle with a brass receiver." Rufus looked at my daddy and said, "You know the gun I'm talkin' about, don't you, Colonel Fountain? It loads by droppin' cartridges down a tube under the barrel."

Daddy nodded, his eyes twinkling, and said, "You know I do, Rufus. I used to own one. How did Yellow Boy come to get his rifle?"

Rufus spat, wiped the dribble from his beard, and said, "Black Horse took it off some poor pilgrim that was wiped out a-tryin' to get to California. The Indians call those rifles with brass receivers Yellow Boys, and they call Black Horse's son *Muchacho Amarillo,* 'cause they's no difference 'tween him and that old rifle. Wherever he points, that's where the bullet goes, and it hits dead center ever' time. I was teachin' him to shoot, an' he's pretty fair shot. Then he has this here vision up on the mountain behind my ranch and I ain't never seen him miss since then, and that be over twenty year. Never seen anybody shoot as good as him. When he was still a pup, Yellow Boy scouted fer the army against the Chiricahuas on the Crook expedition down in the Sierra Madre in 'eighty-three but he quit 'fore Geronimo surrendered in 'eighty-six. He's still got his army coat and a hat like mine. He splits his time between his wife on the reservation and the one in Mexico, who is his first wife's sister."

Mrs. Darcy pushed a strand of hair out of her face and said, "If I were one of those sisters, I don't believe I'd like that sort of arrangement." She paused and asked, "Where did you meet this character?"

Rufus squinted and said, "First time, he was with *Caballo*

Negro. Ol' *Caballo,* he remembered me, when his son couldn't hit a durn thang with that rifle. Caballo knowed I was a purty fair shot and brought him to the ranch for me to train. So we had us a talkin' instead of a shootin'. We weren't exactly friends, ye understand, but we weren't enemies, neither. We made us an agreement, and I told him I was glad to teach the boy to shoot and fer 'em to use my water and to stop anytime. He told me in purdy good English he'd be back for the boy in three moons and that none of his people would bother me. And they ain't since neither."

I asked, "Rufus, is this Yellow Boy a better shot than you?"

Rufus nodded. "He shore as hell is, Henry. It's about like comparing ye to me, as to compare me to him. He could be a big time *pistolero* if he wasn't no Indian. But he just shoots when he needs food or to defend himself or to settle accounts against enemies, but that there is another story fer another time."

Rufus took the opportunity to spit, and then he said, "Yellow Boy carries that there Henry ever'where. He's like a ghost when he travels, too. Has this black-and-white pinto he rides, but once he slides out of sight into the mesquite and creosotes, he just disappears. It's a-scarifyin' the way he becomes invisible like he does. The soldiers and tribal police purdy much leave him alone 'cause they respect him, and they know how well he can shoot. They ain't stupid."

Daddy said, "Rufus, how'd you say you got your first cattle? Weren't they from Mexico?" I knew Daddy was going ask that question because of his business with the grand jury in Lincoln. Maybe he thought Rufus was stealing stock for his herd, too.

Rufus nodded and spat again, making a little *ping* sound in the spittoon. "Yes, sir, durin' the 'forty-nine gold rush and the war, stock got free from wagon trains passin' through El Paso. Then they was some from the free ranges north of the Rio

Grande that just wandered across the river and started breedin' wild and free down there in the Bosque along the river. I had a few cows and was just barely gettin' by. Then Mr. Fremont come by my shack and told me about this bunch of strays south of the river in Mexico. Said he was a-gettin' a crew together to git stock fer their ranches and wanted to know if I wanted to come along. He said he'd give his crew members a quarter of any stock caught to split between themselves, plus some wages. I said shore, so we spent about a month runnin' and brandin' cattle out of the Bosque along the river on both sides. I managed to wind up with about fifty head, and they's a real bull with 'em. Hell, I ain't needed to buy no stock since."

Daddy laughed and said, "You're right there, Rufus. Keep that bull busy, and you won't need to find stock in the Bosque anymore."

Rufus grinned and spat again in his little spittoon. Tobacco juice etched the corners of his mouth, and his Sunday-best white shirt showed a few more brown spots and streaks. He said, "Well, sir, I'll tell you, that old bull is about as run-down as I am, but I ain't heard the cows complainin' yet, and none of this old bull's herd is, either." Daddy laughed again, and I saw Mrs. Darcy blush. At that point, she excused herself to bring out more hot apple pie for dessert.

I thought I'd died and gone to heaven. At the end of the meal, everybody just leaned back in their chairs, dropped their hands down by their sides, and sighed. I wasn't even sure I could get out of my chair. I felt like a fat pup after that meal, and my belly was about as swollen as a fat pup's belly, too.

It took Rufus and me another couple of days to finish repairing the fence around Mrs. Darcy's backyard. On Tuesday night, Mrs. Darcy and Rufus sat in the kitchen talking for a long time. Daddy sat in her parlor reading his notes from the grand jury meetings, while I read *Huck Finn*. After a while, Mrs. Darcy came out of the kitchen, brought me a glass of buttermilk, and brought Daddy some coffee. Her eyes were red, and she didn't look very happy, but she spoke kindly to both of us before she returned to the kitchen.

The next day, Rufus loaded up his pack mule with his supplies, saddled his riding mule, and told Mrs. Darcy good-bye. She laughed and joked with him, but I saw her eyes begging him to stay. I watched him swing into Sally's saddle with a grunt and a groan. When he was aboard, he leaned over the saddle and stuck out his hand for mine.

I said, "Rufus, be careful going through White Sands. Daddy says he heard there's some new bushwhackers from Texas roosting in there."

He spat a dark brown stream of tobacco juice several feet and said, "Thanks fer remindin' me, Henry. I've heard that, too. Reckon I'll cut around the big mesquite thicket on the south side and miss it all together. Y'all be careful, too. Take care now." He touched the brim of his hat with a one-finger salute toward Mrs. Darcy and said, "I'll see you in a few months, Sarah." Then he headed down the road toward Mescalero while Mrs. Darcy and I waved him out of sight.

CHAPTER 10
THE NOTE

After Rufus left, Daddy and I were in Lincoln another eight to ten days. With Rufus gone, I played in Mrs. Darcy's backyard and read some more of *Huck Finn* while Daddy was with the grand jury. Sometimes, I'd even go over to watch Daddy presenting evidence to the grand jury. They were a grim bunch of businessmen and big ranchers who didn't ask many questions and always voted the same way on the evidence: indict. Daddy told me the evidence he had collected was tight and impressive. He also said the grand jurors knew that any indictments they returned were likely to get men killed on both sides.

We left town a day before the end of January. On the morning of our last day in Lincoln, the grand jury returned about thirty indictments, so Daddy knew there was going to be war. Several of the big ranchers in the association Daddy worked for had come to Lincoln to watch his progress and to do a little dickering on beef contracts with the army up the road at Fort Stanton. Up on the second floor of the courthouse where the grand jury had returned the indictments, the big ranchers were standing around talking, all jovial grins, slaps on the back, and cigars.

Daddy wasn't grinning because he knew men were about to die over a few cows. Even so, to Daddy, stealing was stealing, and it had to be stopped. Each side thought they were in the right. The big ranchers and Daddy believed they had the law on their side, and they were determined to set things right. Even at my tender age, I could sense that Daddy was calmly holding a lighted match while standing on a keg of gunpowder.

After the grand jury completed its business, I helped Daddy collect his papers as he packed them into his trunk. Mrs. Darcy swept through the door to the grand jury room, spied us, and rushed over to hand Daddy a small, white envelope.

Breathless, she said, "Mr. Fountain, a man I've never seen before stopped by my house and asked me to give you this. I told him you were just across the street, but he said he knew you were busy, and he was in a hurry to get on the road."

Daddy thanked Mrs. Darcy for her kindness in bringing the envelope to him, and she gave a funny little curtsy. It looked kind of like a semi-bow combined with a one-step jig. "Won't you and Henry have lunch with me before you leave? I have plenty, and you've been such wonderful boarders. It's my treat."

Daddy nodded and said, "Why, thank you, Mrs. Darcy. That's very kind of you. We'll be right over. Tell me, just out of curiosity, what did this gentleman look like?"

She put a hand to her jaw and thought for a moment, then said, "Well, he either had only one eye or he squinted on one side so much that it looked like one eye was gone. He was dressed like a rancher going to church, but it looked like he'd been out in the sun too long without his hat because his face was very red. He had a long, red beard with gray streaks that reached to the middle of his chest, and he wore his hat pulled down close to his eyes, and it was creased and rolled like a Texan's."

Daddy thanked her and said, "You're very observant, Mrs. Darcy. You'd sure make a good witness in a court of law."

Mrs. Darcy blushed and smiled. Then her face darkened a bit, and she said, "I'm not so sure he was a rancher, though, because his hands were smooth, and he wore a big forty-four on his hip and had another pistol holstered under his coat."

Daddy nodded and said, "Hmmph. I don't believe I know the gentleman." He packed the last of his papers away and said, "We'll be right over for lunch, Mrs. Darcy." She grinned, curtsied again, and swept out down the back stairs.

Daddy opened the envelope and took out a single folded sheet of paper. I was standing right beside him as he read, "If you drop this, we'll be your friends. If you go on with it, you'll never reach home alive."

After he read it, Daddy just snorted and mumbled, "Sorry cowards." Then he saw me staring at the paper and realized I had seen it. He folded it, put it back in the envelope, and stuffed it in his jacket with one hand while he tousled my hair with the other. "Henry, you're white as a sheet. Don't let that note bother you. Cowards who were afraid to give it to me personally wrote it. Those cowards won't have the nerve to face me. Everything will be fine."

I said, "Yes, sir." I knew Daddy never let anybody scare him. Even so, I wished I had a gun to help protect him.

We slid the trunk down the steps to where we could pick it up as we left town and crossed the street to Mrs. Darcy's. That meal was a lot more than just lunch. It was more like Sunday dinner. There was a pot roast, various preserved vegetables from her garden, and a big slice of her apple pie. Daddy drank several cups of her strong coffee, and I had a couple of glasses of buttermilk.

As we were leaving, Mrs. Darcy became teary-eyed. She shook hands with Daddy using both of hers. Then she leaned down to give me a tight hug against her big, soft bosom. She shook her finger at Daddy and said, "Now you men have a real safe trip, and be sure to stay with me whenever you're in Lincoln."

I nodded and said, "We will, Mrs. Darcy. You sure make good pies." She smiled when Daddy said, "Henry's right about that,

Mrs. Darcy. Thanks for the great lunch and all of your many kindnesses. We'll be sure to stay with you the next time we're here."

Right on time, a stable boy brought Buck and Sergeant prancing up the street from the livery, all hitched to the wagon and ready to go. Daddy sauntered across the street and got the trunk with his indictments and other papers. He loaded up the rest of our gear while I scrambled onto the seat. Daddy, not far behind me, stepped on board, and taking the reins, he softly said, "Hey, Buck."

Mrs. Darcy stood in her doorway and waved good-bye as Buck and Sergeant high-stepped it out of town.

CHAPTER 11
AN EVENING WITH DOC BLAZER

That afternoon was one of those cold, bright days where you almost had to squint your eyes shut to see. The sky was deep blue; there were no clouds; there was no wind; and there was no sound except the steady rhythm of our horses strutting along and the jangle of the harness. The stillness that had settled in the air relaxed us for a time. Daddy drove as if lost in thought, and I watched the sides of the trail for birds, jackrabbits, and other varmints to shoot with my finger pistol. We headed up the north road toward the Mescalero turnoff with Buck and Sergeant snorting and prancing along, obviously glad to be out and moving again.

A few miles up the road, Daddy stopped, pulled the rifle out of its scabbard, filled the magazine, levered a cartridge into the chamber, set the hammer to safety, and put it across his knees. He checked the load in his revolver, too. "Just being careful, Henry," he said. After that, it wasn't long before we turned off toward Mescalero. Daddy wanted to visit and stay the evening with Doc Blazer, former dentist, sometime innkeeper, and trading post operator in Mescalero who played a big role in keeping the peace between Apaches and whites. Doc had a sawmill he and the Apaches operated, and he and his wife made a little money on a few rooms he rented out to travelers in his big old adobe house.

Daddy had been friends with him for years. He said Doc and his Indians knew more about what was going on in the Tularosa

Basin cattle country than any reporter or politician in El Paso, Mesilla, or Las Cruces, and Daddy wanted and needed that news. He also wanted Doc's advice on tracking down some of the names on the grand jury indictments.

The ride to Doc's place was through tall pines growing along a road that wound back and forth and up ridges and down passes through the mountains. There were patches of snow on the ground, and I could occasionally see Sierra Blanca, white and majestic, rising through breakouts in the trees. It was colder going up to Mescalero than down in the valley on the road from Lincoln. The shade from the big trees holding court along the road cast sleepy shadows where the sun managed to break through. Even up high in the mountains, there wasn't any wind that day. It was an easy ride.

We got to Doc's place well before dark, but the shadows from the mountains were making it hard to see much in the distance. I remember Doc Blazer as a big man with a gray beard, and although he must have been close to seventy then and rounded in the shoulders, he still had all his teeth. We tied the buggy up under the porch that wound around the second floor and provided shade for the first. Daddy asked the housekeeper who met us at the doorway where he could find Doc. She smiled and pointed to the stairs that ran up to his second-floor office.

Doc gave a little whoop when he saw Daddy and me walk into his office. He hopped up from his desk beaming, shook hands with me, and said, "I'll declare, Albert, who's this new law partner of yours?" Daddy told him I was Henry, his youngest son, his assistant, and a fine candidate to become his new partner.

I noticed a concerned squint around Doc's wide-set eyes when he then shook hands with Daddy and said, "I heard about the indictments from some stay-overs that had supper here with us last night. Albert, they were saying people around here won't put up with any harassment from you and the big ranchers and that there's big trouble coming."

Daddy grinned and said, "Let me guess. One of them had a long, red beard, one eye, and carried a gun in a shoulder holster."

Doc's mouth dropped open, and he raised his eyebrows in surprise. "How in the hell did you know that?"

Daddy smiled and said, "Nothing special. I got a note from him earlier today, but I didn't have the opportunity to visit with the gentleman face-to-face. I reckon I won't have a chance to hear his views. Doc, Henry and I were hoping we could visit and stay the evening with you."

Doc made a big, sweeping gesture toward the porch stairs. "We'd be delighted to have you. Dinner ought to be just about ready. Let me get somebody to stable your horses and bring your gear in. Come on. Y'all get washed up, and I'll let Tikila know she needs to set a couple of extra places. By the time you fellows clean up, supper will be on the table."

Doc gave us one of his bedrooms and some hot water. As I was washing my face, I got real homesick and wished I were getting ready for supper in our own house on Water Street. I sighed and thought, *Just two more nights, and we'll be home.* I'd learned a lot traveling with Daddy, but I was ready to see Mama, my sister Maggie, and my brothers. I missed them all, especially Mama, and remembering her, I felt the horse head watch fob in my pocket she had given me to be her knight and protect Daddy and how good she and Maggie always smelled and how soft and warm they were when they hugged me.

Doc Blazer laid out a feast fit for a chief and even broke out a bottle of his best Madeira wine. Of course, all they gave me was just a little taste. I made a face that made them all laugh. I couldn't imagine why anyone wanted to drink that stuff, but

Daddy and Doc smacked their lips and sipped it. Tikila laid out a venison roast, fry bread, boiled potatoes, and peaches out of a can. Tikila was an old Apache woman, fat and covered with wrinkles, and she sure knew how to make great fry bread. I thought it was the best I've ever had.

A couple of Apache men, No Foot and Quick Knife, who worked with Doc at the mill and who were friends of Daddy's, had supper with us. They didn't say much but obviously felt at home eating with Doc and Daddy. No Foot was an old man, still strong, nothing but sinew in his arms and legs. Doc said he had survived many battles with the whites in his younger days. Daddy introduced me to them and told me he and No Foot had become friends after he got No Foot out of the army's lockup for being off the reservation.

I ducked my head under the table, saw that the man had two normal feet, and asked, "Why do they call you No Foot?"

Daddy gave me a sharp look and said, "Henry—"

The old man interrupted him and said, "It's okay."

Then Daddy relaxed a bit and said, "He's called No Foot because of his uncanny ability to avoid leaving tracks anywhere, anytime, even in snow."

I looked at him in awe and said, "Golly," drawing a laugh from all the men. No Foot understood and spoke English very well and laughed aloud at the stories Daddy and Doc told as they reminisced about the old days.

Quick Knife must have been about forty. He was short, and I could see his shirtsleeves bulge when he flexed his arms. Of course, I could guess how Quick Knife got his name, but I sensed Daddy wanted to honor him by telling me when he turned toward him and said, "This man is called Quick Knife because he's deadlier and faster throwing a knife than most men are at shooting a revolver. He scouted for the army, tracking Geronimo in the early days."

Quick Knife gave the faintest smile and said, "Your father, he keep me from get sent to Florida with Geronimo after surrender to General Miles."

Later, during a lull in the conversation, I asked the Apaches, "Do you know Yellow Boy?"

Their smiles disappeared as they cut their eyes to Doc Blazer. Doc looked over at me and, laughing, dropped his fork onto his plate.

He wiped his chin, waved his hand at them, and said, "It's good. You can speak. Henry and Albert have silent tongues."

They relaxed a little and No Foot said, almost in a whisper, "Yes, Yellow Boy we know. He's our friend. He hunts far now. He's not here."

Doc Blazer said, "Yellow Boy is off the reservation hunting somewhere, or maybe he's slipped back down into Mexico to see his second wife. In any case, according to the army, he's not supposed to leave the reservation, but he's not breaking any rule because I gave him a pass letter. Unfortunately, that damned agent Stottler thinks *he* makes the rules. You'll see the best hunters often quietly leave the reservation and come back. I don't know when they go, but they always come back because their families are here."

I nodded and asked, "Does he still have his Yellow Boy rifle?"

No Foot spoke up quickly, "Yes, he still has the Yellow Boy. He shoots best among us. He never comes home without meat."

Doc Blazer leaned back in his chair and sucked through his teeth as he said, "Henry, I've seen Yellow Boy drive a ten-penny nail through a board at two hundred yards with a bullet from that rifle. It was so far that the only way I could see the nail at all was an occasional glint from the sun off its head. His shooting skill is impossible to believe until you've seen it. He might even top Oliver Lee, who I heard hit a plank at nearly a mile with a Winchester one Fourth of July a few years back."

Daddy said, "Come on, Doc. I've heard that story, too, but I don't believe it. A man can't even see a plank at a mile using iron sights."

Doc raised his brows and looked at us over the top of his glasses. "He sure as hell can if you tie some ribbon to it." Daddy nodded and let the subject drop.

After dinner, Doc poured some brandy for himself and Daddy, gave No Foot and Quick Knife cigars, and gave me a sarsaparilla from out of the spring where he kept the bottles cold. We sat around the big adobe fireplace relaxing, telling stories, and letting the dancing fire warm us through to our bones. Sleep was filling my eyes when I heard Doc ask Daddy about the Lincoln indictments. I snapped awake. Even No Foot and Quick Knife leaned forward and cocked their heads to listen.

Daddy took a swallow of brandy and said, "Well, I got thirty-two indictments, nearly all of which will send men, and in a few cases prominent men, such as Oliver Lee, to jail. Many people are not happy about those indictments. If Lee and his crowd don't do away with me or my witnesses, they're gone off this range to being behind bars at Fort Leavenworth."

Doc's eyes narrowed in concern. "Do you mean someone will try to murder you, Albert?"

Daddy pulled the envelope with the note out of his pocket and handed it to Doc, who read the note aloud, then stared at the fire for a couple of minutes. When he handed it back, he said, "Damn, Albert, that's a murder threat if I ever saw one. Are you going to back down?"

"No."

Doc nodded and said, "I was afraid you'd say that. Now, listen to me. The army is sending an escort here the day after tomorrow for Quick Knife to haul a load of lumber to Las Cruces. You wait here a couple of days and ride across White Sands with that escort. At least you'll get back to Las Cruces alive."

Daddy shook his head. "Thanks for the offer, but we have a family we haven't seen in nearly three weeks. I've been all over this country since I married. I've fought outlaws, Apaches, and Mexican bandits. I've been wounded five or six times, and once I thought I'd probably die. I've killed several bad *hombres* who made the mistake of threatening me. I've come close to shoot-outs with Albert Fall and Oliver Lee over this and other business, and I've always come out on top. There's a crowd in Las Cruces and Mesilla who think I'm protecting myself by hiding behind Henry here because they think nobody would deliberately hurt an eight-year-old boy. Well, I intend to prove that I'm not afraid of those cowards. I can take care of us without any help from the army."

Doc slumped further down in his chair and silently gazed at the fire. There was no sound except the crackle of burning piñon. I reckon he knew how stubborn Daddy was when he got his dander up. I sat back in my big chair there in the warm glow of that room, listened to them argue about our safety, and thought, *Nobody can beat my daddy.*

Then No Foot spoke up. "Fountain, you're our friend, a good friend. All of us here owe you much." He waved a hand between himself and Quick Knife. "Quick Knife and No Foot will ride with you tomorrow. Some other man can drive the lumber wagon for Doctor Blazer. He will give us a paper to go with you, and you will be safe. Young Henry will be safe. Your woman and children will be happy you come home. We're strong, good fighters. Men will not attack you when we are there. You know this is true."

Daddy stared into the fire after No Foot spoke. I could tell he was giving No Foot's offer serious consideration. A long time passed as they waited for him to make up his mind. Finally, he shook his head, and, looking directly at No Foot and Quick

Knife with watery eyes, he said, "You are true friends. Any debts to me you have paid many times over. Friends have no debts with each other, and that's as it should be. I'm honored that you want to travel with us to protect Henry and me, but I've lived in this country a long time, fought many battles in the desert and in the courts, and I know these men who threaten us. If I show the first sign of fear, they'll be like wolves that smell blood early in the hunt. I must show them I'm not afraid and that I can defend my family and myself. I must never show them I need help when I'm threatened. If you ride with me tomorrow, then they'll know they've given me fear, and the threats and intimidation will only get worse. I cannot and will not live like that. My young son here, I know he doesn't want to live like that, either. Do you, Henry?"

I said, "No, sir." I was ready to leave right then if it meant facing and beating those men who were trying to scare us. I thought Doc had the saddest face I'd ever seen, but Daddy grinned real big and said, "See, gentlemen? I'm raising a warrior."

No Foot grunted, "I understand, Fountain. A man must go where his spirit leads him. Tomorrow travel safe. You are in our hearts. We go to the warmth of our wives' beds now."

After they left, Doc tried once more to get Daddy to travel with them, but he wouldn't have it. They were quiet for a while and then started talking about reservation business. I was warm and comfortable sitting in that big chair by the fire and dozed off.

The next thing I knew, Daddy was shaking me awake in our bedroom and telling me to get dressed. It was time to get on the road. I could smell fresh bread baking down the hall as I rolled out of bed, splashed some water on my face, and got dressed. Daddy said, "Hurry up, Henry. We have to eat and get on down the road. We'll be home in one more night, and you can finally sleep all you want in your own bed."

Tikila had fixed us a hot meal of bread, bacon, fried potatoes, and strong black coffee. It was good eating. The sun was just starting to give good light at the top of the canyon when Quick Knife brought the horses and wagon around, and we loaded up. Some doves were calling, and everyone's breath made steam. I pulled the buffalo robe over our seat while Daddy checked the loads on his guns. Once more, he levered a round into the rifle's chamber, put the hammer on safety, and laid it under the seat where he could reach it without hesitation. Smiling through her mass of wrinkles, Tikila gave us a sack lunch and said, *"Adios, señores."*

Daddy said, *"Gracias, señora."* He and I shook hands with Doc, and Daddy said, "Don't look so worried. We'll be fine."

Doc nodded, gave a little hand salute, and said, "I sure hope so, my friend. I sure hope so. I wish you'd wait. Be real careful on the White Sands road."

CHAPTER 12
THE ROAD TO TULAROSA

We said *adios* and took off in the deep, dawn shadows along the road. The way the cold air caught our breath and that from the horses, people might have thought we were a small steam engine rolling down that rocky road with streamers of light shining in the mists through the trees. Daddy and I were in good spirits. We were headed home.

After two or three miles we rounded a turn, and there sat an Indian on his horse holding a beautiful, little brown-and-white pinto on a lead line. Daddy handed me the reins and reached for the rifle, but, as we rolled slowly toward the Mescalero, he relaxed, put the rifle back where it was and took the reins back from me. We stopped within ten feet of the Indian, who had one leg crooked around the horn of a McClellan cavalry saddle, its bronze-colored patina scarred and scratched from years of use and abuse. Daddy told me this was Man Who Sees Far. He sat straight on his pony. His long, gray hair was tied back with a red bandanna, and his face was covered with streaks of dark shadows from deep wrinkles.

Without speaking, Man Who Sees Far waved his hand out from his chest and flicked his palm up in a hello. Daddy said, "Man Who Sees Far is on the road with the coming light. Why do you wait here?"

Man Who Sees Far said, "Fountain, you helped me with the man who cheated me in Tularosa. I have a debt. This pony is part of what I owe to you."

I thought it was about the prettiest paint pony I'd ever seen and hoped maybe Daddy would let me ride it when we got home.

Daddy shook his head and said, "No, Man Who Sees Far, I don't have any need for your pony. I told you when we settled with that shopkeeper that you didn't owe me anything."

Man Who Sees Far didn't move but said, "I owe you, Fountain. You take pony now."

Daddy shook his head again, much to my disappointment, and said, "I don't need that horse. You keep it."

Man Who Sees Far still didn't move, and, looking over at me said, "If you don't take it for yourself, then take it for your son. Take it for your children. You take."

I saw Daddy's jaw muscles rippling in impatience. I knew he wanted to get on down the road to Tularosa and not sit there arguing with an immovable Mescalero. Finally, he gave a little nod and said, "All right, Man Who Sees Far. Just tie the pony onto the back of the wagon, and Henry here will have it. Then we must be on our way. We have far to go."

Man Who Sees Far gave a little grunt of satisfaction, rode around to the back of the buggy, and tied the pony onto the back rail. Then he held up his right palm and said, "*Adios,* Fountain. Ride in peace."

I chirped up, *"Muchas gracias, señor."*

Daddy said, *"Muchas gracias,* Man Who Sees Far. It's a good pony. *Adios."*

Without another word, Man Who Sees Far turned and rode back up the road toward Mescalero. I don't think Daddy said another thing until we got to Tularosa early that afternoon. I studied every inch of that pinto as we rode along to Tularosa. It was hard to believe that such good fortune had suddenly just appeared for me right out of nowhere. I smiled. I knew it was going to be a fine day.

We went another two or three miles before we went around another bend in the road and saw a breathtaking sight. Spread out before us was the Tularosa Basin, and, off in the distance, was the big sweep of White Sands reaching right up to the edge of the San Andres Mountains. I had never seen it from up high before, and although Daddy said he had seen this view many times, he stopped the buggy to marvel at its majesty. The sand was blazing white; the sky, a gossamer blue; and the San Andres, fuzzy gray with streaks of light brown. We stopped long enough to have a couple of good swallows from the canteen and to give the horses the last of our oats. Then we rolled off again toward Tularosa.

I kept looking back over my shoulder to study that paint pony and imaging how I would ride and play with it when I got home. Then, about an hour before we reached Tularosa, I noticed two men were trailing along behind us, one on each side of the road. They had beards, long beards, and they stayed far enough behind that I couldn't make out their features. I could see, though, that one of them had a red beard. It stood out well from the shadow of the man's hat, and they wore long, duster overcoats. I told Daddy about them, and he just nodded and said, "I know, son. They've been on the road for the last mile or two. It's a free country. They're probably just going into Tularosa to have a good time on Friday night. The saloons in that place can get rowdy."

We finally reached Tularosa and stopped at Adam Dieter's store. I was rubbing the paint pony while Daddy gave Sergeant and Buck a long drink at the trough in front of the store. I noticed Daddy kept his coat open with that .45-caliber Colt revolver both easy to reach and to see as our two distant companions slowly rode down the street toward us. Both of them had red faces, as if they'd been out in the sun too long without a hat. I remember thinking that wasn't very smart for men who worked outside.

I stared at Red Beard. As he passed, I saw that he was missing an eye. He gave us a twisted grin, touched his hat with a flick of his fingers in a kind of wave, and said howdy, as he and his partner rode by. Daddy seemed to be paying attention to our horses, but I saw his eyes following their every move. He told me to get the feed sack as they casually wandered out of sight down the street.

We went inside Mr. Dieter's store. After being out in that cold air all morning, the heat off the big, pot-bellied stove in the middle of his store was like a gift from heaven. A couple of local farmers and several old-timers had gathered around it, smoking or chewing tobacco, whittling, and talking. Mr. Dieter was leaning over his counter a little distance from the stove. When he saw Daddy and me, he said, "Well, look who's here, gentlemen. It's Colonel Fountain and his new law partner." The men all turned their heads toward the door and the room got quiet as they watched us walk over to the counter.

Mr. Dieter said, "Let me get you gentlemen some lunch. We just ate about an hour ago, and I think there's still some *frijoles* in a pot there on the stove. We'd all be mighty interested to hear your views on what the Lincoln indictments mean for this part of the country, wouldn't we, boys?" Heads nodded like they were all attached to the same string.

Daddy shook his head. "We just had a sack lunch a little while ago. Thanks just the same, but we're eager to get home and need to get on down the road. I do need forty pounds of oats for the horses, though. Henry has the sack." When a murmur of disappointment rose from some of the men, Daddy said, "Next time any of you gentlemen are in Mesilla, I'd be happy to have a smoke with you and talk about what those indictments might mean."

The men nodded again and returned to their conversations. I gave the sack to Mr. Dieter, and he told me to take a peppermint stick out of the jar on his counter while he sent his clerk in the back to fill up the sack. Mr. Dieter and Daddy talked quietly while the clerk was gone. I only heard snippets of their conversation, but I remember Daddy asking Mr. Dieter if he knew who Red Beard was, and Mr. Dieter wrinkled his forehead in concentration, shook his head, and said something about Texas.

The clerk soon reappeared with the sack of oats thrown over his shoulder, and we followed him out the door to show him where to put the sack on the wagon. Before we left, Mr. Dieter shaded his eyes with his hand and said, "Albert, you and that partner of yours be careful. Those strangers with the beards sound like trouble. Watch out for 'em."

Daddy said, "We will. See you next trip, maybe in the late spring." Mr. Dieter waved and said, "*Adios,* you two. *Vaya con Dios.* See you when you come back through." I saw him shaking his head as the door to his store closed behind him.

CHAPTER 13
VISIT WITH DAVE SUTHERLAND

From Tularosa, we drove over to La Luz to have supper and stay the evening with Dave Sutherland, another old friend and political ally of Daddy's. La Luz had been a prosperous little village before the drought came in '89. There wasn't much left when Daddy and I stayed that night with Mr. Sutherland. It was an easy buggy ride from Tularosa, and we could see the southern end of the White Sands and the black Valley of Fires in the distance to our right, as we trotted along. Mr. Sutherland owned a store in La Luz and had his home, an adobe *hacienda,* next door. We tied the buggy up and watered the horses before we stepped inside. With the sun falling behind the San Andres Mountains, it was already getting colder.

Mr. Sutherland was leaning over the counter, talking to a short Mexican man, when we walked through the door. When he saw us, he yelled, "Well, I'll be! They haven't killed you yet, have they? Come on in here out of the cold, and let's have a hot toddy and some hot cocoa for your partner there."

Sutherland was a tall, gangly man with a big, bulbous nose and a hunched back caused by years of bending over account books. When I first saw him, I thought of Ichabod Crane from the *Legend of Sleepy Hollow.* Even so, Sutherland had a gracious air about him that commanded instant respect. Daddy reached out, pumped Sutherland's hand, and said, "We almost froze our tails off getting here, Dave. Those hot drinks will be lifesavers."

Dave laughed and said, "Serves you right for riding up and

down the road in the wintertime." Then he looked at me and asked, "How are you doin' there, *Señor* Henry? You cold, too?"

I stuck out my hand and said, "I'm fine, Mr. Sutherland, just cold is all, and that hot cocoa sure sounds good." I was glad to be in the warm store. It had all those good smells of ground coffee, pipe and cigar smoke, new cloth on the bolt, saddle and gun leather, gun oil, lavender soap, and even the musty smell of oats kept in the back room.

Dave said, "Boys, just settle in there by the stove while I get the refreshments." He disappeared behind the backroom curtain, and I heard him say, "José, run next door and have Glorietta make a couple of rum toddies and a hot cocoa, and bring them back when they're ready. In the meantime, take Mr. Fountain's things on the wagon and put them in the back bedroom. Then take his rig over to the stable and have Riggs put the horses up. Tell him they'll want to leave shortly after first light in the morning."

By the time Sutherland came back out, Daddy and I had our backsides well roasted, standing up next to that big, iron stove. He said lightly, "Gentlemen, refreshments are on the way." He paused and, clearing his throat, looked slyly at Daddy and asked, "So, Albert, did you manage to get a grand jury indictment against Oliver Lee?"

Daddy turned around, held his hands out and flexed his fingers to catch the stove's warmth, and said, "Yes, sir, I sure did."

"Hmmph," Dave grunted. "Good work, Albert. I guess when you convict him, Albert Fall will lose his chief enforcer. We oughta have free rein in the next election and not have to worry about being hustled for weapons by the sheriff's deputies every time we go to town." He glanced over at me, winked, and said, "That'll be real fine, *Señor* Henry, real fine. Your papa there is doin' the civilized people around here a real service, goin' after

Oliver Lee."

I didn't have the foggiest idea what he was talking about, so I just stayed as close to the stove as I could and nodded like I understood what he meant.

They talked about the impact of those indictments on local politics through the toddies and cocoa, through supper, and well after I dozed off in Sutherland's parlor. Daddy finally shook me awake to walk down the hall and climb into bed under a down comforter. It felt good to drift back to sleep, knowing I'd be out of the cold and sleeping in my own bed the next night. It felt like years since I'd seen Mama, Maggie, and my brothers.

Next morning, we were up early for breakfast. Glorietta cooked some fine *huevos rancheros* and a big pot of hot coffee. She had spiced them up good with dried red chilies.

Soon, Mr. Riggs brought the buggy and horses around, and we loaded up and were ready to go. Daddy made sure the rifle was loaded and easy to reach under the seat, and he slid his holstered revolver up his side a notch. Sutherland said, "Wish you'd wait another day or two until you had some company on the way, Albert."

Daddy squared his jaw and said, "No, it's time to get on home. We're lonesome for the family, and we'll be there tonight. You know I can take care of business if there's trouble, and I've got a good man with a gun right here with me, too, so we'll be fine."

Sutherland was somber as the wind whipped his long black coat around, and he said, "All right, you know best. I'm sure you'll be fine. It's just so damn windy and cold that it's not gonna be a pleasant trip. *Vaya con Dios.*"

We waved good-bye and headed down the road toward White Sands. The sky was mottled in black and gray clouds that swirled along at a good clip, and it looked like it might rain. I didn't care. We were headed home, and nothing was going to stop us.

CHAPTER 14
FRIENDS ON THE ROAD

We were just a mile or so outside of La Luz when three men from the direction of White Sands rode up onto the road in front of us. As soon as they appeared, Daddy said, "Hmmph." Two stayed on the left side, one on the right. They were too far away to recognize any of their features, and as we rode along, they stayed just far enough in front so we couldn't recognize them. It was obvious they weren't letting us out of their sight.

When we stopped to let the horses rest, they stopped too, but they kept their distance. When we started again, Daddy put the rifle on his lap. He also pulled the stay strap off his Colt in its holster and checked its load. Usually, he kept an empty chamber under the hammer, but I saw him drop a cartridge into it so he had a full load.

I grinned. We were finally going to have it out with those men who had threatened us. Maybe it would be a fight like he'd had with *El Tigré,* and I would get to see it. It never occurred to me that with all the lead flying I might get killed or wounded.

I wondered when he would give me the rifle so he could use his revolver. I was grinning and burning for action, thinking this was just like a game with my school friends, but Daddy was deadly serious. I noticed him glancing over at me once in a while. I guessed he wanted to see if I was scared, and he seemed satisfied that I wasn't.

In a little while, a rider passed the other three and came toward us. Daddy said, "It's Judge Hill, Henry. I wonder why he's out on a cold day like this." Judge Hill was a justice of the peace. I knew he and Daddy had known each other for years, and Daddy affectionately called him "Hump." He was a big, jolly man whose vest buttons strained to hold his blue floral print vest closed over a big belly that hung over his pants. His white shirt showed between every button on his vest. His porkpie hat was pulled down close to his eyes, and his big duster overcoat flapped in the wind. He had a big, crooked pipe jammed in his mouth and rode a big, bay mare, and she was moving down the road smartly.

We stopped and waited as he rode up to us. The judge stopped and said, "Morning, boys. Kinda cold for a ride, ain't it? Lookin' for varmints with that rifle?"

Daddy nodded and said, "Morning, Judge. Yes, sir, we're looking for varmints all right. Hump, did you notice if one of those men you just passed had a red beard and one eye?'

Judge Hill's brow wrinkled in concern as he took the pipe out of his mouth and looked back up the road toward the men who were moving slowly out of sight. When he turned back to us, he said, "Why, no, none of them looked like that. I didn't recognize them. They just nodded howdy to me as I passed. I thought they were just regular cowboys headed back to Texas. They all had Texas rigs. Why?"

Daddy hesitated, then said, "Well, I've been threatened since I got all those indictments in Lincoln. Got a note from a red beard with one eye, who, along with another fellow, followed us down from Doc Blazer's to Tularosa yesterday. He was riding a gray, and one of those cowboys up yonder is, too. I have a Winchester and a Colt, so I can take care of myself, but now I'm worried about Henry here catching a stray bullet if there's a fight."

I was indignant but afraid to say so. I could take care of myself. Daddy didn't need to worry about me, no, sir, not me.

Judge Hill looked back up the road again. The riders had disappeared in the distance. Turning back to us, he said, "They looked all right to me, but you never know about killers, do you? Why don't you stop at Luna's Well and wait there to ride back with the mail wagon from Las Cruces? I'd ride back with you now, but I've got to be in La Luz for some business with Dave Sutherland Monday."

Daddy shook his head and said, "Thanks, I'll give waiting at Luna's some thought, Hump. Tell Sutherland you saw us and we said hello. We stayed the night with him last night, and Glorietta packed us up a big lunch. Well, we gotta get on down the road to Mesilla before it gets too late. *Adios.*"

The judge tipped his hat, grinned around his pipe, said, "*Adios,* gentlemen," and we passed on.

It couldn't have been more than another mile before we saw the three riders again. They seemed to have paused in the road, and then they were riding again in the same formation, still too far away for us to see who they were and what they looked like.

Daddy kept the rifle on his knees. In a couple of hours, we got to Pellman's Well on the northern edge of White Sands. We hadn't seen another soul except the men in front of us. It was nearly noon, so Daddy pulled into the corral, watered the horses, and put their feedbags on. My little paint pony was a good traveler. We hadn't had a bit of trouble with him following us. Under a gray sky mottled with dark clouds, we ate our lunch. We took a full hour to eat and let the horses rest, since it would be a long pull up San Agustin Pass later in the afternoon.

Daddy stayed on the wagon, but I got out and ran around in the corral, using my finger as a pistol barrel to shoot at bad guys through the corral bars. Our escorts had disappeared up the road again, but Daddy kept the Winchester at hand while he ate and rested.

★ ★ ★ ★ ★

We got back on the road and were almost to Luna's Well when we met the La Luz mail wagon. Santos Alvarado had just left the mailbags from Tularosa off at Luna's Well for pickup by the mail wagon from Las Cruces. He was wrapped in a big, wool *serape* and had a quilt over his knees and another thrown over his shoulders. About all you could see under his hat were his black eyes, bushy eyebrows, and a big mustache under a wide, flat nose. Daddy stopped the team as Santos pulled up and stopped almost axle to axle with us.

Daddy said, *"Buenos tardes,* Santos. *Como esta?"*

Santos grinned, apparently honored that Daddy had spoken to him in his own tongue. He replied, "I'm fine, but it's a cold day for a ride, Colonel Fountain. I guess you're on your way home from Lincoln, eh?" He nodded toward the rifle and furrowed his brow questioningly.

Daddy grinned and said, *"Sí,* Santos. We're going home, finally." He nodded toward the rifle and added, "There've been some threats made against us, and we just want to be prepared if they're more than threats. Did you pass three men on the road before you got to us?"

Santos nodded. *"Sí, señor.* One on a big gray and two others on bays. When they saw me, they turned off the road and galloped toward the Sacramentos. They were too far away for me to tell too much about them, but they looked and rode like cowboys. Why do you ask?"

"Well, they've stayed out in front of us most of the day, and we were followed by a couple of men from Doc Blazer's yesterday. I've got the feeling that some ranch hands are being used to keep an eye on us for some reason. It's probably nothing. Keep the mail rolling there, Santos. We've got to get on home. *Adios."*

Santos nodded with a light smile and said, *"Adios, señores.*

Hace un paseo bueno a su casa." (Have a good ride home.)

The horses loped right along in that half walk, half canter of theirs, and Daddy seemed to relax after Santos had told him the three riders had ridden off toward the Sacramentos.

We passed Luna's Well and were two or three miles from the Black Mountain cut just before Chalk Hill when we met Saturnino Barela driving the Las Cruces mail wagon to make the pickup at Luna's Well. He was another friend of Daddy's. He looked like a wild man, but he loved Daddy.

He didn't wear a hat like most people, and his hair was long and whipped into twists and snarls. Most of his face was covered by a big, wooly beard that reached halfway down to his belly. He had two of the brightest eyes I've ever seen. Sitting on his wagon seat, he blocked the view of a wide span of the Organs behind him. He had big, gnarled hands and didn't wear gloves, and, sitting out in that cold wind, all he had on was a wool shirt and a leather vest. He left the shirt open for two buttons down from the collar. I could see what looked like bear hair all over his chest and the backs of his hands. Between the hair and those piercing eyes, he looked like a man a body wouldn't ever want to cross, a troll straight out of a Hans Christian Andersen fairy tale.

I knew Saturnino usually drove alone, but that day, there was a group in a wagon riding along with him. An old man drove the other wagon and had two women with him, and there was a young man, maybe eighteen or nineteen, riding a horse alongside them. I could see the tension on Daddy's face relax as Saturnino pulled up, stopped, and nodded hello.

Daddy said, *"Buenos tardes, Saturnino. Como esta, hombre?* Aren't you freezing out in this wind without a coat?"

"Buenos tardes, Señor Fountain y Enrique, mi muchacho. Es bueno to see you. This little breeze? It's nothing for a man who grows his own bear coat, eh? Hahaha." His laugh came rolling

up from his belly in a deep, guttural roar, and we laughed with him. I could tell he was a man who liked to laugh. When he recovered a bit, he took in a deep breath, then asked, "*Hombre,* what are you doing with that big gun on your knees, trying to find a bear to make a coat? Hahaha."

Daddy and I laughed with him again, and then Daddy, eyeing the people with Saturnino, said, "No, no bears, just extra comfort. Who are your friends here?"

Saturnino looked back over his shoulder at the wagon and said, "This is *Señor* Ruiz and his two daughters on their way back from visiting family in Las Cruces. I just met them at Chalk Hill." *Señor* Ruiz nodded his brown, weathered face toward us with dignity, but he didn't say a word. The women had quilts in gay Mexican patterns wrapped around them, and they smiled and nodded hello but said nothing.

Saturnino turned his right hand toward the boy on the horse, but before he could say anything, the boy said, "It's a pleasure, Mr. Fountain and Henry. My name is Fajardo. I work for *Señor* Ruiz and his family. He has *un ranchito* near the *norte* end of the Jarillas. I speak Americano *muy bien, si?*"

Saturnino scowled at him for his impertinence and for interrupting his introduction to Daddy, but Daddy just laughed and said, "It's a pleasure to meet you, *Señor* Fajardo, and yes, your English is very good. Where did you learn to speak English? From *Señor* Ruiz and his family?"

"Oh, no, *Señor* Fountain. When I was a *muchacho* like *Señor Enrique,* I worked in *Señor* Dieter's store in Tularosa *por mucho años* (for many years). I learn *nuevo* (new) words each day and practice with all who understand *mi mal* (my bad) English and will listen. I wanted to speak with those three men about a mile in front of your wagon when we saw them, but they rode off the road and kept their distance. They didn't even wave at us. I've never seen them before, and they didn't wear their hats like any *vaqueros,* uh . . . cowboys, I know. I ask *Señor* Barela who see them also, but he think they are just cowboys. You see them, *señor?*"

Daddy shook his head, and I saw he was gritting his teeth. He looked like he had that night in Tularosa when Jack Stone and Charlie Bentene walked over to our table and called our friend Roy a liar. Pure blazing fury is what I saw. I knew then that if I were a grown man I'd never want to cross him.

Saturnino stared at the cloud over Daddy's face and frowned. "Something is wrong, *Señor* Fountain?"

"Those men have been staying just in front of us for miles, just far enough away that we can't recognize them. I received a death threat after the grand jury recessed in Lincoln. There were even threats before I left Mesilla. Yesterday, two men followed us out of Mescalero. Powerful people want me gone, and I believe they may have hired these men to ambush us. I'm not concerned about myself, but I have Henry with me, and I don't want him to be around when the bullets start flying because I'll kill those bastards. They know Henry is riding with me, and it doesn't seem to make a bit of difference."

Fajardo stared at Daddy, his jaw hanging open in surprise. I could tell *Señor* Ruiz understood very little of what was said, and neither did the women. They just sat there and surveyed the mountains while they waited for the roadside chat to end.

Saturnino's eyes glowed from his shaggy head as he looked at Daddy and then over his shoulder toward where they had seen the men. He said, "*Señor* Fountain, why don't you drive back to Luna's Well with us and stay the night? It's not far. Then we can travel back to Las Cruces together in the morning. It would be my pleasure for you and *Enrique* to accompany me. *Por favor, señor,* do this thing *por* Barela."

Daddy must have sat there for four or five minutes looking at the mountains and thinking. I could see his jaw muscles work-

ing and understood he was trying to swallow the fury he felt
and to think rationally. His fingers nervously tapped on the rifle
stock. We all waited for his answer. I hoped he'd say no. I was
tired of traveling, and I wanted to see my mama. I was thinking
those men were just trying to scare him off. I hoped we'd have
a chance to get them.

Finally, Daddy said, "*Muchas gracias, Saturnino.* But I just
can't let them scare me off. If I back down once, I'm done for
as a prosecutor in this country. I know Henry's tired, and I am,
too. We want to be sitting by the home fire tonight. If they try
anything, I won't hesitate to blow holes in all three of them, and
they know it. They'll leave us alone. Saturnino, you're a good
friend. Come by the house for a hot toddy tomorrow evening,
eh?"

Saturnino smacked his lips together in a pucker of delight,
grinning broadly, and said, "*Oh, sí, señor.* That will be very fine.
Vaya con Dios. Hasta mañana." With that, he waved *adios* as he
and his little group passed.

We sat there for a minute. Daddy looked over the countryside,
and I figured he was trying to think where he might have to
confront those riders in front of us. He checked the rifle's load
again, pulled out the Colt, cocked it, and let the hammer back
down slowly as he took a deep breath and relaxed.

He offered me the canteen. I took a couple of big gulps and
handed it back to him. He had a swallow before screwing its top
back on and tossing it down by our feet where it would be easy
to reach.

He said, "Henry, if those men come after us, get down on the
floor here under the seat, take the reins, and make those horses
run while I use the guns."

I rubbed my hands together and asked, "Do you think there's
gonna be a lot of shooting?"

"I hope not, but if anything happens to me, you get as far

away as you can with this wagon and try to hide in the desert. When it gets dark, make your way back toward the road and hide so you can see the people that pass by. Don't let strangers see you. If we don't get home by tomorrow night, there'll be a big uproar, and Albert and Jack will come running with friends and posses. You'll get cold, tired, and thirsty if you have to hide, so take that quilt with you and the canteen. Don't lose your courage, and you'll be fine. Do you understand, boy?"

I nodded, slowly beginning to understand that this was serious business. Daddy hugged me and playfully gave me a gentle punch on the shoulder. He said, "We'll be fine. We just need to be ready for the worst, and we'll expect the best. You can handle it. I know you can. You've done a lot of growing this trip, and I'm real proud of you."

All I managed to say was, "Yes, sir. I can take care of myself. Don't worry about me."

Daddy said, "That's my man." Shaking the reins, he got Buck and Sergeant moving toward the cut leading to Chalk Hill. It felt like it was getting colder, although the wind had died down a little. Daddy flipped his watch open and said, "It's nearly two thirty." He sighed and said, "We ought to be home in time for one of your mother's good dinners. It sure will be good to get home, won't it?" I nodded, too cold to say much as I sat there shivering in the wind.

CHAPTER 15
ATTACK

The road toward San Agustin Pass cut through a Black Mountain spur that was about a mile long. The banks on either side were about ten feet high, and when you pulled up out of the cut there was a little chalky outcropping everybody called Chalk Hill. Not far from Chalk Hill was a big green creosote bush.

We were less than fifty yards from that bush when the one-eyed man with the red beard stepped out from behind it with a rifle to his shoulder. Daddy had the reins in both hands. He dropped them as soon as he saw Red Beard and reached for the rifle on his lap. I heard Daddy say, "Oh, no you don't, you son of a bitch!" Red Beard didn't hesitate. He fired before Daddy had his rifle halfway to his shoulder.

It was worse than any nightmare because I knew it was real. Everything I remember happened like time had slowed to minutes between clicks of a big clock. I heard Red Beard's rifle boom and felt Daddy fall back against the seat. He managed to hold on to the rifle with one hand and throw the other up to his chest. The roar from Red Beard's rifle and the loose reins made the horses rear up, neighing in surprise, then plunge forward. Red Beard stood where he was, coolly levering another cartridge into the rifle still braced against his shoulder.

In a gurgling whisper, I heard Daddy say, "Henry, grab those reins. Get us out of here. Hurry."

I took the reins, slapped them down on the horses' backs,

and yelled, "Get up, Buck! Get up!" I saw the end of Red Beard's rifle following us. He had another aim point on Daddy. Buck and Sergeant took off as if a mountain cat was after them and ran a little off the road to get past Red Beard. I could hear the air gurgling in Daddy's throat. The wagon was bouncing across the ruts so hard I nearly fell out, and I was desperately afraid Daddy would fall out, but somehow he managed to hold on. Remembering what he'd told me, I dropped down into the floor under the seat and managed the horses as they charged up the road. All I knew was we had to get out of there and get away from the man with the rifle.

The wagon had swept past Red Beard on the far side of the road. He was gritting his teeth in a carnivorous grin that showed snarling, yellow teeth against that big, red beard. It made my heart freeze in fear. I saw his rifle smoothly following us. He was steady and cool. It was an eternity before I heard the pounding roar of his next shot.

The second bullet made a low *whump* sound when it hit Daddy in the back. He grunted like someone had smashed him with a heavy club, and the impact pitched him out the right side of the wagon. He did a complete roll, coming out of the wagon and landing faceup on the side of the road. The riders who had followed us all day were flying back down the road toward us.

I jerked back on the reins yelling, "Whoa! Whoa, Buck!" The horses wanted to keep running, but I wasn't about to leave Daddy. The riders' lead man brought his horse to a skid, and, coming up beside me, caught the team within a few yards of where Daddy fell out of the wagon. Red Beard levered another cartridge into the rifle, put the hammer on safety, and casually walked over to Daddy, the rifle on his shoulder and a big grin on his face, enjoying every moment of the murder he had just committed.

I jumped out of the wagon and ran over to Daddy. The front of his shirt had a big spreading bloodstain over his right lung where he'd been shot from behind, and a stain from a smaller hole to the left of his heart. Blood was practically pumping out of his mouth, but his eyes were open, and he was fighting for every breath. I wanted to cry, to hug him, to beg him not to die, but I couldn't. I just knelt down by him and took his hand. I felt him feebly squeeze mine. He was able to turn his head and look at me as the light began to fade from his eyes. All he whispered was, "Henry. Go."

Red Beard walked up, squatted by Daddy's head, looked him in the face, and said, "Reckon I've killed you, Fountain. You was easy. I've seen Meskins that was harder to kill than you." He spat on the ground and wiped his mouth on the back of his sleeve. "Guess you won't be puttin' no more small operators in prison or helpin' no more redskins and greasers, now will ya? I bet ol' Oliver Lee will be happy to know I got rid of his problem fer him. Hell, he might even pay a little extry for the good job I done. You was easy money, Fountain. Easy money."

He turned his watery blue eye toward me and said, "Howdy, kid. Guess you remember me, don't you?" He nodded toward the wagon. "You just go on over there and sit in that there wagon nice and easy whiles we see to yore old man. Ain't nuthin' you can do fer him, and he ain't gonna live but a bit more. Go on now."

When I didn't move, he grabbed my coat collar in a powerful grip that jerked me off my knees and shoved me toward the wagon. I stumbled back up onto the wagon and sat down as they gloated while Daddy drowned in his own blood. I didn't doubt they were going to kill me, too, and I wished they would. I wanted to die.

I slipped my hand into my coat pocket and curled my fingers around the horse head, the emblem of a knight, watch fob

Mama had given me. What would she think of me? I had let my
Daddy get killed. It was my fault. I'd been in the way, and I
hadn't protected him like I'd promised Mama I would. I wasn't
even her knight.

I sat there shivering in the cold wind and felt like some wild
animal was tearing at the inside of my throat. To keep back the
tears, I looked up at the puffy, black and gray clouds in the sky.
Those murderers weren't going to see me cry before they killed
me. I looked back over at Red Beard squatting by Daddy and
grinning as he talked. All I could see was Daddy's shirt covered
with blood, and as the blood oozed out of the wounds, it had
bubbles in it. Every gurgling breath I could hear was weaker
than the last.

Jack Stone was with the riders who came racing back down
the road at the first shot. As he reined in his horse, he said to
Red Beard, "By God, you did it. Red Tally, if you ain't the
damnedest son of a bitch I ever saw. You're worth every penny
we're paying you. Shoulda brought you up here two years ago."
He had a piece of grass dangling from his lips as he talked. He
pushed his hat back on his head as if he were at a church social.
He was laughing, swearing, and slapping his knee. He and his
riders walked their horses over to where Daddy was lying and
just sat there looking at him. One of the other riders was Charlie Bentene, the hook-nosed man with the big mustache and
bad teeth I'd seen with Stone in Tularosa.

Stone studied Daddy with his wolfish blue eyes and said,
"Look at that high and mighty bastard now, drowning in his
own damn blood, sucking wind through a couple of holes in his
chest. Damn if that ain't a purty sight, by God. I know a bunch
of people that'd pay money to see old Fountain sucking his last
wind. Too bad Oliver ain't here. Why, I bet he'd pay a thousand
dollars just to see this." He looked over at me with that snarling
grin, and then gazed back down at Daddy. He said, "I hope, by

God, you suffer a while before you die, you son of a bitch. We're just gonna sit here and have us a little smoke while you do. You're sure as hell not gonna put any more of us outta business." Red Tally looked over at me with his one seeing eye that had no more life in it than the blind one. Stone continued to run his mouth as Daddy died.

The cold wind picked up and brought me to my senses. I'd been shocked into a dreamlike state. Then I remembered Daddy's last words to me. "Henry. Go." And I remembered what he'd said to me earlier about getting away.

When I couldn't hear the gurgles in Daddy's breathing anymore, Stone flipped the last of a cigarette he'd rolled off into the bushes and said, "Sounds like he's done. If he ain't, it don't make no never mind. Charlie, you and Jake come on over here and take that piece of canvas you brought and wrap Mr. High and Mighty here up in it and throw him over a horse."

Charlie Bentene and the cowboy they called Jake had been sitting on their horses in front of the team. They walked their horses over to where Daddy lay. I watched them slowly and deliberately dismount and take a roll of canvas off the back of Charlie's saddle to wrap around Daddy. Daddy stared at the sky with no light in his eyes. I knew he was gone.

CHAPTER 16
ESCAPE

A voice in the back of my head told me if I was going to get away, it had to be then. I slid down on the floor in front of the wagon seat, grabbed the reins, slapped the horses as I yelled, "Get up, Buck! Get up! Hi ya!" The team jumped in the harness and took off straight up the road as if ghosts from hell were after them. They started so fast they almost threw me out of the wagon, but I managed to hang on. I looked back as we charged up the road in a flat-out run. Stone and Red Beard were laughing, and Charlie and Jake were just standing there with their mouths open. I thought, *Yeah, you'll be laughing when my brothers and I get you. We'll hang you in front of everybody. They'll know you murdered my Daddy.*

They didn't chase after me. I thought I might escape after all and get help after I got to Organ, but I didn't know they had a man up the road as a lookout. The horses charged up the slight grade just before the hard pull up toward the pass. They had been trotting all day and were already starting to tire. When I saw the lookout sitting on his horse a mile or so up the road, I managed to turn the team off the road and headed straight out into the desert. I climbed back up on the seat and looked back. The lookout wasn't following me, but I was leaving a trail my sisters could follow.

In a few miles, the wagon sailed over a shallow little wash, took a tremendous bounce, and threw me out. Buck and Sergeant kept on running. I landed hard. My right forearm hit a big rock and snapped, and I felt something warm running down my face. I also had the wind knocked out of me. I lay there for a minute, choking to catch my breath. I knew I had to get off my back and hide because I'd be a goner if they found me. Finally, my breath came wheezing back.

I rolled over on my left side and pushed myself to a sitting position, then to my knees. As I staggered up, I was shaking all over. My arm hurt and throbbed so badly I gagged as the bushes in front of me spun out of focus. When I finally got steady and could see straight, I felt a big knot on my right forearm halfway between my wrist and elbow. When I touched my face, the fingers of my mittens came away bloody.

I took a deep breath, surprised I was still alive. I didn't have the canteen or the quilt, but I wasn't dead yet, either. Daddy would have been proud that I'd at least managed to get away and make them work to find me.

As banged up as I was when I landed, where I landed was the reason I lived, because the spot was on a path cattle followed through the mesquite and creosotes. Their tracks had churned up the dirt everywhere. The men who searched for me would never see my tracks in that chewed-up dirt. I saw a big stand of mesquite up the wash and decided I'd run up there and hide. I thought maybe with a little rest, my arm would stop hurting as badly as it did and my face would stop bleeding.

I ran for my life, holding my arm and getting blood from my face all over the front of my coat. I was already thirsty, and the wind was sharp as it swept down off the Organs. It was getting colder. My face felt like it was freezing, but I didn't dare touch or cover it for fear it would start bleeding again.

I made it to the mesquite thicket, lay down on my back, and slid up under one of the bigger bushes that had caught some tumbleweeds close to the ground. I managed to get positioned behind the bush and under one of those big balls of tumbleweed so I could peep out through a fork in the trunk close to the ground. I had a line of sight not more than a foot or two wide through the grass and overlapping bushes down the path to where I was thrown out of the wagon. I just hoped Buck and Sergeant had run for a long time so it would take the murderers a while to catch them. That way, I'd have more time to hide and get back to the road. In fact, I wished they'd just run all the way home, so my brothers would come running. I didn't want the murderers to have Buck and Sergeant or my new pony.

After a while, my arm settled into a steady, dull throb. I knew it would need to be set and bound in a splint if I was ever going to use it again. I remembered my brothers' tales about pioneers alone in the wilderness who set their own broken arms, but I didn't have the strength or knowledge to do it myself.

The ground was still damp under the mesquite bush, and my pants were starting to soak up the moisture and get cold. My hat was still on the wagon. I was getting the shakes from the cold, and my face was throbbing and burning. It started to think maybe I was going to die. If those murderers didn't catch and kill me, the desert weather would do it for them.

I decided I should get back to the road, but just before I started sliding out of my hiding spot, I saw the four riders pass through my line of sight down the wash. One of them was leading a horse with a big roll of canvas tied over the saddle. I knew that bundle had to be Daddy. I chewed my lip until it bled to keep from crying out for him.

The riders didn't seem to be in any hurry to catch me. I figured out later that they'd felt sure they'd find me with the wagon, or, if not, close by. They thought I was going to be easy pickings, easier than finding a stray calf.

I tried to think. It was amazing how clearly I could think, even as young as I was, when my survival was on the line. I had to figure out whether to run or to stay where I was until dark. I knew the killers were sure to come looking for me because I'd seen them commit the murder. They'd have to get rid of me, so I couldn't identify them. I figured they'd believe I'd take the paths the cattle made moving around the range because that was the easiest walking, so that's where they'd look first. If that was true, I might as well be sitting in the middle of the road waiting for a mail wagon to run over me. On the other hand, if I struck out off those paths, I'd leave a trail any granny could find.

I had to hide under the mesquite until dark, and then make it down a cow path that led back toward the road. I thought that maybe a little rest would give me enough strength to get back to the road by morning even as cold and shaky as I was. If I didn't make it, then I'd just hide out again until I got to the road or one of Daddy's friends or my brothers found me, maybe, in a day or two. I burrowed further down under the tumbleweeds, sticks, and leaves under those mesquites as much as I could without disturbing them enough to draw a rider's attention. Fortunately, my coat was colored about like the tumbleweed I'd wedged myself under, and, with a few leaves and sticks over me, I knew I'd be hard to see. I was still cold, but out of most of that icy wind. I warmed up a little and felt some better.

When the wind passed through the mesquite, it made a low rumble, like a flag being whipped about. It seemed to say, *Hey, he's right here.* I wished it would stop. Lying on my back, I could look up at the overcast sky and see occasional small patches of blue beginning to gallop past. I wanted to sleep, but my arm and face were hurting, and the images of Red Beard coolly murdering Daddy kept playing in my head. I thought I'd never sleep again.

The stillness in the desert was my only comfort, and it was powerful. It opened my soul. In soundless whispers, I started praying. I prayed that Daddy was with Jesus and that Mama would be all right. I prayed that I might be rescued, and if I were rescued, I would do whatever Jesus wanted of me. Mostly I prayed for revenge. I prayed that God's justice would be delivered to my daddy's murderers, especially Red Beard and Jack Stone and that His power would burn their ashes to nothing. I prayed I'd see Oliver Lee get his reward, too. Most of all, I prayed that I'd be the instrument of God's justice. With gun or knife, I wanted justice, and I wanted to be the one who made those murderers pay for killing my daddy.

The patches of blue sky I could see were getting that rich, deep blue that comes just before dark when I heard horses walking in the wash, and, very faintly, men's voices. My first impulse was to get up and run, but I didn't rise more than two or three inches before the mesquite's thorns grabbed my coat and held me fast. I could have jerked from them, but that would have raised enough ruckus for the riders to have found me for sure.

Nighttime was coming on fast. I could only hope that if I were very still, the riders wouldn't see me. I twisted my body just enough to look down the wash. Charlie Bentene and Jake were riding up the path through the wash and leaning over their saddles to scan the dirt, grass, and bushes for some sign of me. Bentene got to my mesquite thicket first and stopped. My heart was beating so hard I thought it was going to pop out of my chest as I waited for him to dismount and drag me out. But he stayed on his horse, looked all around, and then threw a leg around his saddle horn while he rolled a cigarette. Jake came up, stopped, stood up in his stirrups and looked around the tops of the sea of creosotes and mesquites that surrounded them. A cow bellowed in the distance. Jake settled back in his saddle and started rolling his own smoke.

Charlie cupped his hands and snapped a sulfur match with his thumbnail to light up. He gave Jake a light then flipped the hot match over in the mesquite almost right on top of me. He said, "Cold, ain't it, Jake? Seen any signs of the little bastard?"

Jake shook his head, pulled his coat collar up tighter, and said, "Hell, no. Kid that age is small enough to hide in a rabbit hole. Why, hell, he could be hiding in that there mesquite bush, and we wouldn't know it." He took a long drag on his smoke and blew it into the wind whipping around them. "Charlie, it's gonna be colder'n hell tonight. If he ain't by a fire, he'll die, and we ain't got nothin' to worry about. If he don't die, we'll catch him in the mornin', and Red Tally will have to take care of him because I ain't killin' no kid. Come on. I'm starvin'. Let's go get some bacon."

Charlie took a last puff of his cigarette, flipped it in my direction, and said, "It is colder than hell, Jake, but if that kid survives and tells his tale, we'll be in hell a lot faster'n we're expectin', by God. We gotta get out here in the morning before Barela gets to where that wagon run off the road. He'll know something's wrong and hightail it to Las Cruces and have half the town back here looking for Fountain and his kid. But you're right. That kid ain't gonna make it through the night, and I want to eat before Jack heads for Lee's place. Jack said he knew just where to hide the body so nobody will ever find it. Come on. We ain't gonna find that little bastard half-breed in the dark, and he ain't gonna survive without no fire. That's for damn sure."

They rode off down the wash, still leaning over their saddles looking for signs of me in the fading light. I decided the best thing for me to do was stay under that bush, maybe until midday tomorrow, then walk down the wash and back toward the road. I figured they'd be long gone by then and somebody from Las Cruces would find me. When it finally got dark, I noticed the ground losing its heat faster than even at sunset.

CHAPTER 17
A FACE IN THE DARK

I drifted off to sleep after a while. I dreamed I'd been caught and was sleeping between Charlie and Jake when Charlie decided to go ahead and kill me. That woke me up for a bit, and then I drifted off again. I was shivering after a couple of hours and couldn't stop. Then I started having a hard time distinguishing between what was real and what were dreams. One of the times when I was lucid, I knew Jake was right. I was dying. I thought I wouldn't mind dying if I could just have a good drink of water. I was so thirsty. I hadn't known a person could ever be that thirsty.

I thought I was going out of my mind or dreaming again when I saw the big mass of tumbleweeds rise up right off the mesquite bush and sail off toward the other bushes. There was no wind. Then I saw the shadowy, grim face of an Apache with dark, penetrating eyes. He wore a cavalry campaign hat folded up in front and a blue army coat. A big, long-barreled Colt and a long skinning knife hung from a cartridge belt around his waist. A shock of fear ran through me, and I thought I was dead for sure, but instead of killing me, he looked me over slowly, then glanced up and looked over toward the east, seeming to sniff the wind.

I couldn't see much of his face, but it didn't matter. He seemed friendly, and right then I needed a friend more than anything in the world. I started to speak, but he held up his hand, the edge of his fingers on his lips, and shook his head to signal me to be quiet. He looked around again, then reached down and grabbed the hand of my broken arm to help me out from under the bush. When I groaned and gritted my teeth in pain, he nodded, took the other hand and gently helped me up and brushed the dirt off my coat as I stood there swaying. The ground seemed to be spinning. I was so cold. I was shaking all over. He placed a rough hand around my neck to feel how cold I was before squatting, and gently bending me over his left shoulder, he picked me up. He walked about a hundred yards down a cow path to a black-and-white paint pony that snorted in recognition as we appeared out of the darkness.

He put me down and pulled a heavy Mexican blanket off the saddle, wrapped it around my shoulders, and eased me down to sit on it. Then, he pulled a canteen off the saddle horn and offered me water. The cold water sliding down my throat was a gift from heaven, but after a couple of swallows, I started shaking worse. He snatched it out of my hand and whispered, "Not much now. You *mucho frio*. Drink slow or you die." I was surprised that he spoke such good English.

Gently he slid the coat sleeve off my right arm and felt it up and down. Up close, I could see he had a broad, flat nose and thin lips. His black eyes looked like those of a hunting hawk. His rough hands gently felt the knot in my forearm while I gritted my teeth and whimpered. He looked in my eyes and said, "Arm broke. I fix. Then we ride before the men come. *Comprende?*" I nodded.

He disappeared into the dark, so I pulled the blanket up close and just sat there, still shaking but not as bad as when he had found me. He reappeared so quietly I jumped when I saw his boots appear at my feet. He had four short sticks of mesquite the same length, sliced clean of thorns and bark, and some long strips of some kind of gourd vine. He squatted beside me, handed me a stick, and whispered, "Bite stick so you no scream." I realized he was going to set my broken bone, and it was going to hurt a lot. He slid the sleeve up on my arm, took my elbow in a powerful grip, grasped my wrist, and looked in my eyes. I braced myself, bit down on the stick, and nodded. He pulled hard. I felt a huge surge of pain, and then I passed out, drifting in darkness.

I woke up sitting in the paint pony's saddle with my face buried in the front of the sergeant's jacket and the Apache's arm clamping me tightly under my shoulder blades. I wasn't shaking anymore, and between the Apache's body heat and the heavy wool blanket he had around me, I felt warmer than I had a lifetime ago, that same morning when I had gotten out of bed in La Luz. All I remember about that ride is the feeling of the left and right sway in the saddle as the paint tacked back and forth along a trail through creosote bushes, seeing a boulder or two passing in the deep, shadowy darkness, and the moaning wind ripping at my torn face. Soon, I drifted into an exhausted sleep.

CHAPTER 18
THE SHACK

When I woke up, I was lying on a cot staring up through rafters supporting a tin roof that was creaking from the wind. Beams of sunlight burning through a dirty window in a wall opposite my bed made the dust floating in the air look like flakes of gold. I could hear the crackling of a fire and a spoon rattling against the side of a bubbling iron pot. As I looked around, I saw that there was only one room in the place. The walls were two-by-fours sheeted over with planks about a foot wide and nailed in place at about a forty-five-degree angle. The same type planks and two-by-fours made up a rough door that rattled and creaked in the same wall as the window. A rifle with the longest barrel I'd ever seen and a fine walnut stock hung upside down on pegs above the door. Nails stuck in every two-by-four had some piece of clothing, a towel, a pot, a tool of some kind, or a cartridge belt hung on it. There were a couple of stacks of books packed several feet high in the corner closest to my feet.

I turned my head and could see a couple of bedrolls laid out between an old, cast-iron cooking stove and some stools around a rough table. My right eye was swollen so badly that I could only see out of my left eye. Some kind of poultice that stank like wet cow manure had been applied to the cuts on my face and arms. The splint the Indian had put on my arm had been replaced with some nice, saw-cut, smoothed boards tied neatly in place with dingy, but clean, white cloth. I tried to sit up, but was too weak to make it and fell back.

The Indian who had found me was squatting next to the door, resting with his back against the wall, and he fit nicely between a set of two-by-four studs. His rifle butt was on the floor, its stock between his feet so that the barrel rested on his shoulder. His dark eyes followed me.

An old miner's boot nudged the door open, and then a gust of wind flung it wide open as the dark silhouette of a man filled the doorway. I saw the outline of a water bucket and a washbasin, too. The man closed the door, looked over at me, turned to his right, and said, "Well, Yellow Boy, looks like our young friend's finally awake." Then turning back toward me, he said, "Howdy, Henry, glad ye decided to drop in today."

I looked up and saw the silver, wire-framed glasses on the end of Rufus Pike's nose. He looked at me and smiled. His beard had grown scraggly since his time at Miss Darcy's. He had his shirtsleeves rolled up over his long john sleeves, and there was a big bulge of chewing tobacco in his left cheek. Then I looked back at the Indian and realized he was the one I'd heard so much about, the one who never missed with his rifle.

Rufus put the bucket down on a rough-cut table and dipped some water into the basin before he sat it on a stand beside my cot and said, "I didn't expect to see ye again quite so soon. Ain't been home but a few days myself." He took a dipperful and brought it over to me. Sitting on the edge of the cot, he held my head up while I drank. I was dry, and I gulped that good, cold water down. The drink tasted almost as good as the one from the canteen Yellow Boy had given me after he pulled me out from under the mesquite bush. Rufus patted my shoulder and gave it a gentle squeeze of affection as he said, "We're mighty sorry about yore pa, son. He was a great man and shore didn't deserve to die like that. Mostly though, we was worried about ye. Didn't know if old Yellow Boy had found ye in time or not. Ye've been sleeping sound fer two days 'cept fer when ye'd yell yoreself awake. Bad dreams, I reckin."

Rufus pulled up an ancient, dark-stained, three-legged stool and sat down. Reaching in his back pocket, he pulled out the cleanest dirty rag in the shack, dipped it in a pan of water he'd sat by the cot, and carefully dabbed at the poultice.

He said, "This stuff here was made from some weeds the Mescalero women use and recommend fer wounds of every kind. Stinks, don't it?" He wrinkled his nose then grinned as reflected firelight from the open door in the stove danced across his glasses.

There was the barest hint of a smile on the thin line that formed Yellow Boy's mouth, and I smiled, too, in spite of all the hurt I was feeling inside and out.

Rufus tenderly took my good hand and rubbed it. "It's a miracle ye're alive, Henry. Another couple of hours under that mesquite bush, and ye'd have died."

"But I didn't feel like I was all that hurt, Rufus. The cold just gave me a little case of the shakes."

"Well, when Yellow Boy got here with ye," Rufus said, "he told me that when he found ye, ye were too cold to stay alive much longer. He had to keep ye wrapped in a blanket up next to his belly and chest while he brought ye here. Ye don't remember ridin' backwards over Baylor Pass, do ye?"

He looked over at Yellow Boy with the question wrinkled on his brow. Yellow Boy gave a slight nod of assent and cocked his head to listen outside.

Rufus said, "See there, I told ye." He sniffed over toward a big, black Dutch oven sitting on the stove. The room had a pungent, dry wood smell that mixed with the mouthwatering smell of cooked meat, onions, and baked bread and made me glad I was alive. "Stew's 'bout done. Are ye ready to eat yet, Henry?"

"I'm about to starve," I said. "But I'm afraid I can't get food in my mouth 'cause my face feels so swollen up. I can't see out of one eye. Is it gone?"

Rufus chuckled and said, "Naw, it ain't gone. Ye'll see fine when the swelling goes down. Never ye mind about the swelling, boy. We'll get ye fed." He grunted with the weight of his years as he got up and shuffled over to the Dutch oven. Yellow Boy was still listening with his ear cocked toward the door, when he suddenly turned toward Rufus and said in a low, urgent voice, *"Caballos!"*

Without saying a word, Rufus motioned him with spread fingers, waving toward the floor to stay still while he stepped over and squinted into the sunlight pouring through the dirty window.

"It's Buck Greer and some cowboys from over to Drippin' Springs." He looked back at me and said, "Henry, you keep real quiet. Yellow Boy ain't supposed to be here, and I don't know what might happen if those men were to find you all banged up after you've been missing, not what with an Apache here to blame." I nodded that I understood. I could tell the horses were in the yard at that point. "Y'all both be still, and I'll see what they's a-wantin'," Rufus said calmly in a low voice.

Then he flung the door open and closed it just as quickly behind him. I held my breath and listened to him speaking with the horsemen that had ridden up to the porch.

"Howdy, boys, Buck. Looks like ye're goin' on a long huntin' trip with that there pack mule a-loaded up like that."

Yellow Boy's thin lips drew even tighter as he waited with his back to the wall and listened, ready to move if the men came inside. I saw he'd cocked his rifle and curled his finger around its trigger.

A man said, "Howdy, Rufus. Don't reckon you heard the news. Barela, the mail wagon driver over to Luna's Well, got back into Cruces night before last all upset. He said it looked like Colonel Fountain and his boy had come to harm somewhere around Chalk Hill over to the Sands."

Rufus was silent for a moment, as if trying to take in what he'd just heard. Then he said, "Naw, Buck, I ain't heard nothin' about it. What you reckon happened?"

"Seems Fountain told Barela he was worried about some men doggin' his trail. Barela said he saw the men and that they wouldn't stay on the road so he could see who they was when he passed 'em. Next day on the way back, he found where a buggy had run off the road, and he got real worried. When he got to Fountain's place that night and found out that Fountain and the kid hadn't got home, all hell broke loose. Fountain's oldest sons, Albert and Jack, jumped on their horses and took off for the pass without no supplies. Then another bunch in town supplied up and took off, too. A rider come over to the ranch where Fountain's daughter Maggie was spendin' some time with that beau of hers to tell her what happened, and she fainted. They're a-sayin' Fountain's wife is in a bad way, too, almost crazy with grief. The whole damn town's in an uproar."

I heard Rufus step down off the porch, and then he said, "Well, that's a shame in this world."

I hated to hear about my family suffering that way and wanted to get up. I wanted to call out to them and show the men I was all right, but I didn't want to put Yellow Boy in danger after he'd rescued me. Plus, I knew that would make it awful hard for Rufus to explain why he'd claimed he knew nothing about my disappearance.

Buck said, "Mr. Van Patten said José, Pete an' me could ride over the pass and join the search parties. He said we should get back soon as Colonel Fountain and the kid were found, and for shore not to be gone more'n a couple a weeks. We thought we'd tell you the news and see if you wanted to come with us. We shore as hell got enough supplies on that mule so you ain't a-gonna get hungry. You was a tracker back in the old days, wasn't ya?"

Rufus said, "Yeah, I's a tracker for Cap'n Ewell. That was back 'fore the war. We's after Apaches on the El Paso to San Antonio road in them days." He paused, and I heard him spit a stream of tobacco juice before he said, "Boys, I'm mighty sorry to hear about the colonel and little Henry. Why, I was a-talkin' with them 'bout a week ago in Lincoln. I shore hate to hear this, but this here cold and wind has give me a major dose of the gout. I'n hardly walk much less ride, my toes hurt so bad, so I guess I'll leave the trackin' to you fellas. Shore sorry about the colonel and Henry though."

Buck said, "Know what you mean. I get a touch of that gout myself onct in a while. It do hurt. We'd be glad to have you, but if you got the gout, you'd just slow us down. Mind if we water the horses 'fore we head on over to the pass?"

Rufus said, "Naw, boys. Ya'll be my guests. Water trough's over by the corral. Help yourself. I'm about to freeze out in this here wind. Done got too old. I'm going inside now. Good huntin'." I heard the men start riding toward the corral.

It seemed forever, but it couldn't have been more than ten minutes that we stayed nearly motionless in that shack, waiting for the Dripping Springs hands to water their animals and leave. Finally, they left, picking their way down the trail. Yellow Boy stood up and watched them out the window, finally easing the rifle hammer off full cock when the men were gone.

CHAPTER 19
GREEN CHILI STEW

When the Dripping Springs riders were out of sight, Rufus said, "Gentlemen, that there green chili trail stew smell is a makin' my mouth water. Let's eat." He took three big, deep pans like our cook at home used for pies, and ladled out big portions of the stew from his big, bubbling pot into each one. He raised the top on the Dutch oven and got out a toasty, brown biscuit the size of a fist for each of us. Then he got a couple of spoons out of a box on a shelf over the stove and put one in two of the pans. He walked over and handed the one without a spoon to Yellow Boy, who was sitting cross-legged on the floor near the door.

Yellow Boy grunted as he pulled out his big knife with one hand and took the pan with the other. "Ummph, *Gracias*, Rufus. You cook *muy bueno*. I take you *a mi casa* someday. You can cook all the time there. I'll look after you. I won't need a woman then." He grinned, showing his bright, white teeth, speared a chunk of meat, and bit off a mouthful, noisily smacking his lips and grinning as a little of the gravy ran down his chin.

Rufus said, "I don't think ye'd do without a woman, Yellow Boy. Hell, ye just rode over two hundred miles to visit one, didn't ye?" He walked over to the cot and sat a steaming pan down on his ancient stool. "Henry, I know it's a-gonna be hard fer ye to sit up, but rest yore broke arm in that there sling I got around yore neck. Ye need to do fer yoreself as much as ye can as soon as ye can to get yore strength back. Sit up now and cross yore legs. I'm a-gonna put this here stool up on the cot so's ye can eat off it and not have far to go to get the spoon from the pan to yore mouth."

He helped me sit up, then stirred my portion and blew across it to cool it down. I was a little dizzy and sore at first, but eating off that stool was actually pretty easy. The stew was still hot, but I didn't care. It was the best-tasting food I could remember. Because of my swollen face, some of the stew dribbled down my chin as I got the spoon to my mouth, but the pan was close enough to catch the drippings. Handling the spoon with my left hand was awkward, but I learned fast.

Rufus took his pan of stew and sat down on an old, slat-bottomed chair, creating a triangle seating arrangement with Yellow Boy and me. We smacked, chewed, and slurped on that stew and those biscuits without saying a word.

I studied Yellow Boy while we ate. He looked about the age of my brother Albert, who was thirty. His shiny black hair stopped at his shoulders. His face reminded me of a pie pan. It was flat and round with a big, broad nose that appeared to have been broken at least once and was pushed a little to one side. He had two knife slits for eyes. He was short, and I was surprised at how thin he was. Somehow, I'd always imagined Apache scouts to be big and strong, but he looked half starved. We were all sweating a little from the chilies, and he unbuttoned his cavalry jacket to cool off a little, revealing a clean white shirt underneath the dusty jacket.

Before Rufus and I were even half finished, Yellow Boy finished sticking the last piece of stew in his mouth with his knife. Holding the pan up, he greedily drank all the remaining gravy. He said, "Good, Rufus. We hunt together sometime. You cook then, huh?"

Rufus had a mouthful and just grinned and nodded. Yellow Boy wiped the grease from around his mouth with his fingers and rubbed them on his well-oiled boots. He eased back against the wall under the window, once more bracing the heels of his boots on the floor so his knees were about a foot off the floor. He felt around inside his unbuttoned coat, found a black, ball-bat-shaped, Mexican cigar in an inside pocket, and lighted himself a smoke after flicking a sulfur match against his thumbnail. I'd seen cowboys light matches that way. When he smoked, he blew big, blue clouds up toward the rafters as he sat, relaxed and contented, reminding me of how Daddy had looked many times after a good dinner at home.

Then I looked down at my plate of stew, thoughts racing through my mind, roadrunners chasing snakes, juking and jumping here and there, but never making a catch. The day Daddy died felt like a lifetime ago. I knew I had jumped from being a child with no cares in the world to a miniature adult who was weak, who knew nothing about the world he carried on his shoulders. I felt a thousand years old, and I knew in my soul that I could never be a kid again. I remembered what the rider Buck had said about my sister Maggie. She had practically raised me, and I felt so badly for her, I wanted to cry. She had first suggested that I go with Daddy to stop the very thing that had happened to us. Now she must believe we were dead, and I knew she'd think it was all her fault. Lord only knew what Mama was thinking and going through. I wanted so bad to go home and comfort them and then to make those men who killed Daddy suffer before I tore them to pieces.

I remembered tales Jack and Albert told me around a campfire about Apache torture tricks. Maybe I could bury Jack Stone, Red Tally, and Oliver Lee up to their necks in sand and smash their heads with rocks, but not kill them, so they'd know when the rats and ants were chewing on them before they died. I wanted to pour kerosene on their heads and set them on fire. I wanted to cut their guts out. I wanted their blood. I heard a roaring voice in my head and soul that said no matter what, somehow, someday, I'd make them pay for what they'd done.

Again, I looked over at Yellow Boy. So many questions were in my mind that I had a hard time focusing on any one.

I turned to Rufus and asked, "How did Yellow Boy find me? Why did he save me?"

Rufus shrugged his shoulders and said between mouthfuls, "Why don't ye ask him yoreself? He's a-sittin' right there."

"I . . . I thought it was a custom for Apaches not to speak about dead people."

"Well, you ain't dead. Go on and ask him. I'd like to know more about what happened myself. He didn't tell me much in the way of detail 'cept yore daddy was dead and that he found ye on the other side of Baylor Pass nearly dead."

I looked toward the center of the blue haze, through the golden flecks of dust passing through the sunbeams falling through the window. Yellow Boy's eyes were closed, as if he were sleeping. Smoke slowly poured through his nose, and his thin lips curved slightly in an encouraging smile. I said, "Yellow Boy, I thank you, and know I owe you for my life, but why did you help a white boy whose daddy was once your people's enemy? Why didn't you just let me die?"

Yellow Boy's eyes blinked open, and he squinted at me, holding his cigar carefully, gracefully rolling it on the fingers of his left hand, his right hand never leaving the barrel of his rifle. He took a long pull on the cigar and blew the smoke in a long, swirling stream toward the rough underside of the shack's roof as he tilted his head back. Then, looking directly at me with unblinking eyes, he began to speak in English with a little Spanish mixed in.

"I have *una* woman in the *sierras,* the mountains, *sud* of Rio Grande. These people, they only ones left living from last of Geronimo's band and others hiding from soldiers in Mexico.

This woman no stay with me on reservation. She afraid of soldiers. As a girl, she saw many of her people die from hands of soldiers on reservation until my brothers and me help all our women get away. Even so, many Mescaleros get sick when soldiers there.

"Now her belly swells with our child. I go many times to *Sierra Madre,* but I cannot stay. I must come back to my first wife on the reservation. Tribal police and soldiers look for me if I stay too long. My woman in Mexico and my woman on reservation, they are sisters.

"Five suns ago, I left Mexico and ride to reservation through Baylor Pass after I rest here with Rufus. I think not many riders go through Baylor Pass. Many use other pass the *Indah* (white men) call San Agustin, so no one see me. Ranchos on other side of pass have many cows, many *vaqueros.* Move herds to more grass, so hard to hide from *vaqueros.* I ride slow and hide many times. I use *Shináá Cho* to watch road, watch herds, watch riders."

I must have had a questioning look because Yellow Boy reached in the saddlebag sitting next to his knee and held up a big-barreled, collapsible telescope. It was trimmed in brass and very beautiful. He said, *"Shináá Cho,* Apache for *big eye."*

I nodded, and he continued. "I watch road with *Shináá Cho* and wait to ride when *vaqueros* no see me. I saw you and *su padre* in wagon with *Shináá Cho* and also saw *tres vaqueros* up the road from wagon, and one more that ride out from range onto road toward San Agustin Pass.

"This was after Barela went by with his wagon, and with him, wagon with old man and two women, and a man on horse."

I sat up a bit straighter and said, "Yes, that was Mr. Ruiz and his daughters and Fajardo. They stopped to talk with us. Fajardo could speak English well. Where did you learn to speak English so well?"

Yellow Boy grinned, nodded toward Rufus, and said, "I pick up from talking to Rufus and *mi amigo,* Doc Blazer, on reservation."

I smiled and said, "Doc Blazer was Daddy's friend, too. He didn't want us to ride out without an escort, but my daddy didn't want to show fear to the men who had threatened us, so he refused the offer." I sighed and asked, "What else did you see from up high?"

"*Tres vaqueros* stay away from Barela, and Barela didn't see other *hombre* on road. *Hombre* is too far away. Lead rider has much red hair on face. He leave others and hide behind big bush with his rifle, I think, *Indah ambush.* Red beard waits like cougar for deer. I wait and watch. Rider from range waits at San Agustin Pass.

"*Tres vaqueros* walk horses slow toward San Agustin Pass. When your wagon come, Red Hair on Face step out from bush and shoot quick."

I relived that horrific scene as Yellow Boy described what had happened from his perspective. I tried to imagine how it would have been to watch those events unfold from a distance. "Then you must have seen the horses rear up and run," I said.

"*Si,* then Red Hair on Face shoot again *pronto. Su padre* fall off wagon. You stop wagon quick, jump down, run to *su padre.* Then Red Hair on Face comes and watch *su padre* on ground. He laugh. Makes joke, I think, and make you go sit in wagon. *Tres vaqueros* came back quick, talk, smoke, and watch *su padre* on ground."

Remembering the cold indifference to my daddy's death, I bit my lip to keep from crying again. I wondered if Yellow Boy had felt any emotion as he watched that scene. "Do you see me get away?" I asked.

"I see you make wagon run, but riders don't chase you. You brave. You act like little man, not little boy. When you saw other man on road, you took wagon into desert. Wagon goes fast like wind. Hard to see wagon good. The bushes were *muchos grandes.* You ask why I help you. I help *por que* you brave *muchacho,* and you give me warm heart. You were mouse and riders, *gatos.* I think soon they carry you off or kill you. I want to find you and not let *gatos* get mouse."

I felt a surge of pride when Yellow Boy said I was brave. "How did you find me?" I asked. "The riders didn't find me."

"I found trail of your wagon and hid my horse. I waited until dark, tracked wagon on foot. *Es muy difícil.* I found where you fell out of the wagon and saw blood sign on rocks. I followed trail to big mesquite and find you. You *mucho frio.* Shake *mucho.* I set broken arm. You bite stick and no made sound. You no make water in eyes like little boy. Rufus is *Indah.* Knows many *Indah.* I thought Rufus know *su casa* and take home."

Yellow Boy finished his smoke, got up, and tossed the butt into the iron stove. Then he turned to Rufus and said, "*Muchacho is* brave *hombre. No es muchachito, el es hombrecito,* little man." He looked at us and shrugged his shoulders as if the things he'd just described happened every day.

CHAPTER 20
PACT

Rufus finished his plate, sat it on the floor, wiped his mouth with the back of his sleeve, and tilted his chair back on two legs while he cut himself an after-dinner chew. He looked over at Yellow Boy with a raised eyebrow and said, "When ol' Yellow Boy rode up to the door with ye 'fore daylight yestidy mornin', my old hound Cody started raisin' hell." Rufus winked and said, "I named him after Buffalo Bill 'cause he can make more noise and pass more gas than a bugle band."

I couldn't help giggling.

Then Rufus said, "I grabbed my shotgun and run outside in my long johns and socks. It was colder'n hell, and I's 'bout to git frostbit inside the back flap of my long johns while I was off a-lookin' to see if there was a cat after my stock. 'Bout made me mess my drawers when that there Indian just floated in outta the dark with somebody on the front of his saddle. Soon as he showed me who it was, I 'bout puked, I's so upset, but I thanked God at the same time. It didn't take no lawyer to figger out ye and yore daddy had come to no good and that somehow ye, at least, had got away. Yore face was a mess, and Yellow Boy had splinted yore arm. He said ye had the cold shakes when he found ye, but ye had gotten better a ridin' next to him comin' over Baylor Pass. I carried ye inside, and fixed this here spot fer ye with a cot over close to the stove door so's ye'd stay warm and thaw out. Worked too, didn't it?"

I nodded and smiled. I didn't feel like talking much, but I

knew Rufus didn't expect me to.

"Yellow Boy hid his horse up the canyon and then we doctored yore arm with a splint that'll last a while longer than his mesquite sticks. He come back with weeds he'd found fer the poultice. That there is gonna be a nice scar, Henry, but it ain't deep, and it don't need no sewin'. After that, we waited fer ye to get yore sleepin' done. I told him to go on back home, that I'd get ye home soon as ye were strong enough to sit a horse, but he wouldn't leave until he knew ye were a-gonna make it."

Rufus paused a moment to spit into an old coffee can he used for a spittoon, and then he said, "Now I'm a-thinkin' Yellow Boy needs to lie low here until the other side of the mountains settles down from those posses riding ever' which away. Then he can get through without being seen or caught. Them posses, though, they ain't a-gonna find nothin'. Bastards that killed yore daddy, they's long gone. I 'spect Yellow Boy can get through in three or four days. So maybe in a few days he can take off fer the reservation, and we can ease on down to Mesilla and take away a little of the grief your family's a-feelin'."

At this, Yellow Boy said, "I watch. I go when my Power says go."

I finished my plate. Rufus took it and set it inside his on the floor. I looked at Yellow Boy, who was sitting between two wall studs while listening to Rufus with his eyes closed for a little while, and then he'd look at Rufus, who had that earnest look I remembered from talking to him in Lincoln. I hung my head, thinking about the miracle of salvation visited on me by those two good men.

I remembered seeing the glazed look in Daddy's eyes and the bubbles in the blood coming from his chest, and those murderers just sitting and laughing, while they smoked and waited for him to die. The dam finally broke, and I hung my head and cried. I cried from my guts like I'd never cried before. I couldn't stop.

Rufus just reached over and patted me on the shoulder. He said, "Go on and grieve, Henry. Ye're due. It don't make ye less a man that ye loved yore daddy that much."

Yellow Boy just sat and watched. Then he said softly, "Show eye water now, *muchacho*. When you become man, no longer make sound of woman with heavy heart for one gone to grandfathers."

I finally stopped crying and wiped my eyes. I sighed, and I felt better.

Rufus said, "Did ye hear anything, boy? Did ye hear anything at all that'd tell us who those men were that killed yore pa?"

I nodded, still snuffling up the snot and tears. I forgot about how tore up my face was and wiped my nose with my sleeve. It hurt like the devil. It felt like someone tore at my face, and I felt the poultice crack and shift a little, but somehow it hung on.

I said, "Jack Stone, Charlie Bentene, and a cowboy they called Jake were up the road before the shooting started. I remembered Stone and Bentene from when we stopped in Tularosa on the way to Lincoln. I think Red Tally is the name of the man who shot Daddy. He said he was going over to Oliver Lee's to see if he could get more money, said Lee oughta be real grateful 'cause he'd made life easier for him by killing Daddy."

Yellow Boy crossed his arms and stared at me. Rufus frowned as he spat into the old coffee can. He shook his head and said under his breath, "God a'mighty damn."

"Tally and a couple of others followed us down from Mescalero after we stayed with Doc Blazer. I heard Stone say he wished he'd had Tally come and kill Daddy two years earlier." Suddenly, I felt a violent rage rising up inside me. I clenched my fists and said, "I hate their guts, Rufus. I hate 'em, and I'm gonna kill 'em all." Then I started crying again. I couldn't help it.

A gust of wind shook the creosote bushes outside the door and made the window and door rattle. Then Rufus said, "We gotta be real kerful here, boys. I hear tell Red Tally is one brutal, mean, son of a bitch. He's deadly at long distances with a Winchester. Most people he's bushwhacked never knowed what hit 'em. Up in Colorado, they say he even shot a preacher standing in the middle of the street whilst he's a-talking to a sheriff. Couple years back, he burnt down a house with a woman and two little 'uns still in it 'cause she wouldn't leave after he killed her man. If they's money to be made, he don't hold back from killing nobody." He stared at me, his eyes narrow and full with anger, and said, "They was gonna kill ye, too. You know that, don't ye, boy?"

I nodded. Rufus scratched his beard and was quiet for a few moments, apparently thinking about the situation. Finally, he said, "I know Stone couldn't afford to pay Tally by hisself, so they's shore to be a group what's anted up to the pot to pay Tally. They's most likely little ranchers 'cause yore daddy was working fer the big ranchers. Oliver Lee is the biggest little rancher. He probably put some money in that pot hisself. He's smart, that one is. If'n he thinks the law's a-gonna come after him, he turns hisself in and lets Albert Fall get him off. I notice ye seen 'em all 'cept Lee murderin' your daddy."

Rufus paused again and gave me a somber look. He said, "Yore word could send 'em all to hell at the end of a rope. Onct they find out ye're alive, they's got to be rid of ye, Henry. If'n ye show up again—" Slowly, he shook his head.

"What should I do?" I asked.

Rufus said, "I 'spect right now they's thinkin' ye froze to death out there on the range or wolves or coyotes made a meal of out ye. If I take ye back to yore family now, it's likely ye'll be dead in less than a week." He stroked his beard and added, "And yore family, too." He turned to Yellow Boy and asked, "What do you reckin we should do?"

Before Yellow Boy could answer, I said, "I want to kill 'em all." I felt fire burning in my belly and added, "If the law doesn't get 'em first, I will. I want to hide until it's done. After all, it's my fault Daddy's dead, and I promised Mama I'd protect him." I began sobbing again. Rufus just stared off into space for a while, chewing, spitting streams of tobacco juice into his can, and wiping his chin with the back of his hand.

Then, with a wrinkled brow, Rufus said, "Let me get this straight. Ye want to stay here with me until ye can take revenge on them there killers. Is that what you're a-tellin' me?"

I nodded and wiped at my eyes.

"Dang, son. Ye sound like ye're twenty or thirty years old. I can agree with what ye said, 'cept fer one thang. It ain't yore fault yore daddy's dead. Ye mustn't think like that."

Rufus sat down and looked out the window, but it seemed to me he wasn't really looking at anything in particular. After a few minutes, he said, "It's smart not to give anybody anywhere a hint ye're alive 'cause, when word gets out, they'll fer a fact come after ye. 'Specially Stone and Tally 'cause they muffed it letting ye get away. They's a-hoping ye're dead. If ye ain't, they'll be shore to shut ye up at the first opportunity. Hellfire. Ye're not more than ten or eleven year old. How do you plan on gettin' them killers?"

All I could answer was, "I'm eight, Rufus, and I don't know how, but I will. Will you help me? Please?"

He nodded and a little trickle of tobacco juice ran down the side of his mouth before he could spit. He chewed a couple more times and spit the whole wad into the can and said, "Hellfire, son, what'd yore mama and daddy do? Cast ye outta steel? Sire theyselves a wolf pup? I've lived a right long time. I might as well die now as later. Yes, sir, I'll help ye. I can at least help keep ye alive until the law catches those bastards. Maybe we might even get one or two of 'em ourselves, if'n Yellow Boy helps us."

I looked over at Yellow Boy who was watching Rufus, and asked, "Will you help us, Yellow Boy?"

His thin mouth cracked a smile, and he said, "*Sí*, I help. We take life for life many times."

"Can we go after them tomorrow?" I said, tingling with excitement. "I'm sure I'll feel better. Can we?"

Rufus roared with a laugh and nearly choked on his fresh chew of tobacco. "Listen to this little chicken hawk, would ye?" Yellow Boy's faint trace of a smile broadened to a big grin as I looked from him to Rufus and back again. I didn't see what was so funny. Now I had some real fighters who could help me get even for Daddy. I thought, *Yes, sir, we're going to make Stone, Tally, and Oliver Lee pay for Daddy's murder.*

When Rufus finally stopped laughing and choking, he looked at me with kind eyes and said, "Now, Henry, ye gotta start thinkin' like a smart scout. Ye gotta be cool and cakylatin'. Now ye're a little boy, a mighty fine one, but still not close to growed yet. To go after these here killers, ye gotta get big and strong. Ye gotta be a expert with a weapon. I watched ye with yore daddy's rifle, and ye was good fer a little feller, even if it was too heavy fer ye, but ye ain't nearly good enough to hunt men."

He nodded to the rifle hanging over the door. "I'll teach ye how to be a expert with that there buffalo rifle. Ye can shoot at those bastards from half a mile away and kill ever' one of 'em with it if'n ye want to, but ye gotta be able to survive in this here desert to do it. Ye was lucky onct. Not likely to be again. I know a few tricks fer makin' do in the desert, but ol' Yellow Boy there, he growed up in it. He'll teach you to live in it and to make it support ye as if it was yore friend. He'll teach ye a lot of other Apache tricks, too. Of that, I'm shore. When the time comes, we'll saddle up and go get those bastards. But it shore as hell is gonna take a while fer ye to heal and grow and git smart and good with that there gun. It's a-gonna be a powerful lot of work. Ye ready to work, wait, and learn?"

I bowed my head and looked at the rough shack floor, realizing how big my talk had sounded when I had no idea of what it meant. I said, "Yes, sir, I can wait. I'll work real hard, and I promise I'll learn everything you can teach me, just so those murderers don't get away."

Rufus nodded and leaned over to give me a gentle pat on the leg. "Don't worry 'bout that. They's justice a-comin'. They ain't gittin' away. We're a-gonna get 'em."

The need for more sleep suddenly rushed over me, and I yawned and said, "Rufus, I'm very tired now."

He nodded, helped me lie back, and fixed my arm so it lay comfortably on my chest. I don't remember much after that except that he and Yellow Boy seemed to be talking from far away as I drifted off.

I woke up in the middle of the night from a troubled sleep with a deep thirst and needing to pee in the worst way. Rufus helped me up so I could pee off the edge of the porch, and he gave me a dipper of water. It was cold on the porch, but the wind had died to a light breeze, and the stars were twinkling in a black velvet sky. Looking down the side of the Organs toward the south, I could see a weak glow in the sky over El Paso.

CHAPTER 21
THE RANCH

When I awoke on the morning after the Dripping Springs men had stopped by, an old coal-oil lantern with a soot-blackened chimney was the only light in the shack. The most delicious smell of frying bacon, biscuits, and coffee I can remember filled the shack. The biscuits were cooking in the old, crusty, black Dutch oven I remembered from the day before. Beside it on the stove, an old, beat-up coffeepot was steaming away.

I pushed myself up with my good arm and asked Rufus, "Where's Yellow Boy? He promised to help us. Has he decided he won't?"

Rufus looked over his shoulder and said, "Naw. He's a-gonna help us. He's just slipped back to the reservation fer a while a-visitin' with his family. Oughter be back in a few weeks, maybe by the time ye're healed up."

My lower lip trembled when I whined, "Are you sure he's going to help us?"

Rufus's grin spread another inch under his whiskers. "Now don't git yore drawers in no wad, Henry. Why, shore, he's a-gonna help us. He's just a-visitin' his wife—you remember, his number-one wife." Rufus stirred a pan of refried beans, then took the bacon out of the pan and put it on a tin plate. "How'd ye sleep, little man?"

I yawned and said, "Pretty good I think. I don't remember any bad dreams. My arm doesn't throb anymore either, but my face hurts."

"Well, git on up then, if'n ye're strong enough I'll show ye around the place after we eat. They's some hot water and a towel over on that little table next to the door. Wash the sleep outta yore eyes and see if'n ye can wash off that there poultice on yore face, too. It's a-needin' changin'. I'll dress it with a new poultice. Then we'll eat, and I'll show ye around the place."

At breakfast, I kept packing my jaws with victuals like a squirrel. Rufus just spread some honey on a biscuit and dawdled with his eating pan. He kept saying, "Don't make yoreself sick eatin' too much now. They's lots to see. I want ye to see it all. Hope ye're a-gonna like it here."

When we finished, he collected the plates and put the rest of the beans and the last bits of burned bacon in our leftovers. He put all the pans and plates out on the porch for Cody to lick clean.

After breakfast, Rufus helped me get dressed. My coat was shredded from crawling under the mesquite, so he threw a blanket over my shoulders to break the morning chill as we stepped out on the front porch.

The view from his porch was spectacular. Sitting there, I could look around the western edge of the tall canyon cliffs and see the Florida Mountains about sixty miles away to the west, and it was easy to see the top of Tortugas Mountain, just outside of Las Cruces. I could also see a few outbuildings around Las Cruces, but that bald little wart of a mountain on the edge of the desert and the valley hid most anything I might have seen in Las Cruces.

The trail up to Rufus's shack from the desert floor had two ruts and was a straight, sandy road that cut up from a dusty, slightly wider road that ran alongside the Organs. That road passed Dripping Springs Ranch, which was five or six miles away, crossed a trail over the Organs by Baylor Pass, and then crossed the road that went over San Agustin Pass. The mesquites and creosote bushes along the steep road up to Rufus's place were just barely separated enough for a wagon to go through, so a wagon couldn't turn around until it got up to Rufus's yard.

"Well, whatcha think of my place?" Rufus asked, after we'd walked out into the yard a ways.

I was too busy taking in every detail to give much of an answer, so I just said, "It's nice."

Rufus had painted the shack a light, turquoise-green color that matched the salt and loco weeds and a few old cacti that grew scattered around the front of his place. Its original color had faded from years of hard sunlight, but it still blended in well with the plants. The canyon walls, rising like guardians on either side of the shack, were rusty red with an occasional black streak down their faces. Those walls must have been five or six hundred feet high, and they shaded the canyon most of the time, except near midday and late in the afternoon, when the sun, setting behind the Floridas, caught the front edge of the shack. It was about a hundred yards between the south canyon wall to the side of the shack. The canyon wall on the north side was about thirty yards from the shack. On that wall about thirty feet off the canyon floor and just about even with the shack was a wide ledge where piñon bushes grew. There were a couple more ledges like it farther up the wall.

Rufus saw me looking at them and said, "I made me a place to hide on that first ledge, even chipped me some hand and toeholds in the canyon wall so I could get up to it fast if I need to. I keep jars of water and some beans and salt pork stashed away up there in case I have to stay there a while to hide from Indians or *banditos.*"

"Can we go look at it?" I asked.

Rufus grinned and said, "Soon as yore arm heals and ye can climb."

We walked back to a small shed Rufus used for a barn. It was about forty yards southeast behind the shack. It sat surrounded by a corral, and the privy was close by on the other side of the corral fence. He'd stretched barbed wire from the corral all the way across the canyon to keep his cattle and his mules from wandering off. A little spring-fed stream wandered down a wide, shallow gully close by the south wall. He had dammed it up, and, using planks that he nailed and tarred together, channeled the water to watering troughs and a holding tank he used for the shack. The barbed wire fence had a big pole gate at the corral that blocked a path disappearing back into the canyon. I could hear cattle occasionally bawling somewhere deep within the walls of the canyon.

When we walked over to his shed, I noticed a pile of rocks. It was about ten feet in diameter and three or four feet high at the center and sat between the house and corral. As I looked around, I noticed other, smaller piles scattered back down the canyon. "What are these for?" I asked.

Rufus thrust out his chest and said, "Well, boy, I intend to make me a first-class place here one of these days. I'm a-gonna use rocks like old Frenchy Rochas did over to Dog Canyon a few year ago. He even made his fences outta rock. So I've been gittin' my buildin' stones together 'fore I start."

"Can I help you get your rocks together? Since you're helping me, I want to help you all I can."

"Shore, boy. That there'd be a mighty big help." He chewed on the wad of tobacco in his cheek a couple of times and said, "Ye know, carryin' rocks to them there piles might be good fer ye. It'd help make ye stronger than anybody might think ye was fer yore years."

"Oh, boy! Can I start this afternoon?" I pleaded.

Rufus laughed. "Naw, son. Ye gotta heal up first. They's plenty of time to work carryin' rocks to them there piles. 'Sides, they's some things ye gotta know 'fore ye start a-pickin' up rocks in this here canyon."

I was puzzled and a little frustrated that I couldn't start getting big and strong right away. I asked, "Rufus, what do you have to know to pick up and carry a rock? Don't you just pick it up and start walking? That doesn't take training, does it?"

Rufus's brow wrinkled, and his eyes narrowed. "Naw, ye don't jest pick it up and start a-walkin'. And don't go a-gettin' smart-mouthed on me now, boy. Lots times they's bad critters under them rocks. Ye know, like rattlesnakes, scorpions, black wider spiders, or hundert leg centipedes. Those thangs'll bite ye. Aye God, ye know ye been bit when they do, too. Why I seed men lose a fanger after a centipede got 'em. Ye gotta be careful when ye pick up a rock around here, son. They's things under 'em that can kill ye."

I understood then I had a lot to learn and a short time to learn it, and I realized that old tobacco-chewing man was all that stood between death and me. I purposed right then to give Rufus the same respect I'd always given my daddy. I nodded, hung my head, and said, "Yes, sir. I didn't mean to smart-mouth you. I won't do it anymore."

Rufus nodded and said, "Ye're a quick study, Henry. Ye'll do fine." He was quick to try to make up and asked, "How's yore arm a-feelin' in that there sling? Are ye warm enough with that blanket over yore shoulders? Ye wanna rest fer a while before we take us a walk up the canyon?"

"No, sir, I'm ready to go now. My arm's not throbbing, and the blanket feels good."

"All right then," he said. "They's some places I want ye to see up there, too."

"Yes, sir. I want to see it all."

We walked back past the shed where he kept his tools, harness, and some grain for his mules. He pulled a couple of poles down to make getting through the fence easy. When we were on the other side, he put them back in place and led off down the path through piñons that disappeared around a curve in the canyon walls. He called back over his shoulder, "Be kerful and don't go a-steppin' in no cow pies. It don't make the shack smell too good if'n ye git that dirt on yore boots." I saw the mischievous look on his face and laughed with him.

We walked about a mile up the canyon. He had over a hundred head of cattle grazing on the best stand of gra'ma grass I'd ever seen. As we neared the end of the path, the sheer face of the cliffs in which the canyon ended rose up before us, dark and overpowering in the shadows. Looking at their smooth walls for the first time, I felt sure they couldn't be climbed. But Rufus showed me a barely visible line of handholds that went right up the north wall cliff and disappeared up over the top.

"I don't know who fixed them places," he said. "It's easy to climb up to the top of them there cliffs using 'em. Why, I even done it myself onct. I 'spect it was Apaches or Pueblos made 'em. They's probably a-fixin' 'em a rabbit hole to 'scape in case they got trapped in this canyon. If'n ye foller them handholds up over the cliff there, ye'll find a trail that takes ye across the Organs and down the other side 'bout where Aguirre Springs is."

I stood there frowning at the handholds, not understanding what Rufus had said about a rabbit hole. "It doesn't look like a rabbit hole," I said.

Rufus put a hand on my shoulder and said, "Naw, and that mesquite bush you hid under out in the desert didn't neither, but it was a rabbit hole nonetheless. Rabbit holes are hidin' places and 'scape routes. A real rabbit hole always has two 'scape routes. Think on that next time ye need to pick a good hidin' place, Henry."

I looked back up at the handholds in the cliff, and Rufus leaned down, looked me in the eyes, and said, "Now don't ye go gittin' no ideas 'bout goin' up them thangs. One slip up high and ye'd be a goner fer shore."

I nodded and asked if I could see what they were like, and he let me walk over to it. I could barely stand on my toes and reach the first handhold with my unbroken arm.

Rufus pointed toward a small crack in the south wall that was maybe twenty yards wide and ran for several hundred yards perpendicular to the main canyon before becoming impassable. To me it looked like a great place to play hideout. I noticed that there were mounds of dirt all the way down the length of the little canyon, every fifty or so yards, and it looked like bits of glass were scattered on the tops of them. "See that there crack in the world? What do ye think I use it fer?"

I could only shake my head at the mystery.

"See those mounds of dirt? I put 'em in there myself. They hold up my targets, usually bottles I git from the saloons. Them mounds is 'bout fifty yards apart, and they's ten of them. That there is five hundert yards. It's where I practice with that there Sharps a-hangin' over the door. Soon as yore arm's well, I'm a-gonna teach ye how to be a deadly shot with that there old rifle. Think ye'd wanna learn that kinda shootin', son?"

I was so excited at the prospect of shooting that big old rifle I could only smile and nod. Rufus spat a long, brown stream, smiled, and tousled my hair.

"Well, soon as yore arm's mended, we'll start a-shootin'. Let's git on back to the house." He started to go, then turned again and said, "Oh, I almost fergot the main reason I brought ye up here today." In the east cliff wall, he pointed out the source of the spring that fed the little stream that watered the canyon. "That there spring is the reason this place survived the big drought, and its water is our lifeblood. Defend it with yore life, if ye have to."

"I will. I promise," I told Rufus.

"I know ye will, boy," he whispered as he headed on. About halfway back down the path, he stopped and pointed my attention toward the canyon's north wall. "Notice anything peculiar 'bout them bushes over there?"

I stared for a little while before I realized there was a faint outline of some kind of a bulge about the size of a big door on the canyon wall behind the bushes. Pointing toward it, I said, "All I see is something that looks like a little bulge in the cliff. It kind of reminds me of the door to a cave in Ali Baba's adventures when Daddy used to read to me and my brothers. Is it a door? Will it open if I say *open sesame*?"

Rufus grinned and said, "I'll be a-hornswoggled. Dang, if ye ain't got sharp eyes an' a good memory. Ain't nobody else seed that door till I pointed it out fer 'em. Yes, sir. It shore is a door. Made it and fixed it up to look like part of the mountain, I did. It's to cover up the entrance to a little mine I started. It ain't very deep, but it's dry, so I keep my extry supplies there. Wanna see inside it?"

"I sure do." We walked off the trail, and it was easier to recognize the door as we got up close to it. Rufus had made it out of wood then covered it with a thin cloth sack filled with a layer of rock and dirt the same color as the canyon wall. Then he'd used plaster mixed with dirt to hide the doorframe that held it in place.

He fished around near the bottom of the door to find the latch that held it tightly closed. A blast of stale, cool air came floating out as he swung it back. He lighted a coal-oil lantern hanging on the back of the door and held it up so I could see inside. To me, the inside looked better than the US Treasury. It was filled with barrels of stuff, animal hides, an old saddle or two, a harness, tools, some old apple crates filled with potatoes, and a stack of neatly folded canvas tarps. Toward the back, I could see the dim outline of a half a side of beef hanging from a small scaffold.

He said, "Now, I'm showin' this here hole to ye so ye know where it is, what's in it, and how to get in it if ye need to get supplies or tools fer us or to hide yoreself. Only thing ye gotta remember is snakes like this place, too. They think it's a dad-burn hotel. They'll generally mind their own business if'n ye don't bother 'em none. If they's one here, just take that stick there and toss him outside. Ain't no need to kill 'im, lessen ye have to. He'll keep the rats and other vermin gone. Do ye foller me, son?"

I nodded, but, in the back of my mind, I was certain I didn't want to fool with any rattlesnake, especially not with just a stick. If I found one, it was going to be a goner.

We left the mine, and Rufus closed the door and latched it again. He stepped back to admire it for a few seconds before he said, "Now don't fergit to latch that there door after ye're in there, or they'll be more snakes than that there stick'll take care of." I nodded, and he led me down the path toward the house.

By the time we got back to the house, I was worn out. Rufus helped me lie down on the cot for a *siesta* and said he was going to sit outside and whittle a while and enjoy the sun until it was time to cook our supper. That old cot sure felt good. It wasn't more than two or three big yawns before I drifted off to sleep.

CHAPTER 22
EDUCATION

One day in late winter, we were sitting on the porch step watching one of those brilliant sunsets over the Floridas when Rufus asked, "Henry, what was the last thing ye read before ye left school to go to Lincoln with yore daddy?"

I thought for a minute and said, "I got a copy of *Huckleberry Finn* for Christmas, and I had read about half of it when we left for Lincoln. I took it with me, but I lost it on that wagon ride when I was trying to get away."

"Ye read purdy good, then?" he asked.

I nodded and said, "Daddy started us out early. We were reading before we went to school, and he made each of us read something aloud every night by the time we were in the first grade, and we'd all listen to one another read. Sometimes my older brothers would read papers Daddy had written. That's how I learned about the work Daddy did."

Rufus squinted with one eye and said, "Well, sir, ye had a good start. I don't think ye should go to bein' ignorant now that ye're a-livin' here with me. Go inside there and find *The Iliad* in them two stacks of books over in the corner. That's a good 'un to start with. I want ye to start readin' some ever' day. Can't have ye illit'rate when ye git back home."

I had to get the old coal-oil lantern and light it to read the titles. His book stacks were nearly as tall as I was. Rufus read often himself, so there wasn't much dust on them. I found *The Iliad* and *The Odyssey* in one volume about halfway down the first stack. Rufus had practically worn the gold letters off the green leather binding. I restacked the other books and took it outside with the lantern. I sat down by Rufus and opened it to the first page. He spat a long stream against the green creosote bush by the porch and said, "Read some to me, boy. I ain't seen that tale in a while."

I found the book very hard to read. Every night, we'd sit on the porch or at the table with that old lantern casting its soft, yellow glow, Rufus chewing and spitting, leaning back in his chair with his arms crossed and his eyes closed, listening, while I tried to sound out the words. Whenever I asked him, he'd tell me the correct way to say a word, and then he'd tell me what it meant. I worked hard to learn fast and not forget what he taught me.

Over our dinners, Rufus and I usually talked about what I'd read the evening before. I'd say something like, "That was a great trick the Greeks played with the Trojan horse. They didn't give up after ten years of war. I think it's funny they finally were able to beat the Trojans with a trick."

Rufus would reply with something like, "Yes, sir, that was purdy clever. But it don't make no never mind that it took the Greeks ten years to beat the Trojans. What mattered was that the Greeks wouldn't quit no matter what, and neither should ye. Ol' Ulysses didn't quit a-goin' home, neither. When he got home, he set things right, even though he looked like a beggar an' they's men trying to take his wife and property. Shot 'em ever one with his bow an' arrer an' made things right. Aye, God, that's what ye need to do, Henry. Ye gotta set things right fer yore family and fer yore daddy."

Of course, Rufus was just reinforcing what I had already promised to myself and to him. He was teaching me I wasn't the only one who'd had to struggle to find justice. But I wasn't about to quit. No matter how hard it was to bring my daddy's murderers to justice, I was going to do it, and I was going to get back home and see my mama, too.

After the *Iliad* and *Odyssey* I read most of Shakespeare's plays and learned a lot about the doings of men and women, kings and queens, and human nature in general. I read *The Three Musketeers* and *Treasure Island* and learned the true value of friends like Rufus and Yellow Boy. We continued our readings and discussions this way as the weeks sped by, but Yellow Boy did not reappear. After a while, I became convinced he wasn't coming back.

One day Rufus examined my arm splints closely. After he felt my broken arm all over, he asked me, "Does it hurt anywheres, son?" When I told him it didn't, he pulled his long knife out of his belt, the one he said he'd used to take scalps back in his scouting days, and said, "All right, looks like it's about time fer that thang to come off. Ye ready?"

"Yes, sir, cut it off."

His scalping knife sliced up through the splint ties in one smooth motion, and the splint sticks fell away. My arm, although thin and wasted-looking, felt good as new. It was filthy because I hadn't been able to wash it while the splint and bandages were covering it.

"Does it hurt to move it around?" Rufus asked.

I swung it back and forth a couple of times and wrapped it around my body. "No, sir, a little sore, maybe. But other than that, it's great."

Rufus said, "Now, son, we can start a-gittin' ye strong. We're a-gonna start working on the rock pile tomorrow, and we're a-gonna start yore lessons with that there gun, too."

The next morning we had breakfast while it was still dark, and we were out the door at dawn. Rufus rummaged around in his shed until he found a crowbar and an old pair of miners' gloves, which he handed to me. Then he took a steel pry bar about his height and a pair of gloves for himself. He called Cody, and we walked to the stock gate and down the path toward the back of the canyon.

When we got to a rock pile, Rufus said, "Now look at them there rocks. They's about the size of yore head. That there is the size ye wanna git. They's rocks scattered all over the canyon floor, but ye're most likely to find the right size uns up along the canyon walls. When ye find one, check fer critters, then pick 'er up an' haul 'er over to this here pile. Old Cody's a-gonna let us know if'n they's any snakes around. It's cool in the mornings, so them varmints can't move too fast, and they's usually found a place to rest fer the day by the time the sun's up."

He started walking through the bushes toward the canyon wall and said over his shoulder, "Come on, an' I'll show ye how to get one without gettin' bit by snakes or them other critters I warned ye 'bout."

He walked about thirty yards before he stopped in front of five or six rocks scattered about that were just about the right size. He motioned me over to the nearest one and said, "Now, first, jest look all around to be shore they's no snakes around the rocks or the bushes. Usually, Cody will let ye know if they is, but sometimes the old fart fergits to do his job, so ain't no harm in bein' real kerful. If they ain't no snakes nearby, then all ye gotta do is roll the rock over with yore pry bar there so ye can see if'n they's any other bitin' or stingin' varmints under it. If they is, crunch 'em with yore bar, then carry the rock over to the pile, but first, jest stick the bar in the ground where the rock was so's ye can find where ye found yore rock. Go head an' try it."

Eagerly, I walked over to the first rock, slid the pry bar under it and flipped it over with a little strain. I saw nothing on it or in the dirt where it had rested. I started to stick my pry bar in the ground to mark the spot, but the end of Rufus's pry bar landed with a thump in the center of the place where the rock had been. It surprised me, and I jumped back. I looked at Rufus and yelled, "What're you trying to do, scare me?"

He grinned, nodding toward the place where the rock had been, and said, "Naw, son. Take a look at the end of my bar there." I looked. There was a small rattlesnake twisting in its death throes. It was almost the same color as the sand under the rock and maybe five or six inches long. Rufus said, "Ye gotta look close, boy. He ain't big, but a bite from that little bugger can make ye real sick or even kill ye. Now see if'n ye can carry that there rock over to the pile."

Humbled, I bent over to pick up the rock, but before I could lift it off the ground, Rufus said, "Not that a-way, Henry. Bend at yore knees, and use yore legs to lift it, not yore back. Usin' yore back to lift heavy thangs can ruin a feller."

I did as he told me. It was easy enough to lift the rock that way, but the reality was that it was a lot heavier than I'd thought it would be. My right arm was still sore and weak. I strained a little to hold it. It was only about twenty yards to the pile, but by the time I got halfway there, I was struggling to keep hold of that rock. I clenched my teeth and strained to hold on until I finally made it to the pile and let it fall.

As I walked back to him, Rufus asked, "Too heavy fer ye, Henry?" His brow was furrowed. I shook my head, although both my arms felt like they wanted to float off my body now that the weight was gone. Rufus said, "I know that was a strain fer ye, but ye held 'er. That was real good. Git the rest of them rocks there, and call it a day. We'll do a little more ever' day while ye git stronger. In a month or two, ye'll be strong enough to work three or four hours like I do. Careful now an' don't drop one on yore foot."

I got the other four rocks. I found no more snakes, but I did uncover a couple of scorpions, which I promptly dispatched with my pry bar. Each new rock, although about the same size as the first one, seemed heavier than the last, and the distance to the rock pile seemed to grow longer and longer. The last one I carried, I dropped twice on the way to the pile. I was worn out after only an hour of that heavy labor. When I got the last rock to the pile, Rufus, who had been carrying two or three rocks to the pile for my one, said, "Go on to the shack and git me some water will ye?"

Once inside, I drank several dippers of water and carried Rufus half a bucket of water, which he nearly emptied. Then he wiped his face with the old red-and-white bandanna dangling from his back pocket and said, "You go on back to rest on the porch. I'll be along in a while."

Rufus was right. Within a month, I was spending three or four hours a day carrying those rocks. Every step I took with one, I put it down to what I owed Stone, Tally, and Oliver Lee. *Someday . . . someday,* I kept thinking as I carried those rocks. *Someday you're going pay, and I'm going to collect for what you did to Daddy and me. Someday I'm gonna kill you. I promise you, someday I will.*

I was so tired after the days we carried rocks, I slept soundly. However, on Saturdays and Sundays, we rested, and for several years thereafter, on Saturday and Sunday nights, I nearly always had a nightmare in which I was chased by shadowy men who wanted to kill me. Stone's cold, wolf eyes kept sizing me up. Tally was jerking me up by my collar to go sit in the wagon while he watched Daddy die. Big, bloody streams were pumping out of Daddy's chest while he drowned in his own blood. I suppose that nightmare spurred me to start thinking deeply about why my daddy ever allowed the situation to come to that.

Many times, especially on Saturdays, when Rufus went to

town to get supplies, I'd get out the ivory watch fob Mama had given me and think about my family. I began to see that Rufus was right. It really wasn't my fault that Daddy had been killed, but I didn't blame Mama or my sister Maggie for nagging him to take me along. Mostly, I blamed the men who planned his murder, and sometimes, when I was honest with myself, I even cast a bit of the blame on Daddy.

CHAPTER 23
SHOOTS TODAY KILLS TOMORROW

After my first rock-carrying day, Rufus had finally come to the porch in mid-morning and had a cup of coffee. He sat on the porch and rested with his back to the wall, mopping his sweat-covered face with his old red bandanna. After he sat there for about an hour, he pushed himself up and staggered inside. I heard him rummaging around and then heard something sliding across the floor. Soon he stepped out, a box of cartridges in one hand and the buffalo gun that hung over the doorpost in the other. He grinned at me and asked, "Ready to start yore shootin' lessons with this here old thunder stick?"

I jumped up, my heart pounding, and said, "Yes, sir."

He nodded and said, "Well, run in the shack and grab several of them there old, empty whiskey bottles in the box close to the stove, and we'll walk down to the shootin' range and see what you can do."

When we got to the back cliff, he said, "Put them bottles on top of that first pile of dirt."

I ran to the dirt pile and placed the bottles on top, side-by-side, about six inches apart. When I turned around, it took a couple of moments for me to spot Rufus, who was standing a few yards back from where I'd left him, up close to the north face of the cliffs, neatly camouflaged by the bushes and shadows. He was sitting in the shade of a big piñon tree about fifty yards away from the dirt mound. He motioned me to come and patted the ground for me to sit next to his left side.

When I was seated, he said, "This here rifle is a eighteen seventy-four Sharps. It has a barrel that's thirty-two inches long, and it shoots a forty-five-seventy cartridge that has 'bout an ounce of lead in the bullet. Yellow Boy calls it 'Shoots Today Kills Tomorrow' because of its long range—well over a mile. You can shoot at a target a thousand yards away, and it will take about three seconds after you pull the trigger before the bullet hits the target. It can shoot all the way through a buffalo at a thousand yards. Ye know how far that is, Henry?"

I slowly shook my head, my heart pounding harder with the thought that I might get to fire the cannon Rufus lovingly held in his hands. "Well, sir," he said, "it's a little less than two thirds of the length of the path back to the fence." My jaw dropped in wonder. I was amazed at the idea that a gun, any gun, could actually shoot that much lead that far.

Rufus reached in his pocket and pulled out a huge cartridge, its brass shining golden in the sun, its lead short, silvery, and flat-nosed protruding from the brass casing. Nearly two and half inches long, it was a giant compared to the regular .45-caliber shells I had shot in Daddy's rifle.

Rufus grinned at my awe. "Now pay attention, son. This here is how ye load her up. First, ye pull the hammer here to half cock. Half cock is a safety feature. The rifle won't fire with the hammer there." He thumbed the side-mounted hammer back until it clicked. Lowering the end of the barrel until it pointed toward the piles of dirt, he said, "Then ye drop the breech-block." He pulled on the wide, heavy trigger guard until it came forward, and the heavy breechblock dropped down from the stock end of the barrel. "Now ye're ready to slide yore cartridge in. Sight down the barrel first to be shore it's clear the first time ye shoot her. Be shore the cartridge is all the way in, so's the breechblock'll slide past 'er when ye pull the lever back." He slid the cartridge into the breech end of the barrel, then pulled the lever forming the trigger guard back up so the breech closed with a reassuring snap. "Did ye git all that, Henry?" he asked with a smile, and I nodded.

He reached in his shirt pocket, pulled out a couple of lumps of bee's wax, and handed one to me. "Here. Pinch off a couple of pieces an' roll 'em up so's they fit in yore ears. Ye need to do this when ye shoot this here rifle a lot of times at one sittin'. Ye can't hear a thang fer hours afterwards if'n ye don't." I nodded.

"Now watch, Henry. This here is how ye cock and fire." He pulled the side hammer back until it clicked once more. Then Rufus pointed to the back trigger and said, "This here trigger is the set trigger. Pull that trigger back 'fore ye fire, and it'll set the front trigger so it's real easy to pull. See that there little screw between the triggers? Well, ye just adjust that screw with yore fingers until the first trigger has just the pull pressure ye want to use. Some folks want a hair trigger. Some don't. I like an easy pull myself. Onct ye pull back on that set trigger, the pull pressure ye set will make 'er shoot. Ye ready to fire?" I nodded with excitement, trembling, and unable to speak.

Sitting in the dirt, Rufus rested his elbows on his knees and sighted the rifle on a bottle. He squinted down the sights for an instant, and then he pulled back the set trigger. The front trigger made a little click forward. In a smooth motion, his trigger finger found the front trigger and paused for half a heartbeat before the rifle roared and the end of the barrel bucked up about six inches. Echoes filled the canyon, and some cattle that had been watching us headed for the front fence. I was expecting the noise, but I still jumped, amazed at the booming thunder from the report and the obvious power in the weapon. It wasn't at all like Daddy's Winchester, which seemed almost a toy by comparison.

Rufus grinned at me and nodded down range through the gray haze of smoke lying in the still air. One of the bottles had completely disappeared. "See if ye can do what I jest showed ye," he said, handing the rifle over to me. I took it and almost dropped it because it was so heavy. "Be careful where ye point the barrel, and always assume it's loaded. Here, sit cross-legged, and rest it across your knees while a-pointin' toward them bottles." I did, and he said, "Good. Now pull the hammer to half cock and push the trigger lever down, and it'll throw out the empty shell." I had to strain and use my whole hand to pull the hammer back to half cock. The spring on the lever was stiff, and I had to strain a little with both hands to get it to drop the breech, but the spring soon released, and the shell came sailing out of the breech right into Rufus's waiting palm. "Save yore brass," he said. "It's costly, and I reload 'em as often as I can and like I want 'em."

He reached in his pocket again, brought out another cartridge, and handed it to me to load. I first squinted down the empty barrel as he had said to do. It was still shiny with a little smoke vapor left. The cartridge slid smoothly into the breech. I had to pull hard again to make the lever move up to close the breech, but it snapped into place when I finally put both hands on it and leaned back. Rufus said, "Now see if ye're strong enough to hold it up with yore knees like I did." I got the barrel pointed in the general direction, but it waved all over the place. Rufus took it out of my hands grinning. "Still got a few more beans to eat, ain't ye, son? Here, stretch out on the ground on yore belly an' rest 'er on that there piñon stump."

Rufus positioned me at about a forty-five-degree angle to the line of site, raising me up on my elbows, and fit the barrel of the rifle on the stump with the forestock in my left hand and the stock snug against my shoulder. It was a lot more comfortable and steady that way. "Can ye see the bottles through the sights?" he asked. I nodded. "All right, line up on a bottle. Aim about a third of a bottle low cause the rifle is sighted for a lot longer range. Got it?" I nodded. "Now pull the set trigger back until ye hear it click." I squeezed hard against with my forefinger and it finally clicked. "Good. Now get your line of sight and put yore finger on the front trigger. Don't pull at all yet. Jest take a deep breath." I did. "Now let about half of it out an', sightin' where ye want, start squeezin' the trigger."

Daddy had taught me the same procedure with his Winchester. I had just started to squeeze the trigger when the rifle roared, slammed up against my cheek, and kicked hard backwards. I felt like I'd been kicked by a mule. I lay unmoving for a few seconds, stunned by the recoil punch. Slowly, the smoke drifted away. A second bottle had disappeared.

There was a big smile showing though Rufus's whiskers. "Henry!" he yelled. "Henry, danged if ye ain't gonna be a first-class marksman. One shot, one target, by damn."

Rufus watched and coached me as I shot about twenty rounds before my shoulder got too sore to shoot anymore. Then he practiced some. He promised we'd practice nearly every day until I was consistently hitting targets at the end of the little canyon, about five hundred yards away.

When we got back to the shack one Friday, we had our afternoon *siesta,* and then Rufus got up and made us some supper. As twilight came, Rufus and I sat out on the shack porch while I read some more of *The Iliad* to him. As I was reading, I noticed Cody's ears perk up. I looked up and jumped in surprise. Rufus grinned and said, "Howdy, Yellow Boy. Headin' to Mexico again?"

Yellow Boy nodded. *"Si.* My woman, she waits. *Hombrecito,* he is better, *si?"*

Nodding, Rufus said, "Yes, sir, thanks to ye a savin' his hide, I reckin he's done healed up. How long ye with us this time, *amigo?"*

"One sun. Then I leave and return in a moon. Soon I teach *Hombrecito* Apache ways. Make him ready for war on men who kill *padre*."

Rufus nodded and said, "I reckin we got a lot of teachin' to do." He shoved a thumb toward the front door and said, "They's *frijoles* and *tortillas* on the stove that's still hot. Go help yoreself. We'll talk while ye eat."

Before he went inside, Yellow Boy turned and tossed a packet tied with rawhide strips to me. The clothes I'd been wearing when Daddy was killed were coming to pieces after a couple of months of living with Rufus. I untied the packet and found that Yellow Boy had brought me boot moccasins and Apache clothing to replace my tattered clothes.

I followed him inside, thanked him, and put them on, delighting in the feel of them. Rufus looked at me and said, "Well, look at that. He could easily pass for a half-breed Apache child now that his hair's gone uncut for several months. He'd even look full Apache if his hair didn't have little curl to it."

Yellow Boy grunted, nodded, and continued to gobble down the remains of Rufus's cooking.

CHAPTER 24
THE GOING HOME TALK

The next day was Saturday, and Rufus rode Sally into Las Cruces for supplies, as he always did on Saturdays. Yellow Boy decided to go hunting to see if he could get a deer, but he refused to take me with him. "You make *mucho* sound," he said, after I'd sworn to keep quiet for the third time.

"I won't talk a bit," I argued.

"No talk, *pero* still make *mucho* sound," he said.

I wasn't able to convince him I could move through the mountains as quietly as an Apache, although I wished mightily that I could. I finally quit begging to go along and resigned myself to doing my chores and reading.

Yellow Boy returned in that afternoon with a buck and had dressed it, taken a portion for our dinner into the shack, and hung the rest in Rufus's cave by the time Rufus came riding up the trail. Rufus waved at us as he rode by the porch and headed for the corral. After he took care of Sally, he lugged his burlap sack of supplies to the cabin and said, "Come on in and eat, boys. We need to talk."

I looked at Yellow Boy, and he looked at me. Neither of us had any idea what was going on, so we just shrugged our shoulders and went inside.

Rufus said, "I see ye got us some fresh meat, Yellow Boy. I 'preciate it."

Before long, Rufus had his usual pot hung over the fire and served us up a supper of beans, chilies, steak, and tortillas. He didn't appear to have much to say, and Yellow Boy and I ate in silence, waiting for him to speak.

It was strange for Rufus not to say anything. He was usually bubbling over with news from town, but during this meal, he just stared past Yellow Boy at the open door. Yellow Boy, as always, finished eating first, belched his appreciation of the meal, and pulled a Mexican cigar from his vest pocket. He lighted it, smoked to the four directions, and, squinting through the smoke, said, "You talk now, Rufus?"

I said, "Yeah, tell us what you found out today."

Rufus wiggled his nose, trying to nudge his wire-framed glasses up higher. He dropped his fork on his plate, folded his hands in front of him, and said, "Well, fellers, here it is. I've been a-worryin' and a-scratchin' my head about this ever since ye came here, Henry. I ain't slept good fer a lot of nights a-worryin' about what I oughter do. I've tried out all kinds of schemes in my head to make it happen, but I always find they ain't a-gonna work after I think out all the angles."

Yellow Boy took a deep draw on his cigar, making the ash glow brightly in the twilight gloom of the shack. He rolled the cigar between his fingers and said, "Speak straight, Rufus. *No comprendo* when you say you no sleep good. You make big noise in your sleep. You sound like you sleep plenty good." He grinned and winked at me.

Rufus, however, remained grim. He pushed his half-eaten supper away and cut himself a chew of tobacco with a short, deliberate knife stroke. He chewed in silence for a while, and then he sighed and said, "Maybe I'm just a kidnapper." Looking sadly at me, he said, "Henry, I prob'ly shoulda carried ye back to yore mama a long time ago. Maybe it's long overdue that I do. They was a-talkin' today in the barbershop about how yore mama still wears black all the time and nobody ever sees her smile. Fact is, some folks in Cruces think she just went plain crazy with grief after she lost ye and yore daddy. It ain't right she's sufferin' like that when her son she thinks is dead ain't but twenty mile away, playin' and helpin' me."

I wanted to cry. I remembered how sad Mama had looked when Daddy and I left for Lincoln. I knew my absence was keeping her in dark places. I imagined her sitting by herself in a dark house, going through hell.

Rufus suddenly shouted, "Damn it to hell! I'm the one who's made her crazy 'cause I didn't carry her son back to her."

Yellow Boy took a long draw on the cigar and stared at him, waiting.

I said, "Rufus, have you forgotten what you said? You said if you took me back to Mama, Stone and Tally wouldn't waste any time getting somebody to finish me off, along with whoever was with me."

I paused a moment to think and plunged on, dangerously close to shedding tears. "You and Yellow Boy promised you'd teach me how to be a warrior so I . . . so we, can bring those . . . those . . . bastards to justice. Has any of that changed?"

Rufus winced like I'd just hit him. He sat rubbing his neck and watching the last sunlight fill the doorway. Finally, he shook his head, looked at me through his dusty lenses, and said, "Naw, Henry. Ain't none of that changed."

I heard Yellow Boy grunt beside me. He leaned back in his chair and crossed his arms as he stared at Rufus.

Rufus stared back, slowly scratching his week-old chin stubble with his stubby fingers. Then he sighed and said, "Somehow, this still just don't feel right. I like the boy, and I enjoy his company. Maybe I am just a kidnapper."

Yellow Boy leaned toward him and asked, "What does this thing you say, *kidnapper,* mean, Rufus?"

"Well, I reckin it means someone who's a-grabbin' a body and a-holdin' him fer money or as a slave. Hell, yore people used to raid down to Mexico and up here, too, fer women and young'uns to keep as slaves, wives, or even sons. Sometimes ye even sold 'em back again fer money or maybe swapped 'em fer guns."

Yellow Boy held up one hand and asked, "Rufus, did you steal *muchacho*?"

"Naw, but I shore as hell kept him."

"Is *muchacho* slave? *Muchacho* works. You make him sweat much, carry rocks. *Muchacho* uses Shoots Today Kills Tomorrow good. He shoots many times. Is *muchacho* prisoner? *Quien es,* Rufus?"

Rufus shook his head. "Ye're right. He ain't no slave or prisoner. He earns his keep, but that don't make him no slave. He's been a-makin' hisself strong a-carryin' those rocks, an' I've been a-teachin' him to shoot over long ranges with the Sharps. He can come and go when he wants outta this here shack, so I reckin *kidnapper* ain't the right word. Still, I ain't took him home yet, and it's hurt his mama mighty bad to think her little boy's lying dead somewhere out in that desert. I don't think that's right."

"Rufus, is *muchacho* better dead or alive?"

"Why, hell. Alive. Ain't no doubt of that there."

Yellow Boy leaned forward again with his elbows on the table, his arms still crossed, and the cigar still stuck in his jaw. He said, pointing back at his chest, "I pulled *muchacho* from the mesquite bush and brought him to you." Then he slapped the table and almost whispered, "I took mouse from *gato.* He hurt *muy mal,* almost die. You fix him, make his arm strong and his face good now. He now carry good scar, warrior scar. Now, he is no more *muchacho. Hombrecito* is little man. Without us, he die in desert. Now we teach him many things. In maybe ten harvests, he avenges *padre. Hombrecito* cannot learn what he needs to learn from *mamacita.* If he goes home to her, *gatos* kill him, kill her, maybe kill all family. *Hombrecito* hides here, learns all man needs know."

Rufus stopped chewing and stared at Yellow Boy, then at me as the shack faded into darkness. The only light was the glow of Yellow Boy's cigar and the coals glowing in the open door of the old, cast-iron stove. Rufus didn't move to get up and light a lantern.

It seemed like time just stopped until Rufus finally stirred and walked out the door, and we followed him onto the porch. He stood leaning against a porch post, staring toward the Floridas as the last purple and orange streaks filled the sky across the Mesilla Valley.

At last, he eased himself down on the porch step with his hands folded in a prayerful attitude and his elbows resting on his knees. I sat down beside him. Yellow Boy squatted off to one side, making the ash on his cigar glow brightly as he puffed contentedly. Cody got up from his corner of the porch, stretched, yawned, and padded over to flop down beside me. The only sounds were the spring crickets and Cody's tail flopping on the porch floor while I scratched his ears. Yellow Boy finished his cigar and ambled over to the corral to rub the nose of his horse.

Rufus smelled of sweat and tobacco with just a faint scent of lilac toilet water he had slapped on his face in the barbershop. He finally spat his chew out, wiped a brown tobacco dribble off the bottom of his chin, and said, "Aw hell, boy. I tried imaginin' ever' way I could to get ye back to your mama. I ain't thought of one that won't get at least one of us killed, most likely along with your mama or some other members of yore family."

"Like what?" I asked, feeling a twinge of hope that I could help him find an answer.

"I thought about just riding up with ye and saying, 'Look a-here who I found, but ye can't tell nobody he's here.' Yore family might not tell, but a servant, a neighbor, or even a passerby might see ye or tell somebody else, and the news would be all over town in an instant."

I considered this and decided it was true. My sister Maggie would be the most likely culprit in that scenario. It also struck me that, if I went home, I'd have to stay in the house nearly all the time, and that wouldn't be much fun.

"I thought about sending yore mama a note saying I had ye and she can come see ye anytime she wants. Then yore brothers Albert and Jack would be up here a-fillin' me full of holes fer kidnappin', and Pat Garrett would be right behind 'em. I don't trust that son of a bitch. I also thought about writin' a note and tellin' yore mama to get on a train east and I'd meet it somewhere 'tween here and Dallas with ye and that she couldn't tell a soul. She'd do that, but all it'd take is fer someone on that train to know who she was, and the news'd spread like wildfire. Henry, I believe they's just no way to hide it if ye go back to your mama. And, if ye go, ye'll be killed, and—"

I looked up and calmly said, "Rufus, stop. We're talking in circles."

He sighed and said, "I reckin we are. Looks like ye're stuck here."

CHAPTER 25
DESERT LESSONS

As the seasons and years passed and I grew bigger and stronger, in addition to carrying rocks, I helped Rufus with other chores around his place, feeding and watering the stock and chickens and carrying water and wood to the shack. When Yellow Boy came visiting, after the chores were done and it got cool, we'd sometimes walk or ride Sally back into the Organ canyons or down to the desert behind Tortugas Mountain. That's when he and Rufus started my desert training. I learned what plants could be eaten, how to find water in cactus, how to find springs and rain tanks, how to catch and cook rabbits and other little ground animals, to avoid snakes—the Apaches didn't have anything to do with snakes or things that ate snakes—and, most important, how to hide anywhere at any time.

Yellow Boy became my physical trainer, and he started me out running up and down the length of Rufus's canyon. I found it very hard at first. I had pains in my side and usually had to stop and vomit before I completed the circuit. After two or three days of that, he said, "*Hombrecito,* no run so fast. You run. You finish, even if run slow. Get better *poco a poco* (little by little)." After that, I slowly built up speed.

I enjoyed running in the early morning when birds sang in the canyon bushes. The creosote bushes and the piñons had a smell about them near daybreak that made me want to fly, especially if it had rained in the night. I enjoyed running even more as I became better conditioned.

The first few weeks, I just ran the path back to the shooting spot once a day. Then, when Yellow Boy decided that was too easy for me, he'd make me run it again. On the days when he was gone, he had me run it early in the morning and again late in the evening.

Before long, he had me running the canyon in the heat of the day, which was hard. The first time, my lungs felt on fire, and I started vomiting again, so Yellow Boy had me slow down again and build into it.

During these runs, I sometimes carried that ivory watch fob in my right hand and thought about Mama and Daddy and my vow to avenge his death. As I've mentioned, earlier, I came to realize that Daddy's pride was partly responsible for his death. Not long after that, I'd begun resenting the way he'd put me at risk. *If he was such a tough man,* I'd wondered, *why had he caved in to Mama's demand to take me with him?* I began struggling with such questions as I ran up that canyon every day in scorching heat.

I wondered why Daddy had felt he *had* to get back to Mama on that fateful day. I knew he'd promised her to come back as fast as he could, and he had already stayed two nights with friends on the way home. I guessed that maybe part of his reason was just guilt for not getting home sooner. I knew he was always fearless in fights and had always come out on top, so I guessed he had felt he had no reason to be afraid, even if protecting me was something of a handicap. But then, surely he'd known someone could shoot him from long distance, and me, too, for that matter.

He was right, though, I thought, in believing that if he backed down even once, the threats and attempts at intimidation would grow worse. The way I saw it, Daddy had been in a box— damned if he backed down in order to protect me and damned if he didn't. I'd heard him say he felt he wouldn't be able to live and work as an attorney in southern New Mexico anymore if he showed the least fear.

As I pushed my body to run through the heat day by day, answers to my old questions formed. It came to me that Daddy had learned his ways of doing things through trial and error. His personal code required that he be fearless, even in the face of great danger. It required that he always do what he believed was right, and that he must never back down from any opponent or any threat, regardless of the consequences. I had to feel proud of him for that.

The more I pondered it, the more I felt he honestly believed that if he faced those men trailing us, he'd come out on top. It seemed he'd just never learned that living to fight another day was better than being dead. I figured that on the day he died, Daddy wasn't really thinking of the consequences or that his personal code just might not apply at that time and under those circumstances. I reckoned it just hadn't been possible for him to factor me into the risk he took, and I forgave him for that.

About three years after I'd come to live at Rufus's shack, Rufus returned from Las Cruces with news that made my rage over my daddy's death run even deeper. I knew Pat Garrett had been looking for Oliver Lee and his friends, Gililland and McNew, because Rufus had told me he was convinced they'd killed my daddy. Then Rufus came in and told me there'd been a big shoot-out at Wildy Well, and Lee and Gililland had gotten away. "But ol' Lee was smart," Rufus said, "and after a while, they turned they selves in. Said they's innocent and knowed they'd git 'sonerated. Now they's about to go to trial fer yore daddy's murder up to Hillsboro."

His words made me so angry, I had to stand silent and stare at the ground for a minute. I said, "Do you expect they'll convict Oliver Lee when he goes to trial?" I realized my voice was cold and flat, just like Daddy's had been when he was speaking to Stone in the cantina Charlie Esparza ran in Tularosa.

Rufus frowned and said, "I doubt it, son, 'cause they's saying down to the barbershop that the murder case is all circumstantial evidence and that Fall will get him off."

About three months later, I learned that Lee had been found not guilty. I calmed my fury by telling myself that Lee might get exonerated in a court of law, but he need not expect mercy at my hand.

Somehow, I believe it was the fury I held inside that helped me get used to running the canyon in blazing heat. Each time I ran, Yellow Boy would say, *"Rapidamente.* Get stronger. Go faster, *Hombrecito."* After a while, I had enough strength to run that distance as fast I could. At that point, Yellow Boy said, "Now you run in desert. Be fast as lion. Be steady as mule. Make *mucho agua* on skin. Make body strong."

I balked and said, "I can't run in the desert. I look too much like an Indian. Somebody might shoot me if they see me." Yellow Boy said, *"Hombrecito,* be from the land of grandfathers when you run."

It took me awhile to figure out that he wanted me to be ghost-like, transparent to anyone who might see me. He taught me how to be a desert ghost, starting with a few simple tricks. I ran when the light was bad in early morning, twilight, or even at night. I never wore anything that could reflect light and never silhouetted myself against the horizon. I stayed down below the top edge of ridges and hills. I moved so I didn't disturb bushes. I knew where I was all the time and was prepared to hide at the first sign of detection.

I knew Yellow Boy came and went off the reservation and crossed the Tularosa Basin as often as he pleased using those techniques, and he never got caught. Of course, he later taught me many other tricks that weren't so simple.

He had me run down the trail toward Las Cruces. He kept extending the distance: two miles, then three, four. Then he had me run all the way to Tortugas Mountain, which was close to ten miles round-trip.

When I ran to Tortugas Mountain and back, Yellow Boy made me do a trial that's used with Apache boys. He gave me a canteen one morning before I started and said, "Take water in your mouth, and hold it as you run. Spit it all out when you come back. Now go. Be fast." Then he climbed up on a big rock so he could watch me as I ran. The first time I tried it, I had swallowed it all or lost it by the time I got to Tortugas Mountain. When I got back there wasn't a drop to spit out, and I wanted water from the canteen.

I've never seen him more disappointed. Looking at me he said, "No Apache *aqui*. Your heart isn't strong. You weak. You must be strong or you die. If you Apache boy, I beat you. You must learn strength in your heart. Now I go *por una luna en* Mexico. I come back, you do this, *si*?"

I was so shaken that he was so disappointed in me that I had to bite my lip to keep from crying. Rufus walked out of the shack and said, "He ain't old enough fer those kinds of tests yet, and ye know it."

Yellow Boy shook his head and said, "Any Mescalero *muchacho* that tall runs two times distance and not lose *agua*. He have not lived like Mescalero boys, so he slow. He get better soon. I know this is true. He is *Hombrecito*."

It was then I realized that Yellow Boy didn't expect me to do as well since I wasn't an Apache. That made me angry and made me want to work harder to show him I was as good or better than any Apache my age.

Rufus just shook his head, but he didn't say anything else. The next day, after Yellow Boy had gone, I tried again. I made it back with a little of the water that time. I kept trying, and after about the fifth or sixth time, I made the whole route without losing very much. When Rufus saw I had done it, he said, "Good work, Henry. That there'll show old Yellow Boy you have the heart of an Apache."

Upon Yellow Boy's next return, I proved to him that I could meet the challenge, spitting the mouthful of water by our feet. He nodded and said, "Ummph. *Bueno.*" Though his reaction disappointed me, I told myself I shouldn't have expected much more from Yellow Boy. After all, he'd claimed Apache boys my age could do the same after running twice as far.

It wasn't until after dinner that evening that I saw any evidence that he was particularly pleased with me. Rufus, Yellow Boy, and I were sitting on the porch in the cool of the evening. After Yellow Boy finished his cigar, he came and stood by me, smiled, and said, "Today, a warrior was born. Give your hand to me, *Hombrecito.*" I reached to shake with him, but he took my wrist in a strong, yet gentle grip. His big knife with the razor edge appeared in his other hand like magic. "We are same blood," he said. "You now *Hombrecito*, brother of *Muchacho Amarillo.*" I felt the blade slice smoothly, but not too deeply, across my palm, the warm blood flowing freely. He put a slice in his own hand and held my cut against his. Again, he said, "We are same blood."

CHAPTER 26
BEST IDEA EVER

By the time I was fourteen, I had spent nearly six years helping Rufus carry twenty-pound rocks to the piles we made for his new shack and fences. I was very strong for my size, my muscles as hard as the rocks I'd carried. I must have weighed about a hundred and twenty pounds, and I could lift my body weight over my head. Rufus had trained me to be a sharpshooter. Even though the Sharps weighed close to ten pounds and kicked like a mule, I hit bottles or cans ten times in ten shots at four hundred yards, from a prone position, with the forestock resting on crossed sticks. At that distance, whiskey bottles were so small that about all I could see of them was an occasional glint.

I'd read *The Iliad* and *The Odyssey* twice for Rufus, the Bible, and some of Shakespeare's plays. I understood what I read, and that was even more important than just the reading. I was probably more literate at fourteen than ninety-five percent of the grown men in southern New Mexico.

Yellow Boy had taught me to live alone in the desert and survive, to run miles in dry searing heat and do without water, and to be dependent only on myself. His lessons had made my mind tough and my body capable of extraordinary endurance. Rarely was an Anglo or Mexican, rancher or townie, able to endure the desert as I could. I knew I was tougher than most white men who worked the ranches and cattle, and, at fourteen, my hormones raged for a challenge to prove I was a man.

Early one morning, I had already started down the trail on a run to Tortugas Mountain and back when I caught sight of a cowboy riding up the trail toward Rufus's shack. He was jingling along with his head tilted back and his eyes closed, letting the rising sun warm his face. I swung off the trail and hid, perfectly still and close to the ground, just the way Yellow Boy taught me. As the cowboy rode by, never dreaming I was hiding within ten feet of him, his horse flicked his ears and snorted as if it had heard or seen something. I heard him say, "Damn, horse. If we was still fightin' Apaches I'd have my hands filled with cocked guns the way yore a flickin' yore ears around. What're you seein'? A snake?" I recognized the voice of Buck Greer, one of the men who'd stopped by Rufus's place right after Yellow Boy had found me and who paid Rufus a visit once in a while. Lucky for me, Buck never guessed why the horse was acting that way. He just kept riding.

His old gray hair, like straw, poked out from the edges of his hat, and his big, bushy eyebrows lay under a forehead covered with wrinkles that looked like the network of dry washes up by Warm Springs.

Following Buck back to the shack without getting caught was a game for me. I got within ten feet of the shack porch, where he and Rufus were talking, without Buck knowing I was there. I saw Rufus frown just a little when I crept into my hiding place behind some creosote bushes, and knew he probably concluded I was there even if he couldn't see me.

I heard Buck say, "Yep. Cap'n Van Patten's a-usin' three or four of his hands to drive wagons back and forth from Cruces carrying eastern dudes up to that hotel he's a-building."

Buck chewed about as much tobacco as Rufus, and he sent a stream of tobacco juice towards Rufus's creosote bush next to the shack porch. He was sitting on the porch steps, leaning back on his elbow next to Rufus, his hat pushed back, watching the morning shadows of the mountains creep toward them as the sun floated higher.

Rufus asked, "What brought ye over this a way, Buck? Not that I ain't damn glad to see yore ornery hide onct in a while."

Then Cody must have caught my scent because he lifted his head and cocked his ears. Looking straight at the bushes where I was, he gave a little woof. Buck looked at Cody and said, "What's the matter with yore hound, Rufus?"

Rufus rolled his jaw a couple of couple of times before he spat and said, "Aw, they's a wild bitch in heat he's been after for the last three or four days. She's out there in the bushes a wanting him to come out and play. I think she's done wore the old fart out, and he don't wanna get up this early to fool with her."

"Hot damn, Rufus," Buck said and laughed. "Yore ol' hound's a doing better'n both of us put together. There's yore old hound, and the ladies is a coming to him. Damn, if that don't beat all. Best I'n do is 'bout a onct a month visit to Juanita's place down to Juarez." He paused and scratched his head for a moment, then asked, "Hell, I ain't seen you down there in a long time. How's you and that widow lady in Lincoln a-doin'?"

Rufus, who had started whittling while they spoke, grinned big and put another brown stream on the creosote bush. Then he grimaced at me on the side of his face Buck couldn't see.

I smiled because I'd never before considered that Rufus and Mrs. Darcy could be lovers. I might have laughed aloud if Yellow Boy hadn't trained me so well. I'd figured by the time a man was Rufus's age the women would be after young men, not old-timers.

Of course, Rufus had not done a thing to further my sex education. I had Yellow Boy to thank for that. He'd told me about the ways of men and women one evening when I was about eleven years old, after I'd asked him about two deer I'd seen rutting.

Buck laughed again and said, "Still being discreet, huh, you old devil? Or am I wrong about that? I reckon she's too proper for an old geezer like you."

Rufus said, "I don't know, but I'd like to find out," and they both laughed again.

Then finally Buck got down to business. "Rufus, the reason I come by was old Cox, Jack Stone, and Oliver Lee is puttin' a herd together to sell to the army. They plan to drive it down to Fort Bliss next week. Cap'n Van Patten is gonna sell a few head to 'em. We're a little short on the number of cattle he promised to sell 'em and thought maybe you'd want to sell a few yoreself. We could round 'em up for you and drive 'em over to San Augustin Ranch with our herd if you want. Course you understand you'd have to wait until we was paid 'fore you got yore money. I believe Stone plans to pay us off when we deliver our stock on Saturday over to Cox's corral, so I could bring yore money over on say Monday or Tuesday, if that'd be all right."

Jack Stone, Oliver Lee. The names hit me like a slap in the face. I grew sick and hot in the face every time I thought of them. Here Buck was wanting to sell some of Rufus's herd to the men who'd murdered Daddy. *Well,* I thought, *it'll be a cold day in hell before that happens.* Nevertheless, Rufus grinned and said, "Why, shore. That's mighty neighborly of Van Patten and yoreself. If yore boys will take about twenty or thirty head, I'd be grateful. That money'll keep me in beans fer another year or two."

I was madder than a stepped-on rattlesnake. Why was Rufus helping those low-down, murdering skunks? I couldn't understand it. I wanted to shoot them, and here these two old geezers were selling them their stock.

Rufus and Buck chewed and spat while they talked cattle and politics for nearly an hour. The sun was a quarter of its way to its zenith, and I felt the sweat rolling down my face when Buck finally got up and stepped off the porch. He tightened his cinch, climbed in the saddle, and, leaning over his saddle horn, said to Rufus, "I'll send some boys over to get yore stock in two or three days. You just show 'em which ones, and we'll take care of gettin' 'em over to Cox's place." Rufus nodded with a grin and saluted, touching the edge of his raggedy, old hat with his left hand. He said, "That's mighty neighborly of ye. 'Preciate it. I'll be lookin' fer yore crew. Ride kerful now. *Adios.*"

Buck turned and rode off down the trail then called over his shoulder, "Get that old hound to teach you a trick or two, Rufus. Then I'm shore Juanita'll be glad to see you and yore money."

Rufus laughed and yelled back, "Hell, he's taught me too many tricks already." He sat on the porch step and watched Buck disappear down the trail. In a few minutes he said, "Ye gonna stay hid out there all day, boy? You'n come out now."

I appeared from behind the creosote bushes and flopped down by Rufus on the porch step. Cody came over and stretched out beside me, yawned, rolling his long, red tongue, and waited for me to scratch him behind the ears. A flock of quail ran out of cover across the trail and disappeared under some mesquite. It was quiet and getting hot quick. I knew Rufus could tell I was mad. He wasn't any too happy, either.

He said, "Ye're lucky, son. Ye hid well. But damn it, don't ever try to hide when they's a dog close by. They'll give you away ever time. That's why the Apaches always tried to kill the dogs around a house before they snook up to git the rancher living there. Ye's this close"—he made a narrow gap between his thumb and forefinger—"to old Buck catching yore tail. Then, aye God, I'd a-had some fancy explaining to do about why some Indian kid was a-hidin' on my place. It's a good thing I'm a damn good liar."

Humbled by his review of my bush craft, I wasn't too mad anymore about Rufus selling those cows, but I still asked, "Why're you selling stock to Jack Stone and Oliver Lee? You're helping the men who helped kill Daddy make money. That's not right."

Rufus spat on the green bush and wiggled his nose to edge his glasses up. In a soft voice, he said, "I know how you feel, son. I need the money, and it's time to sell. Buck's offer couldn't a-come at a better time. It don't make no difference if I sell them cows to Stone or Mary the Virgin. They's gonna be et all the same. Just get down off yore high horse now and get to runnin'. We got a lot to do to get ready fer them riders from over to Drippin' Springs."

In my heart, I knew Rufus was right, but it still stirred anger and hate down in my guts. As I was runnin' up the trail back to the shack that morning, I kept repeating to myself, *Someday I'm gonna kill 'em, someday.*

I was nearly finished with my run when I thought I had just about the best idea I'd ever had. I couldn't believe how clever it was. Rufus always got up early on Saturday to go down to Ellis's barbershop, listen to the latest gossip, and pick up supplies at Lohman's store in Las Cruces. As soon as he left, I decided I'd take the Sharps and, following the shortcuts over the Organs at the back of the canyon Rufus showed me, I could run over to San Augustin Ranch in two or three hours. Or I could even sneak around through Baylor Pass and still get there in four or five hours. Once I was at the Cox place, I'd pick me out a good spot where I'd hide and watch where the cattle were penned up. If I was lucky, I'd get a good sight picture on Jack Stone and put a .45-70 slug right through his head. *If I'm real lucky,* I thought, *I might even get a chance to drop Oliver Lee.*

It occurred to me that what I'd read in the Bible about God delivering David's enemies into his hands was the same situation I had. David was just a little boy, and he killed a giant. I was just like David. I was going to kill a giant, maybe two or three of them. God was about to deliver my enemy into my hands, and I meant to kill him just like David, who, when he was about my age, had hit a giant right on his temple with a rock. But I didn't have to depend on rocks. I was going to put a bullet right between Stone's eyes.

CHAPTER 27
LONG SHOT

By Saturday morning, excitement was buzzing in my brain like bees around the hollyhocks growing behind the shack and it was all I could do to act my normal sleepy self. Rufus was usually up by four thirty every day. On Saturday mornings, he'd stoke up the fire, put some coffee on, eat a little something with me, and saddle up Sally. He'd tell me with a grin, "Now, Henry, don't go a-gittin' into any meanness, but if'n ye do, don't git caught." Then he'd stomp out into the cold, early, morning air, climb up on Sally, and disappear down the trail toward Las Cruces.

I could hardly wait for him to leave. I told myself I'd been waiting six years for this opportunity and I was ready. I'd carried tons of twenty-pound rocks, shot hundreds of shells through the Sharps, and run hundreds—no thousands—of miles all over the Organs and Mesilla Valley, while getting strong and smart.

Wasn't I a crack shot? Didn't I know how to hide and survive in the mountains and desert? Why, I'd be back before dark, and Rufus wouldn't even know I'd been gone.

After we'd had our beans and tortillas for breakfast, Rufus sniffed and spat before asking, "What ye thinkin' so hard about, Henry?"

"Oh, nothing, except some stuff Yellow Boy's been teaching me about living in the desert." That was the first and only time I ever lied to him.

I felt the lowest of the low for lying to him, but I reckoned what I was planning to do was my destiny. I was going to do it regardless of what I'd promised about waiting until I was fully-grown.

That morning, when he told me not to get into meanness, he gave me an evil-eyed squint that seemed to tell me not to do whatever I had in mind. I knew Rufus couldn't read my mind, but it sure seemed that way.

As soon as Rufus left, I climbed up on a chair and took down the Sharps. Rufus made sure I kept it cleaned and oiled, and it gleamed in the lantern light. I ran my hands over it, feeling the smooth, octagonal barrel and easy-to-grip stock.

Scratching around the cabin, I put ten cartridges, an old brass telescope Rufus had found in a wagon train massacre years ago, and some jerky and roasted corn in the possibles bag he had given me. I filled a canteen only half full of water because I wanted to keep the weight down so I wouldn't wear out with all the running I had to do. I tied my hair back and stripped down to just my breechcloth and Chiricahua moccasin boots Yellow Boy had given me. I knew it was going to be a long, hard run.

I decided I'd take the long way around, over Baylor Pass, to the Cox place. I didn't want to risk dropping the rifle while try-ing to get up the little trail of toeholds over the cliff at the end of Rufus's canyon. When I started running, the cold air and darkness painted with black shadows made me feel as though I was in the nether regions of a womb, surrounded and safe. The trail along the western side the Organs toward Baylor Pass went by tall cliffs, making it hard to see for a while, but I had run it so often I could do it with my eyes closed. My feet knew every stone and pebble along the way. The Sharps' weight was a big-ger burden than I'd thought it would be, so I was glad I hadn't tried to climb the cliffs with it. I was ready to rest when I topped

Baylor Pass on a thin little trail through the piñon and yuccas that ran within several yards of the trail the cowboys used. The sun had been up a couple of hours, but, at this elevation, the air was still very cool and comfortable. I drank from the canteen and ate a little corn. Sitting concealed on a boulder back in the bushes, I used the telescope to find Cox's cattle pens before I eased on down the trail toward the ranch.

Before midday, I'd found an ideal spot where I was able to watch the cattle pens and set up to shoot. It was a large, reddish-brown boulder sticking up out of the ground at about a thirty-degree angle in the middle of a good stand of grass and a few small mesquites. When I crawled up on that boulder and looked over the top, I was just below the top of the grass.

I studied the area for a way to hide or get out of there quick. There was a large, dark, green thicket of piñon trees growing back toward the pass. I thought that might give me the best opportunity to hide or escape if I had to run. I lay down across the hot top of the boulder and felt like my belly was frying in a hot skillet as I balanced the Sharps in a prone position to feel how steady the sight picture was. I picked out a corral fence post about six hundred yards away and held on it steady as the rock. I nodded with satisfaction. Perfect. I was sure I could hit a target at six hundred yards or more if that was what fortune brought me. My spot was about four hundred yards from the cattle pen fence. If Stone showed up, I knew I had a real opportunity to kill him. I pulled the old brass telescope out, wrapped it in my shirt so glints wouldn't give me away, and surveyed the cattle pens. The Dripping Springs herd had arrived early that morning.

There must have been a couple of hundred head squeezed inside the fence. There were five or six cowboys lounging around as if they were waiting on somebody. I took that to mean Stone and his partners hadn't come yet to look over the final herd.

This was going to be my lucky day. I crabbed down the boulder backwards and sat with my back to it to eat some parched corn and jerky and drink from the canteen while I figured out how I'd get away after I'd killed Jack Stone. I thought, *God has delivered my enemies into my hands. There's gonna be justice this day.*

As I looked back the way I'd come, I decided that I'd use the piñon thicket as my rabbit hole for escape after I shot Stone. I knew there was a good chance of being caught if I went back along the Baylor Pass route without first hiding in the piñons, and it was far too dangerous to try to go straight up the spires and over to the handholds in the canyon cliffs at Rufus's ranch. From the piñon thicket, I'd make my way back up to the same trail I had come down to get back to Rufus's place. I felt sure I was strong enough to outrun anyone who came after me.

It was getting hot, and I was restless just sitting and waiting. I decided to ease back up the boulder. I gritted my teeth against its heat when I put my belly to it, stretching out to survey the cattle pens and cowboys with the telescope. Buck Greer and a couple of the hands from the Dripping Springs Ranch were familiar, but I didn't know any of the others. Swinging the telescope towards Cox's ranch house, I saw several horses tied to the hitching post in a shady spot. A couple of Mexican women worked in the plants around the front patio, but still no one to hold my attention. I waited.

Just past midday, five men walked out of the ranch house. They were rubbing their bellies, engaging in jovial conversation, and smoking cigars. One of them stood out in a brilliant white shirt, a vest, and a string tie. I remembered Rufus had told me about how peculiar W. W. Cox was about wearing clean clothes and a string tie. These had to be the men putting the herd together. When I studied them through the old brass telescope, my whole body twitched. A wave of fright and hate rolled through me, making my heart pound as sweat rolled off my forehead in rivulets.

Jack Stone was swinging into his saddle. Laughing and joking with the others, he didn't appear to have a care or any sense of how close to death he was. There was no sign of Red Tally.

Hearing the rapid thump, thump, thump of my heart, I eased the rifle forward to a shooting position. Pulling the hammer to half cock, I dropped the breechblock, slowly slid a shell in, closed the block, and laid out three more shells within easy reach, just in case I needed them.

W. W. and the others climbed on their horses, and they all rode toward the cattle pens together. Apparently, they wanted to look over the stock before they started the drive toward Fort Bliss in El Paso.

I tried to steady my nerves by breathing in long, even breaths and by focusing on the spot by the pens that would give me the best shot to kill Stone. I guessed he and the others would ride over to the ranch-house side of the pens and sit in their saddles while they did a final look-see and head count, so I picked a spot about the middle of the fence line and at about the height Stone should be on his horse. At that range, it was an easy shot. Trying to focus and calm myself, I waited. I knew I had him. At least Daddy was going to get a partial payback that day. All those days of practice staring through the sights on the long Sharps barrel and feeling the now familiar punch in my shoulder from its recoil, all those days of carrying rocks, all those days of running, all those days were finally going to help give justice to Daddy.

The cowboys gathered around their bosses as they rode over to the pens. Stone was the middle rider in the group of five. They all rode up to the spot I had picked. I took a deep breath and felt as steady as the big rock under me. I sighted down the long, octagonal barrel and thought, *God is with me this day.*

Vengeance is mine. This is for you, Daddy.

Cox climbed off his horse and started to climb up to the top rail of the cattle-pen fence. The man riding next to him started swinging off his horse, too. Stone paused. I remember his image as if it were frozen in a photograph. He turned to say something to one of his men. *God is with me this day.* I pulled the hammer back to full cock. The smell of gun oil was strong and intoxicating in the hot, bright light. I sat the Sharps' double trigger, took a deep breath, and aimed for Stone's head. It was just like shooting bottles back in Rufus's canyon. *Oh, joyful God! This day is mine. Die, you son of a bitch.* I let half my breath out and carefully laid my finger on the hair trigger. Stone moved, starting to dismount. I tried to relax my finger. Too late. The trigger setting was too sensitive, and the Sharps roared my rage. Stone's hat went flying, but his head stayed on. The bullet thunked into a big fence post on the far end of the pens and sent big splinters flying. Thunder from the shot snapped across Cox's cattle pens, making men and animals show the whites of their eyes. Stone continued his dismount as a flying belly flop onto the ground in front of him.

The cowboys around the pens hit the ground, their revolvers instantly out, cocked, and pointing in every direction as they jerked about under whatever cover was available, desperately trying to find their attacker and defend themselves. The roll of thunder from my rifle echoed off the mountains, apparently confusing them about my location. Cox had jumped off the fence into the cattle pens, finding protection behind its rails. Horses bucked and jumped around until they jerked free of their bridle ties then ran off down the wide trail to the ranch house.

CHAPTER 28
LONG RUN HOME

I was frozen in disbelief, suspended in time, as my brain tried to digest the situation. I had missed. It was an easy shot, and I had missed. Wasn't God supposed to help me? A murderer was supposed to get justice. I had failed Daddy again.

The yelling men below finally penetrated my daze. Cox's arm was through the fence, pointing to my left. I looked up and saw a little cloud of smoke from the Sharps drifting on a whisper of breeze about ten yards from where I lay. Some of the men began firing toward the cloud, but it was much too far for a revolver to hit anything. The shots fell far short, kicking up dust and sand.

One cowboy with hair so gray it was nearly white rose up on one knee and held his revolver in both hands. He fired a long arching shot that struck the boulder about five feet below my spot and ricocheted away with a sound like a broken guitar string. That shot jolted me.

The old cowboy was on his feet, bent over, and running side-to-side, headed in my direction. I scooped up my extra cartridges, scrambled back down the boulder, collapsed the telescope, threw it in the possibles bag, and, grabbing the canteen, ran in a crouch below the top of the grass toward the piñon thicket two hundred yards away. I stepped on as many exposed rocks as I could. Yellow Boy's lessons taught me to leave no trail wherever I went, and there was very little sign around the boulder that I had been there.

Reaching the thicket, I was sucking wind, and the disappointment I felt made my legs feel as though they were wooden posts with no bounce at all. I passed the first of the bushes, and, stopping, crawled up under one to scan my shooting place. I was shaking with rage and fear as I levered the empty shell out of the Sharps and put a new cartridge in the chamber. In a couple of minutes, I saw several hats floating above the grass near the boulder as they looked for signs that could point them toward the shooter.

I pulled out the telescope and watched them stomping around in the grass, looking in every direction. The gray-haired cowboy found my boulder and climbed up on it. He lay down on top of it as I had and yelled something at the others. He turned around and, squatting on his heels, looked back toward the mountains and slowly surveyed the near rocks and bushes where I might be. He stared toward the piñon thicket where I was hiding for a good while before turning his attention to other spots.

Stone and the other ranchers rode up to the boulder, their men right with them, and every one of them had a rifle set on full cock. There was a nice, round, ventilation hole on both sides of Stone's big, flat-brimmed Stetson, just above the top of his scalp line. His face, even under the shadow of his hat, was pale, grimacing, and filled with rage. His partners and the men continued to swing their heads, scanning the mountains in front of them for some sign of the shooter.

From where I sat, I heard Stone screaming, "Find him! Find that son of a bitch! A hundred dollars to anybody that finds him! Just don't kill him. I got to talk to him before he's hung!" He pointed his rifle toward Baylor Pass and said, "Damn it, you're lettin' him get away! Come on, boys, if we ride hard, we can catch him before he gets to Cruces."

They thundered off in a cloud of dust. Cox rode up to the boulder and said something to the old-timer. He just shook his head and stayed where he was before pointing toward my stand of piñon. Cox nodded then rode off to join the posse heading toward Baylor Pass.

I knew I was in trouble. The old-timer was coming my way, and he knew what he was doing. I had to find a place to hide and fast. He'd come slow, looking for signs. That was to be my only advantage. I could try and outrun him, or I could hide and get behind him and take my time to get home. Either way, I wasn't about to shoot him. He just happened to be at the wrong place at the wrong time.

I decided to put some distance between us, then hide and let him get past me. I grabbed up my gear and took off, trying to keep a stand of juniper between us. After about half a mile, I stopped, and, looking back, saw that he had his revolver drawn and was studying the ground around the piñon thicket where I'd stopped. I ran on.

The weight of the rifle was tiring me out faster than I had expected. I was a mile or so from Baylor Pass and breathing hard when I found a good place to hide under a shelf of rock fronted by some piñons growing a few feet below it. I crawled up under the shelf so I could watch back down the trail. I had just managed to get organized and lie comfortably along the crevice formed by the shelf when I saw the old-timer slowly riding up the trail.

I eased the Sharps up alongside me until it was in front of me and I could reach the triggers if I had to. I glanced toward the end of the shelf, back in the direction of the old-timer, and saw the biggest rattlesnake I had ever seen. It was a foot or two longer than I was tall and must have been four or five inches in diameter. There was a big lump in its middle section, so I figured it had made a kill earlier in the day. It stared at me, but it didn't rattle. I stayed perfectly still while it raised its head a few inches and flicked its tongue at me trying to figure out what I was. I didn't move. I tried not even to breathe.

Soon, the old-timer stopped on the trail just in front of my hiding place. He stared at the bushes in front of the shelf crevice for a long time. Finally, he threw one leg over the saddle and slid off. I heard the hammer of his revolver click back, cocked, and ready to fire. My mouth was dry, but my heart had stopped pounding, and my nerves were steady. He started moving toward the shelf.

The snake turned its attention from me to the new creature advancing on its sanctuary. In the dim shadowy light in the crevice, I could see its forked tongue flicking faster as it sampled the confusing smells we created. It was cool there under the shelf, but I could feel the sweat running off the end of my nose. The snake refused to give itself away with a warning rattle.

The old-timer slowly moved closer. It was obvious he wanted to look behind the brush directly into the shelf crevice. When the old-timer was about fifteen feet from the piñon in front of the shelf, I picked up a handful of dirt and gently threw it at the snake, hitting it about where its lunch was digesting. It didn't do anything except continue to flick its tongue toward the old-timer, who had stopped and cocked his head, listening. He swept the revolver back and forth toward the shelf, trying to see through the bushes and the dark, shadowy underbelly of the crevice.

I grabbed another small handful of dirt and threw it again. This time bits of gravel hit the snake on its head. That made it angry. It raised its head almost to the top of the crevice, rapidly flicking its tongue toward the man outside and furiously shaking its rattle.

The old-timer's eyes got wide. He kept his revolver pointed at the crevice but slowly backed toward his horse. I heard him mutter, "No thanks, brother. Don't think I want to poke my nose in yore house today." The horse was nervous and ready to run, but the old-timer grabbed the reins, holstered his revolver, and swung into the saddle in one smooth motion. He trotted away from the crevice smartly, following the trail up through Baylor Pass that Stone's posse had taken.

After the old-timer rode on, the snake finally stopped rattling and lay there quietly staring at me with cold unblinking eyes. I waited a bit and wiggled back out from under the shelf, took a long swallow from the canteen, and started running up the little path that paralleled the Baylor Pass trail. I wanted to catch up with the old-timer and keep him in sight so he wouldn't wind up behind me. I still hadn't found him when I topped Baylor Pass, but I found fresh horse apples that told me he was no more than a few minutes ahead of me down the trail.

I'd been running with that heavy rifle and possibles bag up the steep path to the pass for nearly two hours. Despite my conditioning, I was leg-weary and needed a rest. I drank the canteen almost dry, ate the rest of the corn and jerky, and lay back against a boulder for a little while, watching the western sun casting long shadows on the Mesilla Valley. I forced myself to start moving again. I had four or five more miles to go to get back to Rufus's shack.

I stayed high up on the Organ ridges and followed the path that cut past the southern wall of Baylor Canyon, expecting the old-timer to keep on into Las Cruces with the rest of Stone's posse. I followed the path all the way around to the western side of the Organs. I found the dry wash the drovers used to push the herd over to Cox's ranch and followed it all the way down to the road that ran in front of Dripping Springs Ranch. Then I followed that trail back toward Dripping Springs until I recognized a spot where I could get back on the trail I had run along going to Cox's ranch. I ran easily, thinking that I might still even beat Rufus back home.

I stopped to rest and was about to start on when I heard a horse snort on the trail below and behind me. Looking for the horse, I blinked in surprise when I saw the old-timer standing off the south side of the trail with his back to me, watering some bushes. Easing down behind a thicket of cactus and creosotes, I waited for him to get in front of me again so I could keep an eye on him. For some reason, he had decided to turn down the road that ran past Dripping Springs rather than head toward Las Cruces. I realized how lucky I was he hadn't caught me. He was trail-smart and relentless.

The old-timer got back on his horse and continued to ride along. He rode slowly, studying the ground in front of him for signs and stopping often to look back over his shoulder like he thought someone was following or watching him. I ground my teeth in frustration that I couldn't go any faster and get around him. It occurred to me that I needed to go a mile or so past Rufus's place, and cross the trail again to make him think I was headed for El Paso.

I saw him turn from the southern trail that ran parallel to the Organs and follow the one toward the Van Patten place. I ran past Van Patten's on my path then moved down the slopes and crossed the trail toward Rufus's place, making sure I left a little sign that I was still on the trail south. Then I got back on the path above the main trail and followed it past Rufus's place for another mile, crossed it again, and backtracked toward Rufus's house. I found a place to rest and drank the last drops of water in the canteen. I was worn out. The sun was nearly down, and the breezes off the Organs were cool and sweet after that long run across the mountains.

It was a good two hours after the sun dropped behind the Floridas when I finally got back to Rufus's place. Coming up the trail, I saw Sally watching me from the corral. I knew Rufus would likely be mad that I had taken his rifle and tried to shoot Jack Stone. After all, I had promised I'd wait until we were ready. I didn't have any idea what he'd do. Sitting on the porch step, watching me come up the trail, he rested his elbows on his knees, his hands clasped together between them, and he had a big wad of tobacco in his cheek. Cody, stretched out on the far end of the porch, woofed at me and beat a thump-thump hello with his tail.

Rufus nodded at me and said, "Howdy, Henry. Glad yore back. I'm just a-sittin' here thankful I ain't gonna have to saddle up Sally and go over to Cox's place to get yore body in the mornin'. Are ye hurt?"

"Wh-why would you think that, Rufus?" I stammered, not having a clue how he knew I had been at Cox's place.

He spat toward the big, green creosote bush and squinted at me through his dusty, round lenses. "Ol' Pete Catron was by here 'bout sundown. I rode with Pete years ago when we was a-tryin' to catch Victorio. Told me about how somebody had nearly put a bullet through Jack Stone's head. Said he thought he might be on the assassin's trail. Said whoever he was trailin' was mighty crafty. He thought maybe whoever he was might be an Indian or an Indian fighter. He just wasn't shore he had come this direction, although he saw signs that maybe he had. He was just followin' a hunch. I give him some beans and tortillas, and we chewed the fat about old times fer awhile 'fore he went on his way."

I was as weary as I've ever been. I just nodded to Rufus, went inside, and drank several dippers of water. I unloaded the Sharps and dragged the stool over to the doorway so I could reach the pegs to hang the Sharps up until I could clean it. I filled a tin plate with beans out of the pot, took a couple of tortillas, and walked outside to sit down beside Rufus.

After covering nearly fifteen miles of mountain trails and eating nothing but parched corn and jerky, those beans and tortillas tasted like one of the best meals I'd ever had. Rufus didn't say a word or look at me. He just chewed and spat, watching the stars fill a cloudless night.

I finished shoveling down the beans and tried to apologize. "Rufus, I'm sorry. I understand now what a fool trick it was and—"

Rufus spat and looked at me a moment, his jaw slowly turning the wad of tobacco in his cheek into more brown juice. He shook his head. "Don't never back up, boy. Say what ye mean to say and do it. Ye're mighty young and inexperienced to do what ye did. But, aye God, ye nearly pulled it off." He reached over and grabbed my shoulder with a big grin on his face. "Just the luck of the draw you missed. It's even luckier ye weren't caught. Now, tell me what happened."

I told him everything, including how I'd decided to do it because David had been able to kill the giant with God helping him. I figured God wanted to punish Jack Stone, so He'd help me, too, but He hadn't, and I didn't understand why. Rufus just sat and nodded as he listened.

I told him what an easy shot it had been and how I couldn't understand how I'd missed. Then I told him about how Pete Catron had nearly caught me in that shelf crevice with a rattlesnake.

Rufus laughed aloud at that one. I had to laugh, too, when I thought about it. I told him how I'd backtracked from farther down the trail, trying to throw Pete off. When I finished, Rufus was quiet for a long time, just sitting there in the dark, chewing and spitting, as he whittled a stick down to a toothpick.

The moon began to fill the canyon with its soft, yellow light and stark, black shadows. A warm breeze rolled up from the valley floor. Rufus spat and sighed. He said, "Henry, ye did all right. Ye just made one or two big mistakes and several small ones, but, for a child yore age, ye did mighty fine. Yellow Boy will be real proud of ye, too."

My weary body, once near collapse, wanted to stand up and

dance in the light of that praise from a man with years of fighting experience. All I could say was, "I did well? I thought you would want to beat me for taking the Sharps without your knowing it or being with me to guide me along. What mistakes did I make?"

Rufus leaned back on his elbows and looked at me. Even in the dark, I could feel his eyes fully on my face. "Yore biggest mistake was ye didn't go fer a body shot. It's mighty hard to hit a man in the head at a long range, son. A head moves a lot. If ye'd gone fer a body shot ye'd probably have hit him in the heart or lungs, and he'd a-been dead one way or the other 'fore ye topped Baylor Pass. The other big mistake was ye should have shot through a hole in some bush so the smoke from the shot would break up and be a lot harder to see.

"But ye was smart hangin' back and followin' the people tryin' to catch ye. That there's an old Apache trick. Did Yellow Boy teach that to ye?" I shook my head. "Well, son, ye're a natural, then. Only difference 'tween yore trick and theirs is the Apaches would have attacked again from the rear and wiped out the ones chasing 'em. Ye oughter've thought about how to hide out until everyone was a-chasin' some phantom up the trail and not got in front of Pete. If he'd just realized ye was a little fart, he'd probably caught ye right there in that shelf. Might even have shot ye tryin' to shoot the snake through those bushes. He just didn't want to waste cartridges. Ye understand what I'm a tryin' to tell ye?"

I nodded and said, "Yes, sir. I know you're right, Rufus, except—"

"Except what, son?"

"Why do you suppose God didn't help me today like He helped David?"

Rufus was quiet as he tilted his face up to look at the stars and scratched at the stubble on his face. He said, "What makes ye think He didn't help ye today? Physically ye're just a boy. Ye covered about fifteen mile worth of mountain trails today, packing a ten-pound weapon and another five pounds of food and water. Ye came within a couple of inches of puttin' lead between the eyes of the man who had yore daddy killed. Henry, ye survived when by rights ye oughter be dead. Don't tell me God didn't help ye. Why, it's a damn miracle ye're alive."

I nodded. Rufus was right. It wasn't luck that got me through. It was providence. Maybe next time the giant would fall. I said, "Rufus, can we rename the Sharps?"

"What do ye mean, son?"

"Well, I want to name the Sharps 'Little David.' You know, like David and Goliath? Because today I almost brought down the giant in front of everybody, and it was like using little David's slingshot."

Rufus grinned. "Well, that old rifle ain't had no name before 'cept when ol' Yellow Boy calls her Shoots Today Kills Tomorrow. I reckon Lil' David is a good name, especially if ye use it to wipe out those men who killed yore daddy. Ye just be shore you clean Lil' David first thing in the morning. We a-goin' to need him."

"Why are you saying that?"

"Well, I 'spec we oughter to see Jack Stone and his boys by here in two or three days. He's a goin' to be madder than hell 'cause somebody took a shot at him. He ain't got no idea why exactly, but I bet it could be fer all kinds of reasons. Ol' Pete will think he might have trailed the shooter past my shack. Pete told me he believes it was a Sharps that was used to shoot at Stone, and he knows I got a Sharps, too, but that I ain't got no reason to be shootin' at Stone with it. We got to find ye a good hidin' place and figure out how to handle Stone when he comes. It ain't goin' to be purdy. I jest hope Yellow Boy gets back here soon to help us."

CHAPTER 29
JACK STONE COMES CALLING

Stone and four other riders showed up at Rufus's shack about suppertime a couple of days later. Rufus said he was just serving up our plates when he looked out through the window and saw the first rider top the trail to the house. He rode into the yard like he owned it, followed by the other four. I was at the spring getting a bucket of water. Rufus came out of the shack, careful to close the door behind him. He was hoping I had heard the men come up and had hidden myself. I was about halfway back to the house when I heard Cody barking and then strange voices. I hid the bucket behind a bush and tried to find a place where I could see and hear what was going on.

When I finally maneuvered within sight of the yard, there sat Jack Stone, Charlie Bentene, and three cowboys I'd never seen before. Those three stayed back on the edge of the yard while Stone and Bentene rode up close to Rufus. Stone was resting his forearm on his saddle horn and leaning forward. Bentene, with his big hooked nose, sat straight in the saddle with his hand on his revolver watching every move Rufus made. As soon as he came out the door, Rufus tied Cody to a porch post. Cody stood with his teeth bared; a low growl was in his throat.

I heard Stone say, "Sorry to intrude on you like this, Mr. Pike, but some son of a bitch put a big hole through my hat a few days ago. We've been looking for him ever since. Pete Catron thinks the rifle used to do it was a Sharps and that the shooter came this way. Told me he thought you owned a Sharps.

That true, Mr. Pike?" He bared his teeth in a menacing grin.

Rufus spat a stream at the green creosote bush and stared back at Stone unblinking. "Yep, I have a Sharps. So do about a hundert other folks on this here side of the mountains."

Stone said, "Yes, sir, you're right about that. But you're the only one that does on this trail, and Catron thinks the shooter rode by here. You got anybody living with you inside that shack, Mr. Pike?"

Rufus stared straight at Stone and said, "Nope."

"Well, do you mind if my partner Mr. Bentene here takes a look?"

Rufus spat another stream in the dirt where Bentene would have to step and said, "Hell, yes, I mind. I'm a-tellin' ye now to git off my place. Ye ain't got no business in here."

Stone drew his Colt. He pointed it directly at Rufus. Slowly cocking it as his finger curled around the trigger, he said, "Oh, we got business here, and you don't care if we look, do you? Step inside and look around, Charlie."

My heart was pounding. I was crazy with anger and scared to death they were going to do something to Rufus. If Bentene looked inside, he'd know that there were two of us there. I was going to get caught, and I still owed those two for my daddy. I tried to think what Rufus would tell them, but he said nothing as Bentene swung down off his horse, pulled his revolver, and cocked it as he walked around Cody, who was making a deep-throated growl. Pushing the door open, he stepped inside.

In a couple of minutes, Bentene came out grinning like a coyote that's caught a quail. He had the Sharps, and he said, "He was getting supper ready for two people, Jack, and there's a bedroll on the floor next to the fire. Here's the Sharps. Looks like it's been shot often, but it's clean. There ain't no telescope for it that I saw."

Stone said with a barely concealed snarl, "Two people? Why,

Mr. Pike, you said nobody else was living here. Charlie, see if you can't persuade Mr. Pike to tell us who the other fella or lady is."

Bentene nodded. In one smooth motion, he viscously swung his revolver into Rufus's face, making his head jerk to one side and his glasses go flying. The blow bloodied the left side of Rufus's head and knocked him backwards, but he caught himself on a porch post before he fell. Cody was going wild, barking, straining with all his might on the rope to go for Bentene's throat. I was sick about what they had done to Rufus because it was my fault. I wanted to kill 'em, and I would have, too, if I'd had the Sharps. I did the only thing I thought I could do. I appeared from behind the bush and walked over to the house ready to die, ready to confess that I had shot at Stone.

I wanted to vomit, and my knees had turned to water. I had failed Daddy. I'd never see Mama again. Now Rufus would probably get shot or beat up or worse. I gritted my teeth and forced my feet to move forward. The riders stared at me like I was a ghost. Then Stone's ugly grin turned to a snarl as he squinted at me with his wolf's eyes. A shadow of uncertainty fell over his face. I reckon he hadn't expected a kid to come walking out of the bushes. I saw him frown.

I started to speak, but Rufus spoke up and said, "The kid's just helpin' me for a few weeks with chores. He ain't nothin' or nobody ye're a-wantin'. His daddy lives over to the reservation. He ain't hurtin' nobody. He don't even speak good English. Ye afraid this kid's gonna shoot ye, Stone? Leave him alone!"

Stone looked from me to Rufus and said so low I could barely hear him, "Calm down that goddamn dog, or I'll kill him. Give me that rifle, and get on your horse, Charlie." Bentene holstered his gun. He stepped off the porch, tossed Little David up to Stone, and swung up onto his horse. The coyote grin never left his face.

194

Rufus stumbled inside, dragging Cody. I could hear him speaking to him soothingly as he tied him to a bedpost. Stone and Bentene sat on their horses, waiting for Rufus to come back outside. Cody still barked, but he wasn't going crazy anymore. Rufus had blood running down from a gash on the side of his face, and a big, ugly bruise was forming around it. He wobbled back outside, squinting hard to get a little focus as he looked around the porch until he found his glasses in the dirt at the bottom of the steps. The left lens was cracked and the frames were twisted. He put them back on just as they were. He spat toward the creosote bush and stared up at Stone, apparently unafraid, waiting for his next move.

Stone's eyes were deadly serious as he frowned and searched my face. Finally, he said, "You look like some kid I've seen before. You remember me?" I just looked at him, pretending I hadn't understood a word.

Rufus said, "He don't understand English too good. Now, damn it, leave him alone!" Rufus stood there like nothing had happened, his hands in fists, blood running down his face. It seemed to me he was in charge, ready to attack. I knew they would have to kill him to get me. Rufus wasn't going to be bullied.

"Shut up before I bend this rifle barrel over your head and we have to dig a grave for you, you old bastard," Stone said, clenching his teeth and waving the heavy weapon a few inches above Rufus's head.

Stone continued to stare at me over Rufus's shoulder. He leaned toward me and shouted *"Como se llama?"* as though I were deaf. I just stared at him and didn't say anything. He looked at Rufus and said, "What is he? A deaf half-breed? He's too light to be full Apache. Must have a Mex mama. All right, Pike, so you got a kid working here. Chores for beans, huh? Mighty charitable of you. I bet you're working his tail off for them beans, too, ain't you?"

Stone let the hammer down slowly, holstered his Colt, and scratched his stubble-covered neck as he looked around. He turned back to Rufus. "I know this kid from somewhere. Maybe I've just seen him around." He laughed and said, "I guess it don't make no difference, does it? He ain't gonna be shooting no rifle this heavy, especially at me, seven or eight miles from here. Pike, I'm thinking all the shooter signs point to this here shack. Even so, it just don't make no sense for you to go to all the trouble to be tryin' to bushwhack me at my friend's ranch."

He tossed the rifle over to Bentene and said to Rufus, "Old Charlie's gonna keep that good-for-nothing old thunder gun of yours, just in case you were involved in my hat trick. You lost a rifle and got a little tap on the side of your head. That's nothing, mister. If there's ever another shot from somebody ain't facing me and the trail signs even point to the west side of the Organs, I'm gonna come back here and burn this place to the ground with you in it. Don't ever cross me, Pike. I'll blow a hole in you big enough for that damn dog to run through if you do." Then he turned said, "Let's go, boys."

Stone jerked his horse around and trotted off. Charlie and his other men pulled back, waiting for him to take the lead back down the trail. Rufus stood there watching them go. Blood from his face had covered the front of his dirty long johns. He stood there unflinching, waiting for them to disappear. I ran up to him in tears, so sorry I had caused his misery.

CHAPTER 30
STITCHES

When Stone and his men were out of sight, Rufus swayed, staggered backwards a couple of steps, and heavily sat down on the porch step. Then he laughed, slapped his knee, and said, "That there is one scared son of a bitch, Henry. Ye flat put the fear of God in him, ye did." He rubbed his aching head and said quietly, "Let Cody outta the house, boy, 'fore he gets loose and eats our grub. Then bring me a bucket of water and a rag to wash this blood off, will ye?"

I let Cody out of the shack and ran to get the bucket of water I'd left behind the bushes. When I got back to the porch, Rufus said, "See if ye can find a clean rag over by the wash bucket to clean me up. This 'un I got here in my pocket is dirty."

I found a clean rag, wet it, and began to dab at the blood on his face. The bruise continued to get uglier. His eye had swollen shut, and the broken skin across his cheekbone must have been two or three inches long. I knew he must be hurting badly, but he sat calm and still on the porch step with his hands on his knees while I fumbled around trying to doctor him. When I finished washing him, he said, "Now, fetch me a mirror and that half bottle of whiskey that's under my bed. Here, give me that rag, and I'll do a little extry washin' while ye look fer 'em."

The whiskey bottle was right where he said it was. I gave him the whiskey and ran over to the corral where he kept a washbasin. He had a broken piece of mirror there he occasionally used when he shaved, and I brought that to him.

Rufus looked at his reflection with his one good eye and grunted. He winced a few times when he probed around the cut area with his gnarled forefinger. I stood there watching Rufus doctoring himself and marveled at how much damage the barrel of a gun could do to a man's face. He took a long pull from the bottle, smacked his, lips and said, "Reckin I'm lucky. Don't think my cheekbone's broke. Does look like we'll have to do a little sewing, though. Go get my possibles bag, will ye, Henry?"

I found the bag next to his bed. It was a soft buckskin pouch with fine beadwork on the flap. He rummaged around in it until he brought out a small piece of folded leather, unfolded it, and took out a curved needle about two inches long and several pieces of sinew. He popped the sinew in his mouth to soften it, and struck a big sulfur match to sanitize the needle. "Remember how I taught ye to sew up yore breechcloth when ye tore it a-slidin' across them rocks?" he asked.

I nodded. "Well, now we're gonna see what kinda doctor or tailor ye'd make. Ye're a-gonna hafta sew up this here cut fer me. I ain't got no depth perception with just one eye, or I'd do it myself. I know ye ain't never done nothing like this, but I'll shore as hell make a mess of things if ye don't sew it up for me. This time, when ye sew, just make one loop at a time and tie it off, and then do another. I figure seven or eight stitches ought to do it. A couple more swallows of this here firewater, an' I'll be ready. Grab that little three-legged stool in there by the fire and sit beside me so ye're comfortable while ye work."

He reached in his mouth and pulled out the sinews he'd been softening. "This here is yore thread. When I'm healed up, you'll be able to cut the stitches off my face easy. They's some little sewing scissors in that there sewing kit. Ye'll need 'em to cut the sinew after ye make a loop and tie it off. I ain't gonna feel much, so don't worry about hurtin' me. Now git to it."

I was scared and a little shaky at first, but I knew I had to do it for my friend. I threaded up the needle with a long piece of sinew. I stared at the cut for a while and kind of eyeballed about where I thought the stitches should go while Rufus swilled down some more of his whiskey.

It was easier sewing than I imagined. I pulled the two sides of the cut together with my thumb and forefinger with my left hand. I didn't have to push hard with my right hand to make that sharp needle pass right through the skin on both sides of the cut. I tied the first stitch in the middle of the cut. Then put three on either side of the first one, halving the distance each time. Rufus didn't show the first sign of pain. When I was finished I poured a little whiskey over the cut like Rufus told me, and it made him groan and grind his teeth.

I handed the piece of mirror to Rufus so he could see what kind of job I'd done. He looked at each stitch carefully and said, "Damn, Henry. You'd make a right, fine doctor. That there is a first-class sewing job." I reveled in the glow of his praise.

Rufus said, "Now go get you something to eat. I ain't hungry. I'm just gonna sit out here and watch the sun go down while I finish the rest of this here bottle." I got a plate, sat out on the porch step with him, and ate my supper while he got drunk.

CHAPTER 31
YELLOW BOY'S VISION

For the next four or five days, we went about our business like nothing had happened. I ran twice every day and carried rocks while Rufus started stacking some of them to make the new house over by the barn. I could tell Rufus's face hurt, though, and that he was giving something a lot of thought. When Saturday morning came, he saddled up Sally as he always did, to ride into town for supplies and visit Albert Ellis's barbershop. Just before he left he said, "Now don't git in no more trouble. Stay hid if anybody else comes. I'll be back 'fore sundown." I nodded slowly. He grinned and winked as he rode off.

The sun was beginning to send streaks of gold and purple across the sky when Sally topped the trail into the yard. I ran outside and found Rufus had new glasses. They had silver wire frames and were a little smaller in diameter than his broken pair. He had also bought an old 1873 Winchester. It lay across the saddle alongside a burlap bag of groceries and a few other supplies. As he handed me the rifle and climbed down from Sally, I said, "How were things in town? Do you like your new glasses? Where'd you get this rifle? What's—"

He laughed and said, "Slow down there, Henry. Jest one question at a time, if ye please. I got my glasses at Lohman's. He'd just got in a shipment from back east. I had to get two pair, one pair fer reading and one fer long distance. Reckin my old lamps are a-goin' out. Ain't they fine ones, though? I saw a feller selling this here rifle to Lohman fer some groceries. I knew how much old Lohman paid him fer it, so I offered Lohman a dollar more, and he sold it to me. So now we got us some long-range artillery as well as that damned old pistol of my mine.

"Ever'body wanted to know how I got beat up so bad. Told 'em Sally run me into a post when I warn't lookin'. They all just laughed 'cause the talk was that several other people over on this side of the Organs had run into posts this week, too. They's all speculatin' about who took a shot at Stone. Ellis said he thought there might be several to shoot at him now. Stone and Bentene are supposed to be up in the Sacramentos lookin' over abandoned homesteads to get some more land and water to support their herds. Soon as Yellow Boy comes in from Mexico, we're gonna go get Little David back, and I'm a-gonna settle me some business with Mr. Bentene. Now let's eat. Ye go set out the meal, and I'll feed and water Sally."

It was monsoon season, raining three or four times a week. Rufus and I loved to sit on his porch watching the lightning shows start far down south or to the west, then roll east toward Las Cruces and El Paso. That night, the sky lighted up with streaks of lightning for hours. We could feel the cool breeze and smell the rain as the columns of water rushing out of the heavy, black clouds marched toward us on giant, stubby legs with thunder beating their march. Those storms are fearful to watch from a house down in the valley. From where we saw them, halfway up the Organs, they were flashing wars, clouds striking each other with fiery, crooked strokes that hung in my eyes long after the dark returned. Up where Rufus had his shack, those storms could turn heathens into God-fearers. I knew we'd probably get enough water to fill to overflowing all the natural and other water tanks we'd been working on. No doubt, this rain would fill the trail to the shack with washouts.

The big, blue bruise on his face was starting to heal and turn yellow. The swelling had gone down enough that he could see out of his left eye. In another week, I knew he'd want the stitches cut off of what was going to be an ugly scar.

I said, "Rufus what're we gonna do?"

Rufus spat and said, "You mean about those bastards that stole Lil' David?"

"Yes, sir." I felt tears of frustration rising to my eyes, ready to embarrass me in front of my mentor. "They're getting away with anything they want. It's not just or fair. I can't stop them, and it's my fault we lost any chance of surprise. Now we both know it's only gonna be a little while before Stone figures out who I am, and then he'll be back to finish his business. I'm the one who got you into all this trouble. Maybe I ought to leave. Just go back to Mama and hope for the best. At least then maybe they'd leave you alone."

Rufus chewed and stared at me for a moment, then snorted and shook his head. "Whatever give ye the idee that life's fair? Let me tell ye, it ain't. Men make their lives just by puttin' honor ahead of ever'thang, even their own lives. That's what we're gonna do. We're gonna git us some justice, even if it means our lives.

"As fer ye leavin' to take the heat off me, well, it just don't make no never mind, Henry. They'd know ye had been stayin' here with me and it was likely ye'd told me what ye knew about 'em. That means they's a-gonna have to wipe me out, too, when they come after ye. So don't go down yonder to yore mama and put her in danger fer me 'cause they's gonna come after me anyway. Ye didn't get me into this mess, 'ceptin' I wanted to be there with ye. It was gonna happen sooner or later. It's just happened sooner is all."

Thunder rumbled across the valley again, and I asked, "So

what are we going to do?"

Rufus smiled and said, "The ace we got in this here game is Yellow Boy. They don't know about Yellow Boy. They don't know he's vowed revenge for ye. And, let me tell ye, I nearly laughed out loud when Stone said ye was too little to put that hole in his hat and then outfox Catron to get back here. But, ye did it, didn't ye? Ye was able to do that 'cause Yellow Boy taught ye how to think, and we helped ye get strong in yore body and yore mind."

He shifted his wad to the other jaw and turned his head to spit at his creosote bush. As he turned back to look at me, his jaw dropped, his eyes got wide, and he said, "Well, I'll be damned. Speak of the devil. *Buenos noches, Señor* Yellow Boy. We been hopin' ye'd show up."

I looked over my shoulder where Rufus was staring and saw Yellow Boy, leaning against the corner porch post. One foot was on the porch, one on the ground, and his rifle was between his legs, the barrel resting on his chest.

I shouted, "Yellow Boy!" In three steps, I was standing beside him. Up close, he looked tired and worn out. I hadn't a clue when he had joined us on the porch.

He held up a hand to greet us and said, *"Hola,* Rufus. *Hola, Hombrecito.* I ride hard *por tres soles y tres noches.* I didn't eat, only rested horse. Is there meat in your pot, Rufus? Is there water inside, *Hombrecito?"*

Rufus smiled, and his eyes sparkled with new fire. "Three days and three nights? Damn, Yellow Boy. They shore as hell is some grub in the pot, *hombre.* Be right back with a plateful," he said, as he pushed the door open and stepped inside. I ran inside, too, and grabbed the water bucket and dipper. I handed Yellow Boy a dipperful that was gone in three long swallows. He sipped the next dipperful.

I studied his face as he drank. He looked weary beyond

anything I had ever seen. Even I could tell he hadn't slept in days. He was covered with dust, and the sweat falling out of his hatband made rivulets in the dust down the sides of his cheeks. Normally, he stayed very clean, but this night he had the sharp, pungent smell of old sweat, his and his horse's, and miles of desert dust. I didn't care. I was so relieved to see him I felt as if I'd just been saved from drowning. I thought, *Maybe our trouble with Stone is going to be set right after all.*

"Where's your pony, Yellow Boy? I'll feed and water him."

"This I've done, *Hombrecito.* He eats and drinks with Sally."

I looked around the side of the shack. Sure enough, there was the paint pony next to Sally, with their rumps pointed out of the shed, its covered sides shielding them from the wind and the coming storm.

Rufus came out of the shack with a tin plate running over with what we'd had left in the cooking pot. Yellow Boy took it and ate like a starving man. He filled both cheeks as he chewed while the gravy ran down his chin. He wiped it off with his free hand and licked it, not wasting a drop. Rufus, his smile made crooked by his swollen face, leaned against a porch post and watched him eat.

Yellow Boy wiped the plate clean with the last tortilla, emptied another dipper of water, belched loudly, sighed with relief, and leaned back against his post, closing his eyes for a moment. When he opened them, he looked at me, then Rufus, and nodded. "You safe, *mi compañeros. Bueno.* We must leave! *Rapidamente.*"

Rufus and I looked at each other with frowns of surprise. We had a lot to tell him.

Yellow Boy's voice was earnest as he said, "Sally run you into tree, Rufus? Why are your glasses new? *Que es* Shoots Today Kills Tomorrow?" Then, sighing, he said, "I dream. I come quick. *Prisa. Vamonos.*" (Hurry. We go.)

Rufus's jaw dropped, and his brow shot up. "We have to go now? Why?"

"I dream in sweat lodge Shoots Today Kills Tomorrow finds *Hombrecito*'s enemy. Enemy no die. Enemy, his medicine strong. I see many riders search far for Shoots Today Kills Tomorrow. They find it, take it, see *Hombrecito,* then leave. Enemy remembers *Hombrecito.* He returns. I know I must ride plenty quick, or *Hombrecito* dies. The enemy, he comes *pronto. Vamonos pronto.*"

I stared at him with my mouth open and felt myself trembling down in my gut. Rufus's said, "Aye, God, Henry, run get Sally an' the paint. Take 'em up the canyon. Hobble 'em. Rope off a little corral around that old log back in the corner of the canyon. You know, where we usually try our longest shots. This here storm's a comin', and it'll likely scare hell out of 'em. They'll try to wander back here if they ain't fenced in back there. If you hear shootin', you hide up in the juniper behind where we put targets. Be kerful and don't get on no glass. Don't come back here till I call ye if they's shootin'. If it's quiet, ye come back on the side trail to that overhang I fixed fer us to hide on. Ye understand me boy?"

"Yes, sir, I do."

I was off the porch and down to the corral faster than a quail crossing the road. There was already a strong breeze filling the air with the coppery smell of rain, and I could hear faint thunder off to the west. The storm would be over us in less than an hour. The paint stood with his head down, no strength left except to eat. He was easy to halter. Sally was skittish with the coming storm, but I knew her tricks and got the halter rope around her neck before she ducked out into the corral.

I led them up the canyon to the log Rufus mentioned. The log was an old juniper tree that had fallen over. I'd rested Little David on it many times to shoot at the bottles Rufus used for targets. The paint and Sally were easy to hide and protect some from the storm there. The wind was swirling up and down the canyon when I finished their hobbles and a little rope corral using the log as one side.

I strained to hear against the increasing moan of the wind high above the canyon walls. There was no sound of gunfire. I ran along the path up on the north canyon wall about ten feet above the path we usually took to shoot. I had to run in stops and starts, waiting for the lightning to show me the way. I knew I needed to get to the overhang before the rain came, because the path would become slick and dangerous when it started raining. There was a pause in the wind and a bright flash and crack of thunder just as I got to where I had to climb up to the overhang.

Rufus and Yellow Boy were stretched out on their bellies, staring out into the darkness through the juniper bushes fronting the ledge. I could hear the low mumble of their voices as I came down the path. I had nearly climbed up to the ledge when I heard Rufus say, "Come on up here beside us, Henry."

I stretched out beside Yellow Boy. The old Henry resting in his hands was on half cock, a cartridge in the chamber ready to fire. Rufus was loading the rifle he had just bought. Three boxes of cartridges lay between them. Cody was tied in the shed, chewing on a piece of meat left to keep him quiet. It was darker than a tomb behind those bushes except when lightning flashes spread over everything. The wind began to pick up and blow dust up the canyon, swirling little dust devils up and down its sides. There were droplets of rain mixed with it. In the lightning flashes, we saw a big cloud with a column of rain over on the western edge of the valley and knew it wouldn't be long before the storm was on top of us.

"Are we going to shoot them if they come?" I whispered. I thought, *Now we'll see if you're such a big dog, Stone. Yellow Boy's gonna cut your nuts off.*

Yellow Boy shook his head. "No, *Hombrecito*. It is bad place *por* ambush. There no way out. Here, we have no extra bullets, no food, no water if men stay and shoot back. If we shoot and men leave, they get away easy, warn others. Then maybe we never avenge *su padre*. We must wait. Later, we find good place to spill blood." He paused for a moment and added, *"Pero,* if they find us, we must kill them all. Everyone. *Comprende, Hombrecito?"*

I nodded, and Rufus spat and said, "Yellow Boy, what ye're sayin', that there's a fact."

There was only the moan of the wind through the canyon. We lay there without moving, feeling the wind rise and fall, the smell of water on creosotes from down in the valley getting stronger. I opened my mouth to tell Yellow Boy about my adventure when he reached over and grabbed Rufus's forearm. He nodded toward the trail and cocked his head to listen. The wind was getting stronger and dust was pelting our hiding place. I was gritting my teeth. The blowing dust burned my skin like fire ants were biting it.

The wind was blowing so hard I couldn't hear or see anything. It was darker than Stone's soul. I barely saw Yellow Boy's head, and he was right next to me. Then there was a sudden, short pause in the wind, and I heard a stone rattle down the trail. My heart started thumping so hard it was about to jump out of my chest. I'd have sold my soul for a swallow of water to wash away the dry cotton in my mouth.

There was a tremendous flash of light as a wicked bolt from the cloud over Las Cruces split and thumped three different spots with a roar of white, blinding fury. Thunder ricocheted against the mountains. The flash revealed four riders reined up in the middle of the yard, their rifles across their saddles. The man closest to us was Red Tally. One of the other riders had been with Stone and Bentene when they pistol-whipped Rufus. I didn't recognize the other two. They all wore long black dusters with collars turned up to fend off the wind, and their horses were black.

I clenched my teeth, and heard my heart pounding in my ears. I wished to God I had Little David. I'd settle accounts right then. I didn't care if I died on the spot. At least I would get the man who shot Daddy.

Red Tally bent his head and cupped his hands as he lit a cigarette. Another lightning flash, and I saw the men had their rifles pointed at the shack door. Kerosene lanterns hung off the saddles of a couple of the riders. One of them yelled above the roar of the wind swirling in the canyon, "Come on out, Pike. Bring the kid with you. Come out now or we'll burn you out!"

Flashes of lightning were becoming brighter and more frequent as the storm began skirting the Organs and moving off toward El Paso. Tally looked at the rider next to him and motioned him forward with a wave of his rifle. The rider climbed down and stepped on to the porch, his rifle ready. He walked up to the shack door, kicked it open, and jumped inside, firing several times as he went.

Rufus sighted on the doorway and brought the hammer back on his Winchester, but Yellow Boy grabbed him by the arm and shook his head. Rufus spat in disgust and put his rifle back on half cock. The man in the shack came out and yelled into the wind's fury, "Ain't nobody here! They was though! Fireplace is still hot! You wanna burn 'em out?"

Tally looked around, and, apparently not liking the odds, especially if they went farther up the canyon, shook his head. Raindrops the size of marbles began to pelt us.

He pulled his horse around and yelled, "No! Leave it! Wouldn't burn now anyway, and I ain't riding up that canyon in this rain and dark! I'll finish the job in a day or two! Come on, let's get down that trail before it's too slick and washed out to use!"

They started back down the trail as the clouds dumped more water on us. I raised up on my knees, ready to run back up the canyon and get the paint and Sally, but Yellow Boy grabbed me by the shoulder and held me with a powerful grip, so I couldn't move. He nodded toward the yard. In a moment, a weak flash showed a single rider sitting motionless, waiting at the edge of the yard, rifle drawn and collar pulled up to his hat. We waited, feeling the cold rain wash us clean and new.

The rain passed. As the lighting flashes became farther and farther apart, and the thunder rolled away toward the south, the lone rider finally turned and slowly headed back toward the Dripping Springs road, letting his horse pick his way through the myriad of little streams racing down the trail. Yellow Boy turned to me and said, "*Vamonos. Hombrecito,* bring horse and Sally to shed."

CHAPTER 32
MEAT FOR THE LION

I made my way back up the canyon. It was tricky business because there were gushing rivulets everywhere, pouring toward the big wash that ran on the south side of the canyon. The paint and Sally were soaked but no worse off than I was. We returned to the shed without drowning in the big wash or falling on slippery rocks, and I gave them an extra ration of oats. Rufus had the fire going and had swept most of the water that had blown through the open door out by the time I got back. He fumbled around for the fixings and finally got a pot of coffee started.

Yellow Boy sat on the edge of the porch calmly smoking one of his Mexican cigars. I walked over and sat down next to him. He clasped my shoulder, gave it a little shake, and said, "So, *Hombrecito*, Rufus say you open *un grande* box of trouble, *si*? *Es bueno.* You have brave heart. You did powerful thing against this man, Stone. I am proud. You have warrior's heart. Soon, we take enemies' lives *por su padre*. This we must do *pronto* or die by hand of this man who comes like hunting lion."

I nodded and wondered how it was that the strongest purposes of our hearts often had the weakest outcomes in action, while the weakest had the most profound effects on our lives. This had been my first lesson in being careful what I asked for because I might just get it.

Soon Rufus brought the coffeepot and three enamel cups out to the porch and poured us each a cup of his strong, black brew. The stars came out and fog rose from the ground, swirling about our feet like smoke from a dying fire. Crickets began their orchestra. The danger had blown through; the strong wind filled with uncertainty had gone up the canyon until the next storm.

I had to blow the steam off my cup and slurp loudly to make the hot liquid cool enough to drink. Rufus and Yellow Boy just smacked their lips and drank it scalding hot. They never taught me how they did that.

Rufus said, "Well, boys, what're we a-gonna do? The fat's in the fire now, ain't it? I say we ambush 'em on the road somewhere, just the way they did Henry and his daddy. That there'd be poetic justice."

Yellow Boy frowned and asked, "*Que es* poetek justez, Rufus?"

Rufus grinned over the steaming cup and shook his head. "Never mind. It'd take the rest of the night fer me to explain it to ye."

Yellow Boy asked, "How many we fight, Rufus?" I knew his tactical mind was at work as soon as he asked this.

Rufus thought for a minute and said, "Well, they's the two big ones, Stone and Tally. Tally is the one with the red beard. Then they's Bentene, and I want the pleasure of guttin' that son of a bitch myself fer the pistol-whippin' he give me. They's three that always rides with Tally, and they was three with Stone and Bentene the other night. I reckon they's maybe nine we haffta to take care of. Henry, did you know any of the other riders tonight?"

I shook my head.

Yellow Boy blew a puff of smoke that hung in the cool night air like a small cloud that had stayed behind from the storm. "Where are ranches of Stone, Tally, and Bentene? You know, Rufus?"

"Shore I know. Stone's place is down towards the malpais

and up against the San Andres. Bentene's place is next to Stone's, but Bentene ain't got much of a place. He's mostly Stone's partner. I hear Tally stays the winters with Stone then rides the train with his crew up to Wyoming country to murder homesteaders. I's surprised to see him here tonight. Stone musta sent fer him all the way up to Wyoming. Stone and Bentene's supposed to be up in the Sacramentos now, looking fer more places with water to run their stock during the summertime. Stone ain't been doing too good lately with his stock, though. They say Lee's been a-tryin' to buy him out, but that there is another story. Why do ye wanna know?"

Yellow Boy's eyes narrowed to match the coyote grin on his face. "Hmmph, you know why, Rufus. Mountains are good place for ambush like wolf hunting deer. Ranch house is good place *por* ambush when enemy sleeps there. If we asleep when Red Beard come, he kill us, *si*? Meat for wolf is meat for lion. What kills for Red Beard kills for us *tambien*. Stone and Bentene are in mountains now, *pero* they come back to ranch house. First, we find Shoots Today Kills Tomorrow. Maybe find it at Bentene's ranch. We take back while Stone and Bentene are in mountains, and camp on Sierra Blanca in my land. No man think we use reservation to hide."

Rufus was grinning and nodding. I could tell he liked this plan, and so did I. Yellow Boy continued, "We go once more to Stone and Bentene ranches. Maybe burn. Maybe kill, *si*? Or maybe ambush on road. What you think, Rufus?"

Rufus thought about Yellow Boy's proposal for a few minutes and said, "Aye, God, Yellow Boy, I wouldn't want ye fer an enemy. We'll rest ye and the paint tonight and most of tomorrow. Then we'll take the path Henry used, go over Baylor Pass tomorrow evenin', and go off to the east of Cox's place. We'n lay low in the Jarillas day after tomorrow then hit Stone's and Bentene's places fer Lil' David that night. I got all the supplies we need. We need to git outta here purdy quick, though. The Tally bunch'll probably burn the place tomorrow night anyhow. If'n we get those bastards, Henry can go back to his mama. If we don't, he ain't gonna be goin' nowheres. Ain't that right, Henry?"

I nodded. I had to clench my teeth to hold my cup steady I was so excited. Rufus and Yellow Boy laughed. I knew they understood what I was feeling. Things were happening much faster than any of us had imagined. They couldn't happen fast enough for me. I didn't care if I was fourteen years old. I wanted blood. I wanted it right then. I wanted to see my father's enemies choking on their own blood just like he had. Most of all, I wanted to see my mother and tell her I had settled accounts for Daddy.

Yellow Boy disappeared down the trail toward the back of the canyon. He found a place to sleep the rest of the night and most of the next day in a juniper thicket close by the back cliffs.

The next day Rufus got me up at daylight. We worked our tails off right up until the time we left, late in the afternoon. His mine, the place where he stored his valuables, was about halfway up the path to the back of the canyon. I had been in it only once or twice since he had first showed it to me.

It was dry in the mine despite the hard rain we had the night before. After he opened the door, he took a stick and beat around inside to be sure there weren't any snakes that had staked a claim to his territory. He found one and tossed it, twisting and rattling, outside. He had me lug stuff from the shed and his shack up to the mine while he rode over to Van Patten's place to buy a pack mule and a horse and to ask Buck Greer to keep Cody and keep an eye on the place while he was gone. Buck had become right fond of Cody when Rufus told him that tall tale about a wild bitch coming to court him.

When Rufus returned, he gave me the horse he'd bought from Buck. I liked her as soon as I saw her. He said Buck called her Midnight, and she was the first horse I'd ever owned. She was small, black, and shiny as tar, and she had a white blaze on her face. I watered her and curried her while we got acquainted. She was a friendly little horse and got along well with Sally.

Rufus said, "Buck says she'll never win any flat land races, but a man could ride her right over the Rabbit Ears, and she'd never miss a step. He wanted to know why I wanted a horse when I had Sally. Told him I was gonna do some cattle drovin' and prospectin' down to Mexico, and Sally was just gettin' too durn slow fer them thangs, which ain't true, but it was a good enough reason fer Buck."

Rufus pointed to the pack mule he'd bought and said, "That there mule answers to Elmer. Buck swears by him, too. Says he even lets some of the fancy-pants tourists that come over to the Drippin' Springs Reezort take him fer a ride 'cause he's so reliable and gentle."

We led Midnight and Elmer up to the storage mine. Rufus dug around inside for a while before he came out with an old, dust-covered McClellan saddle, a rough saddle blanket, and an army bridle. He wiggled his nose and said, "I ain't used this rig since I done a little scoutin' fer the army back to 'sixty-eight. Reckon it'll be easier sittin' than bareback, but not much."

I was thrilled. I was going to be riding across the desert, just like the troopers back when Daddy led men against the Apaches and bandits. Rufus went back in the mine again, banged around some more, and came out with a pack frame for the mule. Then he sent me to fill a small keg he'd found with water. After some more rummaging, he found a case of ammunition for Little David and cases of .45-caliber and .44-caliber cartridges that fit his and Yellow Boy's rifles and his revolver. He threw the coffeepot, a skillet, his Dutch oven, some eating pans, spoons, beans and cured meat, coffee, flour, and grain for the horses and mules into some old, worn-out panier sacks that went on the pack frame. He also packed his medical kit, odds and ends to use around a camp, and herbs he used for everything from snakebite to constipation.

Yellow Boy appeared at the shack in mid-afternoon. He yawned and stretched as Rufus gave him the last of the breakfast beans from the pot left hanging over the fire. When he finished eating, he went down to the shed, sat in the watering pool for a little while, and bathed. He finally got out and shook himself to get most of the water off his skin and out of his hair. He sat drying himself in the air as the sun began falling behind the Floridas. Dry and clean, he twisted his breechcloth to wring the water out, slipped it on, then helped us load up the mule and saddle the horses.

CHAPTER 33
THE BEST DEFENSE

Before we mounted, Rufus showed Yellow Boy the cases of cartridges and told him to help himself when he needed ammunition. Yellow Boy nodded, looked at Rufus solemnly, and said, "Is war, Rufus."

"Ye're damned right it is. We're gonna kill those bastards, or I ain't comin' back here alive. I done kept this boy from his mama too long and put up with those bastards a-whuppin' my head fer too long. Hell, yes they's gonna be war, and they ain't a-gonna see it comin' till they's a big hole right 'tween their eyes."

Yellow Boy stared at him for a few seconds and said, *"Bueno,* Rufus. We make Albert Fountain rest in peace. *Vamonos, amigos."*

We made some final adjustments to the pack on Elmer and the saddle gear, took a last look around, and mounted up. The shadows were long in the desert, and the day slowly drifted into soothing dark as Yellow Boy led us up over Baylor Pass. Buck was right. Midnight was easy to ride and sure-footed as we cantered down the trail. Her steady gait made me less fearful that I would embarrass myself riding her in front of Rufus and Yellow Boy, for I hadn't spent more than a few days on a horse or mule in the six years since Daddy's murder. I'd just run most of the time, as Yellow Boy had demanded of me.

Now traveling was easy, and the McClellan saddle felt like a rocking chair compared to pounding the ground with my feet.

We stopped a couple of times early on for Rufus to rearrange the gear on Elmer so it couldn't be heard rattling around as he trotted along, but then we hurried because we wanted to be well beyond Van Patten's ranch before Tally and his men came back. We rode, strung out over about two hundred yards, with Yellow Boy in the lead, me in the middle, and Rufus in the back leading Elmer.

There was nothing but deep, black shadows and bright stars overhead, but Yellow Boy rode the trail as if it were daylight, and we made good time. As we neared the top of Baylor Pass, he turned and galloped back past me, stopped to speak briefly with Rufus, then disappeared into the inky, black shadows of the Organs.

Midnight had her ears up in curiosity, as we waited for Rufus to ride up. He nodded back down the trail and said, "Ol' Yellow Boy's a-gonna ride back to the shack and keep watch down the trail fer Stone. We're a-gonna wait fer him at Aguirre Springs on the other side of this here pass and give these animals a breather 'cause they ain't used to runnin' up and down these here mountains like ye are." His little backhanded compliment made me smile.

We followed the trail over Baylor Pass, carefully picking our way, until a big, yellow moon finally popped up over the Sacramentos and made the trail easy to see on the way down to the springs. It was so bright we stayed in the shadows from bushes where no one could see us, even if they were coming toward us on the trail.

As we neared Aguirre Springs, I saw Rufus stop, pull his Winchester out of its scabbard and lever a round into the chamber while he waited for me to come up.

"What's the matter?" I whispered.

"They's big cats in these here mountains, and they might wanna use that spring to get a little water and maybe get a little dinner from some idjits dumb enough to be stumblin' around in the dark. They's also the chance there might be some fellers camped in there. Here, ye take the lines fer Sally and Elmer. I'll walk in. Ride in behind me slow and easy. If any of the animals start acting up, it's likely they's probably smelling a cat or a camp's horses and mules. Ye whistle in yore hands like a dove if that happens, then ride back up the trail a ways until I come get cha."

I nodded. I was scared. A mountain cat was big enough to carry me off or kill the horses and mules. I didn't have a weapon except for the throwing knife Yellow Boy was teaching me to use. Right then, a knife didn't seem like much of a defense.

Rufus disappeared down the path into the springs, and I followed slowly, my fast breathing leaving a little cloud of vapor behind us. Midnight, Sally, and Elmer moved along with no signs of fear. We found water from the springs running down the mountain in a little stream, but we found no mountain cats or campers. Rufus put his rifle on safety, spat a stream of brown juice between his boots, and said, "I 'spec Yellow Boy will be another two or three hours. Let's loosen the cinches on Sally and yore horse, take the load off Elmer, and get us some rest. Yellow Boy's a-gonna want to move soon's he gets here. We need to be in the Jarillas before dawn, or, likely as not, ranch hands will spot us."

We hobbled the stock so they could graze around the little stream and found us a big, smooth boulder to rest against while we watched back up the trail for Yellow Boy. It was chilly that time of night, but the water rippling over the rocks and the moon glowing over the Sacramentos made the evening mighty pretty and peaceful.

We sat in silence for a while, watching the moon sail across the night sky toward the western horizon, lengthening the stark, black shadows cast by the bushes, but bending them away from us. Rufus cut a fresh chew and stuffed it in his cheek. Then he nodded toward me and asked, "Are ye fearful, Henry?"

"I never really thought about being afraid," I said, trembling partly from cold air and partly from the trip's excitement. "What do you mean?" I asked.

Rufus spat and said, "Well, sir, ye've been a-hidin' now fer about six years. Here ye are, a-runnin' around in the desert with un old fart an' un Apache. Ol' Red Tally, he'd just as soon cut yore throat as look at ye, and ye can bet he'll do it, too, if he has the least chance. Stone, he's got to have ye dead because he knows if ye ever talked to the law, the sheriff'd come get him, and he'd be swingin' from a gallows shore as hell. That jackass Bentene, he just does what Stone tells him, so he'll want to kill ye, too. If'n that ain't bad enough, they probably got fifteen or twenty trusted cowboys that'd ride through hell with 'em, and they'd not hesitate to try to run ye right into the ground if they's the chance. They's comin' after ye, and here ye are, by God, a-goin' after them." Rufus put a hand on my shoulder and said, "That there is yore best defense. Wisht I could say it'll be that easy, son, but these here *hombres* are gonna be hard snakes to kill. *Comprende?*"

"Yes, sir, I do, and that's enough to make me right fearful. I just know it's something I've got to do. If they kill me, then at least I can rest easy knowing I did the best I could to make things right for Daddy. Ain't nobody gonna care if I'm killed except you or Yellow Boy 'cause everybody else thinks I'm dead." I balled up my fists and said, "Somehow, someway, I'm gonna get Little David back. I'm gonna try again and again, if I have to, until Stone's lying on the ground with a bullet hole through his heart. Then it's gonna be Tally's turn, 'cept I'm gonna stake him out over a slow fire and boil his guts in his own juices like Yellow Boy says the Apaches did to the enemies they hated most. I'm gonna settle my score with Bentene, too, and I'm gonna finish with Oliver Lee. He's gonna suffer for what he ordered those killers to do."

The more I talked, the angrier I got. It was slowly seeping into my head that we were aiming to kill three or four men, all of them with nerves of steel, used to facing death, and not afraid of being killed. None of them would hesitate to kill any of us in an instant, but I didn't care. I wanted payback.

"I hate 'em," I said. "I want to tear their hearts out while they're still living and dance on their graves."

Rufus sat there for a while, looking at me in the soft glow of the moonlight. A little stream of tobacco juice trickled out of the wad in his cheek. Finally, he said, "God, A'mighty, Henry. I didn't know you'd gotten so bloodthirsty. When did that happen?"

I wiped my runny nose, sniffed, and said, "I don't know. Every time I ran in the desert, every time I picked up a rock for your house, every time I hid when you had company, I thought about it. I thought about how I was lucky to be alive and to have you and Yellow Boy teachin' me how to survive. Every time, as I was working or training, I told myself I'd make those men pay every last pound and pennyweight owed to justice, or I'd die trying."

Rufus spat a stream of juice on a big beetle that had started across a rock next to him. He said, "That there is a mistake, a big mistake."

"What are you talking about? Those murderers have it coming, and I'm the one who vowed to giving 'em a start toward the arms of hell."

Rufus shook his head, stared off across the basin in the moonlight, and said, "Ye got to be cold and cakilatin'. If ye want to survive bringin' justice to those men, ye gotta be thinkin' all the time. Yore daddy's killin' and them chasing ye is the best of reasons to go after 'em fer shore. But ye can't let yore feelings about 'em tell ye what to do. Jest like ye a goin' after Stone with Lil' David. Yore feelings on that one left ye high and dry when the nut-cuttin' time come. Ye're lucky boy, damn lucky, to be alive."

"Well I almost killed him, didn't I?"

Rufus spat again then looked at me with a squint of cold rationality. "Almost don't cut it. Ain't no reward in that. Almost ain't never killed nobody. Almost ain't brought nobody to justice. Ever' time ye try to kill a man, be damn shore ye do it. Ye ain't likely to get another chance 'fore he kills ye, and he's in the right to do it, too. Now I ain't sayin' ye ain't brave or didn't show lots of courage and shootin' skill tryin' to kill Stone, but this here range is covered with graves of brave men with a lot of skill who didn't cakilate what they was a doin' 'fore they made a challenge. Ye got to be smart when nut-cuttin' time comes. Ye got to be real smart."

I knew Rufus was right. All I could say was, "Yes, sir. What're we gonna do now?"

He said, "Well, we need to swap idees with Yellow Boy, but I'm a-thinkin' we oughta go after Bentene first and get Lil' David back. He's the weakest of the three and oughta be the easiest to git. Then we need to try to pick off Stone and Tally separately, if we can, even if it means ridin' up into Colorado or Wyoming. We can shoot 'em from a mile away if we need to. Hell, I don't care. I ain't proud as long as we get the bastards.

"Now, Oliver Lee? He's different. People 'round here, they's loyal as dogs to him. He's a good man to have on yore side in any fight. He lives by a strict code. I ain't so shore he was responsible for getting Stone and Tally to murder yore daddy. That there is something ye gotta decide for yoreself. Just be shore yore right about him bein' guilty. If we kill him, this here whole countryside is gonna come after our tails."

I nodded, but deep in my heart, I knew I was gonna kill Oliver Lee. I felt sure he had it coming.

Suddenly, Rufus reached over, grabbed my forearm, and gave it a little squeeze for me to be quiet. We cocked our heads to one side, listening. Rufus cupped his left ear with his hand to hear better and pulled the hammer back to full cock on his rifle with the other. I could feel my heart pounding and my breath coming in short, quick puffs. Out in the cold, moonlit darkness, a rock rolled down the trail, making an irregular clicking sound as it bounced from one stone to the next. We rose up in a squat and stretched our necks, trying to see over the bushes and into the shadows. We waited, straining to hear the next sign, or to see the first motion of what was out there in the cold gloom of the moonlight.

"Que pasa?" Yellow Boy asked.

Rufus and I jumped like we'd been jabbed with cactus thorns. There was Yellow Boy, squatting behind us like he'd been there all night. I laughed aloud and sagged back down in relief. Rufus was gagging and wheezing. He'd nearly swallowed the big wad of tobacco in his cheek.

Finally, he managed to sputter, "Damn ye, Indian. Ye scared me clean into tomorrow. How'd ye do that?"

Yellow Boy squatted there, grinning at us, and swung his arm back toward Baylor Pass. "Many big rocks to springs. Easy to walk over with no sound. I make horse walk down trail. You turned eyes to him. *Bueno* trick, huh? Also, plenty easy to find you. You talk much."

Rufus raised his brow, wordlessly asking the dreaded question, and Yellow Boy said, "No fire at your *rancho*. Water still good. Cattle still graze. Stone and Tally, they come, but Bentene no with them. Stone call you and shoot many time *en su casa*. Glass in windows gone. Now roof no stop water when rain comes. Tally laughed and called Stone fool. Stone said he thinks you and *Hombrecito vamos a Mexico*. He said you come back.

He kill you next time."

"Well, boys, I reckon we got off lucky." Rufus stood and spat all the way across the little stream of water. "Now all we gotta do is find 'em 'fore they find us. Let's git outta here and down to the Jarillas 'fore the world wakes up."

Yellow Boy disappeared but soon came back with his pony while Rufus and I loaded up Elmer and tightened saddle cinches on Sally and Midnight. Yellow Boy led the way, keeping us in the same formation we had used riding up Baylor Pass. We passed slow and quiet through the creosotes and mesquites, bypassing little groups of grazing cattle owned by Cox. The curious cattle watched us with their ears up. Once in a while, we saw the low, red glow of a banked fire from ranch hands staying out to keep an eye on the stock.

We got past the Cox ranch and breathed a sigh of relief, as it was unlikely we'd see any more cowhand camps or run into other night riders. Finally, Yellow Boy set his horse to a good canter and headed straight for the middle of the Jarillas, painted in stark shadows from the setting moon.

We reached a little canyon in the Jarillas just before dawn. Yellow Boy said he'd often used it to rest and take cover on his travels back and forth from the reservation to the Sierra Madre, and we planned to hide and rest there for the day. Mesquite and tall ocotillo with long, cable-like stems with sharp thorns hid its entrance. There was a thin trail only Yellow Boy's sharp eyes could pick out in the early morning gloom that wound through the thicket and into the canyon's entrance. Once through the mesquite and ocotillo, it was easy going for several hundred yards on a little winding trail down the center of the canyon. Near the end of the canyon, Yellow Boy showed us a large rock shelf that we could crawl under and use as a shelter from the sun.

CHAPTER 34
RIDE TO SIERRA BLANCA

"Rufus and *Hombrecito*, rest here until sun is there," Yellow Boy said, pointing straight overhead. "I watch for riders from the canyon lookout. Then you watch until sun goes down. You sleep now, *sí*?"

Rufus spat and gave a quick nod of approval. Yellow Boy climbed up the canyon wall on a series of footholds and handholds that led back toward the mouth of the canyon. Rufus and I unloaded the stock, tied them where there would be shade, rubbed them down, and fed and watered them. We ate a little of the cold beans and meat Rufus had brought from his last cook pot back at the shack.

We had come a long way, and I was sleepy and so sore in my thighs I could barely walk. It was just beginning to sink into my young brain what hard work this justice for Daddy and me was going to be.

As the sky in the east started to brighten and long shadows from the mountains began to form, Rufus found an old ocotillo stalk and swept under the ledge for snakes. Finding none, we spread a blanket, crawled up under it, and stretched out for some sleep. Rufus was snoring in minutes, but the night's excitement and the coming light kept me awake until I finally pulled a bandanna over my eyes and passed out from exhaustion.

Mid-morning sunlight was creeping down the canyon walls, driving the dark, cool shadows away from where we lay, when I snapped awake, startled by the sound of distant, bawling cattle and human voices. I raised up on an elbow and started to get up, but Rufus grabbed me by the arm, shook his head, and said in a coarse whisper, "They's just some stock bein' driven by here, probably just headed fer the stockyards in Alamogordo. Nothin' to worry about. Go on back to sleep."

Rufus was snoring again in less than five minutes, but I had a hard time getting back to sleep. It was hot, and since it was the monsoon season, the humidity was high. Some insects kept biting me, raising little, bloody welts on my arms.

I was slowly drifting back to sleep when I felt Yellow Boy gently tapping my foot with the barrel of his rifle. Rufus was already up and pulling on a canteen in long, slow swallows. I crawled out from under the ledge and had a long drink, too.

Yellow Boy put his finger to his lips, motioned toward the handholds and foot notches up the side of the rust-colored canyon wall, and pointed out the best place to sit while on watch. Then he settled down on a blanket and instantly fell asleep.

Rufus climbed up the handholds to the lookout, as I scrambled up behind him to take my turn watching, so he could nap if he wanted. In the spot Yellow Boy had shown us, a mesquite bush had grown precariously close to the edge of a wide ledge and provided a little shade and perfect cover against being spotted by someone on the desert floor below.

The lookout spot was in a crevice about fifty feet up from the canyon floor, and it gave good protected lines of sight everywhere on the west side of the Jarillas. The monsoon rains had changed the range from dull, summer browns to a mottled patchwork of dark, cedar green creosote bushes and delicate, light green mesquite thickets on a carpet of turquoise-colored succulent grasses and weeds. Delicate little flowers in blues and purples, red poppies, and large white and yellow gourd flowers were blooming everywhere. I could see little wisps of smoke from some activity far away at the Cox ranch, its buildings against the Organs lost in the hazy distance. There were small groups of cattle scattered everywhere, filling their bellies with the new green grass. I could see the occasional cowboy far in the distance, trotting his horse down the cattle trails through the creosotes and mesquites. Sometimes only a hat or a horse's head was visible until the cowboy broke into a small opening that provided a quick, full glimpse of the man and his mount.

Rufus and I surveyed the countryside for a while, then, handing me his rifle, Rufus said, pointing toward the middle of the sun's arch on its downside, "Here, Henry, ye watch till the sun is right there, then I'll relieve ye." As I took the rifle, he pulled his beat-up old hat over his eyes and lay back in the shade. He was asleep again almost instantly, and I wondered how he and Yellow Boy managed to sleep so soundly so fast in the heat and with the worry of discovery hanging over them.

I wasn't a bit sleepy at first, and my heart was pounding as I watched the range and tried to be careful not to miss anyone who might ride toward us. The rock where we sat had been absorbing sunlight all day and was hot to the touch. Soon, sweat poured off me, and I drank the canteen nearly dry. Then I began to feel sleepy. Only because of the discipline and self-control Yellow Boy's training had taught me could I endure the tedium and discomfort of being a lookout. I needed all my willpower to keep from dozing off. Being a lookout wasn't fun, but I realized it was necessary if we were to avoid detection and not have to endure someone questioning us with guns to our heads.

I shook Rufus awake in the mid-afternoon. His eyes blinked open instantly, immediately alert. When I shook my head to his inquisitive look, he took the rifle, scratched his scraggly beard, and yawned like a big tomcat just getting up from a nap. He motioned me back into the shade then crept up to the place behind the bush and began surveying the scene. I lay back and swatted at insects that tried to get to the sweat that bathed my face. I yawned once or twice in the soggy, hot air, then fell asleep. I awoke with Rufus gently shaking my foot. The sun was nearly gone. A cool breeze floated down the canyon, giving the evening a pleasant, easy feel.

Getting down from the lookout was harder than getting up because some of the footholds and handholds were far apart and hard to find in the dark shadows filling the canyon. Yellow Boy had made a fire in a shallow pit while it was still light. He'd let the wood burn down to nothing but hot coals so its glow couldn't be seen after dark. He cooked us some fry bread and beans. All that remained of the fire when Rufus and I came in were a few hot coals, but they were enough to make coffee and keep the food hot. After being up on that lookout through the hot part of the day, I thought that meal had to be about the best I'd ever eaten.

Yellow Boy sat with us holding his rifle between his legs while we ate. He said nothing as the sun slowly faded behind the San Andres and long shadows crept silently down the canyon walls. After Rufus and I gobbled down the beans and bread, we gave the tin plates a sand wash and began loading the gear on Elmer and saddling the horses and Sally. When we were ready to travel, Rufus cut himself a chew and sat back to wait for full dark. Yellow Boy rolled a cigarette and lighted it in his cupped hands. The cool air made the heat from the lingering fire coals feel good. We could hear doves calling as they settled in for the night. I lay back, resting my head on my hand, watching down the canyon.

Yellow Boy asked, "Many men between here and sharp mountains today, Rufus?"

Rufus nodded and said, "Yes, sir, seems like right many more than I thought they'd be. They's more stock than I thought they'd be, too. It looks like the range is bein' pushed too far and too hard to support 'em fer long."

"Ummph," Yellow Boy grunted. "Here we are closer to Tally and Stone than at place near Mescalero, but Mescalero place better and safer than here. You think this is true, Rufus?"

Rufus spat into the fire's coals, causing a little puff of steam to rise. "Yes, sir, I reckon that's about right. Do ye know a place we can hide and scout 'round from at Mescalero, *Señor* Yellow Boy?"

I cupped an ear with my free hand to be sure I didn't miss any of their conversation.

"*Sí,* I know place with good *agua* and plenty wood. Tribal police no find us there. Not far from Lincoln. Close to my woman, too, so I sleep warm at night. Good place, Rufus, even if Season of Earth is Reddish Brown find us there."

Rufus spat on the glowing coals again and said, "Close to Lincoln, eh?"

Yellow Boy grinned and nodded. I grinned, too. Had it not been for my training in self-control, I might even have laughed as the image of Rufus hopping into bed with Mrs. Darcy came to mind.

Rufus said, "Well, can ye get us there tonight so we can burrow in and get us some rest? Then tomorrow night, I'll take a little ride into Lincoln and see what I can find out from Miz Darcy. She oughter know the whereabouts of them fellers we're a-lookin' fer."

"*Sí, vamonos* tonight. We there by sunrise if no rain."

I spoke up and said, "Rufus, won't somebody see you in Lincoln and let Stone or Tally know where you are? For all we know, they might even be there now. I thought we wanted to stay outta sight till we found 'em."

"Naw, I ain't gonna be seen crawling through Miz Darcy's bedroom winder in the middle of the night 'cept by Miz Darcy herself. Git my drift, son?" Rufus got up and started kicking sand over the ashes. "Well, come on, then. Let's haul ourselves on over to Mescalero, so's I can rest up fer my ride to Lincoln tomorrow night."

It was full dark when we rode out of the canyon and across the western end of the Jarillas by Monte Carlo Gap in the same formation we'd used the night before. Yellow Boy led us toward the edge of White Sands, but stayed back in the shadows of the bushes, away from the sands gleaming in the moonlight, as the moon came up big and bright over the Sacramentos.

We passed Alamogordo to the west, tracking along the edge of White Sands. Yellow Boy turned northwest after we passed Tularosa to the west. We rode along at a steady pace, but stopped several times to rest the animals in the dark shadow side of big creosote bushes.

Once past Tularosa, Yellow Boy rode up the right branch of Temporal Creek and into Dry Canyon. It was dark and scary down deep in that canyon with the moon casting tricky shadows as it sailed across the night sky. I felt safe enough, knowing Rufus was behind me and Yellow Boy was in front. We followed along a thin, little trail that climbed up out of Dry Canyon. Then the moon began to set, and it was downright scary-looking off the trail back down into the dark pit from where we were climbing. When we topped Dry Canyon, we rode across a gentle slope that paralleled Pete Gaines Canyon and was covered by stands of juniper bushes among the long, fuzzy shadows of tall, scattered pines.

CHAPTER 35
BOW AND ARROWS

When Yellow Boy finally stopped, I could see the first faint glow of dawn. We were above and within a mile of Jose Second Canyon. It was pitch black under those trees, but, looking out across the plateau, I could see that every clearing was filled with juniper bushes or covered with short, deep, green grass that cattlemen often killed for. Yellow Boy led us to a thicket of large junipers in front of a small spring, which dribbled out of a shelf of rocks and collected in a little pool before rolling down into Pete Gaines Canyon. A clear, half-circle-shaped area lay in front of the spring.

Yellow Boy slid off his paint and motioned for us to dismount. He led the paint to the pool and let it drink long, soothing draughts. Rufus came up with the other animals, and we gave them all a good, long drink. In the receding gloom, Yellow Boy swung his arm around and said, "Good place, Rufus?"

"Good? Hell, it's perfect. Suit you, Henry?"

I was cold and tired, and the insides of my thighs were on fire. I doubted if I could ever walk or ride again. If my protectors thought it was good, it was fine with me. "Yes, sir," I said.

"Good. Boys, let's make us a camp, cook a little breakfast, and get some rest. Don't reckin it's necessary fer lookouts in here, is they, Yellow Boy?"

"No lookouts for men. Horses and mules say when bear or cat comes. No worry, fire keeps away."

Fighting off bears and cats was not my idea of a good time,

but I wasn't about to tell Rufus or Yellow Boy I was fearful. After what I'd been through at the hands of men, a bear or a cat was the least of my worries. We unloaded the stock, fed them some grain, and put some hobbles on them so they were free to graze. Rufus set up a little fireplace under a big pine tree a few yards from the spring, so the smoke diffused before it could be seen. Then he made a little lean-to with a tarp next to it so that we could cook, sleep, keep our gear dry, and keep a fire going when it rained. Yellow Boy and I gathered a pile of wood, being careful not to leave any signs for wandering eyes.

Sunlight was finding its way through the junipers and lighting the morning mists in the tall pines when Rufus poured cups of black coffee, and we sat back to eat the last of his beans and tortillas. The air was cool, almost cold, and filled with the scent of pines. It was paradise, and, although I was having trouble keeping my eyes open, I was very glad to be closer to the lair of the men we were after. A little later, while Rufus and I washed up the pots and pans, Yellow Boy checked his weapons then sat and smoked.

Rufus filled a pot with water and opened a big sack of beans from the supplies. He scooped two double handfuls of the beans and tossed them in the pot to soak and grow large before he put them on the fire to cook. He rummaged through the supplies again and dug out the coffee beans, corn meal, dried fruit, potatoes, and bacon to put them where they were easy to find when he was ready to cook. Yellow Boy watched with a smile on his lips and after a while said, "Rufus you make my women look bad with your cooking." Rufus grinned, shook his head, and said, "Yellow Boy, I didn't know you could tell such tall tales. Why if yore first wife, Juanita, heard that she'd whack you with one her sling rocks." Yellow Boy grinned and nodded.

We all stretched out on our blankets to rest, and I fell into the deepest sleep I can remember. Rufus woke me as the sun was starting to slide behind the mountains, casting long shadows from the peaks and hills. Yellow Boy was gone, and Sally was saddled. After I returned from a trip to the bushes, Rufus handed me a cup of coffee and a plate of beans from the bubbling pot hanging over the fire. "Here ye go. Careful now, it's hot. I'm a-gonna light out fer Lincoln now and visit Mrs. Darcy. Yellow Boy's gone down to visit Juanita. Said he 'spects to be back sometime tonight. I got to take the rifle. The only thing ye gotta worry about till Yellow Boy gets back is cats and bears. I scouted around fer an hour and ain't seen no sign, so ye oughter be fine. If'n one shows up, remember that they's afraid of fire. Ye'll be all right, won't ye, Henry?"

He spoke with such concern but with such obvious longing to be gone, I had to laugh. "Sure, Rufus. I'll be fine. Go on and see Mrs. Darcy, and find out what you can. How soon you reckon you'll be back?"

Rufus scratched the back of his head and said, "Aw, I'd guess in a couple or three days. I'll put a bee in her bonnet about what we need to know and then wait a day or two while she sniffs around. Don't worry, though. I'll stay hid."

With that, he swung up onto Sally. I handed him the rifle, and he was off through the juniper bushes and trees down into Pete Gaines Canyon to find the trail to Lincoln.

I spent the rest of the daylight hours scouting around the area, memorizing the locations of hiding spots, paths through the bushes that led into camp, and potential getaways down into the canyons or across the ridge back toward Tularosa. I felt free, somehow released from a burden I'd felt for a long time.

The sun dropped behind Sierra Blanca, and it was soon full dark. I stayed close to the fire. When Yellow Boy appeared in its circle of light, I jumped up in surprise and relief.

He grinned and motioned me down with his hand. Then he

disappeared into the darkness for a few moments and then re-appeared, holding a short bow and a quiver full of arrows.

He said, "I make this for you. It is good weapon. I give it sooner, but Rufus was teaching you to use Shoots Today Kills Tomorrow. Now you learn to use bow. I teach you."

He put the bow and quiver of arrows in my hands. It was a short, recurved bow, no more than about four feet long, the kind used by horsemen. It was made of mulberry wood, carved smooth with the heartwood on the inside, and its back, reinforced with sinew. A leather cord around its handle provided a steady grip, even for a sweaty hand. It was a work of art, and I wanted it as soon as I saw it. Upon trying it, I found I could pull it back to full draw and hold it only for a few seconds before my arms started to fail me.

The arrows, made of cedar, were tipped with sharp iron points and fletched with wild turkey feathers. They were a little longer than my arm, and when Yellow Boy showed me the balance point on one, I saw that all the other arrows balanced in almost exactly the same place on the shaft. The quiver was made of cougar hide because, as Yellow Boy said, "Cougar is great hunter, quiet, always finds game."

I was so thrilled I could only mumble, "*Muchas gracias, Señor* Yellow Boy. *Es muy bueno.* I'll make you proud. I'll shoot a strong bow."

"Ummph, *Hombrecito.* Bow is not your strength. It is arrow. Find good arrow. Shoot straight with any bow, and you kill. Your arrows good. I make them. *Mañana,* you begin."

"*Bueno.* I'll work hard to learn this new weapon, brother," remembering the day he'd told me, "We are one blood." I put the bow and quiver of arrows by my blanket. Yellow Boy pulled a cigar from inside his cavalry jacket and lighted it with a twig. He lay back with his hands behind his head and stared up at the night sky, puffing contentedly.

Early the next morning, when the sun had just floated over the mountaintops and the shadows from the ridges had pulled away from our spot, the bow-shooting lessons began. At fifty yards, Yellow Boy could easily put all twenty of my arrows in a tree a foot in diameter. I was lucky to hit the forest, but he was patient and taught me how to balance the arrow, aim, and follow through. I soon learned the key to accurate shooting was having the concentration to keep my eye on the target and to concentrate on form and follow-through. We quit after a couple of hours when I was getting tight and tired in my back muscles, and the tips of my draw fingers were nearly bloody from the sinew string. As I got sore, my accuracy grew worse.

Later, we sat by the fire and had some coffee and bacon. The air was cool, and birds sang in every bush and tree. Yellow Boy finished his coffee, handed me his cup, and went for his pony. He brushed him down while I cleaned up the frying pan and toted a bucket of water from the spring.

When I returned, he handed me a piece of buckskin that had an odd design laid out on it and said, "Cut leather. Follow lines to make cover for your bow fingers. Your fingers don't understand string and must grow hard. With fingers covered you still learn until fingers know bowstring. Shoot many times today. Get better. I go now. When sun is gone, I return. *Adios.*"

I saluted him as he disappeared through the junipers and down the little trail. I worked on the bow, shooting nearly all day. My target was a big piece of elk hide strung between a couple of saplings. As I learned to focus on the elk hide, shutting out every distraction, the arrows clustered closer and closer to its center. When the light began to fade, I was shooting twenty arrows out of twenty into the elk hide at a range of fifty yards. My shoulders and arms ached, but the leather shooting patch I'd cut from Yellow Boy's pattern saved my fingers.

★ ★ ★ ★ ★

For the next three days, he patiently instructed me in the use of the bow and arrows. As I learned to sink all my arrows into smaller and smaller circles on a target, I began to feel more confident I could survive anywhere. In addition to weapons training, Yellow Boy started me running again. At midday, every day, I ran up a path through the tall trees toward the ridges below Sierra Blanca and back down again. Near the top, the air was thinner, making it hard to breathe, but the air was cool and fresh, the running, exhilarating. Yellow Boy cautioned me to run quietly and be aware of my surroundings because bears were there, and men might be nearby. Five days passed, then six. Still, Rufus had not returned.

CHAPTER 36
RUFUS RETURNS

I thought maybe Stone or Tally had murdered Rufus as they had Daddy. Maybe Sally had stumbled and thrown him or rolled over on him, breaking bones or killing him. Maybe he'd been snakebit, or a cat or a bear had killed and dragged him off. When I broached these ideas to Yellow Boy, he just shook his head and said, "No, Rufus *es bueno.* He come back soon." Even as he spoke, I saw the slightest frown of doubt on his face. I could tell he was trying to decide what to do about finding him.

On the night of the eighth day, I lay down to sleep in a black despair, certain Stone or Tally had killed Rufus and were trying to find me. That meant I'd have two murders to avenge. I twisted around in my blanket, unable to sleep, trying to figure out what to do next. The coals from the fire and a quarter moon were the only light.

After a while, I started to doze off, and then I felt Yellow Boy squeeze my arm. He put fingers to his lips and sat up on his blanket, cupping a hand to his ear. I strained to hear anything for a couple of minutes, and then I heard the steady breathing and push of bushes as some animal moved toward us. My heart started pounding, and I heard Yellow Boy cock the Henry.

I moved up on my knees, pulled my knife, and waited. Yellow Boy was on one knee, in a crouch, with his rifle sighted toward the marauder. The sounds drew closer and stopped. Whatever it was, it was sizing us up.

An irritated voice floated on the cold air saying, "Now where in the hell did I leave that boy?" I can't explain how overjoyed and relieved I was.

Yellow Boy said, "*Aqui,* Rufus."

"Don't kill me, boys. I'm a-comin' in."

Yellow Boy nodded at me, and I started adding wood to the coals and blowing hard on them to get a flame. In the time it took for the firelight to grow, Sally's long mule face moved into the light, and there sat Rufus, big as you please, with his rifle across the pommel of his saddle.

"Howdy, ladies. Did ye miss me?" He tossed me the rifle and swung down from Sally. I saw Yellow Boy give a quick nod and move toward the fire. I ran up to hug Rufus, but he stuck out his old, gnarled hand, and we just shook hands like grown men. At that point, I realized he wasn't about to let me act like a little boy anymore.

"Where were you?" I asked. "We were . . . I was scared Stone or Tally and their crowd had caught you and made you disappear."

Rufus waved his hand toward the ground and said, "Nope. Ever'thang's fine. Fact is, it couldn't be better. Unsaddle Sally and brush her down fer a tired, old man, will ye? I'll have a little coffee, and then I'll tell y'all about my little trip. We's gonna have to move fast to take ker of business."

Then he glanced down at my sleeping blankets and said, "Great day in the morning, Henry. Where'd you get the bow? That there would make any Apache proud. You know how to use it?" He looked over at Yellow Boy and winked.

"I sure do," I said. "Yellow Boy made it for me, and the arrows, too. He's been teaching me to use it."

"Well, that's a mighty good thang to learn."

Rufus wearily sat down by the fire as I led Sally up to the spring pool for a drink.

It wasn't long before we were all sitting around the fire having coffee. Rufus had pulled off his old miner's boots and was wiggling his toes next to the flames to get the blood circulating. He pulled out a briar pipe and a tobacco pouch I hadn't seen before and filled its bowl while Yellow Boy and I waited to hear his story.

"This here pipe and fine tobac was a present from Miz Darcy. Some drummer left 'em at her place, and since she didn't have any idee where to send 'em, she just give 'em to me. Said she'd rather kiss me if I smoked than if I chewed. Still got my chewin' tobac fer working, though."

I liked the smell of his pipe filling the night air. Rufus said, "Well, boys, I woke Miz Darcy up around midnight on the day I left, scratchin' on her winder screen. Guess I's lucky she didn't plug me when she stuck her dead husband's big dragoon pistol under my nose and nearly dropped it when she saw who I was. Well, sir, she let me crawl in and visit with her."

"You have good visit?" Yellow Boy asked, a knowing smile barely on his lips.

Rufus grinned and nodded, raked a hand through his hair, and continued, "I told her I needed to know the whereabouts of Bentene, Stone, and Tally and that I didn't want 'em to know I was a-lookin' fer 'em. She told me, the last she'd heard, Tally was a whorin' and raisin' hell in El Paso. She was shore somebody had mentioned Stone was down to Fort Bliss with Cox trying to haggle a new beef contract. He's supposed to catch the train up from El Paso to Alamogordo and meet the ranchers he's a-representin' fer the contract four days from now."

My heart started beating faster at this news. *Just four days, and I can have another shot at Stone.* "Will Bentene be with him?" I asked.

Rufus took the pipe out of his mouth and tapped its ashes in his palm before throwing them to sparkle in the fire. "Prob'ly so. Ol' Bentene come into town, got juiced up, and took a little target practice on the post office sign and the winders of a saloon. Got throwed in jail. When the deputy finally turned him loose, he told him he'd better not catch him in Lincoln when the sun was down or he'd put him in irons, trot him down to Las Cruces, and let him deal with the sheriff."

Rufus dug more tobacco out of his pouch with his pipe. He casually asked, "Wanna hear the good news?"

Yellow Boy and I leaned toward Rufus. I could see the glint in Yellow Boy's dark eyes that spoke of the joy of the hunt. I was feeling it, too.

"Ol' Bentene said he was right sorry fer shootin' up the place and said he'd just camp outside town with his men and come in sober durin' the day until he was ready to ride down to Alamogordo. Deputy said that was fine. Guess where ol' Bentene's a-sleepin', right now, this minute?"

I didn't have any idea and shook my head. Yellow Boy just looked at Rufus and waited for him to tell us.

Rufus looked at me and asked, "Remember that there little canyon outside of Lincoln where we went a-target shootin' one Sunday with yore daddy? The Bonito River runs by it."

I nodded, and he said, "Well, he's right there. I've been a-watchin' him fer the last three days. Most of his boys sleep in Lincoln blowin' their pay on whiskey, cards, and whores. But ol' Bentene, he sleeps on the sand by their fire and gits outta his blankets well after the sun comes up, and then goes to Lincoln to eat and maybe visit a whore or play cards mosta the day. 'Fore dark, he'll buy another bottle and ride back to camp with his cowhands that's too broke to buy a whore fer the evenin'. He studies some kind of map while he drinks, until he passes out. His men git up way 'fore he does and ride off to town.

Yesterday, one of 'em told Miz Darcy they's all supposed to leave fer Alamogordo around midday tomorrow and then meet up with Stone and Cox in a few days when their train comes in."

When he said that, I gasped. Suddenly, I was practically shaking with excitement. I said, "That means we have to leave right now if we expect to get him before—"

"You know what else?" Rufus said, interrupting me. "He's got Lil' David in his camp gear. Yes, sir. I seen it!" Rufus was practically shouting with excitement when he told us this. "Ye're right, Henry. I think we oughta go over there tonight, git my rifle back in the mornin', and settle accounts fer yore daddy. Ain't gonna be no better time."

Yellow Boy, his mouth set in a straight line and eyes narrowed to fine slits, was up and moving toward the stock. He called over his shoulder, "I get my pony. We ride now, find Bentene while still dark."

CHAPTER 37
RETURN OF LITTLE DAVID

I saddled Midnight and Elmer because Rufus needed a fresh mount if we were to get to Bentene before sunrise. We moved down the trail into Pete Gaines Canyon a quarter of an hour later with Yellow Boy leading the way because he knew a faster, but rougher, trail than the one Rufus had taken to Lincoln. We stayed close together and rode as fast as we dared on the dark trail. I was glad I was on Midnight because she was sure-footed and seemed to anticipate every move Yellow Boy's pony made as we crossed running creeks, moved over rocky ridges, and picked our way down steep passes.

As we rode along, I thought about what we'd do when we found Bentene. Somehow, it seemed a shame to kill him in his sleep. *Shouldn't we make him suffer for what he'd done?* I thought maybe we could sneak into his camp while he was sleeping and get the Sharps back. Then Yellow Boy could hold his gun on Bentene and have Rufus bust him across his face with the butt of the Sharps a couple of times before he shot him in the gut and left him to die a slow death. It seemed only fair to let Rufus kill him after Bentene had pistol-whipped him.

In another scenario, I imagined walking up to him while Rufus and Yellow Boy hid in the brush, covering me. Bentene would have this surprised snarl on his lips when I told him who I was, then, too late, he'd reach for his revolver, as Yellow Boy shot him before he could get it out of his holster. I'd take his gun, and while he lay dying, I'd make a speech about how he was paying the price for killing Daddy and how we were going to get Stone and Tally, too.

The stars were disappearing into the night sky, and it was the deep black just before dawn when Yellow Boy dismounted on a high ridge next to a spring and motioned for us to do the same. He signaled for us to be quiet. We fed and watered our stock, tied them for a quick getaway, and then carefully worked our way down to the bottom of the valley below us.

When we were very near Bentene's camp, Yellow Boy squatted by some juniper bushes and pointed toward a dark mass of trees to our right. I heard Rufus say under his breath, "I'll be damned."

There was a rutted road not fifty feet in front of us, and the mass of trees were not more than two hundred yards beyond and below it. As we squatted there, I realized we were directly across from the little canyon where Rufus, Daddy, and I had been shooting on that Sunday so long ago.

I heard some faint noises down in the trees, like horses or cattle moving around, and then the faint tinkle of steel cinch rings knocking together and leather being slapped. The low, red glow from a small fire began to grow down in the trees, and I heard occasional grunts and curses as more of Bentene's men began to stir, followed by distinctive clicks as Yellow Boy and Rufus half-cocked their rifles to safety. My heart began to pound.

The sky was just getting gray when a cowboy rode up out of the trees and onto the road, his horse kicking up little puffs of dust as he cantered toward Lincoln. Two others soon caught up with him. We waited another half hour as the day became steadily brighter, but there were no more sounds from across the road.

Yellow Boy rose in a half crouch and motioned for Rufus and

me to follow. He was hard to see in the weak light as he moved from juniper to juniper, then across the road. Birds began to call from the bushes, as it got lighter.

When we were across the road and well into the trees, it was easy to see a bright, flickering glow from the fire, but we heard nothing. Creeping closer, a hundred yards, seventy-five, fifty, Yellow Boy finally stopped, kneeled on one knee in a clump of grass, and motioned us to stop. Rufus was about five yards to his left, and I was just to the left of Rufus. A nice fire was burning under a big cottonwood tree, and there was a black coffeepot sitting on a couple of flat rocks. All the bedrolls around the fire, except Bentene's, were empty. Bentene's horse was tied to a picket rope. A few minutes passed, and I saw the blanket from Bentene's bedroll fly up, and he stood upright. He stretched, yawned, and scratched himself.

It was hard to get my breath. Then I remembered what Rufus had told me about being cold and calculating, and I tried to force myself to be that way. I realized we hadn't discussed a plan, so I assumed Rufus or Yellow Boy had one.

Bentene reached down for his hat, turned away from the fire, and staggered a couple of steps before he hiked a leg and let a tremendous fart, followed by a giggle. Then he wandered into the shadows, and soon we heard water splashing on the rocks.

I heard Yellow Boy bring the Henry to full cock, but in that dim light, I never saw him move, never even saw his chest rise or fall, as he stared toward Bentene like a wolf waiting to pounce on a rabbit. Rufus was a statue, too.

Soon Bentene reappeared back in the firelight. He picked up his blanket, threw it over his shoulders, and moved up against the big cottonwood. Easing himself down against it and stretching his legs out, he yawned again. He pulled the blanket over his shoulders, then pulled his hat down over his eyes to block out light after the sun was up. He didn't move for a couple of minutes. Then I heard a little snore.

I was ready to move closer and looked toward Yellow Boy for some sign to creep forward. He didn't move but continued to stare at Bentene. The Henry came up in one smooth motion. I could see the reflection of the fire in the brass receiver. Yellow Boy sighted down the barrel for an instant before pulling the trigger. The bright flash from the end of the barrel momentarily blinded me, and its thunder echoed up and down the little canyon, making my ears ring.

Yellow Boy was up and running toward the fire through the smoke of his shot, levering a new round into the chamber. Keeping the stock against his shoulder, he visually swept the area around the fire for anyone we had missed as he ran.

Rufus paused for half a heartbeat, staring toward the camp for any movement. Then, he, too, was running toward the fire, crouched over his rifle and ready to shoot if anything moved.

I was frozen in place. It was like a dream. I could see every move they made in slow motion. The ringing in my ears disappeared, and I realized I was being left behind as Yellow Boy and Rufus ran toward the fire. Then I started running, too. Yellow Boy jumped the fire and stood waiting with his rifle still shouldered as he stared at Bentene, not six feet from him. In a few moments, the Henry came off his shoulder.

Rufus said in a hot whisper, "Help me find Lil' David, and then let's git 'fore anybody else shows."

Yellow Boy nodded and started poking around the bedrolls with the barrel of the Henry. I ran up, breathing hard, and stopped to stare at Bentene. He looked as though he was still sleeping except there was a greasy-looking, perfectly round hole in the hat's headband where it crossed the bridge of his nose. I could see the firelight reflecting off dark liquid running down the bark of the tree, and there was a strong smell of fresh feces. I suddenly felt sick and wanted to vomit. Rufus walked up beside me and put his hand on my shoulder. "That there is justice. Take a good look at it. Just the way it oughta be, swift and clean. No jawin' about nothin'. Only thing wrong with this is that the son of a bitch never felt a damn thing, didn't suffer like yore daddy did." Rufus turned and spat in the fire. "Damned son of a bitch. I hope he's a-burnin' in hell right now."

I swallowed several times to keep from vomiting and asked, "Rufus, what's that smell?"

"Man dies like that, his bowels usually turn loose and they's blood and brains blowed against the bark of that cottonwood."

I shook my head and said, "No, Rufus. I mean that other smell sort of like rotten meat."

Rufus took his hat off, wiped his forehead with his handkerchief, sighed and said, "That there is the smell of death. Most men never notice it above the rest."

Just as we turned to look for Little David, Yellow Boy said, "Here, Shoots Today Kills Tomorrow." He held up a beautifully finished saddle scabbard, pulled the Sharps halfway out of it, and handed it to Rufus.

Rufus grinned with delight and said, "I shore am glad to have ye back, Lil' David." He pulled the rifle out of the scabbard and admired it as some men admire a beautiful woman. Then he shoved the Sharps deep into the scabbard and said, "Now, let's git."

Yellow Boy motioned us back up the ridge. "You and *Hombrecito* go now. I wipe out tracks. We ride *pronto*."

Rufus and I ran crouched over so we'd be harder to see in the morning light. Yellow Boy took some twigs from the firewood and lightly brushed away our tracks as he backed up, moving toward the road.

Rufus and I tried to step on big rocks as we moved up the ridge toward the trees where we'd tied the horses and mules.

Yellow Boy took his time and did a thorough job on our tracks. No tracker would be aware we were there unless they found where we had tied our animals, and that wasn't likely. We were saddled and heading down the back side of the ridge as the sun rose over the mountains and the shadows began falling away from the canyon walls.

CHAPTER 38
A DEATH WITHOUT HONOR

We were back in our camp on the ridges of the Sierra Blanca by early afternoon. I was so tired and emotionally drained I was ready to fall off Midnight. Yellow Boy and Rufus didn't move too fast, either. We took care of the stock and ate, and then Yellow Boy and Rufus had a smoke, but I lay down and fell into a deep sleep. I dreamed about Daddy's murder again and saw Bentene sitting nearby, watching him die. I wanted to yell obscenities at him, then the dream turned, and I was standing in front of Bentene after Yellow Boy had shot him. Suddenly, he reached up, lifted his hat, and opened his eyes. He'd sprouted a new eyeball in the bullet hole.

I must have yelled or moaned because Rufus shook me until I awakened, startled and thirsty.

"You have a bad dream, Henry?" he asked.

"Yes, sir," I said, and I told them about my dream.

Rufus wiggled his nose to pull his glasses up. "Well, you ain't got to worry about Bentene no more. We took care of that son of a bitch this mornin'."

It was dark, and the stars were out. I went to the bushes to relieve myself, got a drink from the spring, and walked back to the fire, where Rufus and Yellow Boy were talking about how to get to Stone and Tally. When I sat down, I turned to Yellow Boy. "Can I ask you a question?"

He was stretched out, looking up at the stars, and contentedly puffing a cigar. "Hmmm. *Que es, Hombrecito?* I will answer."

"I'm glad Bentene is dead, but why did you just shoot him between the eyes? He never knew who killed him, and he didn't suffer or have time to think about what he'd done. Shouldn't we have told him? Shouldn't he have suffered? Was there any honor in killing him that way?"

Yellow Boy said nothing for a while. He just puffed on that cigar and watched the stars. Finally he said, "You ask many questions, *Hombrecito*. *Si*, Bentene died quick. He didn't know who kills him or why. Bentene was weak. He no die like a warrior. I no give him honor of good death, so he no suffer." He held up his palm and showed the scar left by the knife and said, "You are my blood. Do you believe this?"

I held up my hand to show my scar and nodded. "Yes, sir, I'm your blood. I believe it."

"Though still boy, you man in heart, warrior in heart. Still much to learn before killing men who murdered *su padre*. I take your part. I kill. I help you kill. This I must do. It is the way of my people. Men who take life from my family must die. This I do as your blood. *Comprende?*"

I nodded. I'd never thought of dying slowly as an honor. If it was, then Bentene died as he should have, without honor, alive one second and dead the next.

Yellow Boy touched my arm and said, "To speak with man before he dies gives *nada* (nothing). Bentene bothers you *no mas*. He kills men in desert *no mas*. He drinks burning water *no mas*. He lays with women *no mas*. It is enough *por* Bentene. It is what he deserved. I speak no more of this dead man. *Comprende?*"

I gave a quick nod and looked over to Rufus, who put two fingers to his lips and moved them away in a wave as he said, "Yellow Boy speaks true."

"What will we do about Stone and Tally?" I asked.

Rufus said, "Here's the plan: Tomorrow we'll ride across the reservation, using a trail 'round by Cloudcroft and over to the Eyebrow Trail that leads down into Dog Canyon. Dog Canyon's where ol' Frenchy Rochas used to live till he was murdered back in the winter of 'ninety-five. Ain't nobody much been back in there since."

I'd heard Rufus speak of the place in his stories and knew the Apaches used to sucker their enemies into chasing them up the Eyebrow, then roll rocks down on them to knock them off the trail down into a two-thousand-foot drop.

Rufus said, "I reckin that there trail climbs nearly a mile. They's real good water in there and plenty of places to set up a ambush with good close lines of fire."

I shifted my weight on the blanket I was sitting on and asked, "Do you reckon Stone knows Bentene's been shot yet?"

"Yep, and I reckon he's a-startin' to sweat a little, what with the long-range bullet Yellow Boy put through his hat and all. It coulda been anybody killed Bentene. Stone probably thinks we lit out fer Mexico 'cause we was gone when he come to git us, so he'll think it ain't us he's got to be worried about."

I smiled and said, "That gives us an advantage, then."

Rufus spat into the fire and said, "It might, but I want him to know who's after him. I figger he may come down to Alamo- gordo a day early to sniff around and try to find out who mighta killed Bentene. Or maybe he jest don't give a damn and will come on the day he planned."

I scratched my head, unable to follow Rufus, since we'd taken some trouble to make Stone think we'd gone to Mexico. "Why do you want him to know we're after him?"

"Just 'cause it'll make him madder'n hell. That's sure to cloud his judgment." Rufus leaned closer to me and said, "When he steps off that train in Alamogordo, we're a-gonna make sure he sees us. We'll just ride along the road outta town like we don't have a care in the world. He'll send somebody to follow us and find out where we're a-campin', and then he and Tally will come after us."

Suddenly, I saw what Rufus had in mind. I said, "We'll ride back to Dog Canyon and set up a little surprise party for 'em."

Rufus laughed and clapped me on the back. "That's right, and if we can't kill 'em and they have help come, then we'll ride up the Eyebrow and hope they foller. If they do, we'll take care of 'em just like the Mescaleros used to wipe out people that chased 'em."

At first, I liked the plan, but then I frowned and asked, "What if they don't fall for it?"

"If they don't foller, then we'll just have to wait to catch 'em again. It might be a long wait, too, Henry. I 'spect we'll have to hide out with Yellow Boy's people down to Mexico fer a while in that case."

Yellow Boy, who had been smoking and staring off at the sky as if he wasn't even paying attention, said, "I cover you from off road when we ride back to Dog Canyon from Alamogordo. I won't let them kill you before we set trap."

By now, the excitement of the whole plan had set my heart to beating faster. I hoped Yellow Boy wouldn't have to shoot them that way because it would spoil my chance to personally set things right for Daddy. I looked over at Rufus, who was stroking his beard, apparently in deep thought.

After a moment, Rufus said, "Course if they make it to Frenchy's shack when we bushwhack 'em, it could be a long standoff, but I think it's a risk worth takin'. Whadaya think, Henry?"

I sat there for a moment trying to see how the whole setup would work, and then said, "Rufus, will you give me another chance to take Stone and Tally?"

"Yes, sir. I believe ye'll drop Stone this time, but they's no shore thing when it comes to killin'. We might be the ones gits kilt."

I clenched my fist and I said, "I don't care. Just so I get another chance at Stone and Tally."

Rufus touched my shoulder and said, "Good. Looks like ye're 'bout three or four days from gettin' some justice fer yore daddy."

"I'm counting on it."

Next morning, after eating and cleanup chores, Rufus tossed me the scabbard with Lil' David. "How 'bout cleaning him up, Henry?"

I checked it over, thrilled to simply hold this long-lost treasure again. The saddle scabbard Bentene had put it in had pockets on the side for cartridges and cleaning gear. I sighted down the barrel and dry fired it a couple of times, dropping the breech each time. Giving it back to Rufus, I said, "I don't think they ever fired it. It's clean, and the trigger pull is still the same."

"Hmmph," he grunted. "Well, Henry, this here seventy-three Winchester works just fine fer me. Why don't ye take Lil' David and use it on this here hunt, unless I need to swap with ye?"

Rufus laughed at the expression on my face. I'm sure it was one of surprise and pure joy. "Yes, sir," I said with a big smile. I put it with the things Rufus wanted me to carry on Midnight.

"Where's Yellow Boy?" I asked.

"Aw, he rode down to Mescalero to visit his wife fer a while. He'll be back later today 'fore we're ready to go. Here, come help me slice up this haunch of venison and get these here supplies ready to go."

We worked through the morning and had everything set to travel by mid-afternoon. When Rufus gave me two hundred rounds to carry for Lil' David, I said, "Rufus, that's a lot. We're not going to war."

He looked back at me with just a crack of a smile and said, "Oh, yes, we are. Here, maybe ye'd better take another hundred rounds now that I think about it." I took the extra cartridges, never believing we'd use anywhere near that many.

Yellow Boy appeared just as we finished eating an early supper. Rufus offered him some meat and beans, but he said, "*Mi mujer,* she feeds her man. We travel now?"

Rufus nodded. "Just as soon as we get this here pot washed and the animals saddled and loaded."

Yellow Boy shrugged his shoulders. "Hmmph. I smoke by fire and wait."

In half an hour, we were moving down the trail. We had about three hours of daylight left, and Yellow Boy set us a good pace over the ridges and canyons. After swinging around the little village of Cloudcroft, he followed a thin trail through tall pines along the western edge of the Sacramentos. We rode until he stopped at a place where the trail appeared to drop off into a steep, black hole.

Yellow Boy spoke softly to Rufus and me. "Here trail into Dog Canyon. Rest horses and mules now till daylight. Then we go." He pulled his pony off the trail a few yards and unsaddled, hobbled it to graze, and then sat down with his back against a tree. Rufus and I unloaded the horses and mules and made ourselves comfortable near Yellow Boy. I was too excited to sleep, so I took the first watch. By the time I shook Rufus awake, I was ready to sleep.

CHAPTER 39
THE EYEBROW

I woke to the singing of thousands of birds down in the canyon, as sunlight cast dusty beams through the shadows of the trees. Rufus and Yellow Boy were already up, saddling the animals and putting the supplies on Elmer's rig. Throwing off my blanket, I walked over to the opening in the trees a few yards away to relieve myself.

The opening was at a cliff's edge that just seemed to roll off into space, and the view of the other side, the basin flats, the far Organs, and White Sands took my breath. The Organs must have been fifty miles away. They were clear as a close-up photograph. The view across to the south-side cliffs made my heart stop. They looked like towering vertical walls made from pillars of stone stacked together without a toehold of any kind for man or beast. The treetops at the bottom of the canyon looked the size of pinheads.

The cliffs on the south side had rust reds, soft pinks, an occasional dark green splotch from bushes that managed toeholds in the stone faces, and there were soft brown beiges and dark, almost-purple colors in some places. They were spectacularly beautiful. Their sheer height and vertical reach . . . I just couldn't believe there was any kind of trail down those walls. I turned back, the sound of my heart pounding in my ears. I wasn't afraid of heights, but the Eyebrow around those walls was too much. What was Yellow Boy expecting us to do? Go down those walls on a rope?

Rufus laughed when he saw me. "Henry, did ye see a ghost? Ye're as pale as milk. What's the matter?"

I swallowed to keep the contents of my stomach down and asked, "Rufus have you been down the Eyebrow before? I don't see how we can ride or even climb down those walls yonder."

Rufus nodded toward them. "Yes, sir, I been up and down 'em a time or two, and I was a-prayin' they warn't no Apaches waitin' to pitch rocks on me and send me to the grandfathers via a quick trip to the bottom. Reckin I was just lucky those times. Ain't no need to be fearful now, though."

"Has Yellow Boy been down it?" I asked.

Rufus spat a brown stream toward the edge and nodded. "Yellow Boy's rode up and down that there trail many a time. It ain't a bad trail 'cept in the part that's called the Eyebrow. The trick is when we start down the trail, just sit back, relax, and let yore pony find her way. She's shore-footed. Ye'll be fine. Don't know nothin' about how Elmer'll do on a narrow windin' trail, but I think he's got the right temperament fer it, and he'll follow Sally near anywhere. Ye ride down 'tween Yellow Boy and me, jest as usual."

All I could do was nod and swallow again. Yellow Boy and Rufus checked the cinches on the horses and Sally and the pack rig on Elmer twice. Then we mounted and followed Yellow Boy down and around the steep, convex curves off the top ridge.

The trail we followed started in the north corner of the canyon and tracked down the southern back wall. It wasn't as bad as I thought it would be, at least not until we got about halfway down the southern wall and hit a narrow squeeze between the cliff and a long drop down. This was what they called the Eyebrow. I could see why. It hung on that vertical cliff like the eyebrow on a giant. This was where the Apaches used to lure their pursuers before pushing boulders and stones down on them.

I still remember feeling the cool morning air floating up around me from below, the calls of birds in the lush trees down in the bottom, and above us, nothing but a great empty hole with blue sky. As Rufus had instructed, I just let Midnight pick her way along, and we eased past that scary, narrow stretch. Elmer jogged along as if he had lived on that trail all his life, and, for all we knew, he might have already been up and down the Eyebrow a few times.

Below it, the trail widened out, and the descent, while steep, was much easier. At the southwestern corner of the canyon, the trail made a sharp right turn and began tracking down the southern face cliffs.

It took us most of the early morning to work our way down. As the trail incline became less and the trail widened, we crossed several small streams. Near the bottom of the canyon, Rufus pointed to the remains of a rock wall and said, "Frenchy Rochas built that 'bout ten or fifteen year ago."

As we neared the mouth of the canyon, we saw Frenchy's small, stone house. Rufus said, "It's only got one or two rooms, but it's strong as a fort. It's the reason I decided I'd build one, too. 'Spect it'll last a while, that one will."

Yellow Boy stopped and surveyed the scene, looking toward one spot, then another, as if weighing the value of each. In a few minutes, he turned back up the trail we had just traveled and led us unerringly to a small spring hidden by a thicket of bushes next to the northern wall. It was within a quarter mile of Frenchy's cabin.

The canyon there was passable on a mount for no more than two or three hundred yards before the walls became so steep a rider had to get off and walk. A good stream of cool water ran right down the middle.

Turning to Rufus and me, Yellow Boy said, "Safe here. *Agua es bueno.* We see all range toward south and riders when they come. Rest animals now, then ride to Alamogordo."

Rufus and I unloaded, fed, watered, and rubbed down the animals. Then we all lay back and rested. I stared at the cliffs and found it hard to believe I had ridden down them. We were not far from the mouth of the canyon. Looking south, we were still high enough to have good view back toward the Organs and White Sands, and we could see little black groups of cattle scattered here and there over the range.

Rufus pointed toward some buildings three or four miles away and asked, "Know what those buildin's are, Henry?"

They were obviously part of a ranch, but whose ranch I had no idea, so I just shrugged my shoulders.

"Well, sir, that there ranch is owned by Oliver Lee."

He had my attention then, and I studied the ranch house and outbuildings closely. How ironic that we were planning to kill the men he'd had murder my father within sight of his own ranch house. I hoped when he heard what we'd done, he'd know I was coming for him.

As we rested, Rufus and Yellow Boy looked over the canyon and picked out spots that formed a triangle from which to set up a cross fire in the canyon, two places on either side of the canyon and a point farther up the canyon, all well protected by brush and boulders.

Our strategy was to get Stone, Tally, and their riders to come up the canyon several hundred yards past Frenchy's house. Then the shooters on either side would lay into them, while the shooter up farther would keep them from escaping that way.

The major weakness of this plan was that it would be mighty hard to get them out, if they retreated and reached Frenchy's house. We debated about whether one of us should get in the house, but then we decided that if any escaped, they would ride past it to try and get away. If the house was open, at least they'd run for cover there and we'd have them. We chewed on that for a while and decided it was worth the risk to leave Frenchy's place open.

CHAPTER 40
FISHING IN ALAMOGORDO

After sleeping for a couple of hours, we saddled the horses and Sally and rode through the brush across the hot flats toward Alamogordo. Once we found the dusty road running to Alamogordo from the San Agustin Pass, we made good time. Yellow Boy hung off several hundred yards to one side of us and out of sight, in case we needed him. Within a half mile of Alamogordo, he pointed toward a thicket of mesquite where he'd wait to escort us back to Dog Canyon.

Rufus and I planned to ride into Alamogordo, visit some stores to get a few supplies, ride up and down the streets, and generally make sure anyone from Stone's outfit knew we were there. If we were lucky, they'd follow us back to Dog Canyon. Then all we'd have to do was wait for Stone and Tally to arrive.

Since I hadn't been in a town for over six years, the place seemed very busy and filled with people. Rufus told me Alamogordo was a railroad town built in 1898. There were businessmen, who were providing ranchers and miners supplies; and ranchers and cowboys, who were in town for a little entertainment, or to buy, sell, or ship cattle and horses. Mexicans and a few Chinese laborers, who worked for local merchants, hurried up and down the streets or sweated in hard labor around the rail station. There were hundreds of horses, either in corrals or tied to anything that wouldn't move. Fancy women walked up and down the streets under colorful parasols. All of the saloons and whorehouses stood over in what was called Block 50.

I saw cottonwood saplings planted everywhere, and I couldn't remember ever seeing so many small trees in one spot before. A train filled with passengers and cattle was just starting to roll toward El Paso and gave a long farewell whistle as it chugged passed us. Rufus laughed in good humor as he watched me take it all in.

We rode up and down several streets in Block 50, but we saw no one we recognized. Finally Rufus said, "Henry, what's say we tie up to that store over there and get me some chewin' to-bac? We'll find you a cold sarsaparilla, and then we'll sit in them chairs in the front of the store fer a while and see who we can see." I nodded, still speechless at all I was seeing.

Rufus motioned me to sit in a chair while he went inside. I could hear him talking and laughing with the man at the counter, as if he had known him for a long time. Then I noticed a cowboy leaning against a post under a big red sign for a gun and ranch supply store and staring hard at our side of the street. I had an uneasy feeling I recognized him, but I had no idea where I'd seen him before. I watched the riders and buggies moving up and down the street. Each time I took my eyes off them and looked back, the cowboy was still staring.

Rufus came out and handed me a cool bottle of sarsaparilla. Before I took a swallow, I pointed with my chin and said, "That fellow has been staring at me ever since you went inside."

Rufus nodded and said, "Yeah, I kinda 'spected he would. When we rode by, I seen him watching us. I'm purdy shore that there is one of the fellers that was with Stone the first night he come up to the shack and stole Lil' David. Finish that sarsaparilla, son, then we'll mount up and see if we got us a fish a-trailin' our bait."

The sarsaparilla was a real treat. I hadn't had anything cool and sweet like that since the night Daddy and I had visited Doc

Blazer. I took my time drinking it, and then we mounted up. The cowboy under the red sign still hadn't moved. Rufus swung down the street toward him, and I followed. We just ambled along down the middle of the street looking in storefront windows. When we reached the cowboy, Rufus paused and stared for a few seconds. Then Rufus's eyes got large, his jaw dropped, and he quickly turned his head and set Sally at a trot down the street. I had to kick Midnight to keep up with him. It was the finest acting job I'd ever seen. I shot a quick look back and saw the cowboy climbing into the saddle on a dun-colored mustang.

I caught up with Rufus well outside of town, as the cowboy followed us at distance. Rufus looked over his shoulder, grinned, and said, "Looks like we found us a fish. Yes, sir, fishing here in the desert is fun, ain't it?"

CHAPTER 41
CHALLENGE

Yellow Boy confirmed that the cowboy who followed us out of Alamogordo had come all the way to the mouth of Dog Canyon then turned back toward Alamogordo, riding at a pretty good gallop. We figured Stone's cowboys might be back that night. That didn't happen, but we were ready and watched in shifts all night under a big moon that would let us see them coming from a couple of miles away.

When dawn came, Rufus cooked us a little something to eat in his Dutch oven before he and Yellow Boy jawed for a while. They decided Stone still must be coming in on the ten-o'clock train from El Paso. Rufus wanted to be sure Stone and Tally came after us while we had the advantage in Dog Canyon, so we saddled up again and trotted off toward Alamogordo. Yellow Boy hid in the same big mesquite thicket outside of town to cover us when we rode back. It was close to train time when we got there, and a small group of ranchers waited on the passenger platform when we rode by. Rufus had tied Little David in the expensive saddle scabbard so it was easy to see on his saddle from Sally's right side.

We rode a couple of blocks up the street past the train station, then stopped and dismounted and led Sally and Midnight into an alley to wait for the train's arrival. Rufus said, "Now, when that train comes, we're a-gonna ride back down the street slow and easy, like we're ridin' to church. I'm gonna be on the side closest to the tracks 'cause I want Stone to see us. I want him to see Lil' David tied to my saddle. He's gonna believe right off I's the one that put a hole through Bentene, and he's gonna know I ain't hidin' out in Mexico a-peein' in my pants 'cause I'm 'fraid of him, neither. I'm hopin' he gits madder'n a cornered rattler when he sees us ridin' down the street big as you please. That way, he won't waste no time in comin' after us. If'n that happens, we got him." Rufus clenched his fist and shook it as if he had Stone by the collar.

We waited about half an hour before we heard the train's whistle moaning from the tracks back toward El Paso. Then we mounted and eased partway out of the alley so we could see down the street toward the train station. Soon the engine with a couple of passenger cars and several freight cars rumbled past the station and stopped with the passenger cars beside the platform. Rufus and I slowly rode out of the alley and down the street toward the station.

We saw several women and children, followed by Stone, Red Tally, and a couple of well-dressed men in derby hats, stepping down from the train just as we started moseying along. The small group of ranchers and cowboys that had waited on the platform walked over and surrounded Stone and Tally. They were shaking hands, slapping backs, and laughing at jokes. I saw Tally's eyes catch sight of Rufus and me and begin tracking us like a hawk watching a rat scramble for cover. Rufus stared right back at him. Tally gently put his hand on Stone's shoulder and wrinkled his brow toward the street to turn his attention toward us. Stone paused in the middle of a big belly laugh, his eyes narrowing to slits when he saw Rufus and me sauntering down the street. Rufus looked toward him, nodded with a grin, and spat a big, brown stream of tobacco juice toward the train as we continued our leisurely trip out of town.

When we were out of sight, Rufus said, "Won't be long now,

boy. Let's git!" We rode at a fast jog back to Dog Canyon. When I looked over my shoulder from time to time, I saw no one following us, and that was a relief, even with Yellow Boy off to one side covering us. We unsaddled Sally and Midnight at our little camp behind the thicket, then tied them to bushes next to water and grass about three hundred yards up the canyon from Frenchy's house. We took care to make sure they weren't easy to see but still visible. Farther up the canyon, Rufus built a small fire that put out just enough smoke to smell and for someone to see if they were riding up the canyon looking for camp signs.

CHAPTER 42
AMBUSH

From the canyon entrance, Yellow Boy kept watch for riders while Rufus and I set our trap. It was well into mid-afternoon when he rode up the canyon and said, "*Cinco hombres,* they come. They are here when shadows reach tree." He pointed toward a scraggly apple tree that had probably been planted by Frenchy Rochas years before.

Rufus nodded and said, "We got 'bout an hour, Henry. Onct ye're in place, keep the barrel of Lil' David back in the leaves so some eagle eye in the bunch don't spot it. Ye take the first shot, and try fer Stone. I'll try to git Tally. Yellow Boy, drop the others then shoot fer Tally, too. We gotta get him fer shore. If'n they turn back and run, shoot the horses. That'll make 'em run for Frenchy's cabin. They ain't gonna git outta here alive without no horse." He paused, turned to me, and said, "I know ye ain't reluctant to shoot at Stone. Can ye shoot horses, too, Henry?"

My heart was pounding, and my mouth felt like I'd had no water in days when I said, "Yes, sir. I can."

Rufus squeezed my shoulder and smiled. Looking me square in the eye, he said, "Don't be shy 'bout shootin' the sons of bitches. They earned ever' round we can put in 'em. An' don't be foolish and aim for Stone's head. Put one in his lungs or heart, an' it'll all be over fer him. Now git up there and drop Stone like I taught ya. Today's payback. Good luck, fellers." I nodded without a word and took off.

Yellow Boy started his pony up the canyon. Rufus and I

walked back to the thicket. I pulled Little David out of the scabbard and picked up a saddlebag heavy with cartridges. Rufus loaded his Winchester and put an extra box of cartridges in his grimy old vest pocket and handed me a canteen.

My spot on the south side of the canyon was about ten feet above and a hundred yards from where we hoped to catch Stone and Tally in a crossfire. Some piñons stood right in front of two big rocks that lay side-by-side, forming a nice notch in which to steady the rifle while sitting down behind them in cover. I opened a box of cartridges. Although I'd looked forward to this chance, I was so nervous I wanted to vomit, but the velvet smoothness of the stock, the smell of gun oil, and the feel of that first .45-70 brass cartridge in my hands made me steady up, and my nervousness soon vanished.

I dropped the block on the Sharps and slid a cartridge into the breech calmly and deliberately. I tried, as Rufus had taught me, to be cool and "cakilatin'?" as I pulled the Sharps' breech closed. As I rested the barrel forestock in the rock notch and looked along the sights, trying to imagine the sight picture on Stone, *Judgment Day* kept running through my mind. Sighting on the notch of a nearby piñon limb, I was able to hold the rifle steady on a sharp point. I was ready. It was a good day for justice, and if we weren't successful, then, it was a good day to die. I pulled ten more cartridges from the box and lay them side-by-side on a little shelf protruding from the rock. I dropped the breech, reloaded, and sighted several times for practice. Then eased the rifle down and sat back to wait.

The water running down the middle of the canyon made the air much cooler than it was out on the desert, but it was still hot enough to bake bread. Sweat ran down the back of my neck in little rivulets. Reaching into my pocket, I felt the ivory watch fob my mother had given me, closed my eyes, and remembered the last time I had seen my father. He was lying on the ground, wheezing and gasping for his last breath, and his chest held two dark, bloody holes. Stone and Tally sat watching him die, glad to be rid of him, and patting themselves on the back for the superb job they'd done killing him. I remembered sitting in the wagon frozen in shock, not believing or fully understanding what had happened.

I thought of how cold I'd been hiding under the tumbleweeds caught in that big mesquite bush and seeing the mass of tumbleweeds lift up as Yellow Boy found me. I remembered all the years I'd worked with that Sharps, all the rocks I'd carried for Rufus to get strong, all the miles I'd run in the desert, and all I'd learned in order to survive and be as tough and hard as any Apache boy or man.

Lastly, I thought of my mother, and I hoped I'd be able to return to her soon. Perhaps I'd get my life back again if I tore it away from the men who had murdered my daddy and stolen my childhood.

An hour passed, and there was still no sign of the riders. Birds were everywhere. Large flocks of canyon wrens covered the bushes, chirping. I wiped the sweat off my face with my sleeve and looked out through the notch hoping for some sign of the men we meant to kill. On the northern wall, close by Rufus's spot, a coyote loped down a path through the bushes. His tongue was hanging out, and he stopped at the water to lap up a drink, roll in the stream, shake dry, and then lope on down the path on the other side. I sat back and had a pull from the canteen. The shadows were becoming longer and starting to fill the canyon. I wondered if Yellow Boy had misinterpreted the direction of the riders he had seen or if, perhaps, they were not connected to Stone and Tally. I thought maybe they were just some of Oliver Lee's cowboys coming in from work.

Then it got quiet in the canyon. Even the breeze stopped.

The wrens stopped chirping, and then, as if on command, they flew up the canyon in several clouds that grew in number as they disappeared toward the south wall we had come down two days before.

I heard two rocks grind together and a splash or two in the little stream that shouldn't have been there. My chest tightened as I plugged the canteen and sat it down carefully before creeping up to look through the notch.

Five riders were spread out across the center of the canyon, about five yards apart. They were moving slowly, looking from side to side with rifles drawn, pointed up, and cocked, ready to fire. The riders on the wings held back about ten yards from the point man, who splashed in and out of the winding little stream. Stone was on the south side between the point man and the flanker. Tally was on the north side between the point man and his flanker. Their arrangement couldn't have been better if we had designed it. They passed Frenchy's house, and a rider stopped momentarily to look in through a window, I assume to verify we weren't hiding there.

My breath was coming in long puffs as if I'd been running. I felt the quiet stillness around me as I picked up the rifle and felt a serene calm as I pulled the hammer to full cock. Stone couldn't have been more than fifty yards away. It was a shot I could make with my eyes closed. The riders had stopped and were straining to look up the canyon. The lead was pointing with his rifle toward some bushes further up the canyon where Sally was sticking her head right out where they could see her, pricking up her ears in curiosity. Putting the sight picture in the middle of Stone's back, I pulled and felt the reassuring light click of the set trigger. Stone nodded toward Tally, who started to dismount. It seemed there was no resistance at all when the firing trigger came back.

A roll of thunder, the voice of judgment, echoed up and down the canyon as the Sharps thumped against my shoulder like a thrown fist, the long barrel kicking up three or four inches. I threw the breech down, and the ejector sent the big shell case flying. I focused on being steady as my fingers slid a new cartridge in the breech and flipped the block closed. I heard Rufus's Winchester roar three times, its echo in time with mine as it bounced up and down the canyon. Yellow Boy's Henry, adding to the echo, put out two evenly spaced shots, held two counts, and then fired again. I looked through the notch to find a new target.

Chaos whirled below me. Stone lay on his back staring at the sky, a bright red stain on the front of his shirt just below and to the left of his heart. The two outriders were down, and, like Stone, unmoving. A bright red stain spread on the head of the man who had ridden next to Stone up the canyon. A horse kicking in its death throes pinned the leg of the rider closest to Rufus. His pistol was drawn, and he was wildly firing in every direction, the bullets ricocheting off nearby boulders. I sighted on his head and cocked the Sharps.

There was a loud report from up the canyon, and his head jerked as if he'd been hit with a club as he wilted before my eyes. The outrider closest to me was on the ground screaming in agony with his hands pressed over his belly. Tally had a crease of blood across his left cheek that was starting to color his beard a deeper red. His horse lay kicking in its final death twitches.

Two horses bucked and kicked as they nervously danced around, screaming in fright, the whites of their eyes showing their terror. They tore off up the canyon as fast as they could run. Stone's horse also bolted up the canyon, straight toward Yellow Boy's position. One of the bucking horses gathered his wits and ran toward the mouth of the canyon, and then, inexplicably stopped, not a hundred yards down the trail from

Frenchy's cabin.

Tally managed to reach the cover of a boulder and returned Rufus's fire. The bushes at Rufus's back blocked Yellow Boy's line of sight. The point man had escaped unscratched. He lay behind some boulders near the stream, levering fire toward Yellow Boy's position. He fired several rounds then stopped, waiting for the shooter above him to make a mistake and show himself.

Stone continued to lie on his back where he had fallen, unmoving, not making a sound, just staring at the sky with open eyes. The bloodstain was spreading across the entire front of his shirt. The stain was too low for him to have been hit in the heart and killed instantly, as I wanted. He was still alive, but he wasn't going anywhere.

Yellow Boy dropped four or five rounds close by the bush that screened Tally, then stopped. He wouldn't shoot at a target he couldn't see. I figured he must be coming back down the canyon to get a better shot. If that were so, then he was in immediate danger as soon as the point rider saw him.

I saw brief snatches of Tally's shoulders behind the rock he used to screen himself as he raised up to squeeze off a shot at Rufus. Although it wasn't a long shot for the Sharps, his motion and short, small exposure made it a hard one. I tried anyway and missed. The thunder of the Sharps, mixed with his return fire and Rufus's shots, filled the canyon with an apocalyptic roar. Tally snapped off a shot in my direction, the bullet ricocheting off the canyon wall a couple of yards to my left. As soon as he fired toward me, Rufus covered the rock Tally was hiding behind with five or six quick shots then stopped.

I dropped the breech and reloaded again. Rufus couldn't see the point man on the ground. I had to kill him or see Yellow Boy put at high risk. I couldn't stand the thought of Yellow Boy getting shot. Less than sixty yards and a still target, it was an easy shot, even though I could only see the point rider's legs sticking out behind the boulder where he waited. I pulled the hammer back and held a cartridge between my fingers for a fast reload. I knew, as soon as I shattered the rider's leg, his reflex to the brutal pain would make him jerk up and show himself. I aimed for his knee. The Sharps roared, and there was a scream of pain as the rider jerked forward and momentarily exposed his upper body. I was reloaded and aimed before he sat fully upright, and there wasn't any sound of pain after my second shot. The rider just flopped backwards and was still. I thought, *Ride with murderers, die with murderers.*

The echoes from the shots faded away, and it was quiet except the gut-shot rider's pitiful moans and pleas for water. Soon, his moaning stopped. It was still as death, except for the blood pounding in my ears. No birds, no breeze, and nothing to rattle the bushes as the shadows got longer.

Then the steady clop of horse hooves filled the stillness. I saw Yellow Boy's pony moving down the stream. There was no sign of Yellow Boy anywhere. I knew he wanted to take Tally alive if he could. He wanted to show me how Apaches made their enemies pay blood for blood. I saw the barrel of Tally's Winchester roll up and over from the direction it had been pointing toward Rufus. It pointed back toward Yellow Boy's paint. Tally fired and a bright red stripe appeared on the pony's rump as the bullet bounced off the walls up the canyon. The horse screamed and kicked, then disappeared, running back up the canyon. There was kicking and bucking from Sally, Elmer, and Midnight as they jerked free behind their bushes and followed him.

I shot at Tally's rifle barrel, the only thing I could see close to him, but I missed. He must have seen the smoke from my shot because he returned fire and splattered lead on the boulder not a foot from my notch. Rufus covered his hiding place again with a quick succession of rounds, stopped, and waited, hoping Tally would make a mistake and show himself.

Suddenly, Tally was up and running, weaving and bobbing, toward the protection of Frenchy's cabin. I took a shot with the Sharps and saw his hat go sailing off and an ear disappear. Another round knocked Tally's revolver holster right off its belt, but he got to the cabin and disappeared inside it. I thought, *Not only is he the most murderous man I've ever known, he's the luckiest.*

I swept the cabin, looking down the barrel of the Sharps, but saw no sign of him. Rufus crouched and ran down the canyon from boulder to boulder toward the house. Yellow Boy soon joined him. I saw Rufus wave, motioning me to stay where I was and cover them. I waved back that I understood and watched as they studied the cabin for a couple of minutes.

Then, before they made a move, Tally dived out a window on the far side of the cabin, rolled to his feet, and took off for the outrider horse that had stopped below the cabin.

Like a fool, I didn't shoot the horse, but tried to hit Tally again and missed. I yelled at Rufus and Yellow Boy, "Shoot! Shoot! He's running for the horse!" They ran toward the cabin. By the time they got there, Tally was already mounted and headed down the trail. I cursed with skill far beyond my years and thought, *Will I ever learn?*

I looked up from the Sharps' sights and through the small cloud of gun smoke surrounding me. Yellow Boy was stripping down to his breechcloth and moccasin boots as he talked to Rufus. His long knife was sheathed at his side. I grabbed the Sharps, cartridges, and canteen and ran down to them.

When I reached Yellow Boy, who was kneeling by the stream and drinking deeply, I asked, "What are we going to do?" I was overflowing with guilt for not shooting the horse, and I knew we were in big trouble.

Rufus rolled a quid he had been chewing to the other cheek

and spat. "It's liable to take an hour or more to run down them animals. By then Tally'll be long gone or will have found help to come back and git us. Damn it, I knowed we shoulda shot the horses right off. Hell, Yellow Boy said we oughta, but I wanted to save 'em and wouldn't listen."

He put his hand on my shoulder and gave it a reassuring squeeze. "It'll be all right, Henry. Yellow Boy's a-gonna run him down."

Yellow Boy dunked his head in the cold stream, pulled it out, and swung it back and forth, flinging silvery threads of water everywhere.

"How's he gonna do that?"

Yellow Boy said, "I run. I catch. I kill." He drew a quick finger across his throat.

"But, but . . . you can't catch a man riding a horse when you're on foot," I sputtered.

He smiled patiently. "*Sí*, I catch Tally, *Hombrecito.*" He held up two fingers. "In two days, at canyon in Jarillas, I return. *Adios.*"

He set off down the canyon in a long, easy stride carrying his rifle in both hands. His cartridge belt was strapped across his chest. I stood staring after him, speechless.

As Yellow Boy disappeared in the late afternoon light, Rufus spat again and wiped his mouth with the back of his hand. "A strong man with good wind has more endurance than a horse. They's plenty of tales floatin' around about how Apaches afoot have caught horses by runnin' 'em down. I was almost kilt by an Apache foot chasin' me back in my scoutin' days."

I sat down on the ground and stared up at Rufus, as he continued, "You push a horse hard, you might get sixty or seventy miles in a day out of him if he's in real good shape. I've seen Apaches run a hundert miles in a day across a hot desert, and that'd kill a horse. Hell, they's tales in the cavalry 'bout an ol' Indian in Californy that run nearly a hundert mile across the desert to a fort. He took a little rest when he got there and then run back, making the entire trip in less time than it takes fer the sun to rise, go down, and come back up again."

Rufus sat down beside me and said, "That there was a two-hundert-mile run in a day and a night, Henry," as if he were uncertain I could do the math. "My money says Red Tally is a-gonna be in hell come first light tomorrow."

I found what Rufus told me hard to believe, but I wouldn't dispute him. After we'd rested a few minutes, he said, "Come on, let's round up the stock and git over to the Jarillas 'fore first light. Somebody at Lee's place mighta heard the shootin' and got a little curious. They could come a-lookin' tomorrow mornin'."

CHAPTER 43
DISASTER

We started walking up the canyon, and I asked, "What're we gonna do with the bodies, Rufus, just leave 'em there?"

He spat a stream of brown juice on a lizard scurrying across a boulder and said, "Naw, if they's found, we might have lawmen coming after us for murder. We'll make 'em disappear. Soon as we get the animals, we'll load 'em up on Sally an' Elmer, haul 'em up the Eyebrow, and toss 'em over. They'll land where it's real hard to git to. Thought we'd never git to those cavalry boys the Apaches sent over the edge back in 'eighty-two. We'll have to ride the trail in the dark, but they's near a full moon tonight, and we ain't goin' over the Eyebrow proper, so we oughta be all right. Suit you?"

I nodded. I knew it would be hard, nasty work, but it needed doing. We were lucky in that we found all the animals grazing together after walking about fifteen minutes up the canyon. The hide on Yellow Boy's pony had an ugly cut from Tally's bullet that had grazed him, but it wasn't life threatening, and Rufus said he could doctor it right up. We led them back to our supplies, and after Rufus put a poultice on Yellow Boy's paint, we harnessed the others up. We decided we'd ride the horses and carry the bodies on the mules until we got to the southeast corner of the trail, then tie off the horses and lead the mules by foot to the spot near the Eyebrow where we could toss the bodies over. The animals were skittish and hard to handle. The smell of death, drying blood, and feces was everywhere.

"That smell's gonna draw varmints fast, Henry. Best have us a gun ready in case a cat or a bear sniffs us out. Bring Lil' David and some cartridges with ye," he said over his shoulder as he led Elmer away.

We picked up the north side outrider, threw him over Elmer's back, and tied him in place. Then we got the point rider. I led Elmer over to the equipment and tied him off until we could load up the other two. Then I saw Rufus walk over to where Stone lay and spit a stream of tobacco juice on Stone's shirt. He said, "That there is what I think of yore sorry ass, Mr. Stone."

I was leading Sally over to help pick him up, when I heard Stone wheeze in an agonized groan, "Why'd you back-shoot me, you old bastard?"

Rufus grinned, showing his yellow teeth through his scraggly beard, and said, "Well, I'll be damned if ye ain't still alive." He leaned forward to look in Stone's eyes and said, "Hellfire, Stone, I didn't shoot ye. Henry Fountain did. Reckin this here's payday, jest like it was fer Bentene."

Stone coughed and groaned, "God. This hurts . . . I knew that sorry little pup would get me someday if I didn't find him first." He coughed again and said through clenched teeth, "Guess this just wasn't my lucky day. It ain't yours either, you old bastard!" With his last bit of strength, he threw his revolver up and fired. The bullet caught Rufus in the side and spun him around. His teeth clamped in pain, and, holding his hand over the wound, he began to sit down slowly.

As the thunder from the Colt's report echoed up and down the canyon, I screamed in a sick rage, "No!" I dropped Sally's reins and grabbed the Sharps by its barrel with both hands. I ran up to Stone, not thinking that he might possibly shoot me, too, and swung it as hard as I could into his face. Blood flew everywhere, all over Stone, onto Rufus's back and neck, and onto the front of my shirt. Half of Stone's face had disappeared into the back of his skull.

I ran to see how badly Rufus was hit. He sat there, his face twisted in pain, laboring in long, slow pulls to breathe. "A dead man shot me, Henry, and damn if it don't hurt." He took my hand and said, "Don't look so scart, now. Go find my doctorin' bag."

I left him there and ran where we had our supplies and began rummaging for his medicine kit. It didn't take long to find it and run it back to him. He pulled out some dried moss and a roll of bandaging. "Look at my back, Henry. Did the bullet pass through?" I looked, lifting his bloody shirt. The exit wound was there, a big, black hole oozing blood. Seeing it made my legs feel weak, but I knew I had to stay calm and strong if Rufus was to have a chance.

"It definitely went through, Rufus."

"That's good, that's good," he groaned as sweat ran down his face in little rivulets. "I might make it yet." He coughed a little blood, spat, and then tore off two wads of moss. He rummaged in his kit, found a sack of evil-smelling powder and dusted the moss with it. Handing a piece of moss to me, he said, "Here, boy. Wet it a little then put it on the hole in my back. Start wrappin' this bandage around me whilst I hold some over the front." When we finished, he sat back against a rock and said, "Don't reckin I'll bleed to death now, thanks to you, but I shore don't feel like packin' any bodies up the trail. Can you do it by yoreself while I rest?"

"Yes, sir, I can do that. You just rest here. I'll be back in a while. He coughed and nodded as he held his hand against the bandage and took a long swallow from a canteen.

I tied ropes around the feet of the other two bodies and tied Sally up next to a couple of dead apple trees. I used Midnight to pull the bodies up on her and get them balanced once they were across her back. She pranced around a little, her eyes still wide with the smell of blood and all the shooting that had gone on. Stone's head was leaking blood, and the stench from the gut-shot outrider was terrible.

I made sure Rufus was comfortable before I led Sally and Elmer up the trail toward the Eyebrow. I was lucky the moon was full and was up early that night. There was plenty of light to see the trail. When we got to the narrow neck of the Eyebrow, I nearly slid off the edge myself getting the bodies off the mules. Stone was the last to go. Before I pushed him over, I took two cartridges from his gun belt and kept them to remember this day and the day he'd had Tally murder Daddy. I expected to put one of them in Oliver Lee. I sat Stone on the edge of the Eyebrow, his face and head smashed nearly beyond recognition. He looked like he'd already fallen over the edge once.

I murmured, "Nothing's ever going bring my daddy back, Stone. I just hope Daddy is somewhere, somehow, resting easier now. You got your due this day. Good-bye . . . I'm sure we'll meet in hell." With that, I heaved him off the side and listened as his body bounced down the thousand-foot canyon wall to crash into the trees and rocks at the bottom with a dull sound, like a boot dropping on a thick carpet.

Mounting Midnight, I led the mules back down the trail and didn't waste any time getting back to Rufus. He was sitting against the same rock where I'd left him. He had his rifle across his knees and was smoking his pipe like nothing was wrong at all.

"That job's done."

He nodded and said, "Good boy. Those bastards oughta not be found for a right long time once the varmints get their fill."

"You any better? Why do you have your Winchester out and cocked?"

"I'm a-hurtin' purdy bad, but I can ride. Done had a coyote

through here sniffing at the bloody spots. Wasn't gonna take no chances that cuss was gonna come sniffin' after me." He groaned as he shifted position. "Now, Henry, if you can load up Elmer and saddle Sally, we'll get on over to the Jarillas."

CHAPTER 44
DARK NIGHT IN THE JARILLAS

When we rode out of the mouth of Dog Canyon, the moon still hadn't risen to midnight. Rufus rode bent over, holding onto his saddle horn with both hands. I led the way, taking paths that avoided the glow of campfires in the distance and making as straight a line as I could toward Monte Carlo Gap in the Jarillas. Thankfully, it was a fairly easy ride. We didn't stop to rest the whole way because Rufus wanted to get where we were going, change his bandage, and then rest.

Crossing to the west side of the Jarillas, I found the ocotillo thicket in front of Yellow Boy's canyon and threaded our way through it to the little stream toward the back. I helped Rufus off Sally, got him some water, laid out his bed, and unloaded our gear near the overhang next to the little wet-season stream. He lay back with a hard sigh and motioned me to rub down and feed the animals before I did anything for him. When I finished with the animals, we changed his bandage and found the bleeding had almost stopped. I unsheathed the Sharps, wiped the dried blood off the stock, loaded it, and lay down next to Rufus. I was exhausted. I was even more tired than the night after I'd taken my first shot at Stone.

At least I hadn't missed today, and Stone lay somewhere at the bottom of a thousand-foot cliff with wolves and coyotes sniffing around for a piece of him. My father had a measure of justice. If Yellow Boy caught Tally, then the debt was nearly paid in full, except for settling with Oliver Lee. I was proud of the work we had done that day.

I awoke to voices and the sound of cattle moving past the canyon. The sun was up, and it was already starting to get hot. I looked over at Rufus. His eyes were squeezed shut, his teeth clenched together. His face was covered with sweat, and his breathing, labored. I knew he must be in a lot of pain.

"Rufus! What can I get you? Do you need water?" I was frantic to do something.

"Ummph," he groaned. "A sip outta that canteen is gonna taste mighty good, Henry."

I got the canteen and helped him sit up to drink. After a couple of swallows, he lay back and said, "Been needin' that fer a while."

"Why didn't you wake me?" I asked, angry with myself for not waking to check on him sooner.

"After ye hauled them bodies up the Eyebrow and brung me here? I'd a-died 'fore I'd a-done that." He hooked a thumb toward the cattle and said, "They's been a herd goin' by here since first light. That oughta wipe out any tracks we made gettin' in here. You all right, son?"

"Yes, sir. I'm fine. You look like you're hurtin' bad, though."

"Reckin I ain't ready to swing no gal in a saloon jig." He clenched his teeth again as a new wave of pain swept over him. Then he panted a little and seemed to relax as he smiled and said, "By damn. We got ol' Stone, didn't we?"

"We sure did." I smiled with him and nodded.

"He shore as hell ain't gonna pull any more sorry shootin's on this here range. Tally ain't gonna be a shooter anymore, either. You'll see when Yellow Boy gets back."

I felt a sudden urge to throw my arms around the old man, but I remembered how he'd shaken my hand when I jumped up to hug him after he'd returned long overdue from Mrs. Darcy's, and I chided myself for continuing to want to act like a boy. He wanted me to act like a man, needed me to *be* a man.

A few moments later, he said, "Henry, I want you to slide your hand agin' that hole in my back and show me the blood." He looked at my face and managed a grin. "Remember, son, cold and cakilatin'. Go on now. It ain't a-gonna hurt that much, and I need to see. Gimme a stick to bite on 'fore you start."

I cut a stick off a mesquite bush and gave it to him. He clamped down on it and nodded. I slid my hand up under his back as carefully and easily as I could, but he groaned deep in his throat, and his breath came in short, desperate pants over the mesquite stick. I felt around on the wet spot under the bandage and pulled my hand back. It was smeared with dark blood, not the bright, red kind I had seen when he was first wounded.

Rufus squinted at my hand through his dust-covered glasses as I held it up for him to see. He nodded and relaxed. I guessed that the dark blood was a sign the poultice we'd rigged up was doing some good. The bleeding didn't seem to be that bad, just a slow low-level ooze. His pain seemed to recede as I took the stick out of his mouth.

I stepped over to the little stream and washed the blood off my hand then came back and sat down cross-legged beside him. I felt the warm sun on my back. It was more peaceful now that the herd of cattle had passed by. Canyon wrens were chirping in the bushes.

"Rufus, what does it mean?" I asked. "The blood was dark, almost black. Is your poultice workin'?"

He managed a smile and said, "Naw. Ain't no poultice gonna fix me. Dark blood means I'm liver-shot. I ain't gonna make it more'n a day or two at best. I'm bleeding to death inside."

I felt as though I'd been punched in the gut. "You're not

gonna die, Rufus," I said. "You can't die!"

"Yes, sir. I reckin I am. They's nuthin' anybody can do about it. I'm done. We got to figure out the best thing fer ye to do next. Stone mighta told somebody he was a-goin' lookin' fer ol' Rufus and his kid. If'n he don't come back, and they think he went a-lookin' fer me and you, they's a-gonna come lookin' fer us, too. Ye oughta lay low fer a while 'fore ye go back to yore mama. Yellow Boy is still yore ace. Ain't nobody gonna guess ye're with him."

I felt sick, enraged, and alone, helpless to stop him dying. Even worse, he was going to die because he'd helped me. I wanted to cry in shame and frustration, but didn't dare do it in front of him. All I could do was sit, stare at him, and chew on my lip. This couldn't be happening to me again. Stone had helped murder my father. Now he had killed the man who'd raised me like I was his own. It wasn't fair. I wished I could kill Stone again as the memory of smashing in his face rose in my mind. I felt so helpless and weak.

Rufus squeezed his eyes shut again and clenched his teeth as pain rolled over him again. When he began to relax, he looked over at me and said, "They's nearly a full bottle of laudanum in my kit. It's the dark brown one with the red thread tied around it. Guess now is as good a time as any to use it. It'll make me easy in a little while. Git it fer me, will ye?"

I found the laudanum and gave him a good swallow. Then he took a big swig of water and lay back. As the air got hotter, he began to relax and drift in and out of sleep.

The animals were getting restless. I took care of them, straightened up the camp, and found some cow chips and wood for the fire. The work dulled the ache I felt in my heart and gut knowing Rufus was about to die. I felt like I was staggering around senseless in a nightmare.

I sat by him through the rest of the day, keeping the flies off the bloody bandage and giving him water and laudanum when he asked for it. He became peaceful and slept easily through the heat of the day. I got hungry as the sun was going down and shadows filled the canyon, so I made some stew and ate. Rufus awoke and watched without speaking, and when I asked if he wanted to eat, he shook his head.

"Is the laudanum working?"

He nodded and said, "It's a-doin' its job, son. I ain't a-hurtin' much now. Just feel kinda dreamy. Havin' a hard time a-thinkin' straight. See if'n ye can find a bottle of whiskey in the grub sack, and give me a swaller or two, would ya?"

I found the bottle, and he took two or three long pulls. He smacked his lips and said, "That there stuff ain't gonna do my liver no good, but it shore warms a feller up on the inside. Sit down here next to me, Henry. I'll tell ya what I'm a thinkin' if'n ye'll fire up my pipe fer me."

He corked the bottle and sat it beside him. I found the pipe in his vest pocket and tobacco in the other. I filled and lighted it as I'd seen him do many times. It took some coughing and wheezing on my part to get a good coal in it, and he grinned while he watched me struggle with it. I handed it to him and sat down cross-legged next to him so I could see his face. I stared at his rheumy blue eyes, waiting for him to speak as he pulled long and slow on the pipe.

"Don't feel so bad about me dying, Henry. I done lived several year past seventy. Shoulda been dead a few times 'fore this. My string just run out is all. Bible says we're done after three score and ten anyhow. Guess God gimme me a little extry time to take care of ye and help settle the score with Stone and Tally. It's time fer me to go an' I'm ready."

Again I had to fight an urge to embrace him. Tears rolled down my face. "I don't want you to go, Rufus. I need you here. Please don't die."

He patted my knee. "Ye're a man now, son. I'm mighty proud of the way you handled yoreself yestidy. Yellow Boy's gonna help you along till yore full growed. Ye're gonna be fine, boy, just fine." He grimaced and said, "Gimme another swaller of that whiskey, will ye?" I uncorked the bottle, and he took a couple more long pulls before lying back with a sigh. He was quiet for a while as he pulled on his pipe and sent puffs of smoke floating up into the still, cool air.

"I ain't got nobody else 'cept you, Henry. I want you to have all my stuff and the ranch. Git a piece of paper outta my medicine kit and write what I tell ya."

The only paper I could find was folded up in a flat leather pouch along with a lead pencil. On one side of the paper, creased and yellowed by the years, was a letter from Mrs. Darcy. It read:

Dear Rufus,

Thank you for bringing my Charlie home to me after the Apaches shot him. He was a fine man, and he liked riding with you. Now that he's gone, I'm selling our place and starting a boardinghouse in Lincoln to support myself. Our children are gone, and all I have left are good friends like you. Please come and expect to stay at my boardinghouse whenever you're over in this part of the country. I look forward to a visit soon.

Your friend,
Sarah Darcy.

I showed the letter to Rufus. He brightened at seeing it and said, "Sarah Darcy. Damn good woman fer any man. Go ahead and write on the back of it, Henry. She won't mind a-tall. Now write what I tell ye: Bein' clearheaded and thinkin' straight, I, Rufus Pike, leave all my possessions, includin' land, cattle, mule, dog, and guns to my friend Henry—"

He paused for a moment and said, "Henry I don't think I

oughta call you Henry Fountain since ever'body thinks ye're dead, and they might think I's crazy or ye's a thief." He stroked his beard and asked, "What's a good name to call you in this here will? Uhmm . . ."

I didn't try to answer because I understood he was talking to himself at this point. At last he said, "I think you's saved from Jack Stone by the grace of God, so I'm a-gonna call you Henry Grace. Is that all right, Henry?"

I said, "That's just fine." I thought, *Anything to make him easy.*

"Henry Grace you are, then. Where was I? Oh yeah . . . to my friend Henry Grace. Signed this date, first of September, nineteen-oh-two. Rufus Pike."

He paused again and said, "I know it ain't the first of September, Henry, but I know it's September, so the exact date don't make no never mind. Hand it over here, and let me sign it." I gave him the pencil and paper and the skillet I had turned over to write on. He struggled to sit up straight, sweat pouring from his face, signed it with strong strokes, and then lay back, exhausted. I folded the letter and put the paper and pencil back in the leather pouch.

He took another pull on the whiskey bottle and sighed. "It's a getting cold, ain't it, Henry? Bring me another blanket, would ye?"

It was dark, but the air was still warm in the canyon. I was sweating, and he had a blanket wrapped around his legs. I couldn't understand why he thought he was cold, but I went to get another blanket.

When I spread the second blanket over him, he said, "When ye're ready to use the will, take it over to ol' George Adams in Las Cruces. He's a lawyer who helped me git the ranch recorded and rode with me in the old days. He'll know my signature, and he'll make shore things is done right."

He coughed, spat some blood, and then took another pull on the whiskey bottle, but most of it dribbled down his chin. I reached to hold up his head and steady the bottle for him, and he coughed and choked a little as the liquid fire flowed down his throat.

Rufus was still for a while, and then he turned and said, "Henry, I just remembered they's four sacks of gold coins under the porch post closest to the barn. I took 'em off a freight wagon the Apaches wiped out years ago on the San Antonio road. I buried 'em fer when I needed the money, but never touched it. I 'spec they's about twenty thousand dollars there. Ye take it and git yoreself a good education and a good start. Ye got the guts and brains to be anything ye wanna be. Never stop trying at anything ye wanna do, and it'll happen. Understand me, son?"

I nodded, but I couldn't speak. I knew he was slipping away. The tears trickled down my cheeks, bathing my face in sorrow. I felt so helpless.

He lay quiet, breathing easy for a while with his eyes closed. I sat by him cross-legged, rocking back and forth, my hands clasped together in an attitude of prayer, hoping against hope that somehow he'd live. The moon swung up over the mountains and climbed high in the night sky against puffy, drifting clouds. Stark shadows mixed with golden light filled the canyon. When the moon began its downward arc, Rufus's eyes flickered open. He looked at me with a peaceful smile and said, "Good-bye, Henry. Live a long time, and do good." His spirit left with a deep sigh as he closed his eyes and was gone.

Gently, I pulled the blanket up over his head to cover him. I hadn't been able to cry for my father at the time he was killed, but I cried for Rufus that day. I cried like a man cries, from deep in my gut, feeling the springs at the bottom of my soul opening and flooding a great empty place left in my life.

CHAPTER 45
TALLY MEETS YELLOW BOY

Sitting there with Rufus's body, I wondered if my life had a chance ever to be right again. It was like I was the only person left in the world. I thought that maybe God had cursed me for some reason and that my destiny was for those close to me to die before their time so I'd suffer. I thought about that for a long time. Then I remembered Rufus had often told me that we mustn't blame God for the bad things that happen to us. God wanted justice, and one way or the other, justice happened. Either we helped it along, or we didn't, but it happened.

"Henry," he'd said, "it's all gonna come out even, regardless of what we do. The Good Book says cast yore bread on the water, and it'll come back to ye, and Jesus talked about reapin' and sowin'. That there means if ye do good, ye'll get more a lot more good back than ye ever intended and maybe in ways ye never believed possible. If ye're doin' a good thang for the right reasons, ye don't expect nothin' back anyways. If'n yore works is bad, the payback can be a hundert times worse, 'cause ye always reap more'n ye sow."

The river of grief pouring out of my soul finally stopped. I sat beside Rufus's body the rest of the night. The times we'd spent together tumbled out of my memory fresh and clear. As I thought about it, I realized Rufus must have spent a fortune on cartridges teaching me to be a marksman with the Sharps. I'd probably shot well over three thousand rounds at the targets he put in front of me. We'd probably carried a hundred tons of rock, twenty or thirty pounds to each stone, to make me strong and to build that cabin and fences he'd wanted.

He hadn't had much of a repertoire when it came to cooking, but I'd never been hungry, and he'd taught me to keep beans in the pot and coffee on the fire. I'd read every book he had stacked in a corner of his shack, and we'd spent many a long evening talking about the ideas and beliefs they held. He'd taught me all the mathematics I needed to know for surveying and for using the stars to navigate across the desert. That meant he'd taught me some geometry, trigonometry, and algebra.

The stars were beginning to fade when I realized I wasn't alone. I jumped in surprise and started to get up, but Yellow Boy, standing behind me, put a firm hand on my shoulder and asked, "What happen, *Hombrecito*?"

I had to bite my lip to keep from crying again. I choked on my words as I told Yellow Boy the whole story. When I finished, he flopped down beside me, exhausted. He sighed as he stared off into the dark shadows along the canyon walls. After a long while, he said, "So, at last Rufus goes to grandfathers. He goes with strong arm and courage in his heart. He is welcome there. We lose friend and brother. We smoke and fast to remember him when sun comes. Tonight, we go to his *rancho*. I know place there for his bones."

I nodded and turned my face away from him. Yellow Boy touched my shoulder and said, "Don't be sad for Rufus, little brother. Rufus has trouble no more. He goes to land of the grandfathers, the Happy Land. You must be strong for yourself. Rufus wants you strong."

We sat together with Rufus's body and watched the morning light find high, puffy clouds and slip through the shadows in our canyon. Birds began singing in the mesquite and creosote bushes. I could hear the trickle of water in the little stream just below us, and the mules and horses beginning to stamp around.

I looked over at Yellow Boy, who was gaunt and dirty. Salt sparkled in the light where rivulets of sweat had run down his shoulders and belly. Then I looked up the canyon and saw the horse Tally had taken tied with our mules and horses.

Yellow Boy's eyes were shining and clear, like those of a big hunting cat, when I asked, "Did you get Tally?"

He nodded toward a greasy-looking sack sitting by the fire and said, "Look."

Moving closer, I saw the sack was a bloody pair of long johns with the arms and legs tied in a knot. I knelt down beside it, untied the knot, and pulled it open. The bearded head of Red Tally stared back at me, a bullet hole through what had been his good right eye. I knew Yellow Boy had made sure Tally's head was blind so it would stay that way in the Happy Land. I clenched my teeth to keep from gagging and stared at the head of the man who had brought me so much grief and nearly killed me. The patch over the left eye was gone, and the socket stared back at me never having known my image. The heavy, red beard seemed to engulf the rest of the face in a ball of fur smeared with dark, dried blood.

The nausea passed. I felt grim satisfaction settle in my belly, a meal fully consumed, but leaving a bitter aftertaste. There was nothing but a great feeling of emptiness left in the middle of my chest. What Stone and Tally started so long ago was nearly finished. I still had the bullet I had promised for Oliver Lee. Now I wondered if I would ever use it. My thoughts formed an image of a naked, headless corpse lying somewhere out in the desert for the coyotes and buzzards to pick over. How ironic, I thought. The man who made my father disappear will also vanish without a trace, and here I stand holding the sack with his sorry, rotting head. Again, I thought of what Rufus had said about reaping and sowing. I retied the sack and put it where I knew it would stay in the shade because it was already starting to stink.

Yellow Boy hadn't moved. I sat back down beside him and whispered, "Tell me of this victory. I want to know all."

"First, I drink and wash. Find my *cigarros, Hombrecito.* I tell you while we watch day."

He got up, drank deeply, and bathed in the little stream by the fire. I wrapped Rufus's body in his ground canvas and blankets and pulled him up under the ledge where it was cooler. I rummaged through our gear until I found Yellow Boy's shirt and coat and handed them to him as he pulled the water from his hair, sliding it through his fingers. He tied off his hair with his big, red bandana, pulled on the shirt, and slipped the army jacket over his shoulders. I looked over at his rifle leaning on Elmer's pack rack. One cartridge was missing from the tube magazine.

Yellow Boy found his gun belt and checked the revolver's load before buckling it on. Stuffing some rags, a straight stick, a small bottle of coal oil, and a box of cartridges in an old flour sack, he picked up the Henry and nodded toward the Sharps. "*Hombrecito,* bring Shoots Today Kills Tomorrow and a blanket. We climb up, clean guns, smoke, and speak of end of Tally."

From up on the watch point, we could see a beautiful, clear morning covering the valley. The air was cool. The sky colors over the Organs were delicate, gauzy purples, reds, oranges, and a soul-lifting turquoise that glimmered for a while to the south before it faded into a brilliant morning blue. Small groups of cattle moved through the grass, and mottled delicate, light-green mesquite thickets and rugged, pine-green creosote bushes spread below us. There were no riders anywhere in sight.

We spread the blanket, sat shoulder-to-shoulder with our backs to a boulder, and began cleaning our weapons. I had to work to get the stain left by Stone's blood off the Sharps' stock. For all the abuse I'd given it killing Stone, the stock showed no cracks and no stains that couldn't be removed with coal oil and a little frantic rubbing. Yellow Boy's stick was just long enough to push a coal-oil-soaked patch down its long barrel. It took several cycles of soaked patches followed by clean, dry ones to clean it.

Yellow Boy was smooth and efficient cleaning the Henry. Soon he raised the loading spring tab and twisted the loading gate at the end of the barrel. He carefully slid the cartridges he had levered out of it for cleaning back down the barrel. After the last one was in place, he pulled one cartridge out of his gun belt and let it ease down the remaining three inches left in the magazine tube. The bullet made the magazine full again. He carefully closed the gate, eased the spring tab back down on the cartridges, and laid the Henry across his knees.

Then he reached inside his vest and produced two cigars and a box of sulfur matches. He cut off the ends to be lighted before handing one to me. He bit off the mouth plug of his and spat it away. I did the same. He lighted each one, we blew smoke to the four directions, and then we sat silently for a while in our little cloud of blue smoke as the morning began its race for midday. I trembled a little inside. I knew Yellow Boy's smoking with me meant I'd been accepted as a man.

"Now I speak of Tally," Yellow Boy said.

"Yes, please. I have to know what happened."

"When I run out of canyon, I see dust from Tally's horse. He rides toward El Paso Grande del Norte. *Es* maybe *tres o quatro* long shots for Shoots Today Kills Tomorrow. He rides hard at first, and distance between us gets longer. Then he slows *un poco* and stops to look back. He stares long time for man riding away from death. I raise no dust. His eye didn't find me in mesquite. He stopped too long, and I got one long shot closer. I run close to the earth. At last, he turns and rides at easy trot straight for the Rio Grande and Mexico. I run easy and steady. The earth is warm, *pero* the air is *frio*. Tally, he know he must not ride hard or horse won't make it to the river. I gain on him."

I sat envying him that run as I listened. I knew Yellow Boy probably hadn't even been breathing hard as he gained ground on Tally's horse. Yellow Boy took a long drag on his cigar and slowly blew the blue-white smoke out in a long stream into the morning air above his head. He said, "I know he stops to give the horse water at Jacob's Tank. I think maybe he's foolish enough to rest there. He rides. I run. Soon the night comes. The moon climbs mountains and watches our race. Tally stop at Jacob's Tank. I pass Tally and his horse and find place to watch and rest. Tally gives horse water, then he drink and wash in the tank. He hobble horse, ease saddle, sit by tank to rest as moon climbs high. I rest, watch for a while, and then run for river until moon starts to hide in far mountains. I run far around Jacob's Tank. Tally never knows I am there. Tally rests. I run. I stop at place called Boat Rock."

I nodded and smiled. I knew Boat Rock was way off the beaten path. Yellow Boy took another long drag on his cigar and stared over the valley, apparently reliving those moments. I waited for him to come back to me. Finally, he said, "I stop and climb up rock to rest. My Power says I kill Tally at Boat Rock when the birds sing next day.

"Sun comes. Birds sing. Soon Tally come, and I stand on Boat Rock. I raise my arms, sing, and ask help from grandfathers to kill enemy. Tally stops one long shot from Shoots Today Kills Tomorrow. He sits on his horse and watches me. I see him but don't move. I sing with my arms high toward west, and I hear him laugh."

I could hardly believe Yellow Boy would expose himself that

way, but he often surprised me in his approach to many situations. Over the years, I'd seen his morning prayers and heard his songs to the great Apache god, *Ussen,* many times. In a flash of lucidity I realized how important spiritual things were to him—even more important than the danger posed by Tally.

Yellow Boy continued, "Tally say, 'All right, you dumb red bastard, stand there, and I'll kill your ass.' I no move. He aims rifle and shoots one time. His bullet hits far in front of Boat Rock. I still no move. I sing, but the birds stop singing. I hold Yellow Boy rifle high."

I pictured Yellow Boy standing on that rock in the morning sun, and it wasn't hard to imagine Tally's rage at his first shot being short. I wondered if Tally had any thought he was headed for the Happy Land. I figured probably not.

Yellow Boy said, "Tally rides forward until he is half long shot from Shoots Today Kills Tomorrow, then raises his rifle and shoots again. His bullet hits only Boat Rock and sand. I still no move, just hold Yellow Boy high. He says, 'You damned ignorant heathen, you wanna die, don't you? My pleasure to oblige you. You just hard to see against the damned sun.' "

I smiled, picturing the scene, anticipating the rest.

Yellow Boy allowed himself a tiny smile as he continued, "He walks his horse toward Boat Rock slow, careful. He watches and waits for me to move. I can tell he is ready to spring, muscles shake like lion hunting deer. He moves until he is a bow shot from rock. I see Tally face, his eye, his beard, but I no move, just hold Yellow Boy high and sing to the grandfathers. He stops, lowers his rifle sight, and laughs mighty laugh. Then he raise rifle to aim. I drop to one knee and fire. My bullet hits his eye, and he fall backwards from his horse. I watch, but he no move. I climb down from rock walk over to him and say, 'Red bastard not dumb. Red bastard lives.' "

I burst out laughing at this, and Yellow Boy joined me. It was the first time I'd ever seen him laugh so hard. Then, after we'd settled down, he said, "I pull his body into the mesquite, take his clothes, his guns, his head. Then I wrap his head in clothes Rufus calls long johns and left body there for vultures and coyotes. My father taught me it's not good to cut dead, but this time I decide to take his head so you could see it and do with as you will. Now Tally has no head in Happy Land. He walk forever with no eye, no mind, no head."

I nodded. The image of Tally wandering headless with no mind in the afterworld was satisfying. Once I killed Oliver Lee, my father's death would be fully avenged.

Yellow Boy finished his story by explaining, "When I leave, I take my tracks away and ride Tally's horse to resting place in mesquite until moon comes. Then I ride to Jacob's Tank and drink and rest before I come here."

We sat and smoked until the cigars were gone. Then Yellow Boy touched my shoulder and said, "Rest now, *Hombrecito*. I watch. You watch when sun is there." He pointed toward the mid-afternoon sky. Suddenly, I was very weary. I stretched out on the blanket and began to doze.

Chapter 46
The Cost of Honor

We climbed down from our perch overlooking the basin as it got dark. I cooked us some hardtack and beans over the little fire. After we ate, I took a shovel and walked to the end of the canyon. I climbed up high to the flat spot under an overhanging shelf and buried Tally's head so it wouldn't get washed away and found after a thunderstorm. I shoveled dirt on top of it, packed it down, and swept the area so it looked unused. I stared at the spot for a while, prayed that the price I'd paid for that head was worth it to Daddy, wherever he was, and I thanked the grandfathers for Yellow Boy.

We loaded the gear on Elmer and put Rufus's body, wrapped in the canvas ground cloth, across Sally. She was skittish at first, rolling her eyes and not wanting to carry the smelly canvas-wrapped body, but after Yellow Boy settled her down, she was steady with her load the rest of the night. With the moon on the rise, rifles across our saddles, we trotted out of the canyon and made a long, flat arc south by southwest around Cox's ranch, up over Baylor Pass, and down the other side. We stopped to rest the animals a couple of times before we cleared the pass and again near the back side of Van Patten's ranch. A good hour before dawn, we rode up the trail to Rufus's shack. It had been a hard ride and a hard return with only Rufus's body there with us.

We left Elmer and Sally loaded, and the horses saddled, while we watered and fed them at the corral. I didn't want Buck to look in on the place and find a couple of strangers there with Rufus's body. There was no telling what he might think or tell the sheriff. As the sun began to brighten the eastern sky, we led the animals up the trail toward the back of the canyon as the cattle stared at us.

We off-loaded Elmer at the storage cave. I was wondering what Yellow Boy had in mind for Rufus's body when he led Sally farther up the canyon. After about three hundred yards, he stopped at a pile of rocks against the canyon wall and motioned for me to help him as he picked up the stones, one by one, and put them to one side. Soon the rectangular mouth of a small cave appeared. It was about waist high and three or four feet wide.

Yellow Boy nodded toward it. "One time Rufus dug new mine. He found no gold and no silver, so he stopped digging when mine not far into cliff. He say work too hard for no money."

When we finished moving the stones, I knelt down and looked inside. It wasn't more than ten or twelve feet deep. It was a perfect burial vault for our friend.

Gently we took his body off Sally. Yellow Boy passed me a canteen of water, and I washed Rufus as best I could, crossed his arms, and wiped the dust off his glasses. I backed into the shaft, pulling the body on the ground cloth all the way to the back. By the time I crawled out, the sun was high, and it was getting warm.

We rubbed the animals down and hobbled them so they could graze around the canyon while we washed, ate, and rested. Lying down in the shade of a big boulder on the south wall of the canyon, we slept through the heat of the day. I was physically exhausted and emotionally drained, and my sleep was deep and dreamless.

When I awoke, Yellow Boy was up and had built a small fire

near the mouth of the mine. He sat cross-legged near it, facing toward the sun in an attitude of meditation, his lips moving in a wordless chant.

I washed the sleep from my face and walked about collecting a few wildflowers. I brought these back and left them floating in a bucket of water. Then I walked down to the shack. It was lonely, unkempt, and deserted. When I stepped on the porch, the boards creaked as I walked across them and opened the door. Sunlight streamed through the broken windows, highlighting dust motes slowly drifting in the warm, stifling air. A smell of old smoke, the residue of cooking on the iron stove over many years, seeped from the dry, cracking, wooden walls.

A thin blanket of dust covered everything. Memories of happy times, struggles to learn, stories of battles fought and won, treks made, and thoughts about what the writers stacked in the corner had said flew at me from everywhere. I stepped to Rufus's old cot and his little bedside table and found his Bible. I'd seen him read it often. He hadn't carried it with him on our trip because he'd thought it was hypocritical to have it in his pocket after he had decided he was going to kill someone. However, I knew he'd thought that it was all right to read it after he'd done his crime and made penance. I blew the dust off the old book, looked around the room once more, felt a shudder of grief, and closed the door.

As I walked back up the canyon, the sun was beginning to slide behind the Floridas, turning the long, streaking clouds a brilliant red and orange. Yellow Boy still sat in quiet contemplation, the little fire burning some pungent-smelling sage he had found. The air was very still, and the smoke rose in an arrow-straight plume, slowly disappearing into the darkening sky. I carried the bucket of wildflowers into the mine and lay them carefully near Rufus's canvas-wrapped body.

Then I went outside and found his rifle with my gear. I was

carrying it to the mine to leave with the body when Yellow Boy raised his hand for me to stop.

"Why you do this, *Hombrecito*?" he asked. "He does not want weapon on other side. He wants you to live long time. You keep it, and use it to stay alive."

What Yellow Boy said made sense, so I deferred to his judgment and kept the rifle. I asked him if it was appropriate to read some scripture over Rufus. Since Yellow Boy had been a scout for the army in his younger days and understood what the white eyes did with their dead, he lowered his gaze and said, "*Sí*, book has wise words and sings good songs. Read words. Read while you can still see its tracks."

The dark shadows of the dying day were creeping up the canyon toward us, and the perfume from the flowers in the mine floated out to us as I stepped to the opening with the Bible, faced the setting sun, and turned to the third chapter of Ecclesiastes. Yellow Boy came and stood beside me, tall and straight, with his rifle in the crook of his arm as I began reading:

> *To everything there is a season,*
> *and a time to every purpose under the heaven:*
> *a time to be born, and a time to die;*
> *a time to plant, and a time to pluck up that which is*
>   *planted;*
> *a time to kill, and a time to heal;*
> *a time to break down, and a time to build up;*
> *a time to weep and a time to laugh;*
> *a time to mourn, and a time to dance;*
> *a time to cast away stones, and a time to gather*
>   *stones together;*
> *a time to embrace, and a time to refrain from*
>   *embracing;*
> *a time to get, and a time to lose;*

a time to keep, and a time to cast away;
a time to rend, and a time to sew;
a time to keep silence, and a time to speak;
a time to love, and a time to hate;
a time of war, and a time of peace.

Yellow Boy sprinkled some golden pollen on the canvas with the flowers. Then he made a complete circle about the fire, stopping to face each of the four directions and say something in Apache I didn't fully understand, but I caught a few words, including *power* and *grandfathers*. I stood by, respectful of what he did, as he had respected me and the words I used.

When he finished, he said, "Now, *Hombrecito*, we close this place that holds Rufus's bones." He picked up a stone and put it in the entranceway. I picked up one and placed it beside his. We worked into the night. The last stone was in place as the shadows from the moon came.

When we finished, he took four stones the same size and put them together in a square in front of the pile of stones covering the entrance. Each corner of the square pointed in a cardinal direction. Then he sprinkled golden pollen in their center. He stood up, facing the west. Putting his fist over his heart he said, "*Adios, mi amigo bueno.* Ride with the sun."

He turned to me and said, "Now we eat and smoke. I sweep the tracks away from here. No one knows where Rufus Pike rests. Only me, only you. Go. Fix our food."

I dug a pit and built a small fire near the corral. I didn't want to go back in the shack again, at least not for a while. I cut venison steaks from a deer Yellow Boy had taken earlier in the day and put them on skewers to cook slowly over the fire. Then I cut some potatoes, put them on to boil, and made a pot of coffee. My stomach felt bottomless and reminded me I hadn't eaten much of anything in three or four days.

Yellow Boy soon came and sat by the fire, but neither of us

spoke. Somehow, it didn't seem appropriate to say anything. The smell of fat dripping in the fire and watching the steaks turn dark with flavor made us ravenous. We pulled the meat off the skewers, still hot and dripping, and wolfed our food down like starving men. When we finally sat back to drink our coffee, Yellow Boy offered me a cigar. I shook my head because my throat still felt raw from the last one. He lighted his, blew smoke to the four directions, and studied my face as I watched the fire.

A little later, I cleaned up our cooking site and covered over the fire pit. We left no sign of anyone being around the cabin and kept the animals out of sight up the canyon. We took our weapons and spread our blankets up on the ledge where we'd watched the shack when Stone had come back to kill Rufus and me. For a long while, we lay back and watched bolts of lightning being pitched back and forth between the clouds collecting over the Floridas and south toward Mexico.

Lying there, I began to have doubts about the rightness of what we had done. Revenge left me feeling hollow, a vessel with no bottom. It had left one of the men who saved me as a little boy dead. Now it was keeping me from my family, and it had placed a seed of desire in my soul to kill again.

"Brother," I said.

"Ummph? *Que es, Hombrecito?*"

"We've killed those who murdered my father. You've cut off the head of Red Tally. I shot Jack Stone and smashed in his head. You killed Bentene. The others with Stone, we killed in Dog Canyon. They are no more, but the price has been high. I would give them all back their lives if Rufus could still be alive. This thing we have done, was it a thing that had to be done?"

He was quiet for a long time, not moving. I expected to hear him snoring at any moment, but after a while, he rose up on one elbow and spoke to me, looking straight into my eyes. "What is worse than death, *Hombrecito?*"

My mind was blank. "I can think of nothing worse than death."

"Ummph. You very young, but have seen death many times now. Still, you do not know? I tell you there are many things worse than death. To be separated from your Power, that is worse than death. To live in fear, that is worse than death. To live without honor, that is worse than death. To have no courage, that is worse than death. To leave your family to mercy of wolves, that is worse than death. *Comprende?*"

"*Sí, comprendo.* Perhaps what you speak is true. I do not know."

He nodded and said, "You haven't lived enough to know this is true. It is true. Your Power is your guide. It shows you the light in life. If you find your Power and are not true to the vision it gives, the light goes. Maybe you stay alive, but your life is dead. Fear comes and stays. Fear is a wolf. It always hunts you. Always in darkness it waits for you. If you run, it comes after you. No let you live as *un hombre* lives. It runs from the shadows and tears you to pieces. Then you live as coward, bent over with your burden. You cannot stand straight and face sun. Your honor, *Hombrecito,* is your will to keep the law you make for yourself, law your father gives you, and his father before him. Honor keeps you a man. It says to the wolf, 'You have no power over me.' Without honor, no light is in your life. Without honor, no peace is in your spirit. Walk a straight line, and let no man push you from it. Always keep your honor."

He paused for a moment, probably to give me time to absorb what he'd said. I frowned slightly, wondering exactly how I was to be sure I always kept my honor. I thought it had to be more than just following my instincts.

Then he said, "Other men must know you have no fear. Other men must know you will not let them dishonor you. If they strike you or your family, they must know you will strike them, even if it means dying. There is no greater value than life lived with honor. Men speak of courage and admire it. What is courage? Courage is to know the wolf, but keep your honor even if it means death. *Su padre* kept his honor. He kept his courage. He lost his life for his honor. He lived well. You are proud of him. This I know."

I listened, almost stunned as Yellow Boy spoke. I'd never heard him say so much at one time, but I felt his words resonate deep within my being. He sat up fully, placed a hand on my shoulder, and said, "When Tally, Stone, and Bentene took your father's life, there was no turning from your honor. They had to die, too. That is justice. That is law my father taught me, and his father before him. It is the law Rufus knew. It is law even the *Indah,* the white man, believes but chooses not to follow. White man gives burden of his honor to others to carry. You didn't do that. Rufus didn't do that, and I didn't do that. We pay debt ourselves. Now Rufus has gone to grandfathers. There are many things worse. He had rather be with grandfathers than for his friend to live without honor. That, too, is my belief."

He sat there silent for a while, then lay back and looked up at the stars. I assumed he'd go to sleep soon, but with my grief, memories, and the awareness of decisions I had to make, I knew I wouldn't sleep anytime soon. A few minutes passed, and Yellow Boy asked, "Will you find your mother now, *Hombre-cito?*"

"I don't think I can for a while yet. If those men we killed are found, riders will come looking for us, maybe even with the sheriff. They'll figure out Rufus and I suckered them into Dog Canyon to ambush them, and then they'll want payback, regardless of why we did it. Rufus told us Stone was liked and respected by most of the little ranchers. They won't stand for letting somebody get away with killing him."

I sat there trying to think of what Rufus would want us to do next. Soon the spirit of Rufus spoke to me. "Let's saddle Tally's horse and turn him loose down on the edge of the Van Patten ranch. When he comes in without Tally, they'll think he was thrown or killed by somebody on this side of the Organs. I doubt there'll be much investigation of his disappearance because he comes and goes all the time anyway, and Rufus said most folks were afraid of him. They'll be glad to see him gone." I paused a moment and added, "There's also a score I have to settle with Oliver Lee before I can go back and face my mother."

Yellow Boy brought himself partway up again, propping on one elbow, and said, "You not strong enough to get Lee yet. You come to Mexico with me. Stay with the same People in the Blue Mountains (Sierra Madre) as my woman, my second wife. No *Indah* knows they hide there. You safe there. I teach you more. You learn to shoot *pistola*. Maybe you find wife, too. I know good woman for you."

I sighed and said, "I'll think on it. I know it's a good thing to do. But I'll have no wife for a long time. A woman will only slow me down or hold me back."

Yellow Boy grinned. "You think *muy bien, Hombrecito*. You come with me."

I sighed again and said, "I just haven't figured out what I'm going to do with my life yet."

Yellow Boy's brow wrinkled. He said, "You live your life. You make your honor. You make body strong and have courage. You fight, live as man, and die as man. What *mas* is there?" He pulled himself back to a full sitting position, his eyes boring into mine, and waited for an answer.

I said, "Among the Apache, don't some men choose to be warriors? Don't some choose to be hunters or to make weapons? Don't some choose to work at the sawmill with Doc Blazer? In the white man's world, there are many things a man can choose as his work. I must choose mine."

Yellow Boy shook his head. "They don't choose. Their Power chooses them. My Power told me to be warrior, a killer of witches, a killer of evil like Tally and Stone. My Power told me to go where I want. My Power says bullet won't kill me, so I sang, knowing Tally couldn't kill me with his bullets before I sent him without eyes to the grandfathers. My Power says I should live free with wife in the Blue Mountains and with her sister in Mescalero. My Power chooses how I live my life. My Power helped me find you and make you warrior, too."

"I don't know this Power, brother. How will I find it?"

"Come with me to the Blue Mountains. Fast until weak with hunger. Pray on mountains. Feel cold wind, rain, and snow. Feel hot sun on your body. Your Power will find you. You will know."

I stared at his dark eyes and the sharp outlines of shadows on his face etched by moonlight. Either I had to go with him or go back to my mother. I couldn't face her yet, and I didn't want to be hanged for killing Stone. I knew I could hide out for maybe a year with Yellow Boy in the Sierra Madre. Things would be calm enough by then for me to come back to my family and settle with Oliver Lee. I thought of the horse head on the watch fob resting in my pocket. There really wasn't much choosing to do, so I said, "I'll go with you."

He grinned and said, *"Bueno.* You'll find your Power in the Blue Mountains. We rest until sun leaves *mañana,* then *vamonos."* With that, he lay back down and went to sleep.

I lay awake thinking about what he'd said earlier about honor. I knew what he told me was true. I wanted the burden of courage and of honor. I wanted to be a man, a man like Yellow Boy, courageous and honorable. I purposed I would never give my burden of honor to someone else, and I would submit myself to whatever harsh training Yellow Boy thought I needed. There was some satisfaction in the feel of the hard rock shelf under my body as I drifted off to sleep. I imagined Oliver Lee sleeping in a soft bed and thought, *When I return from Mexico, there's going to be a final accounting, and I'll return as my mother's knight.*

ABOUT THE AUTHOR

W. Michael Farmer, a member of the Western Writers of America, learned about the rich mosaic of historic figures depicted in his books while living in Las Cruces, New Mexico, for fifteen years. He has a PhD in physics and has conducted atmospheric research with laser based instruments he developed. He has published short stories in anthologies, won awards for essays, and published essays in magazines. His first novel, *Hombrecito's War,* won a Western Writers of America Spur Award Finalist for Best First Novel in 2006 and was a New Mexico Book Award Finalist for Historical Fiction in 2007. His other novels include: *Hombrecito's Search; Tiger, Tiger, Burning Bright: The Betrayals of Pancho Villa; Conspiracy: The Trial of Oliver Lee and James Gililland;* and *Killer of Witches, The Life and Times of Yellow Boy, Mescalero Apache, 1860–1951, Book 1.*

The employees of Five Star Publishing hope you have enjoyed this book.

Our Five Star novels explore little-known chapters from America's history, stories told from unique perspectives that will entertain a broad range of readers.

Other Five Star books are available at your local library, bookstore, all major book distributors, and directly from Five Star/Gale.

Connect with Five Star Publishing

Visit us on Facebook:
  https://www.facebook.com/FiveStarCengage

Email:
  FiveStar@cengage.com

For information about titles and placing orders:
  (800) 223-1244
  gale.orders@cengage.com

To share your comments, write to us:
  Five Star Publishing
  Attn: Publisher
  10 Water St., Suite 310
  Waterville, ME 04901